The Lost Girls of Willowbrook

Center Point
Large Print

Also by Ellen Marie Wiseman and available from Center Point Large Print:

The Life She Was Given
The Orphan Collector

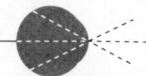

The Lost Girls of Willowbrook

ELLEN MARIE WISEMAN

CENTER POINT LARGE PRINT
THORNDIKE, MAINE

This Center Point Large Print edition
is published in the year 2022 by arrangement with
Kensington Publishing Corp.

The text of this Large Print edition is unabridged.
In other aspects, this book may vary
from the original edition.
Printed in the United States of America
on permanent paper sourced using
environmentally responsible foresting methods.
Set in 16-point Times New Roman type.

ISBN: 978-1-63808-509-6

The Library of Congress has cataloged this record
under Library of Congress Control Number: 2022942239

For my littlest love, Liam—
what a precious gift you are to my world

(It is difficult) to get at the fabric of life in a "city" like Willowbrook. This abysmal and underground city, this dark hellish environment of eight thousand souls, residents and workers together . . . it was a town that was "underground," completely out of the public sight, completely closed off, completely understaffed, completely underfunded. That essentially provided a border place for maximum human abuse . . .

—Dr. William Bronston, *A History and Sociology of the Willowbrook State School*

I mean, the place was a concentration camp, it was, it was a crime against humanity in every corner and every nook and every cranny.

—Dr. William Bronston, *A History and Sociology of the Willowbrook State School*

It is only in taking them onto the wards to see the din and the stench, the misery, heaves and twists and cries that they suddenly and indelibly understand that it is not the handicap which has taken its toll, but Willowbrook. Willowbrook is the culprit.

—Dr. William Bronston, testimony to the New York State Joint Legislative Committee for the Mentally and Physically Handicapped, February 17, 1972

ACKNOWLEDGMENTS

Again I'm happy to honor the wonderful people who make my writing career possible. There's no doubt that I owe my success to their steadfast love, endless encouragement, and unwavering support.

First and foremost, I want to thank my daughter, Jessica Thompson, for giving me the idea for this book. Somehow you knew Willowbrook State School on Staten Island would be the perfect setting for this story, and that what happened there would be another social injustice I'd want to explore. I hope this book makes you proud and excited that I finally wrote about a serial killer. Thank you to Kayleigh Wilkes and Maria Hopkins for sharing your memories of the rumors that surrounded Willowbrook during the 1970s. Your insights provided interesting layers to this story. I'm also grateful to Elayne Morgan for helping me make this book shine. Thank you to Lorna Dollinger, Sue Stearns, and Susan Butler for sharing your knowledge and expertise concerning the Willowbrook Class.

Heaps of gratitude go out to the bloggers, podcast hosts, reviewers, booksellers, and book clubs who celebrate and joyfully spread the word about me and my books, along with a ton of appreciation to everyone who invited me to the many, many Zoom events I had the pleasure of joining over the past year. Hopefully things will get back to normal soon so I can meet all of you in person someday. A thousand more thanks to the booksellers and librarians who took the time to read an early copy of this novel and provide such wonderful endorsements. Your generosity means more than you know.

Extra thanks and big hugs to Bill and Mindy Reilly, owners of the River's End bookstore, for everything you've done for me and my books. Your bookstore rocks and so do you! I'm also grateful to my online friends and readers who talk about my work and make the Internet a fun place to be—Susan Peterson, Nita Joy Haddad, Sharlene Martin Moore, Jenny Collins Belk, Kayleigh Wilkes, Barbara Khan, Andrea Preskind Katz, Jill Drew, Lauren Blank Margolin, Melissa Amster, Linda Levack Zagon, Tonni Callan, Denise Birt, Annie McDonnell, Jackie Shepard, Renee Weiss Weingarten, Vivian Payton, and Suzanne Leopold. If I've forgotten anyone, please forgive me and know that I truly appreciate each and every one of you!

To all my loyal readers, I can never thank you enough for your continued support and for sticking with me. Writing is a solitary struggle, but you remind me every day of the potential power and reach of words. Thank you for inspiring and motivating me. To the people who live in and around my community who continue to bolster me in too many ways to count, you have no idea how much your enthusiasm and encouragement mean to me. Hopefully we can get together again for the launch of this novel because being with you, all of us packed into our little library, makes the hard work worth it. To say I missed seeing your smiling faces when my last book came out is an understatement. And thank you to Patti Hughes for always being ready and willing to celebrate my launches!

Thank you to my friends and family for understanding my crazy schedule, for sharing my trials and triumphs with open minds and hearts, and for always being there when I crawl out of the writing cave, spent and bewildered. I can't begin to tell you how much it helps to know you always believe in me, even when I don't believe in myself.

As always I'm grateful to mentor and friend William Kowalski, who had faith in me all those years ago and made sure I had the tools to succeed. To my brilliant agent Michael Carr, thank you for your friendship and invaluable advice regarding my books and career. To my wonderful editor, John Scognamiglio, thank you for always being a pleasure to work with and for giving me the extra time I needed to finish this novel. Your patience was very much appreciated. To everyone at Kensington, I hope you know how much I value everything you do to get my work out into the world—Steven Zacharius, Adam Zacharius, Lynn Cully, Alex Nicolajsen, Jackie Dinas, Lauren Jernigan, Carly Sommerstein, and everyone else who works so hard behind the scenes, with an extra nod to Kristine Mills for my gorgeous covers and Vida Engstrand for always being right beside me in the trenches. Getting the call that *The Orphan Collector* made the *New York Times* bestseller list was one of the highlights of my life. And it never would have happened without all of you!

To my family, you are the rock I stand on and my reason for being. I could never find the courage or strength to write novels without your love and support. To my mother, Sigrid, you are my hero and inspiration. I wish you could see yourself the way I do. To my husband and best friend, Bill, thank you for always holding me steady when I think things are falling apart. To my amazing, wonderful, brilliant children, Ben, Shanae, Jessica, and Andrew, thank you for loving me, for making me proud every day, and for giving me the most precious gifts in the world, my beloved grandchildren, Rylee, Harper, Lincoln, and Liam. I could write a million books trying to convey the depths of my love for all of you but there would never be enough words to describe how very much you mean to me. You are, and always will be, the most magnificent and priceless blessings in my life.

CHAPTER 1

Staten Island bus station
December 1971

People still search the woods for the remains of lost children.

Sixteen-year-old Sage Winters picked up the bus tokens with shaking fingers and stepped away from the station window, her friends' haunting words playing over and over in her mind like a creepy childhood rhyme. It wasn't the first time she'd heard the warning—everyone who lived on Staten Island understood the need to keep their eyes on the ground when they entered the woods—but the more she thought about Heather and Dawn repeating those words the previous night, the angrier she grew. Why would they say something so awful instead of trying to comfort her? Why would they dredge up old rumors about Satanic rituals being held below the abandoned tuberculosis sanatorium instead of offering to help her find out what had happened to Rosemary? Sure, they'd been drinking, and deep down they were probably scared too, but this was *serious*. Her twin sister was missing. It didn't mean she was dead. It didn't mean that the urban legend they'd grown up hearing was true. "Cropsey" was nothing more than a scary story parents told their children to frighten them into behaving and staying close to home. And Rosemary was a patient at Willowbrook State School—she wasn't out wandering the streets, where a homicidal madman could pick her up. Doctors and nurses and teachers were taking care of her, making sure she was being properly fed, protected, kept clean, and taught basic skills. At least that's what Sage's stepfather, Alan, had told her last night, when he finally admitted Rosemary was alive.

Shivering at the memory of learning the truth about her twin, Sage shoved the bus tokens into her jacket pocket, then dug in her purse for her pack of Kools. She needed a cigarette so bad she could taste it. And a Pepsi too, but the damn soda machine was out of order. On top of everything else, she was totally hung over. Her head was pounding, her mouth tasted like sandpaper, and her thoughts jumbled together in a thick haze. Feeling this shitty made her even more anxious, but she had no one to blame but herself. She must have been an idiot to think drinking six amaretto sours and ten shots of peppermint schnapps was the best way to deal with the shock of finding out Rosemary had been committed to a mental institution.

Still rummaging through her purse for her

cigarettes, she crossed the grimy waiting area, hurrying past the rows of blue plastic chairs as she made her way toward the exit. Considering the weather, it probably would have been a better idea to stay inside the station to smoke, but the place smelled like a urinal, and she didn't want to miss the bus to Willowbrook. The sooner she got on it, the less chance she'd have to change her mind.

But something kept getting stuck under her mood ring, hindering her search through her purse. She stopped. Had she forgotten to put her fake ID back in her wallet after leaving the bar last night? When she pulled her hand out and saw what it was, she swore under her breath. One corner of an empty condom wrapper had caught beneath the ring's stone, and now it hung from her hand like a banner. She pulled the wrapper free, went over to trash bin, and chucked it in the garbage. Still cursing, she dug the rest of the six-pack out of her purse and threw them away too, not caring who saw. One thing was for sure: Her next boyfriend would be man enough to buy his *own* damn condoms. Thinking about Noah, tears burned her eyes. If she hadn't caught him making out with that bitch Yvette the other day, he could have gone to Willowbrook with her. Instead, he was probably still in bed, enjoying the final days of Christmas vacation and dreaming about seeing her later. Well, he was in for a surprise.

She'd slipped a letter under his door, telling him never to call her again. Because if there was one thing she wouldn't tolerate, it was a cheating boyfriend. It didn't matter that he and Yvette had "only" been kissing—cheating was cheating. And she'd vowed a long time ago that she'd never waste a minute of her life with someone like her late mother, who was always unfaithful to her father, no matter how heartbroken she was.

Thinking about her mother, a familiar resentment tightened her jaw. She used to believe her parents were so crazy in love that no one and nothing else mattered. In high school her father had been the star player on the basketball team, and her mother the head cheerleader; they were married right after graduation. It was supposed to be forever. Sage and Rosemary had thought it would be forever too—until the first time they saw their parents fight. The first time their mother threw a martini glass at him. The first time she told him to get out. And the last.

Rosemary never understood why their parents fought all the time—but it had changed her, and not for the better. Sage, on the other hand, knew they had problems but was powerless to fix them, so she tried to ignore their bickering. In the beginning, when she first realized her mother drank every day, she thought her father was having an affair and she'd hated him for it. But then she learned the truth.

The cheaters are the ones who scream and yell, the ones who try to place blame on the other person. As if it were her father's fault that her mother lied about working late so she could have sex with her boss. As if *he* were the one who had destroyed her boss's marriage along with her own. No matter what Sage's father did or how hard he tried, he was never good enough for their mother. He didn't love her enough. He didn't kiss her ass enough. He didn't do *anything* enough. Except he was the one who brought her coffee in bed every morning and cooked dinner every night. He was the one who took Sage and Rosemary to preschool and made sure they had clean clothes. He was the one who decorated the house and bought the biggest tree he could find every year because Christmas was their mother's favorite holiday. No one had ever cared about Sage's mother as much as he did. And she'd never had a reason not to trust him.

Sage had never had a reason to distrust Noah either. A lot of girls hung around hoping to get his attention, but he never gave any of them a second look. Heather and Dawn always asked her if she trusted him, but Sage knew how much he loved her—or at least she'd thought she did. She was used to seeing the other guys partying with different girls, the whiskey and beer flowing, the joints being passed around. But Noah was always with her, laughing at his friends' antics. She never thought he would cheat. The whole year they'd been together, there had never been a note stuffed in his locker, a lipstick stain on his neck, a rumor that he'd even *looked* at someone else. Until now.

She cursed him under her breath again, then blinked back her tears, refusing to cry over a boy. She had more important things to worry about. Pushing the image of Noah from her mind, she trudged toward the exit. He wasn't worth another thought. At least that's what her head said. Heather and Dawn weren't worth a second thought either. At first she'd felt bad about walking out on them last night, leaving them in the bar without paying her tab, but now she was glad she'd left. Her grief over losing her sister six years ago—the horrible, heavy heartache she could still feel to this day—was not something to joke about. They *knew* Rosemary's death was the dividing point of her life. The before and after. It wasn't a hoax or a plea for attention.

To this day, Dawn and Heather still picked on her about the fact that she hated Ouija boards and was so scared of needles that she'd passed out when they'd tried to pierce her ears using a sewing needle and a chunk of ice, so it should have been no surprise that they'd bring up the rumor of Cropsey and the horrible crimes he'd committed when she told them Rosemary was missing. And even that would have been okay, except they wouldn't quit talking about him even after she begged them to stop.

Now, as she neared the double doors of the bus station, she slowed. Help wanted ads, business cards, and what seemed like a hundred missing-kid flyers covered a bulletin board next to the door—row after row of innocent, smiling faces lined up like faded yearbook photos. She'd always hated those flyers: the word *MISSING* in all caps knocking you between the eyes, the grainy photos taken on happier days before the kids were abducted, when everyone was still blissfully unaware that they'd be stolen from their families someday. The flyers were plastered all over Staten Island, inside the grocery stores and post offices, outside the bowling alleys and movie theaters, on the mailboxes and telephone poles. Something cold and hard tightened in her chest. Would her twin sister's face be on one of those damn flyers too? And where were all those poor, innocent kids? What horrible things had they endured? Were they dead? Still suffering? Crying and terrified, wondering why their parents, the people who'd promised to love and protect them forever, hadn't saved them yet? She couldn't imagine a worse fate.

Everyone said it was no surprise that so many kids went missing on Staten Island. After all, it was New York City's dumping ground; it'd be easy for someone like Cropsey to hide the bodies there. The "dumping," as they called it, had started back in the 1800s, when the city abandoned people with contagious diseases on the island—thousands of poor souls with yellow fever, typhus, cholera, and smallpox. Later, the city dumped tuberculosis patients at the Seaview Hospital; the destitute, blind, deaf, crippled, and senile at the Farm Colony; and the mentally retarded at Willowbrook State School. The mob dumped bodies in the forests and wetlands. The city dumped tons of garbage at Fresh Kills, which had once been a tidal marsh full of plants and frogs and fish, but now teemed with rats and feral dogs. Maybe the cops should look there for the missing kids.

Just then a woman in a plaid coat came into the station, bringing with her a blast of cold air that swept through the waiting area and stirred the "MISSING" flyers like the hands of ghosts. The woman hurried into the room, bumped into Sage's shoulder, and, without a word of apology, kept going.

Jarred back to the here and now, Sage turned away from the flyers, pushed the station door open with more force than necessary, and went outside into the colorless light of winter. She lit a cigarette and took a long drag. Heather and Dawn had been right about Noah. What if they were right about Cropsey too? What if he really *had* kidnapped Rosemary? She took another hard drag of her cigarette and started along the sidewalk, telling herself to stop being ridiculous. An escaped mental patient with a hook for a hand or a razor-sharp ax was *not* hunting children and dragging them back to the tunnels beneath the ruins of the old tuberculosis hospital to sacrifice them for Satan. It was just easier to believe in the boogeyman than to acknowledge that there were so many evil people in the world.

But if Alan was telling the truth about Rosemary being safe and cared for in Willowbrook for the past six years, why was she missing? How had she gotten away from the doctors and nurses who were supposed to be watching over her? Had Sage discovered Rosemary was still alive only to lose her all over again? She'd already lost enough people she loved.

Digging in her jacket pocket for the bus token, she clasped it tight in one hand and walked toward gate number eight, where the bus to Willowbrook was scheduled to arrive any minute. If she could just stop the hammering in her head and the roiling in her stomach, maybe she could think straight. The most important thing right now was figuring out the best way to find Rosemary. Not being mad at her friends and her boyfriend—make that ex-boyfriend—not feeling sorry for herself, not worrying about a mass murderer who didn't exist. She needed her wits about her so she could focus on what to do when she got to Willowbrook. Hopefully the search party would let her help in some way. It might have been six years since she'd seen Rosemary, but she still knew her sister better than anyone. Silly things and vague ideas that no one else could see or understand terrified Rosemary; it was perfectly possible that someone or something at Willowbrook had frightened her and she'd gone into hiding. Maybe if she saw Sage looking for her or heard her calling her name, she'd come out. *If* she was hiding. All Sage knew for sure was that she would call her sister's name until her voice grew hoarse, until those three syllables came out cracked in despair, until the last nook and cranny had been searched and the last rock overturned.

Near the corner of the station, a homeless man in a frayed army jacket sat huddled beneath a blanket on the trash-littered sidewalk, his long, greasy hair hanging from beneath a worn Yankees cap. A cardboard sign beside him read: DISABLED VIETNAM VET, PLEASE HELP. He looked up at Sage with sad brown eyes, like wet marbles sunken in his bearded face, and held up an empty soup can.

"Spare some coins for a wounded veteran?" he said.

She could hear Alan's voice in her head, warning her not to give money to the homeless because they'd just use it to buy drugs and booze, especially those "baby killers" who'd fought in Vietnam. But she figured the homeless had to eat too, and it was unfair for all the veterans to be judged by the actions of a few, so she chose to imagine them using what she could spare to buy a McDonald's cheeseburger or an apple pie. She put her cigarette in her mouth, searched her jacket pocket for the change from her bus tokens, and dropped it in the veteran's can. It wasn't much, but it would help.

"Bless you, miss," he said, smiling to reveal a line of crooked teeth.

She nodded once and moved on, her shoulders hunched against the cold. Along with everything else, it had started to snow, and she was wearing a short suede jacket and a corduroy miniskirt with bare legs and wooden clogs. Not the wisest choice for today, but she hadn't been thinking about the weather. Plus, she'd told Alan she was going to the mall with her friends. Of course, if he'd actually been paying attention, he would have realized she hadn't put on makeup or showered. Everyone knew she wouldn't be caught dead in public without clean hair and mascara. Everyone who cared, at least. She supposed she should have been thankful he hadn't noticed—if he'd had any inkling of where she was going, he might have tried to stop her. Or maybe not. It was hard to tell. If it didn't involve hunting, a bottle of whiskey, or watching sports, he didn't care much about anything, especially not her. She could stay out all night as long as the cops didn't bring her home. Alan only cared when her life inconvenienced him directly—like last October, when the school principal caught her smoking in the girls' room and he had to leave his job at the Fresh Kills landfill to come get her. Then he'd screamed and yelled and threatened to lock her in her bedroom for a week—or a month, or however long it took her to learn her lesson. It was only a threat, of course. Following through would have taken too much effort.

Sometimes it was hard to tell which one of them was more miserable, her or Alan. She never understood what her mother saw in him. She'd dated other men after her boss had dumped her—men with good jobs and decent personalities—but maybe Alan had been the only one willing to marry someone with two kids. Except the joke was on him. The mother and her daughters had been a package deal, but now the prize was gone, and he was stuck with the part of the package he never wanted. Sage had learned a long time ago, even before her mother died in that drunken car crash, that she'd never please Alan. Running away had entered her mind so many times she'd lost count. But where would she go? No close relatives lived nearby. No friends had room to spare. Heather shared a bedroom with four sisters in a two-bedroom apartment; Dawn's parents weren't any better than Alan, drinking their money away and leaving Dawn and her little brother to fend for themselves. Not that any of them would have taken in another mouth to feed, anyway. Her maternal grandparents had passed away years ago, and her mother had stopped speaking to her only sister after that. And Sage had no idea whether her aunt was even alive, let alone where she lived. When she and Noah were still together, she might have been able to go to his house, except that his mom thought her little boy was a perfect angel who helped old ladies across the road and was saving himself for marriage. Hell would freeze over before she'd let his girlfriend sleep under the same roof. Make that *ex*-girlfriend.

Worst of all, she had no idea where her father was. No phone calls came at Christmas; no birthday cards arrived in the mail. It was so unlike him. Her mother had insisted he'd started over and didn't want anything to do with his old family, but there'd been something about the way she said it that didn't ring true. Maybe it was the venom in her voice, or how she continued to blame him for leaving. Maybe it was the way she'd treated her daughters like an inconvenience, while he always said they were a miracle. If Sage had to guess why they never heard from him anymore, she'd bet money it was because her mother had never given him their new address or phone number when they moved in with Alan. Still, it seemed like he could have found them if he'd wanted to badly enough.

She always wanted to ask her mother if she knew where he was or if she could call him, but had never been able to bring herself to do it. Because if there was any truth to what her mother said, being rejected for real would have been too hard to take. The first time had felt like an amputation; the second would have felt like death.

She often imagined him with another family and wondered if he had two more daughters, or maybe a son. Sometimes she wondered if she would run into another girl that looked just like her and Rosemary, making them triplets instead of twins. She wondered if they lived in a better neighborhood—if her father had gotten out of the low-rent section of town, away from the broken-down clusters of apartment buildings and two-bedroom houses where almost everyone she knew had a parent or uncle who worked at the Fresh Kills landfill.

Thinking about her broken family, she swallowed hard against the burning lump in her throat. No one knew where she was or what she was about to do. She felt like a feather that could be blown away by a gust of wind and no one would miss her.

Rosemary would have missed her, of course. If she hadn't been sent away.

Rosemary. Her twin. She was *alive*. It was still hard to believe. What was it going to feel like when they saw each other again? Would it be awkward? Amazing? Would they wrap their arms around each other and fall down crying? Would Rosemary remember who she was? Would it be a wonderful reunion or another heartbreaking loss? A shiver of fear-spiked excitement snaked up Sage's back.

Last night, when she'd learned that her twin sister was alive, still felt like a dream or something you'd see in a movie. And if she hadn't been in the exact right place at the exact right time, she never would have learned the truth.

It was after ten o'clock when she'd decided to sneak out and meet her friends. She left her room and crept down the hallway of their fourth-floor apartment, picking her way around hunting rifles and plastic laundry baskets filled with rumpled clothes. She'd hated the place from the day they moved in. Maybe because it felt like her life after her father left—chaotic, messy, uncertain. The kitchen was small and cramped, with a harvest-gold stove and matching refrigerator that had seen better days. The closets smelled like mice and urine, and every noise made its way through the thin walls—someone's hair dryer, women laughing, men yelling at a ballgame on TV, a muffled phone conversation filtering through the plaster along with the smell of someone else's dinner. Any excuse to leave was a good one. Or maybe it was just Alan she hated.

Trying not to trip over the clutter, she tiptoed past the plastic-framed family portraits on the paneled walls—her and Rosemary in matching ruffled dresses; Alan with his arm around their mother when she still looked like Elizabeth Taylor, her black hair in a perfect bob, her silver-blue eyes happy and shining. Alan was smiling in the picture too, a normal-looking man with perfectly ordinary features, content and in love with his wife. But his eyes were cold and calm. Secret-hiding eyes. Sage knew that pictures, just like people, could be deceiving: one moment in time captured on film, everyone looking happy and perfect when the camera clicked—then, a minute later, bickering and stomping out of the room. Or yelling and screaming and hitting.

Before she got to the living room, she checked her jacket pocket again to make sure she still had the cash she'd taken out of Alan's bedside table. Normally she only stole his drinking money to go out on weekends, but it was Christmas break and Heather and Dawn had asked her to go to a new disco over in Castleton Corners because Heather knew one of the bouncers, which meant they'd get in without being proofed. When she neared the archway to the living room, she stopped to listen, praying Alan was passed out drunk in front of the television again. As predicted, the

TV was on, but to her dismay, Alan was talking to someone. It sounded like his hunting buddy, Larry. Edging closer, she peered around the doorframe.

Like the rest of the house, the living room was cluttered, the orange shag matted and worn, the furniture dingy with dust. Alan sat on the edge of the plaid recliner, shirtless and lifting dumbbells, his chest and face shining with sweat. Larry was on the couch, smoking and drinking a beer, his feet on the coffee table; he looked like he'd managed to shower that day, at least. A basketball game was on the TV, the volume turned down. Hoping they wouldn't notice her, Sage got ready to slip past the doorway. Then Larry said something that made her pause.

"How long has she been missing?"

"Almost three days," Alan said, his words punctuated by hard breaths as he lifted the dumbbells.

Sage frowned. Oh shit. Not another missing person.

"Why'd they wait so long to call you?" Larry said.

"Beats me. Maybe they thought they'd find her first. I should have changed our phone number so I wouldn't have to deal with that bullshit."

"Well, they sure took their sweet time lettin' you know. Seems kinda strange if you ask me."

"Nah, it's not strange," Alan said. "You got any idea how big that place is? The guy on the phone said they checked forty buildings. *Forty.* First they thought she wandered off and got lost, maybe ended up in the wrong ward, but now they're searching the woods. He said Willowbrook has three hundred and fifty acres. Can you imagine how many retards they got there? It's gonna take a while to search all that."

Sage racked her brain, trying to think. Who did they know at Willowbrook? The only thing she knew about the place was that it was for mentally retarded and disabled kids, and everyone's parents threatened to send their kids there when they were bad. Even the shop owners scared away troublesome teenagers by saying they'd called Willowbrook to come pick them up. Girls were warned that if they got pregnant too young, the baby would be born with an underdeveloped brain, taken away, and put in Willowbrook. But Sage had never heard of anyone who'd actually been sent there. And if someone were actually missing from Willowbrook—or any other place in the world—why would they call Alan, of all people? What could *he* do to help?

"Are the cops involved?" Larry said.

"Don't think so," Alan said. "Not yet anyway. The guy I talked to said he was one of those shrinks they got there. Guess they didn't call the cops yet because they don't want to cause a panic."

"So why'd they call you?" Larry said. "What the hell are you supposed to do about it?"

"They had to call me," Alan said. "I'm Rosemary's legal guardian."

Sage went rigid. What the hell was Alan talking about? Her sister was dead. She had died of pneumonia six years earlier—fifteen days before Christmas, two nights after they'd finished writing letters to Santa asking for presents they'd never get.

Sage would never forget the instant she heard the news. She'd never forget the way the air disappeared from her lungs, the explosion of agony in her chest, like someone had stabbed her with a white-hot knife. She'd never forget screaming until she ran out of breath. Losing her sister was the worst thing that ever happened to her. Only her father's leaving had even come close. Her twin's death had left a hole in her heart and soul that nothing else would ever fill.

So how could Rosemary be *missing?* Dead people don't go missing. Her mother had already spread her ashes in the Hudson River; neighbors had brought pies and casseroles. It didn't make sense.

She felt a shift somewhere deep within her, as if she were watching old home movies but didn't recognize anyone; like all her memories were being torn away and replaced by something unknown. She felt it in her chest too—a

29

thickening, a hardening, a heavy pressure that made it hard to breathe. She put a hand on her stomach, took a deep, gulping breath, and tried to pull herself together. Maybe she'd heard wrong. Maybe she'd misunderstood. Maybe the television had garbled Alan's words.

No. She'd heard what she heard. Alan said Rosemary was at Willowbrook and she'd been missing for three days. It sounded impossible. Unbelievable. Insane.

She steeled herself, then entered the living room. When Alan saw her, he dropped the dumbbell and stood.

"What the hell are you doing?" he said. "Don't you got school in the morning?"

"No," she said. "We're still on break."

"What do you want?"

"I want to know what you were saying about Rosemary."

Alan shot Larry a nervous glance, then looked back at Sage, his mouth twisted in an ugly scowl. Acting oblivious, Larry took his feet off the coffee table and sat forward to crush out his cigarette in the overflowing ashtray, his eyes locked on the TV.

"Were you listening in on our conversation?" Alan said to Sage in a new voice, one she knew all too well. It was the voice of authority, of lectures, of pretending to impose rules.

"No," she said.

"Don't lie to me. Admit it. You were eaves-dropping."

"No, I was—"

"Sneaking out again?"

She shook her head.

"Then why the hell are you wearing your coat?"

Heat flushed her cheeks. She'd forgotten she was wearing her coat, forgotten all about leaving to meet her friends. "Tell me what you said about Rosemary," she said.

"I didn't say anything about her," Alan said. "Maybe you need to get your hearing checked." He let out a humorless chuckle and looked at Larry, hoping for a reaction. Larry ignored him and picked up his beer.

Anger flared beneath her rib cage. He was lying, like he always did—about paying the rent, about going to parent-teacher conferences, about where he was on the nights he didn't come home. "Yes, you *did*," she said. "I heard you. You said someone from Willowbrook called to tell you she was missing. And that they had to call you because you're her legal guardian."

An ugly sound came from Alan's throat, like the grunt of a burrowing animal. He wiped his brow with the back of his hand. "Well, you heard wrong," he snarled. "Now get out of my hair. Go out drinking or whoring, or whatever you do with your slutty little friends. I don't care what it is, just leave me alone."

"No," Sage said. "Rosemary is my sister. I have a right to know what's going on."

He gave her a blistering look. "You have a right?"

"Yes, you have to tell me."

"Or what?"

"Or I'll tell your boss you drink at work. I know what you put in your Thermos every morning."

He moved closer, his face twisted in rage, his hands in fists. The rank odor of beer and sweat came with him, wafting over her like a pungent cloud. "Are you threatening me, little girl?"

"Tell me the truth or I'll—"

Before the next word left her mouth, he slapped her hard across the face. Her head whipped to one side and her teeth rattled together. She put a hand to her cheek and glared at him, fighting back tears of shock and anger. It had been months since he'd hit her. The last time had been when he found her asleep on the couch with her jeans unzipped, reeking of beer. She'd come home, gone to the bathroom, and forgotten to zip them up again before laying down to watch TV. But he thought she'd been out doing something else, so he slapped her and called her a slut, then followed her down the hall and shoved her across her bedroom onto her bed. She'd been too shocked and drunk to do anything about it then, but she decided then and there that if he struck her again, she'd call the cops.

Larry put down his beer and stood. "I better get going," he said.

"No," Alan said, his voice hard. "I want you to witness this. That way she can't say I lied about anything." Larry sat back down, looking like he wanted to be anywhere else. Alan went over to the recliner, picked up his T-shirt, and yanked it over his head. "I understood why your mother didn't want you to know the truth back then, but you're old enough now to keep your mouth shut."

Locking tear-filled eyes on him, she held her breath, anxious to hear the words he was about to say, scared of them at the same time. "Keep my mouth shut about what?" she said. Her legs started to tremble.

"Rosemary's been in Willowbrook State School for the past six years," he said. "The doctors said it was the best place for her."

The room started to spin around her. She wanted to sit more than anything, but she refused to give Alan the upper hand. "But you and Mom said she had pneumonia. You . . . you said she *died.*"

"I told your mother that lie would come back to bite her in the ass someday, but she wouldn't listen."

"I don't understand. Why did you send her there? And why would Mom lie to me about that?" She shook her head, unable to stop the tears no matter how hard she tried. "It doesn't make sense."

"Oh, come on," Alan said. "Your sister's a retard. Don't act like you didn't know it."

Sage could hardly breathe. She could still see her sister, her best friend: pale, pretty, and thin as a willow. They were a matched pair, two halves of a whole as only twins could be. They'd loved each other, loved all the same things; building fairy houses out of twigs and bark, playing jump rope and Hula-Hoop, watching Saturday morning cartoons. Yes, Rosemary had been different, but mostly in the best ways. The world had come alive in her eyes, and she'd shared it with everyone, pointing out monarchs and dandelions, how the sun sparkled like diamonds on the snow and water, the glow of birthday candles on the ceiling when the lights were turned out.

But there had also been doctors—too many to count—and mysterious overnight hospital visits. It seemed like she was always sick. And yes, Sage had to admit there'd been times when her sister frightened her; like when she got upset and flapped her arms, screaming and hitting anyone in striking distance. Or when she stood beside Sage's bed in the middle of the night, silent and staring. Sometimes she moved the bedroom furniture around, pushing the desk and chairs and toys to the corners of their room while Sage slept, then in the morning saying she didn't do it, that it had been that way when she woke up. Other times she talked in her sleep and had conversations with people who weren't there, or chattered in gibberish, her words all tangled together like knotted yarn.

On her good days, she told Sage she heard voices that said terrible things, and she always apologized for scaring her. While they watched *The Beverly Hillbillies* and counted their mother's green stamps, she made Sage promise to remember the stories she told her, and Sage promised to protect her if she could. Their mother said Rosemary was confused and Sage should come to her whenever she did anything odd, but Sage never wanted to tattle. Sometimes Sage felt like her sister's problems were *her* fault, as if she'd done something to harm her before they were born—taken too much nourishment, taken too much blood, taken too much room inside their mother's womb. After all, Sage had weighed two full pounds more than Rosemary at birth and had fought her way into the world thirty-five minutes sooner. Sometimes it felt like their mother blamed Sage too, making her promise to be extra nice to Rosemary, extra understanding, until they could figure out what was wrong.

But now Sage knew the truth. Her mother had thrown Rosemary away like garbage. Maybe that was why she'd started drinking more. Maybe it was guilt that had killed her.

Sage clenched her jaw. She didn't want to cry in front of Alan any more than she already had—didn't want to give him that satisfaction. "You should have told me the truth," she said.

"It wasn't my decision to keep it from you, so don't go blaming me. Your mother didn't want you blabbin' it all over town. The doctors said Rosemary would never get better, and you know how people are when they find out you got a retard in the family. Your mother wouldn't have been able to show her face anywhere without people whispering behind her back."

"So she let everyone think Rosemary was dead. Including me."

"You should be grateful. We tried to spare you."

"Spare me? Telling me my twin sister was dead wasn't *sparing* me."

"Oh, quit the 'poor me' act. You know how your sister could get. The doctors said she's a schizo, among other things. She was never going to be okay, no matter how much you and your mother wanted her to be. Putting her away was the best thing we could do for her. She was getting worse and we couldn't handle her. The people at Willowbrook know how to take care of retards like her."

Hatred welled up inside of her, burning through her chest and up to her ears, making her head throb like it was on fire. How *dare* he act like he cared! How dare he think he knew what was best for her sister! "If they know how to take care of Rosemary at Willowbrook, why is she missing?"

"How the hell should I know?"

A million thoughts and questions churned like a tornado inside Sage's mind, making her dizzy. For the past six years she'd sensed the lingering ghosts of Rosemary that remained in every corner of the apartment. Her favorite Barbie with the short red hair and crocheted vest. The smell of the lavender lotion she loved to use on her skin. The bottles of meds collecting dust on her dresser. How was she supposed to process the fact that her twin sister was alive? That she had been locked up in Willowbrook all this time?

And who else knew the truth?

"Did you tell our father you sent my sister away?" she said.

Alan looked at her like she had three heads. "What makes you think he'd give a shit?"

"We're still his daughters."

"Is that right?" Alan said. "You could have fooled me." He yanked a cigarette out of the pack on the coffee table, lit it, and took a long drag, then jabbed the air with one hand, the cigarette between his fingers. "Is your father the one putting a roof over your head? Is he the one paying for your clothes and food?"

She dropped her eyes, disgust blazing like a firestorm inside her. They'd had this argument a hundred times, and it was one she'd never win.

Her father was the bad guy and always would be. Even if he had been sending money all these years, her mother and Alan never would have admitted it. And that extra cash was probably the only reason Alan kept her around.

"Did you ever visit her?" she said. "Did you and Mom go see her at Willowbrook?"

Alan picked up a beer from the coffee table, took a long swig, then nodded. "Once."

"Once?" She gaped at him. "You only went once?"

"Your mother couldn't handle it, seeing her kid like that. And your sister didn't even know we were there. She was, like, in a coma or something. Had her eyes wide open, just staring. She had no idea what was going on."

"Oh my God. Didn't Mom want to check on her? Didn't she want to make sure she was okay? Rosemary had to be so scared and confused!"

Alan slammed the beer bottle down on the coffee table, his face red with anger. "Now you listen to me! Your mother did the best she could. None of that was her fault, so don't you go blaming her for anything."

Sage glared at him, not sure if she was going to scream or throw up. Her sister was alive and had been locked in an institution for six years. And her mother had only gone back to see her once. *Once.* Rosemary must have been heartbroken and terrified, wondering what she'd done to deserve such horrible treatment. She probably wondered where Sage was too, why her beloved twin hadn't come to see her, why she hadn't rescued her or even sent a letter or a card. Rage boiled inside Sage's chest. "I would have visited her," she said. "If you had told me the *truth*."

He shrugged. "Don't know what to tell you. Like I said, it wasn't up to me."

"You could have told me after Mom died."

"Why? What good would it have done?"

"I could have gone to see her! I could have told her I loved her. I could have tried to help her get better."

Alan rolled his eyes. "You have no idea what you're talking about. It wasn't that easy. Every visit had to be scheduled a frigging month in advance, and most of the time they'd end up canceling it for one reason or another. Always saying it was 'for the good of the patient.' "

"So you did try to visit her more than once?"

"A few times, yeah. But like I said, it was too much for your mother."

"What about her room? You know how she used to get up and walk around in the middle of the night. Did you make sure it was comfortable and safe?"

He shook his head. "They wouldn't let us in her room. They brought her out to the lobby to see us. And the place smelled like shit."

Tears filled Sage's eyes. Poor Rosemary. "Are

you going to Willowbrook to find out what happened to her?"

"No, there's nothing we can do. She won't remember me anyway. They said they'll call as soon as they find her."

"But we could help with the search," Sage said. "We could help look for her."

"I can't. I gotta work."

"You can call in."

"I said I can't," he said. "And the doc on the phone said it's best to let the professionals handle it anyway."

She could see the anger building up inside him again, in the way his nostrils flared, in the way his jaw tensed. She didn't care. "Yeah, right," she sneered. "God forbid you can't play cards and drink with your buddies on your lunch break. God forbid you care about anyone but yourself."

He came toward her again, ready to explode. "You watch your mouth, young lady. As long as you live under my roof, you'll show me respect."

"I'll never respect you," she spat. "Especially after what you did to Rosemary! Especially after you lied to me about her for years!"

He bared his teeth and raised his hand but before he could hit her again, she spun around and stormed out of the living room. She ran down the hall and out of the apartment, tears of fury and frustration stinging her eyes. She needed a drink. And she needed to tell Heather and Dawn what had happened, so they could help her figure out what to do.

Except her friends had been no help at all. Instead, they'd gotten drunk and asked if she thought Cropsey had kidnapped her sister, and what she would do if, this time, Rosemary really was dead.

CHAPTER 2

Standing on the sidewalk at the bus station, Sage took another long drag of her cigarette, resentment knotting in her stomach. How could her mother have lied to her all those years ago? How could she have said Rosemary was cremated because they couldn't afford a funeral? How could she have watched Sage suffer with a grief so deep it left her unable to eat or sleep for weeks, when all along she had the power to ease her pain by telling the truth? Of course it would have upset Sage to know Rosemary had been sent away, but it would have been better than thinking she was dead; better than thinking she'd died alone and unable to breathe, attached to tubes in a cold hospital room. If Sage had known Rosemary was alive all this time, she could have gone to Willowbrook to visit her, to bring her flowers and cards and toys. To see her and hold hands, to tell her she loved her no matter what.

And how could a mother lock her own daughter away, anyway? Didn't loving someone mean taking the good with the bad, helping each other through the hard things? A mother, especially, was supposed to love and protect her children to the end of her days. Sage would never forget meeting Heather's mother the first time she'd stayed overnight—how she'd asked if the girls wanted to order pizza and joked about them staying up all night to talk about boys, how she'd buzzed around the kitchen the next morning making eggs and pancakes, asking if they wanted orange juice or Ovaltine. Was that what mothers did—ask you what you wanted for breakfast? Sage's mother used to forget to buy bread and milk.

Over the years, Sage had convinced herself that her mother's distance started after Rosemary died. That was the story she told herself anyway, the one that allowed her to keep her heart safe. But she no longer believed it—especially now that she knew Rosemary was alive.

She looked across the bus station parking lot, down the slow incline of the road, along the gray tarmac cutting through the sprawl of buildings and telephone poles and electric wires. Her eyes were naturally drawn across Upper New York Bay toward the Manhattan skyline, where a jumble of skyscrapers floated above the ocean, like the Emerald City in *The Wizard of Oz*. When she and Rosemary were little—still small enough to be under the innocent spell of a world they thought was safe and secure—their father had told them the city would never sink because it was held up by magic, and the millions of sparkling lights in and around the buildings were powered by fairy dust. When he left a few years later, Sage wondered if she could use magic to bring him back. She used to stare at the distant city from her bedroom window every night, begging the fairies and whoever who was in charge of magic to bring him home. It never worked.

What would her father do if he knew what her mother and Alan had done? Would he care? Would he understand? Would he be outraged? If only she could tell him, maybe he'd help with the search. Maybe, once Rosemary was found, they could be a family again. She bit down hard on her lip. It was too late for fairy dust and magic wishes. Her father had left for a reason; he had chosen not to be part of their lives. There was no changing that fact, whatever the cause behind it. All she could do now was look for her sister. What might happen after that was anyone's guess.

The growl of an engine brought her out of her trance. A graffiti-covered bus crawled around the corner of the station, its diesel fumes cutting through the cold air. The graffiti reminded her of the tunnels below the crumbling tuberculosis hospital, the names and gang logos and penta-grams scrawled on the walls where high school kids gathered to drink, do drugs, and scare the shit out of each other with stories about Cropsey. Even without the horror stories, she'd always hated going into the tunnels, where the ceilings

44

and walls could collapse at any second and bury her alive. But everyone hung out there, so that's where she and her friends went too. Maybe the graffiti-covered bus was a bad sign. No. She had to stop thinking like that. She couldn't let her friends' crazy theories get under her skin.

As the bus pulled to a lumbering stop next to the sidewalk, air brakes hissing. Sage dropped her cigarette, crushed it out beneath her wooden clog, and headed toward it. If no one else was going to find out what happened to Rosemary, she would do it herself. She climbed the bus steps, handed the overweight driver her token, and made her way toward the back, shoulders hunched to avoid bumping into the other passengers, hands clasped in front of her to avoid touching the grimy, duct-taped seats. Old food wrappers and the remnants of snacks crunched beneath her feet, and the pungent odors of stale cigarette smoke, diesel fuel, and urine filled the air.

Halfway down the aisle, a guy with a dark mustache and leather jacket gave her the once-over, shooting her a flirtatious grin. She scowled at him, fighting the urge to give him the finger or accidentally-on-purpose smack him in the face with her elbow. Attention from the opposite sex was nothing new to her; she was used to boys and men staring at her body before scrutinizing her face and strawberry-blond hair to see if she was the entire package. And normally she didn't mind, as long they weren't old enough to be her father and didn't look like a health risk. But today the scrutiny made her feel like prey. Maybe she was sick of people who thought others could be lured in with a smile then thrown away like garbage. Like her mother threw her father away. Like Noah threw her away. Like her mother and Alan threw Rosemary away. When she reached the back of the bus, she slumped into a seat near the window, trying not to cry. She hated feeling like this, hating everyone and everything.

While the other passengers boarded the bus and found their seats, she gazed out the window at the fat, lazy snowflakes hitting the cracked pavement. By the time everyone was seated and the driver pulled away from the curb, the wind had picked up and the snow was coming down hard and fast, covering the sidewalks and buildings. Wherever her sister was, hopefully she was out of the storm.

Again, she berated herself for not wearing the proper clothes. How could she help with the search in this weather wearing a mini skirt and clogs? At least she was wearing a long-sleeved peasant blouse and a crocheted vest, but they wouldn't help much. That's what she got for being so hung over. If she hadn't been feeling so sick and anxious, she would have remembered it was winter and put on bell-bottoms and boots instead of throwing on the clothes she'd worn the night before. And she would have brought a snack and a drink. Of course the rocking of the bus didn't help her stomach, and neither did sitting in the back, where turning corners felt like swinging on the end of a giant pendulum. Thankfully Willowbrook was only thirty minutes away. The last thing she needed was to throw up.

Outside the grimy bus windows, apartment buildings and storefronts rushed by, tucked behind car after car parked end to end to end. Trucks and other vehicles whooshed past, throwing up sheets of dirty slush. Then came a strip mall with a beauty salon, a carpet retailer, a bakery, and a hardware store. A group of boys in matching jackets stood under the awning outside a grocery market, watching traffic and looking bored. They looked like the Bay Boys, a gang that wasn't much of a gang; they didn't have a turf and never fought with any of the other gangs, but they attacked prostitutes in the West Village. Some people said Cropsey attacked prostitutes too.

People still search the woods for the remains of lost children.

Her stomach twisted in on itself. She had to stop thinking about Cropsey. It was a waste of time and energy. Setting her purse on the empty seat beside her, she leaned against the window and closed her eyes, trying to ignore the sway of the vehicle and the awful smells. What she wouldn't give to be at the mall hanging out with Heather and Dawn, laughing and making fun of people and being bored. Instead, she was alone and scared, thanks to the thoughts they'd planted in her head. But there was no time for pity parties. She needed to figure out what to say to the people at Willowbrook so they'd let her help with the search. Convincing them that she was Rosemary's sister would be the easy part—they were identical twins, with matching strawberry-blond hair, high cheekbones, and silver-blue eyes flecked with touches of violet. Unless Rosemary had changed. Unless six years locked in an institution had washed her out and used her up.

Every time the bus stopped to let off a passenger or pick someone up, Sage startled upright and looked out the window to see where they were, her heart racing. Watching the people get off the bus and walk along the snowy sidewalks, all of them ready to begin another normal day—shopping or meeting friends for brunch and mimosas, going home after pulling an all-nighter, checking in on a sick aunt—filled her with envy. Even if they lived alone with an old cat, she longed to be one of them instead of who she was: a grieving, unloved girl on her way to a mental institution to look for her lost sister.

She closed her eyes again so she wouldn't see anything or anyone, and tried not to think too far ahead. The best way to deal with whatever was going to happen next was by taking it minute by minute instead of imagining all the things that could go wrong. But the more often the bus stopped and the closer they got to Willowbrook, the deeper her unease grew. Maybe she should have waited until she'd found someone to come with her. Maybe she should have asked Noah to come, even though he'd cheated with Yvette. No, he would have talked her out of it—and she couldn't trust him anyway. She didn't trust herself not to take him back either, especially now when she was feeling so vulnerable. She would do this on her own; she had no other choice. It was too late to turn back anyway.

After several more stops, the only people left on the bus were the driver and an Asian couple, both husband and wife staring sullenly out the window. Before pulling away from the last stop before Willowbrook, the driver closed the door and glanced in the long mirror above his head.

"You goin' to Willowbrook?" he shouted, looking at Sage.

The Asian couple turned to gaze back at her, their pale faces devoid of emotion.

"Yes," she said, nodding. "I am."

"All right," the driver said. "Just checkin'." He closed the door and pulled away from the curb.

She sat up to watch out the window, alert and shaking with nerves. After traveling a few more blocks, the bus turned and lumbered down a long, single-lane drive, past a brown, billboard-size sign that read: WILLOWBROOK STATE SCHOOL. Then they went through a pillared gate, which was held open by padlocked chains secured to thick posts. Next to the gate, a uniformed guard sat in a closet-size guardhouse reading a magazine and smoking a cigarette. After a brief glance at the bus, he waved it onto the Willowbrook campus.

Sage closed her hands into fists, her knuckles turning white. Between the gate and the guard, Willowbrook seemed more like a prison than a school. Maybe it was a good thing she'd come alone. She wouldn't have been able to cope with anyone else's anxiety or apprehension. She could barely contain her own.

For what seemed like forever, the bus traveled along a narrow entrance road passing scraggly, snow-covered meadows and thick woods with frozen creeks. The storm had finally let up, but piles of heavy snow weighed down the evergreens and coated the bare limbs of maple and oak trees. A trio of deer lifted their heads to watch the bus pass, flicking their tails, then went back to pawing through drifts to find grass. The scene reminded Sage of a Christmas card, like something you'd see on your way to your grandparents' house on a winter holiday—everything light and peaceful and calm, a stark contrast to the dark chaos inside her head. It reminded her of her father too, how he used to talk about building a log cabin in the wilderness someday. If only he were here with her now. If only he knew how much she and Rosemary needed him. Surely he would help. Unless his dream had come true, and he'd built that cabin in the woods somewhere. Unless he had a whole new life.

Desperate, she tried a crazy trick she and Rosemary used to attempt when they were young: straining to send thoughts to each other and reading each other's minds. It had never worked, but she tried it now anyway, concentrating as hard as she could to send a message to her father, praying he would hear, or somehow sense, her despair.

We need you, Daddy. We need you now more than ever. Please look for us.

It was foolish, but she didn't care.

After the tangle of woods thinned out, vast snow-covered lawns appeared with perfectly spaced trees and landscaped bushes. In the distance, a stand of willows grew along the bank of an ice-covered stream, their long, bare branches sweeping the ground. Then came a row of four-story brick buildings on each side of the road, low-slung and U-shaped, with black numbers stenciled in white circles on each wing. In front of the buildings, gaily painted benches, swing sets, carousels, and monkey bars dotted the yards, all capped with tufts of snow. But no children played outside. No teachers watched over recess or led groups of students on walks. A man shoveling a sidewalk—oddly without a coat or gloves—stopped to watch the bus go by. Otherwise, the entire place looked deserted.

Sage wasn't entirely sure what she'd expected or what she'd hoped to find. Maybe a search team in orange vests with a search and rescue dog, squad cars and helicopters, and volunteers on horseback heading into the woods. Definitely she'd imagined decrepit buildings with barred windows and overgrown yards. Even barbed-wire-topped fences and uniformed guards. But Willowbrook looked more like a college campus than a prison, where things were cared for and a person could find peace and quiet. Maybe Rosemary had been treated well there. Maybe she'd made friends and found someone to love and care for her. Maybe she'd even been happy—or as happy as a person locked in an institution could be, anyway. Hopefully when Sage walked in, she'd be informed that Rosemary had already been found, no harm done. That her sister had gotten lost in the woods or tried running away, and now she was safely back in her room enjoying a bowl of her favorite ice cream, vanilla. Sitting back in the bus seat, Sage breathed a sigh of relief. No matter what happened next, at least Willowbrook wasn't as horrible as she feared.

Then a six-story building came into view,

appearing like an ancient ship out of an artic fog, with a black roof and brick wings on both sides of an octagonal rotunda, which was adorned with an impossibly tall white cupola that disappeared into the low gray clouds. When the bus made its way around the side of the building, she saw another wing even longer than the others, making the building look like a giant cross. Smokestacks—more of them than she could count—jutted from the multiple black roofs like building blocks scattered on a shelf. Then other buildings emerged like dark apparitions, many of which looked like shops or garages or storage sheds. And everywhere she looked there were more U-shaped, numbered buildings and additional turnoffs leading to other roads. High fences surrounded some of the buildings to keep people in—or out; it was impossible to say which. When the bus slowed, she noticed a lone shoe in the snow and something that looked like a pair of crumpled pants. Goose bumps prickled along her arms. Maybe, even when it came to a place like Willowbrook, appearances were deceiving.

Finally, the bus pulled around to what looked like the main entrance of the cross-shaped building and came to a stop, air brakes hissing. A sign above the double doors read: ADMINISTRATION. The Asian couple stood and moved toward the exit, the husband waiting

53

patiently for the wife to go ahead. Sage took a deep breath and gathered her courage. It was now or never.

Still looking out the window, she reached for her purse, wondering if she should have another cigarette before she went in. But her hand landed on an empty seat. She gasped and looked down. Her purse was gone. *Shit.* She should have known better. She should have kept her eyes open, especially when the bus stopped in some of the seedier neighborhoods. Frantic, she scanned the floor, then got up to search under the other seats. Maybe it had slid off the cushion when they stopped. But it was nowhere to be found. She went down the aisle, looking in and under every chair.

"Is there a problem, miss?" the driver said.

"I think someone took my purse," she said.

The driver rolled his eyes, put the bus in park, and got up to help.

They looked everywhere, over and under and in between every seat, and searched every inch of the floor. Her purse was not on the bus.

"Was there anything important in it?" the driver asked, out of breath and sweating. "Money? ID?"

"Just a few dollars and some makeup, a hairbrush, my cigarettes." There was no point in mentioning her fake ID.

"No driver's license?"

She shook her head. "I don't have a license."

"What's the purse look like?"

"It's a leather saddlebag, with blue flowers stamped on the front."

He returned to his seat, took off his cap to wipe the sweat from his forehead, and grabbed a clipboard from a hook on the dash. "Give me your name and phone number. If it turns up, dispatch will give you a call, but don't hold your breath."

"It's Sage Winters. 212-567-2345."

He wrote the information down and put the clipboard back on the hook. "Okay, got it," he said. "Sorry about that." Then he looked up at her. "You okay?"

No. I'm not okay. Not even close. She nodded and tried to smile, touched by his compassion, and for the first time, noticed his kind eyes. She glanced out the window at the massive brick building. "Do you know anything about this place?"

He shrugged. "Not any more than you do, probably," he said. "I just drop people off and pick them up, so I can't tell you much. I remember Robert Kennedy called it a snake pit, though." He pointed out the open bus door, in the direction the Asian couple had gone. "That couple, they come every other week, and every time I pick them up that poor woman is crying."

She wished he hadn't told her that. "Do you know why?"

"I think they're visiting one of their kids. And I imagine it's got to be an awful sad thing to have someone you love in a place like that, don't you think?"

She nodded, sorrow tightening her chest. Poor Rosemary.

"I'm sorry," he said. "I shouldn't have said that. Are you visiting someone?"

She swallowed hard. "My sister."

"Damn. I'm sorry. Did she just arrive?"

"No, she's been here for six years."

"Oh," he said, then furrowed his brow. "I know it's none of my business, but how come I've never seen you on my bus before? Do you normally come with your parents?"

She would have laughed if she didn't feel like crying. "No, I just found out she's here."

"Oh, man," he said. "I'm sorry. That had to be hard."

"It was," she said. "It is." For a brief second, she thought about asking him to go with her, to take her inside so she wouldn't be alone. But that was ridiculous.

"Well, good luck, kid," he said. He shoved his hat back on his head and turned toward the steering wheel. "If your purse shows up, some-one'll give you a call, but like I said, don't hold your breath. The 'lost' list is a lot longer than the 'found' list on this route."

"Okay, thanks," she said, and started to exit

the bus. Halfway down the steps, she looked out at the massive building again and was struck by a jolt of panic. What she wouldn't give to be getting back on the bus for the return trip home. She stopped and turned to face the driver again. "I guess I'll see you later then, when you come back to pick us up."

To her surprise, he frowned. "Sorry, kid. Normally it would be me, but I'm clocking out early to take my wife out to dinner for her birthday." Then he smiled again and gave her a friendly wink. "You know what they say, happy wife, happy life."

She forced a weak smile. Going out to dinner to celebrate a birthday sounded like the most wonderful thing in the world right now. Hell, going to the dentist sounded better than what she was about to do. "Oh. Well, thanks again for your help."

"No problem." He put his hand on the door lever and waited for her to get out. "Take care now."

At the bottom of the bus steps, snow filled the backs of her clogs, instantly turning her feet to ice. She turned to wave to the driver, but he was already shutting the door. Swearing under her breath, she made her way along the snow-filled sidewalk toward the brick building. At the top of the frozen steps, she hesitated, wondering if she should knock on the imposing double doors or just walk in. She tried the handle. It turned, one side of the door clicked open, and she went inside.

After stomping her snow-covered clogs on the industrial-size doormat inside a short vestibule, she read the plaque on the wall: ADMISSIONS: ACUTE AND CHRONIC PSYCHIATRIC, GERI-ATRIC, CHEMICAL DEPENDENCY, MENTAL RETARDATION, AND CHILD-ADOLESCENT WARDS. She frowned. Was she in the wrong place? Wasn't Willowbrook supposed to be a school? Nothing on the sign said anything about classes or teachers or grades.

The only thing she could do was go in and ask. She went through another set of double doors and entered what looked like a waiting area. Straight ahead, a receptionist wearing cat-eye glasses sat at a desk looking through a stack of papers. Except for an odd, roped-off staircase at one back corner, the waiting room had the false, relaxed feel of a doctor's office, with a tiled floor, cushioned chairs, and paintings of mountains and lakes on the walls. A corner table offered an assortment of magazines—*National Geographic*, *Psychology Today*, and *Better Homes & Gardens*—and a small room off to one side held toys and books and child-size chairs. Then she noticed the sinister-looking gargoyles on the banister of the roped-off staircase and was instantly reminded of the rumors about Satanic rituals being held under the old tuberculosis sanitarium. What the hell were those creepy-looking decorations doing in a school? She shivered, then shook off her uneasiness. This was no time to let urban legends make her afraid.

The room was empty except for the Asian couple from the bus. The wife, sitting still as a stone, stared at the floor with a haunted look in her eyes, while the husband rested a comforting hand on her arm. When he glanced up, he gave Sage a tired smile. Not wanting to appear unfriendly, she smiled back, then made her way toward the receptionist.

"Yes?" the receptionist said, putting down a sheet of paper. "What can I do for you?"

"I'm looking for my sister, Rosemary Winters," Sage said. "She's a student here, but my stepfather got a call yesterday that she was missing."

The receptionist's forehead creased with confusion—or maybe it was distress, it was hard to tell. "Hold on for just a moment, please," she said. She picked up a clipboard, lifted the first sheet of paper, and ran her finger along the next page. After putting the clipboard down, she gave Sage an efficient smile, then picked up the phone and pointed toward the waiting area. "Please take a seat. Someone will be with you in just a moment."

"Thank you," Sage said. She chose a seat

near the desk, straining to listen in on the phone conversation. When the receptionist turned her back and whispered into the receiver, dread settled like a rock inside Sage's chest. Maybe there was bad news about Rosemary and the receptionist didn't want to be the one to tell her. Then the receptionist hung up, wrote something down, and avoiding Sage's gaze, busied herself looking through her desk. Sage clasped her hands together and tried to calm down. No. She wasn't going to think like that. She was imagining things. The receptionist never looked up at the Asian couple either—and why would she? Judging by the size of Willowbrook, she probably saw hundreds of people a day. And she had work to do. There was no time to get emotionally involved with every person who walked in the door.

While she waited, Sage couldn't help but picture her sister in the same room, her mother and Alan talking to the receptionist, then someone taking Rosemary away. Had her mother asked to see where her daughter would be staying? Had she asked if she'd have her own bed, a private room, or roommates? Had she even cared? Sage's eyes flooded. Rosemary must have been beyond terrified and confused.

She thought about asking the Asian couple what they knew about Willowbrook. The sign on the road said it was a school, but it felt more like a hospital. Or worse, an insane asylum. She picked at her fingernails, anxiety quivering in her stomach. It was ridiculous, of course—as absurd as the stories about Cropsey—but she couldn't stop thinking about the other rumors she'd heard growing up. There was the story about doctors experimenting on kids there, and the one that said Willowbrook was built on Staten Island because poison from the Fresh Kills landfill seeped out of the ground, providing more retards for scientific research.

Before she got the nerve to ask the Asian couple any questions, a door opened at the back of the room and a man in a white uniform entered with a boy of about ten years old in an oversize flannel shirt, scuffed boots, and trousers held up by shoelaces. Maybe it was the man's brush cut or the hard angle of his jaw, but he looked aggravated as he led the boy across the room by the arm. The boy walked with his head down, his hands fidgeting beneath his chin, his fingers oddly crooked. A terrible foreboding quickened inside her. The man in the white uniform was no teacher. He was an orderly or an attendant of some kind, the kind you'd see in a hospital or insane asylum. The Asian couple got to their feet and rushed over to the boy.

"Oh, Jimmy," the wife said, taking his fumbling hands in hers. "We've missed you so much."

"Yes," the husband said. "How are you, son?"

61

Jimmy stared at them blankly, his mouth twisted to one side.

"Say hello to your parents, Jimmy," the attendant said.

"Hello, parents," Jimmy said, his tongue lolling out of his mouth at the end of each word. His voice was lower than Sage expected. Maybe he was older than he looked.

Concern creased the mother's face and she put a gentle hand on one side of Jimmy's head, where something dark, like dried blood, lined his jaw and neck. "What happened to his ear?"

"He was roughhousing with one of the other boys and got bit," the attendant said.

"It looks like it needs stitches," the mother said.

"I'll mention it to his doctor," the attendant said, his voice filled with indifference.

"What about the new sneakers we brought last time?" the father said. He pointed at the boots on Jimmy's feet. They looked two sizes too big and were missing the laces. "Where are they?"

The attendant looked down at the boots as if noticing them for the first time. "I'm not sure," he said. "He must have lost them."

The father shook his head, disgusted. "That's the third pair this year."

"Can we take him outside for a minute?" the mother asked. "It's been snowing, but the fresh air will do him good."

"I didn't bring his coat," the attendant said. "Maybe next time."

"I can get his coat," the father said. "Just tell me where it is."

"You know parents aren't allowed in the wards, Mr. Chan. I've told you that a hundred times."

"I know you have," Mr. Chan said. "What I want to know is why? Why won't you let us see where our son lives? What are you trying to hide?"

"We're not hiding anything," the attendant said. "But it can be upsetting for the other residents to see parents in the wards, especially those who never get visitors. You're welcome to visit with Jimmy right here, like you always do."

"And why do we always have to let you know when we're coming or else Jimmy's not allowed a visit?" Mr. Chan said. "Perhaps you can explain that to me too."

Mrs. Chan had already taken Jimmy by the arm and was leading him toward the toy room off the waiting area, lovingly rubbing one hand along his shoulders.

"I don't make the rules, Mr. Chan," the attendant said. "If you have a complaint, you need to take it up with one of the doctors or a member of the administration."

"Oh, I plan on it. The parents' association just met with one of your doctors and we're going to get to the bottom of this, you can bet on that!"

The attendant shrugged. "Do what you have to do."

Mr. Chan shot him another angry look, then followed his wife and son into the other room. The attendant watched until they were settled before turning to leave, then noticed Sage and hesitated, a strange look on his face. Instead of exiting, he went over to the receptionist and leaned over her desk, talking quietly. The receptionist nodded and glanced at Sage. The attendant looked over at her again, then left through the door at the back of the room.

Apprehension gnawed at her insides again. What had they said about her? That there was little hope Rosemary would be found? That they needed to get someone to tell her she was dead? Or was it something else entirely?

She got up and approached the receptionist. "Excuse me," she said. "But I got the feeling you and that man were talking about my sister. Is there something you can tell me? Anything at all?"

The receptionist shook her head. "I'm sorry. I don't know for sure what's going on, but someone will be out shortly to speak to you."

"But you don't understand," Sage said. "I just found out my sister was here. I thought she was dead and I came all this way and—"

Before she could finish, the door at the back of the waiting room opened and the brush-cut attendant returned with a thin man in a tweed sports coat. The attendant pointed at Sage and they started toward her, walking fast, the attendant with his hands in fists, the man's face grave. Her first instinct was to turn and run. They thought she was sick; they were going to lock her up. Maybe Alan had told them she was coming because he wanted to get rid of her. Maybe everything he said about Rosemary had been a lie to get her here. After all, she and every kid on Staten Island had grown up being told they'd be sent to Willowbrook if they didn't behave. Now the nightmare was coming true.

But that was impossible. Alan had no idea she was here. She pushed the idea away. Then, in the next instant, she wilted inside. The attendant and the man in the sports coat were going to tell her Rosemary was dead. She could see it in their eyes and the way they held their mouths. No. Rosemary couldn't be dead—not again! The men looked tense because of this place, because of the difficult decisions associated with their jobs. Maybe they thought she was here to berate them for losing Rosemary.

On watery legs, she went to meet them, her hand out and her chin up, trying to look friendly and confident. Inside, she felt nauseated.

Before she could speak, the man in the sports coat said, "Where have you been, Miss Winters? We've been worried about you."

CHAPTER 3

Sage's mouth fell open in surprise. Then a fiery jolt shot through her, a hot shock of confusion and embarrassment. She frowned at the man in the tweed sports coat and lowered her hand, fighting the urge to turn around and leave. She couldn't do that; she had to find her sister. Instead, she laughed, a nervous laugh full of desperation and misery that seemed to fill the entire waiting room. The man in the sports coat had to be joking. He didn't honestly think she was Rosemary, did he? It was ridiculous. She started to tell him he'd made a mistake when he gestured with one hand, like a king telling a guard to take away a prisoner. Before she knew what was happening, the attendant grabbed her by the arm.

"What are you doing?" she said, trying to pull away. "Let go of me!"

Ignoring her protests, the attendant tightened his grip and steered her toward the door at the back of the room, pulling her so close his sour breath washed over her face. The man in the sports coat followed. She dug in her heels and tried to wrench free, but the attendant seized her with both hands and half pushed, half dragged her across the floor.

"Stop it!" she yelled. "You're hurting me!"

"Everything is going to be all right, Miss Winters," said the man in the sports coat. "You're back now and you're safe here. This is your home, remember?"

Panic plowed through her, stealing the air from her lungs. "No!" she cried, struggling against the attendant. "I'm not Rosemary! I'm her twin sister! Let me go!" Her heart felt like it was about to explode in her chest. "What are you doing?"

In the other room, Mr. Chan looked up to see what the commotion was, but his wife put a hand on his arm to keep him from interfering.

"Don't worry," the man in the sports coat said. "We're not going to punish you. We just need to get you back to your ward."

"But you're making a mistake!" she cried. "My name is Sage! I'm here to look for my sister because I found out she's missing!" She twisted her body and tried to get free. The attendant dug his fingers into her skin. "Get your fucking hands off me!"

The receptionist stood, concerned. "Do you need me to call for help, Doctor?" she said, picking up the phone.

"Yes," said the man in the sports coat. "Have Nurse Moore meet me in room five right away."

Sage dropped to her knees, yanked herself free from the attendant's grasp, and started to scramble away. But he was too quick. He caught her, grabbed her around her waist, and carried her across the room. Her clogs fell from her feet, clattering across the tiled floor. She screamed and kicked and pounded her fists on his chest and face, but he held on.

"Someone, please!" she shrieked. "Help me! I don't belong here! I'm not who they think I am!"

She clawed at the attendant's face, catching the skin beneath his eye. He grunted and turned his head away, then hauled her through the door into a corridor lined with more doors.

At the end of the corridor, he took her into an examination room filled with white cabinets and the sharp tang of rubbing alcohol. He yanked off her jacket and threw it on the floor, then forced her onto on a gurney and held her down, his sweaty hands crushing her arms. She thrashed on the mattress, screaming and crying and gulping for air. The doctor waited near the wall in silence while a nurse rushed in and strapped Sage's ankles and wrists to the gurney railings.

"Let me go!" she screamed. "Someone help me, please!"

When the nurse finished fastening the leather straps, the attendant tightened them, then stepped back and wiped his sweat-covered brow, his shoulders heaving.

"This is for your own good," the doctor said. "So please stop fighting us."

Sage wrenched on the straps, pulling with all her might, but couldn't get free. "Why are you doing this to me?" she cried. "I'm not Rosemary. I'm her twin sister, Sage. You should be out looking for her, not in here tying me down. Please, you have to listen to me!" She stopped struggling for a moment and tried to catch her breath. The more she fought, the less they would listen. She had to act rational and sound calm, despite the fact that inside she was screaming hysterically. "I came here because someone called my stepfather to tell him my sister was missing. You can call him and ask him. He'll tell you who I am."

"Now, now," the doctor said. "You and Dr. Baldwin have talked about this numerous times. Your name is Rosemary, not Sage. Sage is just part of your psychosis and a result of your confused thinking, remember?"

"No, I don't remember because it's not true!" she said. "I'm not my sister, I don't have any type of psychosis, and I'm not confused. We're identical twins. That's why you think I'm her. Just call my stepfather, please!"

At a gesture from the doctor, the nurse opened a cabinet drawer and took out a glass vial and a glistening syringe.

"No!" Sage cried. "Please. Don't do this. Let me up. I won't try to get away, I promise!" Straining against the leather straps, she stared at the needle, horror filling her throat. "Please, I'll behave, I swear! You don't have to do this!"

Pursing her lips with determination, the nurse slid between the doctor and the gurney, yanked up Sage's sleeve, and plunged the needle into her arm.

"No!" Sage screamed. "Pleeeease!"

After administering the shot, the nurse took the bottle and syringe, then left the room without a word, slamming the steel door behind her. The attendant and doctor looked down at Sage.

"You gave us quite a scare again, young lady," the doctor said. "Where were you hiding this time?"

Sage's chest and face felt like they were on fire. She squeezed her eyes shut and swallowed, fighting the terror that shuddered through her body. When she thought she could speak again, she opened her eyes and fixed her gaze on the doctor. "I haven't been hiding anywhere," she managed. "I came here on the bus to look for Rosemary and I . . ." She hesitated, suddenly woozy.

"It's all right," the doctor said. "Everything is going to be okay. We're not going to hurt you. We just want to help. But you already know that, right?"

She turned her head to beg him to listen, but her words felt garbled in her mouth, all soft and squished together like mud. The room grew fuzzy and dim, the corners of the walls curling and blending together in a whirling haze. The attendant's face melted into his white uniform, and the doctor's features went blurry, his eyes and mouth spinning into a gray mass.

"Don't worry, Rosemary," the doctor said, his voice turning slow and deep, like a record on the wrong speed. "You're safe now. Just relax. We're not going to let anything else happen to you, I promise."

"I'm not Rosemary," she mumbled. "I'm . . ." Before she could finish, her eyelids grew heavy and she blinked twice, struggling against the drugs that coursed through her blood, making her limp and helpless. Then she was falling, the room growing dark. She tried to stay awake, to keep talking, but a loud roar started in her ears, blocking out all sound. It was no use. When she shut her eyes a third time, the world disappeared.

Sage knew the nightmare as well as she knew the words to her favorite song. It was the same one she'd tumbled into nearly every night since the day Rosemary died, the same one she fell into over and over, end over end, sleeping and waking, wondering what was real and what wasn't. The difference between this nightmare and the others was that it was actually a horrible memory—the heartbreaking replay of the last time she'd seen Rosemary alive. And there was nothing she could do to stop it from coming—especially not now, tonight, while deep in a drug-induced unconsciousness.

In the nightmare she sat up in bed, roused as usual by her sister's midnight conversations with invisible people. But this time Rosemary's bed was empty, the mattress topped with nothing but a pile of twisted blankets and a crumpled pillow. Sage scanned the dark bedroom to see where her sister was hiding but couldn't make out her pale face. And the harder she stared, the more everything in the room seemed to move, like shadows shifting and changing shape, making her wonder if Rosemary had been telling the truth about the furniture moving around on its own. Then she saw her sister huddled in a corner, mumbling and giggling, her hands like claws over her mouth.

"What are you doing?" Sage said.

And suddenly Rosemary started screaming, an impossibly loud wail that sounded like it was coming from a wild animal, looping over and over on itself, then going weak before booming out into the darkness again.

"What's wrong?" Sage cried. "Stop screaming and tell me what's wrong!"

Rosemary screamed louder.

Sage curled up into a tight ball and put her hands over her ears, but the horrible wail made its way through her trembling fingers. She had promised her sister she would always protect her, but Rosemary had to listen and do as she was asked. Rosemary wasn't doing either. And Sage couldn't see anything she needed to protect her from. "Please stop!" she yelled.

Then the door flew open. Her mother entered and switched on the ceiling light, her face distorted by shadows, frantic eyes scanning the bedroom. "What's going on?"

Alan stumbled in behind her, shirtless and bleary-eyed. "What the hell—"

"Stop it!" Rosemary yelled from the corner. "Stop it! Stop it!"

When her mother saw Rosemary, she went over to her and knelt down, feeling her face and arms and legs, looking for injury. "What is it? What's wrong?" She glanced over her shoulder at Sage. "What happened? What did you do?"

Sage shook her head, her hands still clamped over her ears.

Suddenly Rosemary went silent, scrunching her face up tight. Then her eyes and mouth popped open and she started gasping for air and clutching her throat.

"She can't breathe!" her mother said. "Oh God. Alan, do something!"

Alan hesitated, unsure, then hurried over to the corner and knelt in front of Rosemary.

"It's okay," her mother said. "Everything's okay." She touched Rosemary's forehead and arms with cautious hands. "Just relax and take a deep breath. We're right here. You're going to be all right."

"They're choking me," Rosemary cried. "They won't let me breathe."

"What?" her mother said. "Who is choking you? What are you talking about?"

Rosemary started screaming again. Sage thought it would never stop.

Her mother looked at Alan. "Do something!"

"Jesus Christ, Rosemary," he said. "Stop it! You're scaring your mother half to death!"

"That's not going to help!" her mother said.

Alan gaped at her. "Well, what the hell do you want me to do?"

"She needs a doctor!"

Alan pulled Rosemary out of the corner, picked her up, and started toward the door, struggling to contain her flailing arms and legs. She kept screaming, kicking her feet and pounding him on the back.

"Don't!" her mother cried. "What are you . . . Alan! Be careful!"

"She needs to go to the hospital," Alan said as he carried her out of the room.

Her mother followed, leaving Sage alone on the bed.

The next morning, her mother called from the hospital and said that Rosemary was screaming because she was in pain and had a horribly high fever, and that she was scared because she couldn't breathe. The doctors suspected pneumonia, so she had to stay at the hospital for a few days. In the meantime, Sage had permission to stay home from school. Her mother would call the principal to let him know what was going on.

Then something happened. Sage had no idea what, but the next day her mother came home crying. The doctors had done all they could, but Rosemary hadn't been strong enough to survive.

Sage wanted to curl up and go back to sleep more than anything, to turn on her side and fold her hands beneath her cheek, to slip back into the peace of oblivion. The nightmare had haunted her all night and she was still exhausted, more than she'd ever been in her life. She tried to change positions on the bed, but her arms and legs felt weighed down, as if someone was holding her wrists and ankles, and she couldn't move. Her head felt heavy as a boulder and her body like she'd been in a fight, every muscle aching and sore. The sheet beneath her was cold and wet, the air filled with the stench of urine and bleach. Had she downed too many 7 and 7s again? Done too many shots? No, she'd never had a hangover like this. This one felt different. And horribly wrong.

She tried to sit up, but something lay across her chest, holding her down. She opened her eyes, blinking several times to clear her vision. A domed ceiling light filled the room with a hazy yellow glow. No windows lined the gray walls, only white cabinets and strange metal devices that looked like medical equipment. This wasn't her bedroom. And it wasn't one of her friend's bedrooms either—where was she?

She glanced down at her feet and hands. No wonder they wouldn't cooperate. Leather straps bound her wrists and ankles to a bed railing, and a wide strap lay across her chest. Had she been in some kind of accident? Was she in a hospital?

Then it all came back to her. She was locked up in Willowbrook State School. And the doctors and nurses thought she was Rosemary.

She kicked and fought against the restraints, pulling on them with all her might. "Help!" she shouted. "Please! Someone help me! Get me out of here!"

No sound came from the hall on the other side of the door. No voices answered back. No key rattled in a lock.

"Please! Anyone! I need help!" Panic clawed at her mind, threatening to overtake all thought. She couldn't get enough air. The room spun around like a top, making her nauseated. She closed her eyes for a moment to regain her balance, then lifted her head and yelled again and again, until her voice cracked and gave out.

Finally, out in the hall, hurried footsteps clipped along the hard floor. A key rattled in the lock, the door opened, and a colored woman in a white uniform rushed into the room. Not a nurse's uniform—the shirt and pants of an attendant. Her black hair was slicked back into a tight ponytail, with gray roots circling her forehead. She bent over Sage and grinned, revealing empty spaces on each side of her mouth where molars should have been.

"You're awake!" she said, yelling as if Sage were deaf. Her breath smelled like peppermint. She straightened and brushed Sage's hair away from her forehead.

Sage lifted her head. "How long have I been here?"

"You just relax now, honey," the attendant said, still speaking loudly. "I'm Hazel and I'm gonna take good care of you. You'll be okay, I promise."

"But I don't belong here," Sage said. "Please, you have to untie me."

Hazel's eyes filled with pity. "I'm sorry, but you know I can't do that," she said. "Just hang on if you can, sugar. I'll get the doctor and be right back."

Before Sage could respond, Hazel left, locking the door behind her.

Sage groaned and dropped her head back on the mattress. If they didn't let her up soon, she wasn't sure what she would do. She tried to think, to push away the haze in her mind. How long would it take for someone to realize she was missing? Would Heather and Dawn realize she had gone to Willowbrook when she didn't answer the phone? Would they even call after what she'd done? And what about Alan—would he have any idea where she'd gone? Would he even care? If only she hadn't argued with her friends. If only she'd shared her plan to search for Rosemary instead of getting mad at them for teasing her about Cropsey. They'd probably think she was still pissed if they called and she didn't answer. They probably thought she'd overreacted that night. And they would be right.

Maybe Noah called the apartment looking for her after he found her note, despite her telling him not to. Unless he was happy to be free. Unless he'd been waiting for a chance to be with Yvette. The problem was, even if her friends called, Alan would probably just say the same thing he always said when he answered the phone—that she wasn't there and he didn't know where she was; no explanation, no excuse. And school wasn't starting back up for another week—not that Alan would care if the principal called. He'd probably lie to him too, and tell him she moved. Fear crawled up her spine. How long would it be before someone figured out where she was?

Somehow, she had to convince a doctor or attendant or nurse to call Alan. And when Alan told them who she was and that she hadn't come home, they'd let her go. Except Alan paid little attention to her coming and goings. He never knew when she stayed out all night, partly because he often slept in his truck outside a bar or went home with strange women, but mostly because he didn't care. He never went looking for her or called Heather or Dawn to see if she was with them. So why would he care now? He'd probably be happy to let everyone at Willowbrook think she was Rosemary just to get rid of her.

After what seemed like forever, a man in thick glasses and a gray sports coat entered the room, followed by the attendant, Hazel. He stood near the wall, one hand in his jacket pocket, his mousey brown hair uncombed. Maybe it was the lighting, but his skin looked colorless; his fleshy face as white as the belly of a dead fish. "Hello, Rosemary," he said. "Do you remember me?"

"I'm not Rosemary," she said. "And I don't remember you because I've never seen you before."

"I'm sorry," he said. "I wasn't sure who you were today. Do you forgive me, Sage?"

Her stomach clenched. He was humoring her; she could hear it in the way his voice lifted, like he was talking to a child, pretending to play along with her game.

"It's perfectly normal if you don't remember me right now," he continued. "It's not unusual for someone with your condition to have slight memory loss after experiencing trauma or unusual circumstances. Soon you'll remember that I'm Dr. Baldwin and we've some spent time together before today. How are you feeling?"

The question annoyed her—or maybe it was his condescending tone—and she couldn't control her rage. "How am I feeling?" she said. "How do you *think* I'm feeling? I'm strapped to a gurney and no one believes me when I tell them who I am."

He smiled at her, a smile that was both phony and cold. "I believe you," he said. "You know you can tell me anything and I'll always believe you."

"Then untie me."

"We can do that," he said. "But first you have to promise to behave. Dr. Whitehall said you gave him a hard time when you returned. No more kicking and screaming, all right?"

She took a deep breath, then nodded. She had to be calm and rational if she had any hope of convincing him that she was telling the truth.

Hazel moved forward to undo the straps, but Br. Baldwin put a hand up to stop her. He gave Sage a stern look.

"I need you to say it," he said.

"I'll behave," Sage said. "No more kicking and screaming."

"Do you promise?"

"I promise."

Someone knocked on the door. Hazel unlocked

it and a nurse entered. Without a glance at Sage or the others, she opened a cabinet drawer, retrieved a glass vial and a syringe, set them on a tray, then stood next to Hazel with her hands clasped together, waiting. Sage gritted her teeth. No matter how mad or upset she got, she needed to keep quiet and cooperate—at least until they untied her.

Dr. Baldwin gestured for Hazel to undo the straps, then addressed Sage. "I have to admit I'm a little disappointed in you," he said. "You know the rules are in place for a reason. And you know what happens when you don't follow them. I'd rather not put you back on a double dose of Thorazine, but if you keep running away, I'll have no choice."

Hazel unbuckled the straps one by one, smiling and patting each of Sage's wrists and ankles with a warm hand once they were free, like a mother comforting a child.

"I'd like you to tell me where you went this time," Dr. Baldwin said. "Were you looking for your mother again? Was that it? Did you get lost in one of the other buildings? I know it's an easy thing to do when there are so many. Believe it or not, I've done it myself a number of times."

Hazel loosened the strap over Sage's chest and let it fall to the sides of the gurney, metal striking metal with an ear-piercing clang. Then

81

she lowered one of the railings and stepped back, silent but on high alert.

"Were you in the woods this time?" Dr. Baldwin continued. "Or hiding in the basement somewhere?"

Sage sat up and swung her legs over the side of the gurney, rubbing her wrists. The room spun around her and she grabbed the mattress, closed her eyes, and waited for the dizziness to pass. *For the love of God, please make it stop.*

"Are you all right?" Dr. Baldwin said.

She opened her eyes and nodded, doing her best to look sane while feeling anything but. "I'm fine," she said, and started to get down. Before her feet could touch the floor, however, Hazel stepped forward, pressed a hand against her shoulder, and shook her head.

"Hold on," Dr. Baldwin said. "There's no hurry to get back to your ward. We need to talk first."

"But I—"

He held up a hand to silence her. "I need you to tell me where you've been."

Sage locked eyes with him. "I haven't *been* anywhere," she said, trying to keep her voice calm. "I live over in Mariners Harbor with my stepfather, Alan Tern. He's the one who told me Rosemary was missing from Willowbrook. I didn't even know she was alive until then. That's why I came here, to help look for her. But my purse was stolen on the bus and now everyone thinks I'm her. But I'm not. We're identical twins and look exactly the same."

"I'm sorry," Dr. Baldwin said, "but I've spoken with your mother many times over the years and she never mentioned anything about Rosemary having a twin sister. There's a girl in your ward, I believe her name is Norma, who you call your sister, but that's it. We've talked about this several times since you came to stay with us, and I've explained that it's all part of your condition. Sage isn't real, remember?"

Her breath caught in her throat. "No," she said. "You're wrong. I'm Sage. And I'm real. Rosemary is my twin sister and she's still missing." She pressed a hand over her churning stomach, fighting the urge to swear and scream. How many times did she have to say it? "So why aren't you out looking for her? Why aren't the cops here with a search party?"

He chuckled to himself, as if amused by a private joke. Then, in that same condescending tone, he said, "Let's start over, shall we? Like I said, you've been through quite an ordeal, and it's not uncommon to have short-term memory loss after experiencing trauma. Especially for someone with your disorders."

"But I haven't been through an ordeal or experienced any trauma, up until that other doctor strapped me down and drugged me. And I don't have a disorder or a condition or whatever you want to call it. I'm perfectly sane and I came here to see if—"

"Where did you go again? You forgot to tell me."

She shook her head. Was he trying to confuse her? "I didn't go anywhere. I came here from our apartment in Mariners Harbor. I rode here on the bus and—"

All right," he said. "Let's say you're telling the truth. How did you pay the bus fare?"

"With money, like everyone else."

"Where did you get the money?"

"I stole it from my stepfather."

"I see. And do you have any money now?"

She shook her head, her face growing hot. "No, I gave the change from the bus token to some homeless guy because I thought I'd be coming right back and—"

"According to Dr. Whitehall and the attendant who brought you in, you didn't have a purse or wallet with you. So where did you keep your money?"

"In my purse," she said, starting to shake. "But it was stolen when I was on the bus." If only she'd put her purse in her lap or kept the strap around one arm, they wouldn't even be having this conversation. Then she remembered something. "Wait. I still have the return bus token." She reached for her pocket, then realized she was no longer wearing her coat. The attendant had yanked it off before putting her on the gurney. She glanced around the room. Her coat was draped over a chair in the corner. She pointed at it. "The other token is in my pocket."

Hazel picked up the coat and held it out to her. "We didn't find anything in it, honey."

Sage grabbed it and searched the pockets, an icy sense of dread swelling inside her chest. The token was gone. "It must have fallen out somewhere." Desperate, she scanned the floor, peering into the far corners of the room and the shadowy spaces under the chair and cabinets. The token was nowhere to be seen. Then she remembered grabbing the change from her pocket. She must have dropped the token in the homeless vet's soup can along with the coins. Her eyes flooded. "Please, I'm telling the truth, I promise. Call the bus station. The driver took down my name and number after my purse was stolen. He can tell you I was on the bus."

Dr. Baldwin looked doubtful. "Okay, let's say you came back here on a bus somehow. And your purse was stolen. Did anyone witness your purse being stolen?"

"I don't know. I had my eyes closed."

"Did you tell the driver your name was Sage Winters?"

"Of course I did," she said.

Dr. Baldwin said nothing, instead watching

her with knowing eyes, waiting for her to realize what she'd just said—that she'd told the driver the same thing she was telling him now.

"It *is* my name," she said, her bottom lip trembling. "Sage Joy Winters. And yes, Rosemary and I have the same middle name."

"How interesting," Dr. Baldwin said. "I've never heard of sisters with the same middle name before."

A frantic mixture of anger and terror quaked through her body, making her tremble all over. "What about the telephone number I gave the driver?" she said. "How would I know my stepfather's number if I've been in Willowbrook for six years?"

"Many people can easily recall their childhood phone numbers. Or it's possible you memorized it when we let you call your mother every year on your birthday and Christmas Eve. One of the nurses always helped you dial the phone, remember?"

Sage recoiled as if slapped, a fresh wound piercing her heart. Before she died, her mother used to take phone calls in the other room on Sage's birthday and Christmas Eve. Her mother always said it was her aunt, who only called to ask for money, and Sage wasn't allowed to say hello because her mother didn't want to ruin the festive mood. Now Sage knew why. It hadn't been her aunt calling. It was Rosemary.

"Will you please let me call my stepfather?" she said.

"I don't think that would be wise," Dr. Baldwin said. "Perhaps sometime in the future, but right now I feel it would only add to your delusion."

"I'm not having a delusion," she said, trying to control her emotions. "And if you're so sure I am Rosemary, why won't you let me call him? How could it hurt?"

"There's no need for you to call him. I already let him know you've returned safe and sound."

"And he believed you?"

"Of course he did. What reason would he have not to?"

Her heart dropped like an anvil in her chest. Of course Alan believed him. "What about my friends? Can I call one of them?"

"Your friends are here, remember? I'm here and all your friends in House Six are waiting for you to come back. I'm sure your best friend, Norma, has been missing you. You two are like sisters, remember?"

"I have no idea who Norma is. My friends' names are Heather and Dawn."

Dr. Baldwin nodded agreeably. "Yes, Heather and Dawn are on your ward too."

"That's not what I meant. I'm talking about the girls I go to school with, Heather Baily and Dawn Draper. We're in the same class. We're going to be seniors next year."

He furrowed his brow, thinking. "I don't recall their last names at the moment, but I'm glad to hear they're your friends too."

She slammed a fist on the gurney. He twisted her words and had an answer for everything. "That's not who I'm talking about," she said. "I'm talking about my real friends. The ones who go out to the bars with me. The ones who drink shots and smoke weed with me. The ones I talk to about my stepfather and my sister. The ones I share secrets with, like having sex with my boyfriend."

"Did you meet those friends while you were away?" Dr. Baldwin said. "Did they make you do things you know are wrong and try to get you in trouble?"

Sage looked at Hazel with tearful, pleading eyes, hoping she'd show some sympathy. "You believe me, don't you? Please, someone *has* to believe me."

Hazel shifted her weight and dropped her gaze.

Sage hung her head, terror rising inside her. If she had a breakdown or got hysterical, they'd never listen to her. She yanked at the loose threads on the hem of her corduroy skirt, pulling them out one by one. She'd never been in a fist-fight before, but she wanted to punch the doctor in the face. Then she thought of something and looked up at him again.

"What about my clothes?" she said. "Do you let your patients wear miniskirts?"

"I'd like to say no, but unfortunately we don't have the luxury of being strict about what the residents wear since most of the clothes here at Willowbrook come from donations. The residents wear whatever they're lucky enough to find. Of course, some of the garments are not ideal, but it's better than letting them walk around naked, which as you know, happens more than we'd like."

"What about my hair? Next you're going to tell me Rosemary wore it in the same style."

He nodded. "Long and parted down the middle, yes. But I see you've combed the snarls out of it. Or did someone do that for you? One of the friends you made while you were away, perhaps?"

This couldn't be happening. It couldn't be real. It just couldn't be. Maybe she was having a horrible dream. Maybe she was safe in her bed at home, having nightmares fueled by stress and alcohol. For the first time ever, she wished she'd been brave enough to pierce her ears or get a tattoo, anything that would prove she wasn't Rosemary. She pinched the skin on her arm, hard, to wake herself up. It didn't work.

"Now that I've answered your questions," Dr. Baldwin said, "I think it's time for you to finally answer mine. Where did you go? Were you looking for your mother again?"

"My mother is dead. She died two years ago."

"That's right. I'm glad to know you retained that important information. It took a while for you to accept that she was gone when we first told you. And the last time you went missing was because you'd gone looking for her. Remember, when you ended up in House Fourteen with the five- and six-year-olds?"

Sage shook her head, the fire of panic making it hard to breathe. "I don't know anything about House Fourteen. I don't know anything about Willowbrook or Rosemary, or what's she done, or how she is, or what's wrong with her, or how long she's been here. I told you, I just found out she's still alive. Now, please, you have to let me go. This isn't right." Despite her best efforts to sound calm and reasonable, her voice rattled.

Dr. Baldwin shot the nurse a worried glance. The nurse picked up the glass vial, stuck the needle in the silver-edged neck, and started filling the syringe.

"Are you still having suicidal thoughts?" Dr. Baldwin said.

"I've never had suicidal thoughts," Sage said. "I just want to find my sister and go home, that's all. Please don't drug me again."

Hazel and the nurse moved toward her, Hazel getting ready to grab her, the nurse holding the glistening syringe.

"There's no need to be frightened, sugar," Hazel said. "We only want to help you."

"Please," Sage said. "I won't kick or scream or anything like that. I promise. Just let me call Alan, then I'll do whatever you say."

"As I told you," Dr. Baldwin said, "I already called him."

"But you told him you found Rosemary and you haven't. Please. I just need to talk to him for a minute!"

Dr. Baldwin shook his head. "I'm sorry, but right now you need to go back to your ward and get some rest."

She couldn't take it anymore. She jumped off the gurney, grabbed the doctor's sport coat with both hands, and yanked him toward her, pushing her face into his. "Let me fucking call him!" she cried. "He'll tell you I'm not Rosemary!"

"Let go of me, Miss Winters," Dr. Baldwin said, recoiling as if she had the plague. Despite his composed, firm voice, fear flashed in his eyes. "You don't want to do this. You know what happens to residents who assault the staff. It's an automatic ticket to our state security hospital with no chance of returning to Willowbrook for at least a year. We've talked about this. You don't want to go there again."

Realizing that she was only making things worse, Sage let go and opened her mouth to apologize. The sting in her arm was sharp and immediate. She turned toward the nurse, who was pushing the needle farther into her arm. Her legs went weak and her hands fell to her sides. Hazel rushed over and grabbed her under the arms to hold her up, then dragged her back to the gurney. Sage toppled onto the mattress, and the room started spinning round and round, like a carousel inside her head. Dr. Baldwin yanked a paper towel from a dispenser, frantically wiping off his coat while Hazel lifted Sage's limp legs over the edge of the mattress. Gagging and panicked, Sage turned to look at Dr. Baldwin and the nurse, to beg them to listen, but no sound came from her throat. Everything went blurry and the room started closing in, like curtains drawing at the edge of her vision. Dr. Baldwin and Hazel and the nurse melted together, spiraling in a whirlpool of gray and white, white and gray, gray and white. Then everything went black again.

CHAPTER 4

A searing pain tore at the top of Sage's feet, dragging along her flesh like hot knives and slowly bringing her out of her drug-induced stupor. After several tries, she opened her heavy eyelids, looked around, and tried to understand what was happening. Two people, one on each side, were lugging her by the arms through a narrow passageway, and her bare feet were scraping along the rough, icy floor. She tried to walk, but the aftereffects of the shot still swirled through her, and her legs wouldn't cooperate. She kept stumbling and tripping, and was constantly being yanked upright. She had no idea where she was or how long she'd been unconscious.

When she finally found her footing and her vision began to clear, she realized that two male attendants were holding her up, and they were inside what looked like a stone tunnel. Greenish-gray mildew striped the walls, and rusty pipes ran along the ceiling, dripping a brownish fluid onto the floor. Dusty lightbulbs in metal cages emitted a weak, jittery glow, and the cave-like odor of mold and wet rock filled the air. Except for the lights and the lack of graffiti, the tunnel looked like the crumbling passageways beneath the old tuberculosis hospital.

"No," she cried, struggling to get away. "What are you doing? Where are you taking me?"

The attendants tightened their grip. "Take it easy," one of them said. "We're just taking you back to your ward."

"Please," she said. "You have to listen to me. There's been a terrible mistake. I'm not Rosemary. I'm her twin sister, Sage. You have to believe me." She tried to make eye contact with them, tried to let them see that she was perfectly normal and rational, but they kept their gaze straight ahead, intent on doing their job. The attendant on her left was taller and older, with a gray ponytail and a diamond stud in his ear. The one on the right had a youthful, innocent face, with pimple-pitted skin and a strong jawline. He looked like he belonged in high school.

Neither of them responded.

"Please," she said again. "If you take me back to Dr. Baldwin's office, he'll explain everything. You can't do this to me."

"Shut up," the gray-haired attendant said. "Dr. Baldwin's the one who told us to put you back where you belong."

"But I'm not Rosemary," she cried.

"Yeah, yeah," he said. "That's what you always say. Let me guess, your name is Sage."

Oh God. Had Rosemary told *everyone* her

name was Sage? "Yes," she said. "It is. Please, I'm begging you. I'm telling the truth. My sister Rosemary was sick. She didn't know what she was talking about."

The gray-haired attendant squeezed her upper arm and shook her hard. "I said shut up," he snarled. Then he directed his attention to the younger attendant. "That right there is one of the most important things you need to remember if you want to make it past your first day."

"What's that?" the young attendant said.

"Don't believe anything these retards say."

Sage started to protest again, but stopped. Trying to reason with them was pointless. They were only doing their job. Instead, she focused on paying close attention to where they were going, searching for markers or numbers on the walls so she could find her way back to the administration building if she got the chance. But every tunnel they went down looked the same, and they took so many twists and turns, going this way and that, it felt like they were inside a giant maze.

Finally, they came to the end of a tunnel, where a corroded sign above a rusty door read: ENTRY KEY REQUIRED. The gray-haired attendant dug a ring of keys out of his pocket, then unlocked the door and opened it, revealing a narrow staircase of crumbling stone steps. The attendants took her up the steps and stopped at a landing with another steel door. While the older attendant unlocked the latch and deadbolt, she glanced back at the stairs, wondering if she could make a run for it. She could probably get away from the older attendant if she got back into the tunnels, but the younger one would surely catch her. And she had no idea where to go anyway.

As if reading her mind, the gray-haired attendant pushed open the door and yanked her through it. They came out into what looked like a supply room lined with shelves, mops, buckets, and industrial-size barrels of Pine-Sol. After relocking the door, the attendants led her out of the supply room and into a tile-floored space surrounded by an L-shaped counter, where the air smelled like sour mops, disinfectant, and something that reminded her of dirty diapers. Somewhere, someone shrieked. Someone else moaned. Another wept. Goose bumps rose on her arms. What kind of place was this?

At the counter, a red-haired woman with a bulbous nose turned in her chair to look at them, a cigarette in one hand. When she saw Sage, her penciled brows shot up and her mouth fell open, her red lipstick like a circle of blood. She looked like someone who feasted on orphaned children and puppies. She stamped out her cigarette in a metal ashtray and stood, smoothing her nurse's uniform.

"Holy shit," she said. "They found her."

"Looks that way," the gray-haired attendant said.

"Where was she?" the nurse said. Her dull hair color was clearly a dye job, and the layers of makeup she wore did little to hide her crows' feet and sagging jowls.

"Don't know," the gray-haired attendant said. "Baldwin didn't tell us. Maybe we should ask Wayne."

The nurse rolled her eyes. "Like he'd admit anything."

"Wouldn't hurt to poke around a bit," the gray-haired attendant said.

The nurse shook her head. "I'm not asking him. I was already on his shit list once. That was enough for me."

Struggling to push aside her fear, Sage repeated the name in her head. *Wayne.* She needed to remember his name. "Who is Wayne?" she said, trying to sound rational. "And why would he know anything about my sister's disappearance?"

"Here we go again," the gray-haired attendant said, annoyed. "Had to listen to that bullshit all the way over here."

"Because it's true!" Sage said. She looked at the nurse with pleading eyes. "Can you please help me? I'm Rosemary's twin sister, but no one believes me. Someone from Willowbrook called my stepfather to tell him she was missing. That's why I came here, to help look for her. But Dr. Baldwin thinks I'm her and he wants to lock me up."

The nurse ignored her, keeping her attention on the gray-haired attendant. "You know the drill, Leonard," she said. "Either ignore them or agree with them. It's the only way to shut them up."

"Yeah, yeah," Leonard said. "I know. Want her in the same ward?"

The nurse nodded. "Yes, but be careful. Norma's at it again."

"Great," Leonard said. "Just what we need."

Behind the nurse, out in the hall, a female attendant pushed a high-railed white crib filled with babies past the counter. The babies were all different ages, from a few months to a year old. Three were sitting up, two were lying down, and one was standing up and crying, his tiny fists clutched around the iron crib rails. Two of the babies had the wide forehead and almond-shaped eyes of Down syndrome, one was missing both arms, and another looked blind. Sage watched them pass, horrified. Maybe the rumor about taking babies away from teenage mothers was true.

"Why are there babies here?" she said. "Is this a hospital or a school?"

The attendants and the nurse acted like she didn't exist.

"We still on for tonight?" the nurse asked Leonard.

"Hell yeah," he said. "We gotta show this

young stud how to party with the best crew at Willowbrook."

The nurse smiled at the other attendant. "What's your name, handsome?"

"Dale."

"Nice to meet you, Dale. I'm Vicki, but everyone calls me Nurse Vic. Welcome to Stalag Six."

"Stalag Six?" Dale said.

"That's what we call the houses," Leonard said. "Stalag Six, Stalag Thirteen. You get the idea."

Nurse Vic laughed. "You've got a lot to learn, boy. But don't worry, old Leonard here will teach you the ropes. You ready to have some fun tonight?"

Dale grinned. "The real question is, are *you* ready? I'm pretty sure I can teach you guys a thing or two about partying."

"I doubt it," Leonard said. "I survived Woodstock."

"Yeah?" Dale sounded amused. "So did my brother. But he didn't say anything about seeing any geriatric hippies there."

Sage wanted them to shut up. She *needed* them to shut up and listen to her. Couldn't they see she was terrified? Didn't they know she was falling apart? And what about the crying and moaning coming from out in the hall? Couldn't they hear it? Didn't they care?

Nurse Vic winked at Dale. "We're not as old as you think, honey. We'll see who teaches who."

Leonard and Dale laughed, then pulled Sage toward the end of the counter. She looked over her shoulder at Nurse Vic as they dragged her away. "Please," she cried. "This isn't right!"

Nurse Vic sat back down and lit another cigarette.

When they went around the counter and started down the hall, Sage stopped in her tracks. If the attendants hadn't been holding her up, she would have fallen to her knees.

Young girls, ranging in age from children to gangly teenagers, lined each side of the hallway. They were crowded together by twos and threes in beds and chairs and wheelchairs. Some of the beds were more like carts, with large wheels and handles for pushing, and several of the wheelchairs were made of wood, with rusting wheels and thin armrests, as if they'd been pulled from a Victorian museum. Many of the wheelchairs had long, wooden boxes in place of seats, like coffins without lids, in which girls lay crumpled on grimy sheets, their pale, thin limbs pulled into fetal positions, their wrists and hands curled up to their chests.

Most of the girls were either wearing cloth diapers, in various stages of undress, or naked; all were thin, their spines like pale ridges, their shoulder blades sticking out like sharp wings. Bruises and scrapes covered their skin, and a few had what looked like cigarette burns. At first Sage thought some of them were dead, their features and limbs were so cadaverous, but then she realized they were sleeping, or unable—or unwilling—to move. Several tossed their heads around, blind eyes searching and searching, while others looked at Sage with haunted eyes, reflecting all the horror she felt.

One girl's face was crusty and bleeding, as if it had exploded from the inside. Some were missing body parts, arms or legs or hands, while others had misshapen heads, or deformed limbs or torsos. Dark splotches and brownish-yellow puddles speckled the tiled floor, and moans, honking cries, and gibberish filled the air, along with the stench of human waste.

A black terror grew inside Sage's chest, choking her, closing her throat. The rumors were true. This was no school. It was a nightmare, a dumping ground for the broken and insane and unwanted. No wonder the people in charge never allowed parents in the ward. They would have called the police. Again, she asked herself how her mother could have left Rosemary in such a horrible place.

Dale put his free hand to his nose. "Sweet Jesus," he said. "What is that smell?"

"You'll get used to it," Leonard said, and yanked Sage forward.

Undeterred by her resistance, he and Dale dragged her down the crowded hall, past a young girl inside a coffin-like box stained with something dark and sticky-looking. The girl turned her head and looked up at them, her face full of pain, her eyes pleading for help. An older girl smiled at Sage, gleeful and happy, as if she had a hilarious secret that she was determined to keep to herself. Sage squeezed her eyes shut and tried to cover her ears, but Leonard and Dale kept tugging her arms down. Her heart hammered like a runaway train in her chest. This couldn't be real. It couldn't be. No one would do this to children. No one would treat them like this. Maybe she was dead. Maybe the bus had crashed on the way here and she had been killed. Maybe this was hell.

A loud buzzer sounded and she jumped, the deafening tone going on and on and on. The girls in the hallway grew agitated, flailing and crying out and screaming, impossibly louder than before. A door slammed behind them and a bald attendant with muscular, tattooed arms ran past them, then turned down another corridor.

Leonard and Dale followed his route, taking Sage down the same hall. This one was narrower than the first and was lined with four sets of double doors marked Ward A, B, C, and D. Outside the door to Ward A, a teenage girl in a wheelchair was hitting another girl who was sitting on the floor and yowling, her hands up to ward off the blows. Leonard let go of Sage and pulled the two girls apart, pushing the one in the wheelchair away from the one on the floor. Then he grabbed Sage's arm again and kept going without looking back to see if the fight had been averted. At the end of the hall, they stopped at the double doors to Ward D. Leonard unlocked one side and pushed it open. Wails and shouts and screams erupted from inside the room, along with bursts of profanity. A rancid stench as thick as the paint on the walls wafted over them, making Sage gag. Unbelievably, the odor was even stronger than it had been in the main hall, like shit and piss and vomit mixed with the underlying tang of disinfectant and bleach.

"Oh my God," Dale said, coughing.

"Better buckle up, buttercup," Leonard said, then yanked Sage into Ward D.

It was hard to tell which was worse, the noise or the smell. The air tasted like death; the inhuman, guttural cries coming from what sounded like a hundred tortured souls, rising and falling and rising again, made the hair on the back of her neck stand up. She'd never heard anything like it in her life, not even in the horror movies Noah loved to watch.

Ward D was L-shaped, with a vast main room and a smaller tiled space off to the left that looked like it might be a large, open restroom. Hooded strips of fluorescent lights lined the peeling ceiling, the long white tubes that still worked filling the room with a stark light. What looked like a hundred iron beds filled the main floor, all of them white and crammed together end to end, footboard to headboard, with a narrow walkway in between. Every bed was occupied, some with two girls on each mattress. Many of the girls were wearing straitjackets, sitting or kneeling or lying vacant-eyed; a few were tied to headboards with ropes, while others lay in their own waste. Some of the residents were naked; many wore only cloth diapers, while others were in crude, handmade uniforms. More rail-thin girls in wooden carts lined the right side of the room, while others crawled or jumped from bed to bed, laughing and howling and screaming. It seemed like everyone was moving—rocking back and forth, rolling their heads, licking their fingers, twisting their arms, shaking all over, like a roiling sea of human beings. The few who weren't moving sat still as stones. One young woman sat forward on her bed, her torso bent impossibly flat against her legs, her head between her knees as if she'd been folded in half like a piece of cardboard. Another lay on the filthy floor next to the wall, her ankle tied to a support beam with a chain.

Sage stood in shock, numb and speechless and appalled. Willowbrook, the school where her beloved sister had been locked away for the past six years, reminded her of a concentration camp. She'd seen the photos in history class: the skeletal inmates, lying and standing and sitting in spaces made for half as many, some dirty, others partially clothed, all eyes devoid of hope and sanity. How was this abomination allowed to exist in the United States of America? And in the seventies, no less, when they could record music on an eight-track tape and put a man on the moon? This had to be a nightmare. It *had* to be. How could anyone survive?

Suddenly a high-pitched scream erupted in a far corner of the ward. Sage looked, and saw the muscular attendant with the tattooed arms and a female attendant with a frizzy Afro chasing a naked girl around the room, hopping over beds and stretching their hands out to catch her. The female attendant moved with surprising speed considering her barrel-wide chest and the way she limped when she ran, like she had a bad hip. The naked girl looked to be around eighteen years old, with droopy breasts that seemed too large for her thin body; her pallid skin was covered with jagged scars and boot-shaped bruises. She screamed and spat at the attendants, then ran away before they could reach her. When she raced into the tiled room, they chased her inside. Shouting and the sudden hiss of water echoed out of the room; then the tattooed attendant hauled the girl back out, kicking and screaming and soaking wet. She slipped away from him and ran again. The majority of the girls watched in fear and fascination, some jeering and laughing wildly, a few crying. Others lay or sat or stood silently, with no reaction at all; no furrowed brows or worried eyes, no sadness or fear.

"I'll take it from here," Leonard shouted at Dale. "Go back to administration and find out where they want you next."

"Are you sure?" Dale said.

Leonard nodded. "This ain't my first rodeo, kid."

With a sigh of relief, Dale let go of Sage and hurried out of Ward D. Leonard locked the door behind him, then took Sage by the arm again and led her toward the beds. She dug in her heels, refusing to let him take her in any farther.

"I don't belong here," she said. "This isn't right. You can't do this to me!"

"Of course it's right," he said. He pointed toward the far end of the room. "That's your bed right over there. Now get moving."

She shook her head. "No, it's not. That's my sister's bed! I've never been here before in my life. I'm not Rosemary!"

He gave her a hard shake, wrenching her arm and making her teeth rattle. "Do you want to go back in the pit again? Because that's where they're gonna put you if you don't start behaving."

The naked girl screamed again, louder and higher than Sage thought humanly possible. To her surprise, Leonard turned and watched, waiting to see what was going to happen next. The attendants had cornered the girl behind a chair. She gaped at her pursuers like a caged animal, her breath shallow and quick, her bloodshot eyes darting around the room. The tattooed attendant held out his muscular arms and rocked side to side like a wrestler ready to attack, laughing as if it was a game. The girl lifted the chair above her head, her wiry arms straining with the effort, and smashed it against the floor. The wooden back split in two, cracking like bone. One of the legs broke off and spun across the tiled floor.

"It's okay, Norma," the female attendant said. "Just calm down. We want to help you."

Norma. Why did that name seem important? Then Sage remembered. *Oh shit.* Dr. Baldwin had said Norma was Rosemary's best friend and the girl she called her sister. But that didn't mean it was *this* Norma, did it?

Norma growled and grunted as she ripped off the back of the chair with her bare hands. Splinters pierced her skin, and one particularly jagged piece of wood stabbed her wrist and tore her flesh. Blood dripped from her wrist onto her thighs and feet. She stomped on the chair until its remaining legs broke off, then picked up the pieces, hurled them at the attendants, and bolted toward the door. Dodging the projectiles, the tattooed attendant raced after her. When he caught up with her, he grabbed her by the arm and twisted it behind her back, grimacing with the effort, then gripped her other arm and did the same. Norma screamed again, over and over and over. The female attendant hurried over and slapped her hard across the face. Norma went silent, hung her head, and slumped toward the floor. The tattooed attendant lifted her up and carried her to a bed, the blood from her wrist leaving a red trail. As soon as he set her on the mattress, she tried to escape again, but the female attendant sat on her stomach while the tattooed attendant held her arms.

"Norma, Norma," the female attendant said, shaking her head, her frizzy Afro shaking too. "What are you doing? You finally get to come back to the ward and this is how you act?"

Norma glared up at her, panting through clenched teeth.

"Do you want to sleep in here again?" the female attendant said. "Or do you want to be punished?"

Norma shook her head. "Not punished," she said. "No, no."

"Are you going to behave?" the tattooed attendant said.

Finally, Norma nodded and gave in. She turned her head to one side and closed her eyes, her arms and legs going slack. The female attendant stood, and the tattooed attendant slowly let go and stepped back. They both wiped their sweat-slicked faces, then just stood there for a moment, trying to catch their breath.

"Get some bandages," the female attendant finally said. "We can't have her bleeding all over the place."

The tattooed attendant nodded and started across the ward in Sage's direction, trudging toward the door like a massive robot. The girls and women in his path shrank away—those who noticed him, at least.

When the coast was finally clear, Leonard pushed Sage toward Rosemary's bed, dodging wayward arms and legs and sidestepping dark puddles. When the tattooed attendant was about three beds away, Leonard shouted over to him.

"Hey, Wayne! Look who we found."

Wayne? Sage startled, surprised to hear the name so soon.

Wayne looked over and wrinkled his forehead. "Where was she this time?"

"Damned if I know," Leonard said. "Vic and I figured you could tell us."

"Yeah, right," Wayne said, giving him a dirty look. "You two need to stop with your fucking gossip. You're worse than a couple of old ladies." He picked a girl off the floor and tossed her on a bed, then continued toward the exit.

Sage dropped her gaze, afraid to look him in the eye. Just what she needed—the one person who might know something about her sister, and he looked like he could rip someone's head off. When he was out of earshot, she said to Leonard, "Why do you think he knows where Rosemary is?"

"Don't play stupid with me," Leonard said. "You know why."

"No, I don't. I swear. I have no idea."

"Uh-huh, whatever you say." He continued herding her down the aisle between the rows of iron beds, past the growing puddle of Norma's blood. The female attendant with the frizzy Afro was sitting on the mattress next to Norma, holding her wrist and pulling splinters out of her hands.

"You see that shit?" Leonard said. "You remember anything now?"

Sage shook her head, too overwhelmed to speak.

Those girls and young women who were aware of the world around them stared at her with pitiful, knowing eyes. One laughed, leaned over to a girl in the next bed, and whispered behind her hand. Another reached out and yanked Sage's hair, pulling hard. Sage raised a protective hand to her head and hunched her shoulders to make herself smaller. Someone else touched her cheek, fingers brushing dead cold against her skin. Another woman got up and followed her and Leonard to the end of the row, where a teenage girl sat on the next-to-last bed, watching silently. She looked to be around fifteen or sixteen, with piercing blue eyes peering out of a face covered in scars, marled and red like a slab of petrified beef. More scars covered one side of her neck and the length of one arm.

When they reached Rosemary's bed, Sage could see inside the tiled room where Norma had tried to get away. A row of sinks and low-slung toilets without lids lined one wall, and half a dozen steel trollies lined the other. Most of the toilets were cracked and broken; some had dirty toilet paper hanging over the edge. Brown streaks and yellow puddles seemed to mar nearly every surface—the floor, the sinks, the toilets, the walls. She swallowed the gorge rising in her throat and turned toward the window. Night had fallen and it was snowing outside, sheets of white flakes dropping thick and fast. The wind groaned against the ice-covered windowpanes, forcing snow between the glass and a scratched sheet of Plexiglas that covered the inside. Obviously someone had already thought about breaking the window and jumping out. For the first time, Sage realized how cold it was in the ward, and remembered she no longer had her jacket.

"Do you know what they did with my coat?" she asked Leonard. "It's brown suede with—"

"Nope," he said, cutting her off. "Didn't see it when we picked you up."

"But I had it when I got here. Can you get it back for me?"

He let out a sarcastic laugh. "You're shittin' me, right? You know how it works in this place. If something's gone, it's gone. 'Cept you, of course. You seem to be the strange exception to that rule. You're like a cat with nine lives or something."

"That's because I'm not Rosemary. My sister is still missing."

"Yeah, yeah," he said. "That's what you keep telling me."

"What about a sweater and some shoes? It's freezing in here."

He rolled his eyes. "Does it look like there's an extra sweater or pair of shoes laying around this place? Now sit."

She looked at the bed, searched the thin, grimy blanket for the cleanest-looking spot, then did as she was told. The mattress was lumpy and hard, the frame of the bed nearly poking through on the edges. A stained straitjacket hung over the footboard, like a sweater tossed haphazardly aside after school. She couldn't help picturing Rosemary in it, helpless and afraid, her arms trapped around her waist by the row of leather straps. She was about to ask Leonard if he'd take the straitjacket away when he picked it up.

"Now that you're back where you belong," he said, "do I need to restrain you, or you gonna stay put this time?"

She shook her head. "I'll stay put."

"Good girl. No one's gonna tolerate any more shit from you, you hear? Least of all Marla and Wayne."

"Who's Marla?"

He pointed at the female attendant who was tending to Norma. "How could you forget about Marla? You know you don't mess with her."

She glanced at Marla, grateful for the warning, then looked up at Leonard. For the thousandth time, she tried to think of something to say to make him—*anyone*—believe her. Nothing came to her.

"When do I see Dr. Baldwin again?" she said instead.

He scoffed. "How the hell should I know? Probably not until the next time you try to run away, which I wouldn't even think about if I were you."

"What about classes?" she said. "Do we have any tomorrow?" Maybe a teacher would listen to her.

"Classes?"

She nodded.

He shook his head in disbelief. "Look, you're not gonna fool me by playing stupid. So quit trying." Then he dropped the straitjacket over the footboard of the bed and walked away.

As she watched him go, an odd numbness mixed with growing panic started to spread through her body, icing her legs and arms and heart. What did he mean she wouldn't see Dr. Baldwin unless she tried to run away again? The residents saw doctors on a regular basis, didn't they? She *had* to see Dr. Baldwin again. Or any doctor. And soon. They wouldn't just stick her in a ward and forget about her—would they?

Wishing she could disappear, she started to pull her legs up on the bed, to curl up and make herself smaller; then she noticed the filth on her feet. And she had no way to wipe them clean. She stood and looked down at the blanket. The end near the footboard was dirtier. She lifted the blanket and looked underneath. The mattress was dirty too, but not as bad as the blanket. Rosemary must have wiped her feet on the top of the blanket before getting under it. She sat down again and wiped her feet on the end of the blanket too, careful not to touch the filth with her fingers. Then she sat in the middle of the mattress, her knees under her chin, her arms wrapped around her knees, the black terror needling its way into her every crease and pore.

When Wayne returned to the ward with bandages for Norma, he glanced in her direction, then quickly looked away. Unable to decide if the look on his face was anger or worry, she thought about getting up and approaching him to ask what he knew about Rosemary. But what would she say, and how would she say it? If she pissed him off like Leonard had, she'd get nowhere. Before she could decide what to do, he gave the bandages to Marla and left again.

After bandaging Norma's wrist, Marla went over to a Plexiglas cubicle near the ward door, sat down inside, and put her hand on a light switch. "All right, ladies!" she yelled. "Lights out in five!"

When Sage saw the able-bodied girls and women scrambling beneath the covers of their beds, she did the same. A few seconds later, the ward went dark. She lay down and closed her flooding eyes, every thud of her heart like an explosion inside her skull. She put her hands over her ears to shut out the sounds of human suffering all around her and prayed for sheer exhaustion to overtake her, to release her into sleep. Then something crawled on her leg, inching along her skin. Something else trailed up the back of her neck. She brushed it away, trying not to think about what it might be. Unlike séances and needles and tunnels, insects were not on her list of fears—and Willowbrook made any and all fears seem foolish by comparison anyway— but she'd rather not be under the covers with cockroaches or any other type of pest. She stood up, shook out the blanket and wiped her hands over the mattress, then got back in bed. When sleep mercifully came, several wretched hours later, she dozed in fits and starts, alternating between nightmares of being chased through a tunnel by Cropsey and dreams of drinking and laughing with Noah and her friends. And, of course, Rosemary.

CHAPTER 5

A shriek pierced the air. Sage startled and opened her eyes, the stark glow of fluorescent lights penetrating the thin blanket over her head. As she struggled to breathe through rancid air as thick as wool, a renewed weight of fear seemed to push her toward the center of the earth. Her shoulders and arms ached from hiding under the blanket, hunched up and praying the other residents would leave her alone. Marla had stayed in the Plexiglas cubicle after lights out but had done nothing to stop the other residents from crying and shouting and fighting and jabbering, on and on and on through the night. Instead, she just sat there, reading and dozing and taking sips from a silver flask. At one point Sage thought someone had been fatally injured, their screams going on for what felt like forever. She sat up and looked around the shadowy ward to see where it was coming from, but she couldn't tell. Marla ignored it. Finally, the screams grew quieter and quieter, then stopped all together.

Now, anxiety rattled deep inside her, a jittering spark that quickly ignited into a flame. Her hands shook and her head throbbed. She needed a cigarette. She threw off the blanket and sat up, certain she was going to be sick. Something crawled on her leg. She brushed it off without looking to see what it was or where it went, then took long, deep breaths and tried to calm down. The girl in the next bed kept singing "Ring Around the Rosy" over and over and over again. Sage wanted her to stop.

On the other side of the ward, Marla stood in the entrance to the tiled room, yelling, "Rise and shine, ladies. It's shower day. You know the drill. If you can walk and you can hear me, get undressed, come over here, and wait your turn."

In front of the tiled room entrance, a dozen naked residents lay in steel trollies, while others swayed and cried and fidgeted in a cluster near the wall. More naked girls sat hunched over on the row of toilets, crying and moaning, or sitting with their heads in their hands. Others stood against the opposite wall with their arms up, shoulders bunched, turning round and round while a female attendant in a rain slicker sprayed them down with a hose. After a hasty rinse, the attendant in the rain slicker lined up the drenched residents, haphazardly dried them off—using the same towel for everyone—then ordered them back to their beds to get dressed. Limping as she moved back and forth, Marla helped the residents on the toilets wipe themselves, then took them over to the shower wall to get sprayed down. After helping another group get on the toilets, she steered one of the steel trolleys bearing helpless girls into the shower room so the attendant in the rain slicker could hose them off. When Marla came out again, she stopped, crossed her arms over her barrel chest, and looked down at a young woman who lay in a trolley, one leg splayed over the edge.

"Lordy, Sheila," she said, laughing. "Where's your pride?"

She picked up Shelia's leg and pushed her knees together, then took her into the shower room on the trolley. When she came out with the first trolley-bound resident, she deposited that shivering girl on top of her bed, left her there naked, then lifted another girl into the trolley, undressing her and piling her clothes on the mattress. As soon as Marla pushed the trolley toward the showers, the woman in the next bed snatched a dress from the pile and hid it under her pillow. After loading more trolleys with residents and taking them into the shower room, Marla started going from bed to bed with a laundry cart, removing soiled diapers and clothes. When she reached Sage's bed, she stopped. Sage was sitting up, the thin blanket around her shoulders.

"Come on, girl," Marla said. "Don't give me a hard time this morning. You know I'm not going to put up with it."

Sage had to pee, but she was determined to hold off as long as she could. Hopefully someone would figure out who she was before she had to use those filthy toilets. "I don't have to use the bathroom and I don't need a shower," she said. "I took one yesterday. At home. In my apartment." It was a lie, but she wanted to make a point.

"Uh-huh," Marla said, reaching for her. "Sure you did."

Sage scooted sideways, out of her reach. "I'm not Rosemary. I'm her twin sister, Sage."

"Oh yeah?" Marla said. "I musta forgot again." She impatiently motioned Sage toward her. "Now get up and get undressed so you can use the toilet and get washed. God knows when we'll have the next shower day."

"I'm telling the truth," Sage said. "Please, you have to listen to me. I know my sister is missing. If Dr. Baldwin calls my stepfather, he—"

Before Sage could finish, Marla grabbed her by the shoulders, flipped her facedown on the bed, and started yanking off her clothes. Sage twisted and kicked, trying to shove her away, but it was no use—Marla was strong as an ox. She put her forearm across Sage's neck and pushed down hard, clenching her teeth and pinning her to the mattress like a moth under a rock.

"I told you," she said. "Old Marla is not going to put up with it today. Now you can either cooperate and take your shower, or I can have Nurse Vic come give you something to calm you down. Which is it?"

Sage clawed at Marla's arm, gasping and unable to breathe.

Marla pushed harder. "You gonna stop this crap?"

Sage nodded, her mouth opening and closing like a dying fish. Finally, Marla released her. Sage turned on her side, her hand to her throat, coughing and gagging.

"Get up," Marla demanded.

Sage slid to the side of the mattress and stood on wobbly legs, still coughing and holding her throat.

Marla put her hands on her hips and glared at her. "Now, are you going to get undressed, or do I have to do it for you?"

Sage shook her head, then unbuttoned her skirt with trembling fingers, took it off, and laid it on the bed. She pulled her crocheted vest and her top over her head, put them on the bed, then unfastened her bra and slid it off, keeping one arm over her breasts.

"Speed it up, girl," Marla said. "I ain't got all day."

Still covering her breasts, Sage pulled down her underwear with one hand and stepped out of them, shame and fear burning her face. Then she pushed her clothes under her sister's pillow, trying to cover her pubic area with one hand. Common sense told her that no one but Marla was paying attention to her body and almost everyone else was naked too, but it didn't help.

Marla pointed at the shower room. "Get yourself on over there," she said. "And don't be acting up again or I'll get Nurse Vic after you, you hear?"

Sage nodded and made her way over to the tiled room, edging between beds and wheelchairs and carts and trolleys, snaking between naked, screaming, crying, laughing girls and women. Tears blurred her vision as she glanced down before each step to avoid the yellowish splotches and pools of dark liquid on the floor. Marla followed, limping and barking orders at other girls. When it was Sage's turn to enter the tiled room, she held her breath and went over to the row of toilets. Marla tried flushing some of them, but they didn't work. Toilet paper and feces filled nearly every bowl. Some were clogged by towels and cloth diapers. Cockroaches skittered along the edges of the floor. Sage stood frozen, trying not to breathe or throw up.

"Get yourself on over there," Marla said, motioning at a free toilet. "This ain't no time to be picky."

Sage shook her head.

Exasperated, Marla started toward her, pressing her lips together into an angry, hard line. Before she could reach her, Sage went over to the toilet, closed her eyes, and sat down. She tried to pee but couldn't, despite the fact that her bladder was full to bursting. Unable to hold her breath another second, she exhaled and filled her lungs again, the putrid stench of human waste burning her nostrils and throat. Tears of rage and disgust sprang up behind her eyelids. She squeezed them away and released her bladder. When she was finished, she looked around for clean toilet paper, but there was none to be found. Marla pulled a girl off a toilet and dragged her over to the attendant in the rain slicker, then headed for Sage. Sage stood and hurried over to the shower wall and waited to be hosed down.

When it was her turn, she spat and sputtered and tried to protect her face and breasts from the stinging torrent of icy water, but the attendant yanked her arms up and spun her around with rough hands. Sage turned toward the wall and put her hands over her face, the water slamming into her head and back and buttocks. When she was finished, the attendant patted her down with the soaking wet towel, then moved on to the next resident. Marla ordered Sage back to her bed and told her to get dressed.

Shivering, Sage did as she was told, her teeth rattling. The girls and young women who were lucky enough to have clothes and were able to dress themselves struggled into dresses and blouses and skirts, while the rest of the residents with clothes lay helpless beside their crumpled garments, forgotten. Some, while waiting for a clean diaper, had messed themselves again. When Sage returned to her bed, she put her underwear and clothes on over her still-wet skin, pulling and tugging at the material, then wrapped up in the thin blanket and sat on the bed, rubbing her arms and legs to get warm.

She watched the door, praying that someone would come in and admit there'd been a mistake—Dr. Baldwin had called Alan again; he had explained everything, and now she was free to go home. Money for a bus ticket was waiting in his office, along with her suede jacket and the clogs she'd lost when they grabbed her in the waiting room. Then Dr. Baldwin would apologize. Or maybe Alan was on his way to get her. He'd be pissed he had to retrieve her, but she didn't care as long as he got her out of there. Somewhere in the back of her mind she knew it was all wishful thinking, but it was the only hope she had left.

Once the residents were all showered and diapered and dressed, Marla limped her way around the ward, shouting and pulling those who could stand from their beds, hefting others into wheelchairs and carts. Then she herded everyone toward the door.

"Come on," she shouted. "Let's go. It's time to move."

While Marla unlocked the double doors, the attendant in the rain slicker started to mop the floor, filling the air with the strong sting of

Pine-Sol. Sage stood, grateful to be leaving the ward. Maybe she'd find someone to listen to her. But the scarred girl in the next bed stood at the same time, still naked, then turned to face Sage, blocking her way. The red-marled skin on her face and neck reached over one shoulder and covered part of her chest, including one breast. She held up a dress with a purple top and lilac-covered skirt and frowned at Sage.

"I don't want to wear this one yet," she said. "But somebody took my other one and it'll be weeks before laundry brings more."

"I'm sorry," Sage said because she didn't know what else to say.

"My mom sent it to me, remember? And I hid it under my mattress because I was saving it for when she visits again."

When the girl mentioned her mother visiting again, Sage couldn't help thinking of Rosemary. How many days, weeks, months, *years* had she spent waiting for her mother to do the same? How many times had her heart been broken, longing for someone who would never come? "Does your mother come to see you a lot?"

"You know she don't," the girl said. "It's been two years since the last time. And I don't know when she's coming again, but when she left, she said, 'Tina, I'll be coming again real soon, so behave yourself. And make sure you always wear a nice dress.'"

Sage cringed inside. *Two years?* What made this poor girl think her mother was ever coming back? "How long have you been here?" she said.

Tina looked at her like it was the dumbest question in the world. "Why are you asking me that? We always talk about how hard it is to tell about them things in here. But as far as I can figure, I think it's been about eight years since my mom left and Daddy dumped the boiling water on me. Maybe a little longer."

Oh God. So that was how she'd gotten the scars. And eight years? That meant she'd been a little girl when it happened. "Why did your father do that to you?"

"You know why. 'Cause I'm feeble-minded and Daddy didn't want me no more."

Sage didn't know what to say. How could a father intentionally disfigure his own daughter? And how had poor Tina stayed sane in this awful place for eight long years? If she *was* sane.

"No need to look so sad," Tina said. "You been here long enough to realize I'm not the only kid from a broken home stuck in here." She pointed at a young girl, about seven or eight years old, who was shuffling toward the door with her head down. "That's Ginny. She showed up while you were gone. Her daddy brought her here in a big fancy Cadillac, dropped her off, and said he didn't want no news of her ever again, even if she died. And there ain't a darn thing wrong with her." She pulled the purple and lilac dress over her head and pushed her arms into the sleeves. "Guess I better wear this instead of walking around naked as a jaybird. You been in the pit again?"

Sage couldn't take her eyes off Ginny, who looked sluggish and miserable, moving like a zombie among the rest of the residents. Had the threats about sending disobedient kids to Willowbrook been true too? How many other residents were like Ginny, healthy but thrown away by their parents? That idea was horrible enough, but how would a child ever get put in foster care or adopted if they were trapped in here? And if they managed to survive and get out, how would they ever feel normal again?

Tina waved a hand in front of Sage's face. "Hello? You in there?"

Sage shook her head to clear it. "I'm sorry. What did you say?"

"I asked if you been in the pit again."

"The pit?"

"You know. Seclusion. The rubber room. The pit?"

Sage shook her head again. "No, I wasn't in the pit."

"You been on the experiment ward? I heard they got shiny floors and drapes on the windows over there. And toys and silverware and paper to write on."

"The experiment ward? What is that?"

Tina shrugged. "Where they do experiments. I don't know what kind."

"On the residents?"

"Yeah," Tina said. "That's why they let them have toys and stuff."

A chill passed through Sage. What other rumors about Willowbrook were true? For a second, she thought about telling Tina who she really was, but it could backfire. Tina might not believe her. And if Tina was Rosemary's friend, she might know something that could help. But if Sage tried to convince her Rosemary was still missing, she might get confused, stop trusting her, and clam up.

Tina made a face. "Well, *don't* tell me where you were then, fine. Guess we all got secrets." Then she smiled, and Sage caught a glimpse of the girl she must have been before—innocent and full of hope for the future. It broke Sage's heart and reminded her of Rosemary at the same time.

"Speaking of secrets," she said, "what do you know about that bald, tattooed attendant Wayne?"

Tina furrowed her brow. "What do you mean, what do I know about him? He's awful and mean and everybody's scared of him. That's all I need to know."

"But why would Leonard and Nurse Vic say he might know where . . ." She hesitated. "Why would they say he knew where I was?"

" 'Cause everybody knows he's got a thing for you. They probably thought he snuck you out of here."

"Would I have gone with him?"

The frown line between Tina's eyes deepened. "What the devil is wrong with you? Did you hit your head and forget everything you ever knew? Of course you wouldn't have gone with him! Not willingly, anyway." Then her eyes went wide with concern. "Did they do something to you while you were gone? Did they give you one of those lobotomies or experiment on you? Is that why you can't remember anything?"

Sage shook her head. "No, it was nothing like that. I'm just . . . I'm a little confused right now, that's all."

"Well, don't worry, it'll all come back to you soon enough. Or maybe you don't want it to." For a brief moment, sorrow clouded her eyes. Then she smiled again.

Sage tried to return the smile, but it felt weak and quivery. Still, it was nice to know at least one person who was on Rosemary's side. "I know this might sound stupid, but do you think he took me somewhere? Or do you know where I might have gone? I'm having trouble remembering."

"Sorry," Tina said. "I don't. You kept saying you were going to get out of here. That's it. I thought you were joking."

Sage considered what she said. Maybe Rosemary had escaped after all. Maybe Wayne had helped, or maybe she'd done it on her own. The latter seemed more likely after what Tina said about Wayne; it didn't seem possible that he could have dragged her out of there kicking and screaming without someone noticing. But where would she have gone? And how was she surviving?

Then she had another thought, one that hadn't occurred to her until now, and her heart constricted. What if Rosemary had escaped and was lying dead out in the woods somewhere, slowly being buried beneath the snow?

"Hey," she said. "This is probably another stupid question, but is there any way to get a cigarette around here?" Asking was probably pointless—even if she could sneak a smoke somewhere, she'd get in trouble if she got caught—but it was worth a try. She needed something, anything, to calm her nerves.

Tina crossed her arms and gave her a stern look. "Now, why would you want one of those nasty things?"

Sage shrugged one shoulder. "I don't know, just to try something different."

"Well, that would be really dumb. And I don't know anything about that stuff anyway. You sure they didn't do something to your brain while you were gone?"

Marla yelled at them from across the room.

"Let's go, ladies! Stop your lollygagging and move it!"

Tina looked over her shoulder, then grabbed Sage's hand and pulled her toward the door. "Come on, we gotta go."

Startled, Sage yanked her hand from her grasp. Tina turned to face her, a confused, wounded look pulling at her face.

"What's wrong?" she said.

"I'm not . . ." Sage began, then stopped. She couldn't tell the truth about why she had pulled away because it was senseless and cruel; letting Tina take her hand would mean she was one of *them,* one of the tormented souls who called Willowbrook home. And she would never be one of them. She wouldn't let it happen. "I'm sorry," she said. "I've been feeling sick and I don't want you to catch anything from me."

"Well, that stinks," Tina said. "I hope you feel better soon because I'm really happy you're back."

"Thanks," Sage said. Then, before she could ask where they were going, Tina turned and headed toward the door. Sage rubbed her arms and followed, hoping she hadn't upset the only person who'd been decent to her since she arrived. She needed an ally, someone who knew the ins and outs of Willowbrook and might be able to help her find Rosemary. But it was true that she wasn't feeling well. Her stomach churned with acid and fear. Then she had an idea. Maybe if she told someone she was ill, they'd let her see a doctor; maybe even someone besides Dr. Baldwin.

Nearing the door, she approached Marla with one hand on her stomach. Marla had just finished separating two girls who'd been screeching and yanking on each other's hair, and now she stood between them with her arms out, like a referee between two boxers.

"I'm sorry to bother you, but—" Sage started.

"What is it?" Marla said, giving her a surly look.

"I think something's wrong with me," Sage said. "I need to see a doctor." She bent forward and winced, pretending to be in pain.

Marla shot the girls a threatening glare, then dropped her arms and looked Sage up and down, her lips pursed. "You need stitches?"

Sage shook her head.

"You dying?"

She shook her head again.

"Well then," Marla said, "you know the rules. No blood, no broken bones, no impending death, no doctor." She gestured toward the wooden carts lined up against the far wall. "Now make yourself useful and grab a cripple cart."

"But my stomach," Sage said. "What if my appendix is about to burst or my spleen ruptured?"

Marla put her hands on her hips. "Are you really testing me again, girl? What in tarnation got into you while you were out doing whatever it was you were doing? You need to remember who's in charge around here. Now get your ass over to those cripple carts before I call Nurse Vic and have her straighten you out."

Sage opened her mouth to respond, but Marla turned and limped away.

Fighting the urge to scream in frustration, Sage looked around for Tina but didn't see her anywhere. She made her way through the crowd over to the line of carts, dodging unruly legs and reaching hands and swaying heads. If the attendants didn't allow the residents to see a doctor when they were hurt or sick, how would she ever talk to anyone besides Dr. Baldwin? How would she ever find someone who would listen or care? She tried to calm down. If Marla wouldn't listen to her, maybe someone else would. Maybe she and the other residents were leaving the ward to go to a cafeteria where a sympathetic lunch lady would believe her, or a classroom where a caring teacher would realize she was telling the truth. She took the handles of a cart and looked down at the silent occupant of the wooden box, an adolescent girl wearing nothing but a cloth diaper and staring at the ceiling. No blanket lined the box; not even a thin sheet or a flat pillow. Despite feeling anything but friendly, Sage tried to smile at her to show her she cared, but the girl gave no indication of awareness. Sage thought about saying hello and asking if she was okay but didn't think she could do it without crying. The horror and heartbreak of the poor girl's nightmarish existence—along with every other tormented soul struggling to survive inside Willowbrook—felt as thick and heavy as breathing lead. Instead of trying to communicate, Sage pushed the cart toward the door, concentrated on putting one foot in front of the other, and tried not to run into anyone or step on anything. All she could do now was stay out of trouble and pray for something to change.

Marla propped open both sides of the double door, then steered one of the wheelchair-bound residents into the hall. The rest of the residents followed, those who could walk pushing the ones in the wooden carts and wheelchairs. Out in the hall, more residents and attendants spilled chaotically out of the other wards to join the crowd—young girls and teenagers and adult women; some moving zombie-like, gangly and awkward and slow, others trying to hurry forward, pushing and bumping into everyone around them. Through the open doors of one ward, Sage could see what seemed like a hundred naked women on the floor, sitting or squatting or kneeling or cross-legged or bent over, but all of them rocking, moving, swaying. No beds filled the room. No tables or chairs. Just women.

Sage looked everywhere for her sister, searching every face in the wards and hall. With this many people in one building, she thought it would have been easy for Rosemary to return, unseen and overlooked, to get lost in the endless hordes of women and girls crammed into one floor—especially when so many looked so similar, with hollow faces and vacant eyes, thin limbs and snarled hair. Finding her sister among the other residents was improbable, but she could hope.

Shouting orders for everyone to keep moving, the ward attendants herded the residents forward, funneling them into the main hallway like animals into a processing chute, squeezing them between the beds and carts on both sides. Everyone stood too close. They crowded Sage's space and pressed nearer and nearer and nearer. She was jostled and shoved, her feet were stepped on, and her elbows were knocked into her ribs. It sounded like thousands of people were shouting and weeping, mumbling and screaming. Between feeling crushed, the chaotic din echoing off the walls, and the horrible stench that hung like a thick haze in the air, she could hardly breathe.

"Please move back," she said. "Don't lean on me. Please. You don't need to stand so close."

No one listened.

She forced her elbows out, kept close to the cart, and shuffled along with the slithering, rambling, fitful horde. While looking down to avoid the brown smears and yellow puddles on the floor, she accidentally ran the front of the cart into another resident. She stopped and looked up, alarmed. Hopefully she hadn't hurt anyone. A teenage girl in a cloth diaper and a pink sweater stood bent over, one hand holding the back of her bare leg.

"Oh my God," Sage said. "I'm so sorry. Are you all right?"

"That's okay, that's okay," the girl said, her eyes rolling toward the ceiling. "That's okay, that's okay." Then she straightened, turned, and kept going.

Mortified, Sage held the cart back briefly to see if the girl was bruised or bleeding. Thankfully, no marks reddened her pale skin. No blood ran down her leg.

When Sage started moving again, she stood on her tiptoes and peered over tilted heads and sloped shoulders to see where they were going. She searched for Tina too, but picking one person out of the roiling mob was impossible. At the end of the hall was a set of double steel doors, which hopefully meant they were being taken to classrooms, with desks and a teacher and some semblance of order. Willowbrook *was* called a school, after all. Surely most parents sent their kids there for the benefits of special educators who knew how to work with the disabled. There had to be *some* reason they let their children live there. The tiniest spark of hope ignited inside her. Surely a teacher would listen to her.

Then she saw where they were headed, and a cold slab of dread pressed against her chest.

CHAPTER 6

Standing in front of the nurses' station where Sage had first seen Nurse Vic, two burly-looking attendants allowed one resident at a time to take a plastic medicine cup from a stone-faced woman in a gray skirt and blue blouse. Nurse Vic supervised the process from behind the counter, refilling the water glass and restocking the medicine cups. One by one the residents put the cups to their lips, then took a sip of water from the glass and threw back their heads to swallow. After the woman in the gray skirt took their empty cups and put them back on the counter, Nurse Vic waved the residents on toward the double doors at the end of the hall. The line limped slowly but steadily along. Anyone in a wheelchair or cart who was unable to sit up on their own was heaved upright by the attendants, and the woman in the gray skirt held the cups to their mouths and gave them a sip of water, carelessly letting it spill down their chins and necks. If a resident was uncooperative for some reason, whether sitting or standing, the attendants forced the pills into their mouths with their fingers, without giving them a drink afterward.

Sage didn't know what to do. She couldn't let

them drug her. Couldn't let them turn her into a zombie who slept and swayed and lurched around this hellhole. She'd never get out of there if she was hopped up or knocked out by some powerful psychiatric pill. Then she realized no one checked to see if the residents actually swallowed the drugs—not the attendants, not the woman in the gray skirt, not Nurse Vic. If she was careful, she could hide the pills in her mouth and get rid of them later. No one would know. Surely she couldn't be the only person in Willowbrook who did that. If she got caught, she'd likely be punished, but it was a risk she had to take.

Then she noticed a slender girl with a familiar head of strawberry-blond hair at the front of the medicine line, swaying back and forth as if listening to music. Sage's breath caught in her chest.

Rosemary.

She let go of the cart and sidled up its side, her bare legs scraping the oversize wheels as she fought her way through the crowd toward the nurses' station, determined to get to her sister. Gently pushing the girls and women to one side and craning her neck to see, she tripped over wayward legs and feet, bumped into shoulders and heads, and tried not to lose her balance. Not that there was anywhere to fall; the rocking, jerking, twisting residents were crushed together like kindling, filling every available space.

"Rosemary!" she yelled.

The strawberry-blond girl stepped up to the woman in the gray skirt and took a plastic cup.

"Rosemary! It's me, Sage! Turn around! I'm right here!"

Out of the corner of her eye, Sage saw Marla shove her way into the crowd and start toward her, anger twisting her face. "Don't you leave that cart there!" she shouted. "Get back to it right now!"

Sage froze, adrenaline coursing like fire through her veins. If Marla sent her to the pit or had Nurse Vic drug her, she'd be done for. She fought her way back to the cart and took the handle. Thankfully, Marla stopped, waited to make sure she was staying with the cart, then turned around and waited near the wall. Breathing a sigh of relief, Sage stood on her tiptoes to look for Rosemary.

Rosemary had taken the pills and was returning the plastic cup to the woman in the gray skirt. Sage almost called out her name again, but stopped. There would be time to find her when they got to the cafeteria or classrooms. And they couldn't reach each other right now, anyway.

Then Rosemary turned, revealing her profile, and Sage's heart sank. The girl had a high, round forehead, bulging eyes, and a cleft lip. It wasn't Rosemary. *Damn it. How could you have been so stupid? Did you really think it would be that easy?*

Besides, if Rosemary had returned, Dr. Baldwin would have realized Sage was telling the truth. Rosemary would have been taken back to her ward, and Sage would have been released. Unless Dr. Baldwin decided not to let her go so she couldn't call the cops on him for keeping her there against her will. Unless he was trying to hide the fact that something bad had happened to Rosemary.

No. She couldn't think like that. This was real life, not some horror movie where the evil doctor locked up sane people and hid bodies in the basement. Then again, no horror movie could ever be as terrifying as Willowbrook.

Pushing the ridiculous thoughts from her mind, she cursed herself for letting her imagination get the better of her. She didn't have time for that shit. It was nearly her turn to take the pills, and she had to figure out how to pretend she'd swallowed them. When she steered the cart up to the counter, one of the burly attendants hefted the girl inside into a sitting position, and the woman in the gray skirt bent down to give her the pills, holding the cup to her lips. For the first time, Sage noticed the woman was barefoot, which meant she was a resident, not an employee. Why was a resident helping hand out drugs? It seemed odd.

After attending to the girl in the cart, the woman handed Sage a plastic cup and the glass filled with murky water. Eyeing Nurse Vic to see if she was paying attention, Sage took the glass and the pills, like tiny orange eggs in the cup. When Nurse Vic lowered her gaze to fill a tray with more drugs, Sage popped the pills into her mouth and, using her tongue, pressed them between her upper teeth and her cheek. But when she started to take a sip of water, she hesitated. Everyone had shared the same glass, smearing the sides and rim with fingerprints and lip marks and drool. But there was no time to react, and nothing she could do about it anyway. She closed her eyes and pretended to take a quick drink, trying not to gag, then put her head back and pretended to swallow. When she was done, she gave the cup and glass back to the woman and, without waiting to be waved on, pushed the cart away from the counter to join the others, who were being herded through one side of the double doors at the end of the hall.

With the bitter taste of dissolving drugs slowly filling her mouth, it was all she could do not to choke and cough. She looked around to see if anyone was watching, then spat the pills into her hand and got ready to drop them on the floor. Then she stopped, holding them tight in her fist. What if someone saw and told Marla or Nurse Vic? Maybe it would be better to wait until they got to the cafeteria or classroom or wherever they were going, so she could put them in a garbage can or drop them under a desk.

At the end of the hall, a janitor pushing a mop and bucket came out through one side of the double doors, then stopped and started to open the other side. Sage could hardly resist the urge to plow the cart through the crowd. She needed to get out of the congested hallway. She wanted to yell at the other residents to hurry up and get out of her way, despite the fact that she had no idea where they were going or why. Anything would be better than being trapped in this heaving sea of tormented humans, swaying and moaning and wailing and twitching.

After propping open the double doors, the janitor pushed the bucket along the hallway, staying close to the wall, keeping his hands wrapped around the mop handle. He wore a white shirt and gray trousers, and he looked more like a college kid than a janitor. All the janitors Sage knew were gray haired and wrinkled, with hunched backs and beer bellies and grizzled chins. This janitor reminded her of Dawn's boyfriend, Len, the star quarterback on the football team, with his broad shoulders, thick brown hair, and strong jaw. Why in the world would someone so young want to work at Willowbrook? Shoveling trash at the Fresh Kills landfill would have been better than working in this awful place. *Anything* would.

Then she had another thought. He was younger

than the other employees—maybe he would listen to her. Maybe he'd believe her if she told him about Rosemary. Unless he'd heard that story a hundred times, which was pretty likely, considering how many other residents probably didn't belong there either, or believed they didn't. He'd probably heard all kinds of stories and desperate pleas for help. Suddenly she realized she was staring at him, and he was staring back. She looked away, sweat breaking out on her forehead. Could he tell she was hiding the drugs in her hand? Was he going to tell on her? Instead of waiting like she planned, she opened her fist to drop the pills on the floor. To her dismay, they stuck to her palm, turning her skin orange. She shook them off, but instead of falling to the floor, they tumbled into the wooden cart, landing next to the girl lying inside. *Shit.* She bent down and scraped the pills into the corner of the box, then wiped her hand on her skirt, praying no one would notice. When she looked up again, the janitor had parked his mop bucket against the wall and was weaving his way through the residents toward her, his face a strange mixture of alarm and surprise.

"Hey," he said when he reached her.

She shrank back, keeping her eyes straight ahead. Maybe if she ignored him, he'd go away. Why would he care if she took her pills or not? He was only a janitor. Then he touched her forearm, his nicotine-stained fingers pressing into her skin as if testing to see if she were real.

"Rosemary?" he said.

She shook her head, too frightened and confused to speak.

"Leave her alone, Eddie!" Marla shouted at him from across the hall. "I'm not gonna warn you twice!"

He glanced at Marla, annoyed, then whispered, "We'll talk later."

She wanted to say something, *anything;* her name, a demand to tell her who he was and why he knew Rosemary. But she was overwhelmed. The residents were bumping into her. Someone stepped on her foot. A girl screamed in her ear. A young woman pushed her so hard she almost fell. Before she could form a reply, he had turned and begun making his way back through the crowd. When he reached the mop bucket, he pushed it in the opposite direction, stealing glances at her over his shoulder. She watched him for as long as she could, then turned forward again and trudged toward the double doors, her mind racing. How did he know Rosemary? Were they friends? Were janitors and residents allowed to be friends? Judging by the surprised look on his face, he knew Rosemary was missing, but what else did he know? And how would he talk to her later? Did he know where she would be?

It seemed like her instincts might be right

about someone younger listening to her, at least. Maybe, between him and whomever she could talk to when she finally got to the cafeteria or a classroom, things would get sorted out. She could be released by the end of the day. *If* she could convince one of them she was Rosemary's twin.

Then she pushed the cart through the doors at the end of the hall and a cold block of fear stopped her in her tracks. No classrooms waited on the other side. No gymnasium or cafeteria. Just a vast, windowless room lined with stained couches and plastic chairs. Crude images of Mickey Mouse and Donald Duck had been painted on the cement walls, as if the cartoon characters could lessen suffering. A television hung bolted to one wall near a Plexiglas cubicle housing a small desk, a chair, and a telephone. More plastic chairs and a dozen round tables were scattered as if someone had purposely run helter-skelter through the room, pushing them this way and that across the stained tile floor, which was still wet with puddles and mop swirls. Twin radiators hissed against the far wall, and fluorescent lights with metal shades hung from the ceiling, casting dark shadows under the residents' eyes, turning their skin even more pale and sickly. The overpowering smell of Pine-Sol, along with the ever-present stench of human excrement, burned her nostrils.

Above it all, there was the ever-present

noise—the inhuman howl of wails and shrieks and moans that somehow grew more deafening in the windowless room than it had been in the ward or the hallway. Like the subterranean cries of an ancient, dying creature echoing inside an underground cave, the sounds fused together until they were all one thing—one clamor, one racket, one tortuous wail going on and on and on, swelling and falling and swelling and falling. Every trapped sound seemed amplified a thousand times over—frantic voices, manic laughter, skin slapping against skin, heavy breathing, sobs and shouts and groans and screams. It seemed impossible that the desperate, horrendous din was coming from humans, but the tortured souls making the noises were right in front of her. It was enough to drive anyone mad.

To add to her dismay, Wayne, the bald, tattooed attendant, was herding everyone inside, yelling at them to move to the far end of the room. "Put the carts against the wall," he shouted. "Come on! Move it!"

Sage fought her way across the Pine-Sol-damp tiles, skirting around a bald girl in a frilly dress who sat splay-legged on the floor and a half-dressed woman who looked unconscious. She parked the cart in the haphazard line of a dozen others below a giant image of Donald Duck, his oversize eyes crossed and black. Several of the carts held two or three girls or young women inside—some naked, others in cloth diapers or straitjackets. A few of the girls were sitting up while others lay curled into fetal positions. Still others lay helpless, their bare, skeletal legs draped across the edge of the cart or sticking straight up, resting on the handles.

Sage looked down at the girl in the cart she'd been pushing to see if she was okay. Her eyes were closed as if she were asleep, her limbs safely tucked inside the wooden box. Glancing around to make sure no one was watching, she lifted one of the other girl's legs back into her cart, then moved another one's arm from over her head into a more comfortable position. After one woman grabbed her hand, someone else tried to bite her, and another girl returned to the same awkward position Sage had just moved her from, she gave up trying to help. No matter how bad she felt for them, there was nothing more she could do. And for all she knew, she could get in trouble for even trying. On shaking legs, she hurried over to a chair in a far corner of the room, put her hands over her ears, and hunched her shoulders to make herself smaller. A shoe flew past her and hit the wall, making her jump.

In what seemed like every square inch of the room, women and girls of various ages sat in plastic chairs or lay on the cold, wet floor. Some wore helmets; others were in straitjackets or had leather straps binding their wrists together.

Some sat slumped in wheelchairs or lay in the wheeled wooden boxes, feces and urine covering their legs. Many wandered aimlessly or stood stock-still, babbling incoherently. All seemed to have bruises and scabs and bloody marks on their skin, marking their arms or legs or faces. They clawed at one another and hit one another and pushed one another around. They pounded on the walls and floors with their feet and hands and heads. A girl in ripped pajamas sat close to the television and stared blankly at *The Dating Game* show on the screen, her lips curled back, her tongue thrusting in and out of her mouth. A woman in a hospital gown stood next to her and laughed loudly every few minutes, then paced back and forth wringing her hands. Sage couldn't help wondering what the residents thought about the images on the TV screen, the contestants in their clean clothes sitting calmly in their chairs, laughing and smiling and having fun. What did they think about other shows—the ones that showed warm homes and normal families, teenagers dancing on *American Bandstand*, news coverage of the Vietnam War? Did they *know* there was an outside world? Did they long to be part of it, or remember when they had been? Did it break their hearts?

A trio of girls, perhaps nine or ten years of age, lay sideways and crooked in four plastic chairs like three forgotten rag dolls, their heads shaved, their arms twisted behind them inside filthy strait-jackets. A girl of about twelve smeared feces on the wall, while a teenager in a muzzle stood near the door slapping her own face. A group of naked residents huddled around the steam radiator to get warm, burn marks lining their arms and shoulders.

The chaos reminded Sage of a painting she'd seen of hell, the sinners of the world tangled together like fish in a net, some missing arms and legs, some being eaten by demons, all bleeding and crying and screaming. Bulging, vacant eyes in emaciated faces, giant heads and wasted bodies.

How long would they be held in this torture chamber? An hour? Two? The rest of the day?

To add to her growing terror, Wayne closed and locked the doors after everyone was inside, then made his way around the room like a bristled, breathing beast, a bully stick in his fist. No other attendants stayed behind. No nurses or additional staff. Obviously Wayne was strong and intimidating, but how could he control this pandemonium-filled room on his own? And who would protect her if he thought she was Rosemary?

Almost immediately, she had the answer to her first question, watching in horror as Wayne pulled residents away from one another and struck those who fought back or didn't cooperate.

He wrestled some to the ground and forced them into straitjackets or twisted their arms behind their backs until they calmed down. A screaming teenager jumped on his back and he yanked her off, then beat her with the bully stick. After separating two residents who were hitting each other, he dragged one to a chair and roughly pushed the other across the room, then made her stand in the corner with her hands in the air. The other woman got up from her chair, met him on his way back, and hooked an arm through his, looking up at him and puckering her lips. He pushed her away. A brown-haired girl lifted a chair over her head, getting ready to smash it over another girl's back; he took it away from her, then tied her in it.

When a bald woman got in a fight with a woman in a flowered housecoat over a slip of paper on the floor, he rushed over to break it up, but it was too late. The woman in the housecoat screamed and held a hand to her ear, blood gushing down her neck. Wayne pulled the woman's hand from her head to see what was wrong and she screamed louder. Her bloody ear dangled from her skull by a jagged thread of skin. Wayne dragged her over to the Plexiglas cubicle and made a phone call. Within minutes, Nurse Vic entered and took the injured woman away. After she was gone, Wayne went around the room, yelling at everyone to sit down, threatening them with the bully stick and a balled-up fist. Most cowered and moved away, but others either didn't listen or didn't hear. Once everyone was relatively calm, he went over to the cubicle, sat down hard in the chair, and lit a cigarette, his leg jerking up and down. As he smoked, his eyes skittered around the room, searching for his next victim.

Struggling to control her fear, Sage tried to figure out how to ask him about Rosemary. She could go over there and try to bum a cigarette. It would be a good excuse to approach him and maybe he'd realize she wasn't Rosemary—unless Rosemary had taken up smoking, which seemed doubtful. But then again, asking for a cigarette might get her in trouble. Maybe he'd tie her up or put her in a straitjacket. Before she had time to decide, another fight broke out. Wayne pounded the cigarette out on the side of the cubicle, launched across the room, and pulled two young women apart.

A minute later, the doors opened and Marla and two other attendants entered, pushing food carts. Wayne locked the doors behind them and began unloading trays filled with bowls from the carts. Marla and one of the other attendants took trays over to the tables and started feeding the residents seated there. The second attendant poured orange juice into plastic cups and passed them out to those who could hold them. Wayne helped by forcing the residents at the tables to gulp down their juice, then taking their empty cups. Sage took the cup she was offered and, realizing for the first time that her throat was sore and parched, took a drink. The juice was thin and watered down, but it helped. Then a strange, metallic tang filled her mouth, like the aftertaste of medicine on her tongue. She wiped her lips on the back of her hand and looked into the cup to figure out how much she'd swallowed. Had she taken a big sip? Two big sips? She couldn't remember. When Marla started limping toward her with a food tray, she dumped the rest of the juice behind the chair, praying Marla wouldn't notice.

After taking her empty cup, Marla handed her a bowl of what looked like watery oatmeal. "You know what to do," she said. "Bring the dish over when you're done." Then she moved on to the next girl.

The serving of watery oatmeal barely covered the bottom of the bowl. And there was no spoon. Sage looked around to see if anyone else had a spoon. No one did except for the attendants, who were going around the tables using the same spoon to feed those who couldn't feed themselves. After shoving a few overflowing spoonfuls into a resident's mouth, the attendants made sure their juice cups were empty, then moved on to the next person. No one got any more than those first few mouthfuls before Wayne picked up the bowls and returned them to the carts.

Those who could feed themselves ate with their fingers, greedily stuffing oatmeal into their mouths before Wayne and the attendants took it from them. Some dumped the food on the floor and lapped it up like dogs. The wailing and shouting and shrieking continued through it all, and Wayne had his hands full trying to help and keep everyone under control.

"You better eat," someone said in Sage's ear, startling her. "You know we don't get much. You'll still be hungry when you go to bed."

It was Tina. She stood next to Sage in her lilac-covered dress, twisting a lock of her thin hair between her finger and thumb, back and forth, and back and forth.

"Where's yours?" Sage said.

"Already ate it. Time's almost up, too, so you better hurry."

"Does it taste as bad as it looks?"

Tina shrugged. "I can't remember ever having anything that tasted any better. Been here too long, I guess."

Sage looked at the watery oatmeal. Tina was right. It might look and taste horrible, but whether she wanted to or not, she needed to eat to keep up her strength in case she wasn't released as soon as she hoped. She took a deep breath, lifted the bowl, and scraped two fingers full into her mouth. As expected, the oatmeal, or whatever it was, tasted like paste. She swallowed without chewing, anxious to get it over with.

Across the room, Wayne dragged a woman away from a garbage can next to the Plexiglas cubicle, forced her over to a couch, and tied her ankle to the couch leg. When he walked away, the woman got up and tried to follow him, but she reached the end of the tether and fell, then pounded her fists on the floor, screaming.

"Damn it, Betty," Tina said, watching the woman. "Don't you ever learn? That's what you get for being a picker."

"What's a picker?" Sage said, desperate to distract herself from the slop she was eating.

"Geez Louise," Tina said. "You really did forget everything, didn't you? You know, it's when you pick through the garbage for food." She pointed at a young girl sitting on the floor across the room. "That one's a biter." She pointed at others. "That one's a head banger. That one over there is a grabber. That one's a soiler, and that one's a puker."

Sage grimaced and gave up trying to finish the oatmeal. While she was grateful to have someone to talk to who understood so much about Willowbrook, there were some things she'd rather not know. "Do you know what's in the orange juice? I can't remember."

Tina shrugged. "Some kind of tranquilizer. We

get it with every meal, which is either oatmeal or mush."

"Mush?"

"Yeah, they grind it up so no one chokes. Brown mush is meat. Green mush is some kind of vegetable. And white mush is either potatoes or rice. But most of the time it's mixed together so you can't tell what's what anyway."

"Great," Sage said. Not that it mattered. The food was the least of her worries. And with any luck she'd be released before lunch anyway. "Where do we go after this?"

Tina made a face. "What do you mean?"

"When we're done with breakfast," Sage said. "Where do they send us next?"

Tina let out a humorless laugh. "Sometimes they let us outside if it gets too hot in here during the summer, but other than that, this is it. We stay here in the dayroom until after dinner."

Sage gaped at her, dread pressing against her chest. "But what about school?" she said. "Where do we have classes?"

"Only the kids who live in the experiment ward get lessons."

Oh God. Her fears were real: Willowbrook was a school in name only. "What about doctors? How often do we see them?"

Tina scrunched up the unscarred side of her face, thinking. "Umm, the last time I saw one was when Marla broke my arm. I think that was

156

about a year and a half ago." She regarded Sage, a worried look in her eyes. "Are you sure they didn't mess with you while you were gone? It seems like you forgot *everything*."

The watery oatmeal soured in Sage's stomach. "Are you saying they don't reevaluate the residents every once in a while to see how they're doing?"

"I don't know what re . . . re . . . whatever that word was. I don't know what it means."

"Reevaluate means to look over your case, to see if you're getting better or worse."

"Well, they told me a long time ago I'd never get better."

Sage closed her eyes and took deep, deliberate breaths, trying to beat back the claws of panic.

"You okay?" Tina said. "You don't look too good."

Sage opened her eyes and studied Tina, wondering again how she'd managed to stay sane for so long. Sage hadn't been there an entire day yet and already felt like she was losing her mind. "It's okay," she said, her voice trembling. "I'll be okay." She swallowed her rising anxiety and said it a third time to convince herself. "I'm okay."

After the attendants were done feeding those who needed help—breakfast was done and over with in ten minutes—they finished gathering the bowls and cups, put them back on the carts, and left the dayroom. Wayne locked the door behind them, then sat down in the cubicle and lit another cigarette. The medicated orange juice seemed to be taking hold of the residents, cutting a slight edge off their hysteria, dulling their frenzied voices and chaotic actions. Instead of wailing, they moaned. Instead of shrieking, they cried. Instead of grabbing others and fighting, they fidgeted and pulled their own hair, talked to themselves, or pounded their fists on their skulls and stomachs and legs. Even Tina had quietly taken a seat in a cracked plastic chair next to Sage, still twirling her hair.

The last thing Sage wanted to do was talk to Wayne, but she didn't have a choice. She had to find out what he knew about her sister. Maybe when he heard her speak, he'd be able to tell she wasn't Rosemary. She stood and started toward the cubicle, zigzagging through the ever-shifting sea of residents, moving around puddles of urine and splotches of feces and oatmeal on the floor.

About halfway across the room, a girl in a stained yellow dress stepped in front of her, ruined eyes searching Sage's face. She looked around a year or two older than Sage, maybe more, with lifeless brown hair, a pimple-marked forehead, and a gauze bandage wrapped around her arm. Sage froze, a sliver of fear piercing her heart.

It was Norma, the girl who'd cut her wrist on a chair.

"Where did you go, Rosemary?" she said. "Or are you Sage today?"

Sage tried moving around her, but Norma blocked her way. "I . . . I didn't go anywhere," she said.

"You said you'd never leave me here alone again," Norma said. "So why'd you lie to me? We're sisters, remember? Forever and ever and ever?"

"I'm sorry," Sage said. "I didn't mean to. I . . . I got lost."

Norma bared a mouthful of nubby teeth. "No, you didn't. You left me. You said you'd never do that again. Never, ever, ever." She grabbed Sage's wrist and squeezed, digging her nails into the skin. "But you did. You lied!"

Sage tried to pry open Norma's clawed fingers, but her grip was like a vise. She looked over at the cubicle, hoping Wayne would help, but it was empty. Then she saw him down on one knee next to a girl on the floor who looked like she was having a seizure. "I said I was sorry," she said to Norma. "But I'm back now, okay? Please, just let me go."

Norma squeezed harder, then suddenly turned her head as if someone had whispered in her ear. "I know she did," she said, talking to someone who wasn't there. "I know."

The hair on the nape of Sage's neck stood on end. Rosemary used to have conversations with imaginary people too. "You're hurting me," she said.

Norma glared at her again. "I thought he got you," she hissed. "I thought he got you like he got the others."

"You thought who got me?" Sage said, still struggling to pull away. Norma refused to let go.

"You know who," Norma spat. "Cropsey."

Sage's mouth went dry. "How . . . how do you know about Cropsey?"

"Everyone knows about Cropsey," Norma said. "So stop trying to trick me." She turned away and spoke to the imaginary person again. "It's okay, she already knows."

"I'm not trying to trick you," Sage said. "I just . . . please, let go of my arm."

"He got those girls too, Jennifer and Midge. One minute they were here, the next they were gone." She snapped her fingers. "Just like that. And those girls who died in their beds last week? Everyone says they were drugged and tied down. But Cropsey did it. I know he did. He smothered them."

Sage swallowed, the watery oatmeal threatening to revolt in her stomach. Norma was out of her mind. She'd proven that. But why was she talking about Cropsey killing residents in Willowbrook? What if, after all Sage's doubts and fears, he was real? And what if he got Rosemary? "Do you . . . do you know who Cropsey is?"

Norma shook her head. "Of course not. If I did, I'd kill him." Then, just as quickly as she'd grabbed Sage's arm, she let go. "You know what? I don't want to talk to you right now. Just leave me alone." She spat on the floor, then stomped away, mumbling to the imaginary person inside her head.

Sage trembled with relief and dread, grateful that Norma was gone, at the same time wondering if she should go after her. If there was the slightest chance that Cropsey was real and he'd done something to Rosemary, she had to know. But how could she trust anything Norma said? She examined the fingernail marks on her wrist—red half-moons in a bright neat row, like the smiley faces she used to draw inside her schoolbooks. The skin wasn't broken, but the marks looked deep and angry. She rubbed her arm, then berated herself for being so stupid. She couldn't believe Norma. Obviously, the urban legend of Cropsey had found its way inside Willowbrook and festered like a disease, moving from the staff to the residents. Norma had no idea whom or what she was talking about. Cropsey wasn't real. And even if he was, there was no way he could get inside this place without being seen. Every steel door was barred and bolted, every room under lock and key.

She scanned the room for Wayne again. He'd carried the girl having the seizure over to a couch and laid her on it; now he stood over her with his hands on his hips. The girl looked unconscious, her head to one side, her eyes closed. Sage moved toward him, slowing when she grew near, ready to run if he tried to grab her. Up close he seemed even taller and broader, like he belonged in a wrestling ring.

"Is she going to be okay?" she said.

"Back off," he shot over his shoulder, his voice hard.

She retreated a couple of steps. "Sorry," she said.

"What do you want?" he said.

"She looks like she needs a doctor."

He turned toward her suddenly, dark-eyed and ferocious. "And you need to mind your own business."

Before she could say more, he turned and started across the room. She followed, dodging a chair that came out of nowhere and went flying across the floor.

"Are you going to call someone?" she called after him.

He kept going. "Don't tell me how to do my job," he snarled. "She'll be fine."

"Please, will you just talk to me for a minute?"

He stopped and spun around to face her, a blue vein bulging in his forehead. "About what?" Sweat dampened the armpits of his white uniform, and needle marks tracked the inside of his elbows.

Great. Along with being an asshole and a bully, he was a junkie too. Pressing her hands into fists to keep them from shaking, Sage pretended she hadn't noticed. "I was wondering," she said. "How well did you know my sister, Rosemary?"

He let out an ugly chuckle. "Oh, I get it," he said. "You want to play *this* game again. Don't you think you've caused enough trouble?" Something about his eyes made her pause. They were calm and cold, like Alan's, but murkier. Predator eyes.

She shook her head. "I don't know what game you're talking about."

He moistened his lips. "You know, the one where you pretend you're someone else?" A young woman ran up to him and pawed at his chest. He pushed her away. "That way, whenever you do something wrong, you can blame it on your 'sister.' " He made quotation marks with his fingers around the word "sister."

She shook her head again, panic tightening her throat. Between what Norma had said about being "sisters" and what he was saying about Rosemary pretending she was someone else, no wonder no one believed her. "I swear I'm not playing a game," she said. "I'm not Rosemary. Everyone thinks I am, but I'm not. I'm her twin sister, Sage. I found out she was missing, so I came here to help look for her."

"You came here to look for her? Is that what you're telling everyone?"

"Yes," she said. "But Dr. Baldwin thinks—"

He held up a plank-thick hand. "Just shut up," he barked. "I'm not in the mood for your shit today." He headed back toward the cubicle, shoving residents out of his way.

Trying to keep up, she dodged the girls and women who stumbled in his violent wake. "Please," she said. "I need to talk to you about Rosemary. Nurse Vic and Leonard said you might know where she went. If you were friends with her, maybe you can help. Maybe you know something that would prove I'm not her."

He stopped and turned on her again, crossing his massive tattooed arms over his broad chest. "I don't know what you're trying to pull," he said. "But you know Nurse Vic and Leonard love to stir up shit. And you tell everyone your name is Sage all the time. You never stop." He scanned the room, then pointed at Norma. "You say she's your sister too. Now leave me alone." He walked away again.

"Please," she said again, still following him. "You have to help me. I don't belong here."

"Yeah, that's what you all say," he snarled over his shoulder. "The ones who can talk, anyway."

"It's the truth! Really! Please, I'm begging you. You have to believe me."

When he reached the cubicle, he turned to face

164

her again. "Listen, you stupid bitch. I told you to leave me alone. You've caused me enough trouble."

She drew back. "How did I cause you trouble?"

"You know damn well how. They almost fired me when you disappeared."

"Why would they fire you? Did you have something to do with it? Do you know where Rosemary is? I heard you had a crush on her." As soon as the words left her mouth, she regretted them.

His face turned purple with rage, the blue vein in his forehead looking like it was about to burst. "I'm warning you one last time. Stay away from me or I'll send you to the pit again. And this time it'll be twice as long."

She dropped her eyes, practically wilting under the heat of his seething glare.

"That's what I thought," he said. "Now get lost."

Near tears, she turned and headed back toward the opposite wall, pushing away groping hands and moving around naked bodies. Clearly Wayne was hiding something. But what? And why was he almost fired when Rosemary disappeared? More importantly, how had he managed to get out of it and keep his job? Halfway across the room, she noticed a girl with strawberry-blond hair sitting Indian-style in a chair facing the wall. She had the same slim build as her sister, the same thin arms and legs. Unable to stop herself despite the poor odds, she rushed over and went around the front of the chair.

It wasn't Rosemary. The girl's skin was white as paper, thin as parchment. Gray clouds filled her sightless eyes, but she seemed to sense Sage's presence and said, "Who's there?"

"I'm sorry," Sage said. "I thought you were someone else."

"Is that you, Rosemary?" the girl said. "Where have you been? I've been worried about you."

"No, I'm not Rosemary. I'm her sister, Sage."

"Oh," the girl said. "I'm sorry. I get confused."

At first Sage was stunned that the girl had believed her so easily; then she remembered what Wayne had said: Rosemary called herself Sage all the time. "I don't mean to bother you," she said. "But I've been worried about Rosemary too. Do you know anything about her and Wayne? Were they friends?"

"Wayne isn't friends with anyone," the girl said.

"Do you know why Nurse Vic thinks he had something to do Rosemary's disappearance?"

The girl gasped. "Rosemary's disappeared?" Suddenly she clawed at her head and shrieked, making Sage jump. "Where is she? Where did she go?"

Sage reached for her, hoping to calm her down, then stopped. Who knew what would happen if she touched her? "Shh," she said. "Please. Don't scream. I'm sorry."

The girl screamed again. And again.

"It's okay, it's okay," Sage said. "I'm sorry for upsetting you. I'll leave you alone." She glanced over at Wayne. He was headed straight for them. "I'm going now. But I'll let you know when Rosemary comes back."

The girl went on screaming.

Sage hurried back to the other side of the room, found an empty chair, and sat down hard, her heart thrashing in her chest. Another storm of anxiety gathered inside her, making her tremble. She drew her feet into the chair, wrapped her arms around her knees, and tried to beat the fear back down, to stifle the whirlwind of panic before it destroyed the fragile walls of composure she'd somehow managed to maintain so far. Falling apart now was a bad idea. Then she noticed the brown filth on her toes and soles. She quickly put her feet back on the floor and gritted her teeth, trying not to think about the mix of human waste and Pine-Sol darkening her skin. At least the blind girl had stopped screaming—either that or her shrieks were no longer noticeable above the rest of the deafening mayhem. Cursing herself for not being more careful, she tried to push the incident from her mind. At least she'd gotten out of there before Wayne had reached her and sent her to the pit.

If only she'd talked to Nurse Vic when she was handing out pills earlier. Not that she would have listened this time either, but it might have been worth a try. The next time Sage saw her, she would ask what she knew about Wayne and Rosemary. For now, she needed a break. She needed to think for a minute and figure out her next move. Maybe Tina had more information.

Sage looked around the room for her, searching through the ever-moving jumble of bodies and arms and legs and heads. Finally, she saw Tina sitting cross-legged on the middle of a table, eyes closed, mouth moving as if she were praying or meditating. Maybe it would be better to wait until they were back in the ward to talk. It would be less chaotic, and she didn't feel like fighting her way across the room again anyway. Exhaustion weighed her down like a thousand chains around her shoulders.

Then, to her surprise, the young janitor entered the room pushing a cleaning cart full of brooms and mops. She sat up and tried to remember his name. What had Marla called him? Jimmy? Bobby? Eddie? Yes, that was it, Eddie. After locking the door behind him, Eddie took the cart over to Wayne's cubicle, emptied the garbage can into a bag, then tied the bag to his cart. As Wayne approached him, a gaunt woman in a grimy bathrobe limped over, grabbed Eddie's arm, and began talking to him. It looked like she was begging. When Eddie gently freed himself from her grip, she fell to his knees, clasping her hands together as if praying. Eddie ignored her. She clutched his pant leg and started to weep, her face twisting in agony. Wayne yelled at her to go away, then yanked one of the brooms off the cleaning cart and banged the wooden handle on the wall, once, twice, three times. The woman continued to beg. Wayne raised the broom, threatening to strike her. She cowered and cried out. Eddie put up a protective hand and said something to Wayne. Finally, he lowered the broom, shaking his head and laughing as if it were a joke, and the woman got up and left Eddie alone.

After she was gone, Wayne put the broom back in the cart and offered Eddie a cigarette, then took a second one out of the pack and reached into his pocket for his lighter. While lighting Eddie's cigarette, he jerked a chin in Sage's direction, then said something and grinned. Eddie took a long drag and looked over at her, his face unreadable. Then he turned back to Wayne and said something to him; Wayne shrugged. While they talked, Eddie glanced over at her a few more times with a strange, solemn look on his face.

Sage couldn't decide what to do. Should she go over there and talk to him before he left? Wait and hope she saw him again? Obviously he thought she was Rosemary, and he'd been surprised to see her in the hallway, but there was something in his expression now that she couldn't quite read.

It was hard to tell if it was concern or relief. Or maybe it was a warning to stay away, to not come near him in front of Wayne.

Eddie and Wayne talked a few more minutes, their shoulders shaking every now and then with laughter. Then Eddie put his cigarette out beneath his boot, picked up the stub, and put it in his pocket. Sage unfurled herself from the chair and stood. Wayne would get angry if she approached them, but she could meet Eddie at the door and say something, or ask him a question before he left. She started in that direction, walking slowly, winding her way through the other residents. Hopefully Wayne wouldn't notice.

Eddie had his hands on the cart again. He was getting ready to leave. When he glanced her way, she moved faster, hoping he'd read the desperation in her eyes. Then Wayne laughed and clapped him on the back, pulling his attention away. Eddie laughed too, and started toward the door. She hurried toward him, praying he'd talk to her before he left, that he'd say something important before Wayne came over and pulled her away. She skirted around a woman with bald patches on her head. Only a few more yards and she'd be at the door. Suddenly someone grabbed her arm and yanked her to a stop. She spun around and braced herself, certain Wayne had snuck up behind her.

It was Norma.

"What the hell are you doing?" Norma said. "Trying to leave again?"

"Let me go," Sage said, wrenching free so hard she nearly fell. She caught herself and headed toward the door again. But she was too late. Eddie had slipped into the hall and disappeared.

"Were you going somewhere without me?" Norma said.

"No," Sage said. "I wasn't going anywhere." The truth of her words clogged her throat. She headed back to the plastic chair in the far corner, hoping no one had taken it. Norma followed.

"You better not be trying to escape again," Norma said. " 'Cause I'll tell if you are."

Sage ignored her and sat down. Norma stared at her silently for a few minutes, then turned and staggered away without another word. Sage sighed, relieved. If ignoring Norma meant she'd leave her alone, that's what she'd try to do from now on.

In between breaking up fights, Wayne stared at the television, smoked, or dozed. Sage had no idea how he could sleep with all the racket. Maybe, along with a heart, he was missing a soul too. Or at least that part of his brain that made most people troubled by the suffering and chaos around them. Then again, it seemed like most of the staff was missing that part of their brain, too. Or maybe they'd grown numb.

With no windows or clock to tell how much

time passed, the minutes felt like hours and the hours felt like days. It seemed like she'd been trapped in the torturous dayroom for an eternity. But no one had brought lunch yet, which meant it was still before noon. How was that possible? She put her head in her hands and closed her eyes, the darkness behind her lids a welcome escape from the horror and misery surrounding her. Then she heard Wayne yelling and looked up.

Towering over one of the carts, he pointed at something in his hand and snarled at the occupant. Sage couldn't be certain, but it looked like the cart she'd brought in earlier. How could the poor girl lying in that box be in trouble? She couldn't walk, she couldn't talk, she could barely move. Then Sage remembered.

The pills.

She jumped up and raced over to the cart. Wayne was holding the girl up, getting ready to shove the pills down her throat. "Stop!" she yelled. "I put them there! They're mine!"

Wayne let the girl down and straightened, scowling at Sage. "What did you say?"

"I didn't know what they were," she said, breathing hard. "So I didn't take them. I tried to drop them on the floor, but they fell in the cart instead."

"Bullshit," he said. "They're the same ones you take every day."

"I . . . I forgot."

He held them out to her. "Well, now you know. So take them."

She stepped back, shaking her head.

"Do it or you're going to the pit."

"Please," she said. "Don't make me."

"Oh, I'm going to make you," he said, moving toward her. "You can be damn sure about that. So we can do this the hard way or the easy way. It's up to you."

Fighting tears, she held out her hand. He dropped the pills into her palm, crossed his arms, and waited. She looked at him, eyes pleading.

"I've got all day," he said.

"But I don't need them," she said. "I haven't been causing any trouble."

"Yeah, right," he said. "You've been working on getting sent to the pit all morning. I'm actually starting to think you like it there. Now take the damn pills."

"I don't have any water," she said.

"Too bad," he said. "You should have taken them earlier."

She closed her eyes and put the pills in her mouth, tears streaming down her face. Then she tilted her head back and swallowed hard. The pills were hard and gritty, like hunks of chalk, and they almost lodged in her throat. She swallowed again and again until finally they went down.

"Atta girl. See how much easier it is when you do what you're told? Now sit down and shut up,"

Wayne said, practically growling at her. "I don't want to hear another word out of you today." He turned and walked away.

Retreating to the back of the room again, she slid into a chair, fear tearing at her insides. Weed and alcohol were one thing, but pills were something else entirely. She'd never blown coke or swallowed so much as a Valium, but she'd seen the effect on those who had. And it wasn't always good. Plus, the "Don't Do Drugs" films in health class had terrified her. She dug her fingers into her thighs, considered the room full of howling, lurching, flailing residents, and braced herself for a bad trip. Next to her, the girl who'd had a seizure earlier was lying on a couch, her head still to one side, her eyes still closed. She looked dead. Panic vibrated through Sage's body, running along her nerves like jolts of electricity.

Then her head grew foggy. She stretched out her hands but couldn't see the ends of her fingers. She couldn't remember ever being so tired, ever feeling so strange. She was outside her body somehow. Her skin felt clammy and on fire at the same time, and she tore at her sleeves; she couldn't bear to have the material touching her arms. The monotonous wails and moans of the other residents felt like knives in her ears. She wanted to run, but couldn't. She wanted to scream, but couldn't. Everyone was looking at her, staring into her. *Stop,* she thought. *Stop. Stop!* Terror overwhelmed her. She couldn't move her arms or legs. Her tongue felt like lead, her lips heavy and useless over her teeth.

Then she fell out of the chair, and the world went away.

CHAPTER 7

On her second morning in Ward D, Sage slowly opened her eyes, squinting against the fluorescent lights that glared down from the cracked ceiling. Her head felt like it had been split in two; her mouth and lips were parched and dry, and her eyes felt glazed over. If she didn't know better she would have thought she'd been out on another bender. Except this was worse than any hangover she'd ever had. Her blood felt heavy as lead, the mattress beneath her wet with urine. Her skirt was wet too. The last thing she remembered after Wayne forced her to take the pills was someone feeding her green mush and orange juice. It felt like a nightmare—everything jumbled together behind a blurry, drug-induced haze. She sat up and dragged her hands over her face, trying to clear her head.

How did the other residents survive being drugged every day? Were they used to feeling this horrible? Then again, they were probably addicted by now, numb to everything but the high. And between the pills and whatever was in the orange juice, how could the staff tell how the residents were doing? Maybe they didn't care.

She slid off the bed and stood, testing her legs.

To her surprise, they held her up. She glanced over at Tina's bed. Maybe she'd remember what happened. But Tina's bed was empty. Sage looked over at the tiled shower room. Tina wasn't waiting in line to use the toilet either. She was nowhere to be seen. On the other side of the ward, Norma sat on a bed against the far wall, watching Sage with an angry stare. Sage dropped her eyes and made her way over to Marla, who stood next to a bed removing urine-soaked clothes from a nearly catatonic woman.

"Where's Tina?" Sage said.

"Don't you worry about that," Marla said. "You just mind your p's and q's today and everything will be fine."

"Did something happen to her?"

Marla yanked the sleeves of the woman's damp shirt from her arms and tossed it on the floor. "I told you not to worry about it, didn't I?"

"I know, but she was fine yesterday."

Marla shot her an irritated look. "She'll be back soon enough. That's all you need to know. Now hurry up and use the toilet or you'll be next."

"What do you mean I'll be next? For what?"

Marla raised an impatient eyebrow, struggling to keep the naked woman from falling off the mattress. Afraid to push her luck, Sage did as she was told and got in line to use the bathroom. When Marla said she could be next, was she talking about where Tina was or something that was being done to her? Was Tina being punished? Had she been sent to the pit?

Inside the tiled room, no residents were being hosed off, and no one had cleaned the filthy toilets. Sage held her breath and went inside. If yesterday was any indication of how things were going to go, this would be her only chance to relieve herself until she returned to the ward later, and who knew when that would be. No wonder the residents soiled themselves.

When she was finished, she went to the opposite wall, where everyone had stood to get hosed off, so she could rinse out her skirt and underwear. Lifting the end of the sprayer, which seemed more like a fire hose than something that should be used on humans, she found the water faucet and turned it on. No water came out.

"What in the Sam Hill do you think you're doing?" someone yelled. It was Marla, glowering at her from the main room, her hands on her hips. "Put that down. There's no showers today."

Sage dropped the sprayer and turned off the faucet. "I just wanted to rinse out my skirt."

Marla shook her head. "Come on out here right now," she said. "You're gonna have to wait for clean clothes like everybody else."

Sage started out toward her. "When will that be?"

"You know the laundry don't tell me that," Marla said. "They just show up. Now grab a cart and get ready to go."

Trying to ignore her dank clothes and dreading another day spent trapped in the dayroom with Wayne, Sage went to the other side of the room and grabbed a cart with two girls inside— one in nothing but a cloth diaper, the other in a short-sleeved blouse and diaper—then followed the other residents into the hallway. Hopefully Nurse Vic would be at the nurses' station again; maybe she could talk to her. Shuffling forward within the roiling sea of residents, she slowly rounded the corner into the main hall and stood on her tiptoes to see who was at the nurses' station. When she saw a nurse with silver hair refilling the medicine trays, her shoulders dropped. The stone-faced resident in the blue blouse and gray skirt was there again, passing out the plastic cups like a well-trained robot, but Nurse Vic was nowhere to be seen.

She would have to make the best of it. Who knew—maybe the silver-haired nurse knew more about Rosemary than Nurse Vic did, anyway. Maybe she'd be friendlier too. When Sage finally reached the counter, she addressed the new nurse in the most reasonable-sounding voice she could muster.

"Excuse me."

The nurse set a tray of cups on the counter

and gave her a smile that was both gentle and indifferent. "Yes?"

"This might sound like a strange question," Sage said. "But do you remember my sister, Rosemary? And would you happen to know anything about her and Wayne?"

The silver-haired nurse wagged a crooked, rheumatic finger at her. "Now, now," she said. "You know we don't have time for that nonsense this morning. Take your pills and move along."

"It's not nonsense," Sage said. "Rosemary is still missing and I'm her twin sister. I came to Willowbrook to look for her."

The silver-haired nurse ignored her and kept dropping orange pills into plastic cups.

"Please," Sage said. "I need to talk to someone who will listen. I need—"

The nurse stopped filling the cups and eyed her coldly. "You need Marla to help you take your pills?" she said. "I can get her over here if you'd like."

Sage shook her head, frustration burning her face, then obediently took the plastic cup from the resident in the gray skirt. After hiding the pills in her mouth again, she pushed the cart with the two girls toward the dayroom and, looking around to make sure no one was watching, spat the pills into her hand. As she'd hoped, Eddie came into the hall pushing a mop and bucket, then propped open the double doors to the dayroom. Would he say something to her again? Would he realize she wasn't Rosemary?

But the janitor wasn't Eddie. He was a stick-thin man with black orthopedic shoes that looked too big for his scrawny legs. Maybe Eddie had the day off. Maybe he'd gotten in trouble for talking to her. Could that be why he'd looked so serious while smoking with Wayne yesterday?

When the new janitor walked past pushing the mop bucket, she thought about shouting out to him, asking him about Eddie. But he kept his eyes on the floor, his face a blank slate. He almost seemed scared to look up. If she tried talking to him, who knew what might happen? Instead, she kept going and entered the dayroom, staying as far away from Wayne as possible. Why couldn't *he* have had the day off?

After parking the cart with the others beneath the crude painting of Donald Duck, she looked back at Wayne. Hopefully he was too busy driving the rest of the residents inside, barking orders and yelling like a cowhand herding cattle, to see what she was about to do. She hurried to a far corner of the room, put the orange pills beneath the back legs of a plastic chair, and sat down hard. After the pills were crushed, she stood and brushed the gritty fragments across the Pine-Sol-damp floor with her bare feet, smearing the powder around the floor and pushing the larger pieces under a couch, one eye on Wayne.

When she finished, she sat down again, determined to stay out of trouble until she could figure out what to do next. Along with everything else, hunger began to gnaw beneath her rib cage. She put her hand on her stomach. What she wouldn't give for a stack of pancakes or even a dry piece of toast instead of whatever mush they'd be serving that day, not that she could remember anything but the watery oatmeal. Then she noticed Norma leaning against the wall, watching her. *Shit.* Hopefully she hadn't seen what she'd done with the pills. She pretended to examine her fingernails, praying Norma would get bored and leave her alone.

After the residents were served another breakfast of pasty oatmeal and medicated orange juice—which Sage poured behind her chair again—the janitor in the orthopedic shoes came into the room to empty the trash. Keeping his head down as he worked, he only looked up when a patient got in his way, then left without exchanging a word with Wayne.

A little while later, the silver-haired nurse entered, pushing an unconscious resident in a wheelchair. After locking the door behind her, she pushed the wheelchair across the room and parked it with the other wheelchairs below Mickey Mouse's giant yellow shoes. Some of the residents watched in grave silence, their worried eyes speaking volumes; the rest paid little or no attention. When Sage realized who was in the wheelchair, her breath caught.

Tina sat slumped in the plastic seat, her head lolled back, the scar-free half of her face deathly pale. A leather chest strap kept her from falling out of the wheelchair, and more straps wound around her wrists and ankles. As soon as the nurse walked away to go speak with Wayne, Sage hurried over and squatted beside the chair. A dark spot of dried blood filled the inner corner of Tina's right eye; more blood crusted one of her nostrils.

"Tina?" Sage said. "Are you awake?"

No answer.

"What did they do to you?"

Struggling to open her eyes, Tina lifted her head, straining as if it weighed a thousand pounds. Then she let her head fall back to rest on one of the wheelchair handles, her eyes still closed.

"Can you hear me?" Sage said.

Finally, Tina opened her eyes. But she stared into nothingness, as if she'd gone blind and deaf and mute. There was no eye contact, no nod to show she was listening. No clue she was even there.

"Lobotomy," a flat voice said behind Sage.

Sage looked over her shoulder to see who'd spoken. It was Norma, grave-faced and fidgety, her eyes dark and wild. Sage turned back to Tina, the image of an icepick going through her eye socket and into her brain making her nauseated.

"Why would they do that to her?" she said, her voice choked. "There was nothing wrong with her. She wasn't a troublemaker or anything."

"Probably needed to teach a new doctor how to do it," Norma said. "Happens all the time. So you better be careful."

Sage rested a hand over Tina's. Her fingers felt cold as ice, hard as bones. "But why her?" she said. "It doesn't make sense."

"Why not?" Norma said. "At least she didn't die like some of the others."

CHAPTER 8

Sage shivered beneath her thin blanket while the other residents cried and shouted and laughed and mumbled, jumped and crawled from bed to bed, and wandered around the ward despite it being after midnight. Hungry, cold, and exhausted, she ached for sleep. After destroying the orange pills that morning, the sights and sounds of her day had been crystal clear, and now they played over and over inside her head like a horror movie on a continuous loop. Along with the usual fights and chaos in the dayroom, Wayne had broken one woman's nose and whipped another with his belt; two girls had vomited all over each other; a teenage girl had fractured another teenager's arm; and Sage had tripped over a woman she thought was asleep, only to discover she was actually dead. Along with those ghastly images, she couldn't stop thinking about Tina in the bed next to her, lying silent and still as a rag doll.

A thousand times, she thought about keeping the orange pills the next day to take at night so she could sleep, but she decided against it. She had to keep a clear head. And if God or fate was on her side at all, she'd be released before then. Struggling to erase the grisly pictures in her brain, she tried to stop thinking about the things she couldn't change or control. She couldn't help Tina or anyone else right now—not as long as she was trapped inside Willowbrook—but somehow, some way, she had to help herself. And she had to find Rosemary. She refused to believe she'd stay locked up here forever, day after day spent among the forgotten girls and young women sent away by parents and foster homes, abandoned to battle their way through this gruesome existence until they grew old or died. She had to believe she'd learn what happened to her sister and find a way out. She *had* to. There was no other choice. And yet, it was easy to fall into the deep, dark pit of despair.

As exhaustion finally pushed her toward the edge of a troubled, restless unconsciousness, she sensed a presence above her, looming like a dark weight over her bed, getting closer and closer. Startled, she tore the blanket off her head and gaped into the inky vault of the ward.

Norma stood gazing down at her, a pallid ghost caught in the weak moonlight that seeped through the grimy windows. She held one finger to her lips, the blood-soaked gauze around her wrist seeming to glow in the dark. Sage glanced over at Marla to see if she noticed Norma standing there. Not that Marla would do anything, but if Norma planned to hurt her or do something stupid, at least there would be a witness. As usual, Marla was asleep in the cubicle, her head tilted back in the chair, her mouth open.

Sage peered up at Norma. "What are you doing?"

"I want to show you something," Norma said.

"Go back to bed."

"No, I have to show you." Norma turned toward her invisible friend, listened, nodded, then regarded Sage again. "I can't tell you."

Sage couldn't imagine what Norma wanted to show her. There was nowhere to hide anything of importance or value. Not that she knew of, anyway. Maybe Norma was imagining things, or lying, or trying to trick her. Then she remembered that the best thing to do was ignore her. "You can show me in the morning," she said.

Norma shook her head. "Can't." Crooking her finger, she motioned for Sage to follow her. "You have to come with me."

"Unless it has something to do with my sister, leave me alone."

Norma went still, then stomped her foot, pouting like an angry toddler. "*I'm* your sister."

Sage opened her mouth to explain, but stopped. Pissing Norma off again was a bad idea. And maybe whatever she wanted to show Sage *did* have something to do with Rosemary. Even the smallest clue could help. But if she wanted to get anywhere with Norma, she had to play along. "I'm sorry," she said. "That's not what I meant. I meant unless it has something to do with where I was hiding when I left before, please leave me alone."

Norma smiled, a wide, mischievous grin that transformed her face from that of an angry young woman into an impish child with a headful of secrets. "It might have something to do with that," she said. "But you have to come with me if you want to see." Then she sat on the edge of the bed and roughly petted Sage's head, running her fingers through Sage's hair and catching strands in her nails. She smelled like sweat and sour milk.

Sage went stiff, afraid Norma was going to do something crazy. "Please get off my bed," she said.

Norma sighed contentedly, then stood, still grinning.

Sage sat up and put her feet on the cold floor, ready to push her away if she tried to sit down again. "Why can't you just tell me?" she said.

"Because you need to see it with your own eyes."

Sage started to ask her where it was, but Norma suddenly dropped to her knees and crawled toward the door, moving rapidly in the narrow space between the beds. A coil of fear twisted up Sage's spine. Norma wasn't right in the head, and the eerie, jerky way she moved along the floor looked like something out of a nightmare. This could be a trick, or even worse, a trap. Maybe she wanted revenge because she thought Rosemary had deserted her. But Sage had no choice. If there was the slightest chance Norma might show her something that could lead her to Rosemary, she had to follow her.

"Damn it," she said under her breath, then slid out of bed onto her hands and knees. Norma glanced over her shoulder to make sure she was coming, her face blank, then kept crawling toward the exit. Where the hell was she going? Did she honestly think she could get out of the ward? When Norma reached the middle of the room, she disappeared beneath one of the beds like a spider scuttling under a cupboard. Sage stopped and peered over the tops of the beds filled with residents. Some lay with closed eyes; some were staring at nothing, others weeping, humming, talking, singing—a crumpled gray landscape of sheets and pale arms and legs and heads. Norma reappeared briefly, her head popping up in a narrow aisle, then went under another bed. Sage hunkered down, her elbows on the floor, trying to decide if she should follow her or stay put. Maybe this was a test. Or a game. Or a huge mistake. She peered over the beds again. When she saw Norma this time, her heart almost stopped.

She was inside the Plexiglas cubicle with Marla.

Panicked, Sage crawled as fast as she could back to her bed and scrambled beneath the blanket. Whatever Norma was up to, it was bad, and Sage didn't want to be drugged again, or sent to the pit. A minute later, Norma reappeared at her bedside, dangling a ring of keys in front of Sage's face.

"I thought you were coming with me," she said.

"What the hell are you doing?" Sage hissed.

"I told you," Norma said. "I want to show you something." She turned her head to address the invisible person again. "I don't care. It doesn't matter."

Suddenly, Sage realized this might be her only chance to escape. "Do any of those keys open doors that lead outside?"

"You know they don't," Norma said, annoyed. "*Those* keys are kept at the nurses' stations, and there's only one set on each floor."

Sage had the feeling Norma was either lying or pretending to know what she was talking about. But there was no way to tell unless she tried the keys herself. How that would happen, she had no idea, but it would be impossible if she refused to go with Norma. "What if we get caught?"

"I never get caught."

"You've left the ward before?"

Norma nodded.

"What for?"

"You'll see."

Sage let out a heavy, frustrated sigh. If anyone saw them, there'd be hell to pay—or worse—but if this had something to do with Rosemary or was a possible way out, it was a chance she had to take. "Are you sure?"

Norma nodded again.

Shaking and uncertain, Sage slid out of bed again, got on her knees, and followed Norma across the ward. When they reached the door, Norma stood, quick and smooth as a snake, and put the key in the lock. Sage held her breath, keeping her eyes fixed on Marla. Thank God she was still out like a light. Opening the door just wide enough to slip out, Norma went through first, then let Sage through and quietly closed it behind them. After looking left and right to make sure no one was coming, she relocked the door, then slinked down the hall on her tiptoes, her stained yellow dress trailing behind her like a ghost.

Praying she wasn't making a huge mistake, Sage followed close behind, her heart beating so hard she thought her ribs might crack. Norma flew down the main corridor in the opposite direction of the nurses' station, then took a right down another hallway. At the end of that hall, she unlocked a set of double doors that led into a dim corridor lined with single steel doors, each with a grated window centered above a narrow sliding panel. Muffled sounds and voices came from behind the riveted steel—crying, loud talking, praying, singing, someone howling like a wolf.

"What is this place?" Sage whispered.

"You know what it is," Norma said.

"No, I don't. I can't remember anything since I came back."

"How could you forget the pit? You spent enough time here."

"Why? What did I do?"

Norma looked at her like she was crazy. "Lotsa things."

Suddenly someone pounded on one of the steel doors, making Sage jump.

"Let me out of here or you'll be sorry!" a woman shouted on the other side of the door, her voice strained and muted, as if coming from under the ocean. "My husband is John Lennon and he's going to come looking for me!" She pressed her face against the grated window, tormented and wild-eyed, her skin smeared with something that looked like dirt.

Sage moved to the center of the hallway, an icy mix of fear and sorrow making her shiver. Being locked in one of those rooms had to be torture. And it sounded like Rosemary had spent a lot of time there, alone and afraid, not knowing when she'd get out.

At the end of the corridor, Norma stopped at a door below a sign that read: SUPPLY ROOM. She regarded Sage. "You have to promise not to tell anyone."

Sage nodded. "Okay."

Norma held out her little finger. "Pinky swear?"

Sage hooked her pinky through Norma's and they shook. "Pinky swear."

Satisfied, Norma opened the door, entered the supply room, and pulled a string above her head. A bare lightbulb buzzed to life, casting a yellow glow over an oversize closet lined with stained straitjackets on hooks, coils of rope, a jumble of waste buckets in one corner, industrial-size barrels of Pine-Sol, and battered metal trays piled on wooden shelves. The room smelled like old wood and warm dust, and something that reminded Sage of whiskey. Before she could ask why they were there, Norma squatted and pushed on the back wall with both hands. A wooden panel creaked open and Norma moved it to one side to reveal a knee-high opening. When Norma crawled through it, Sage stood frozen, trying to decide what to do. What if she was right about Norma wanting revenge? What if she had lured her there to lock her in a hidden room where no one would find her? She scanned the room for a weapon, just in case, but didn't see anything she could use other than the metal trays or rope.

Before Sage could act, Norma popped her head out of the opening and gaped up at her.

"You coming with me or what?" she said.

"What's in there?"

"You'll see. Hurry up."

"Shit," Sage said, and got down on her knees. She'd come this far; there was no backing out now. Maybe Rosemary was hiding in there. Maybe Norma had known where she was this whole time.

When Norma backed up to let her inside, a rank odor hit Sage in the face, like a mixture of cow shit and rotten eggs. She recoiled and sat back for a second, then stuck her head through the opening.

"You're blocking the light," Norma said. "You need to come in all the way."

Sage hesitated for a moment, then crawled through and moved to one side, sitting back on her haunches, ready to scramble out again if necessary. Norma stared at her, waiting for a reaction. Sage looked around, one hand over her nose and mouth. The cramped space was half the size of the supply closet, with a slanted ceiling reaching down to the floor on one end. A torn, stained mattress lay among dozens of open tin cans, half-eaten pigeons, and the heads of dead mice. Here and there, dark piles that looked like animal shit dotted the moldy floorboards.

"What is this place?" Sage said behind her fingers.

Norma turned her head and nodded to her imaginary friend. "Yes, I'm going to tell her that too."

"Tell me what?"

"We think Cropsey hides in here sometimes."

A jolt of fear yanked the air from Sage's lungs. She had to get out of there. She turned toward the opening, then stopped. No. Her imagination was running away with her. This hidden room might look like the perfect hiding place for a mental patient turned serial killer, but that didn't make it true. She was just being paranoid and ridiculous. And so was Norma. "Oh my God," she said. "Is that why you brought me here? I don't care about Cropsey. He isn't real."

"Yes, he is. But don't get scared. He only hides in here sometimes."

"Even if that were true, how would you know?"

She shrugged. "My friend told me."

"Which friend?"

"I don't know his name."

Suddenly it dawned on Sage that Norma was talking about the voice inside her head. She had no idea what was true and what wasn't. Sage should have known better. "Is that why you brought me here? To show me this room?"

Norma nodded.

"Is this where Rosemary . . . I mean, is this where I was hiding when I was missing?"

"I don't know where you were. You never told me."

"But you think Cropsey hides here sometimes, so you wanted me to see it?"

Norma nodded again.

Sage clenched her jaw. This was a waste of time. The room was creepy as hell, and she couldn't imagine why it existed, or who'd been doing God knows what in there, but if it didn't have anything to do with Rosemary, she needed to leave. Norma was only thinking about Cropsey, and Sage had risked getting caught for no reason. "We have to go back before someone notices we're gone," she said, turning toward the opening. She crawled out and waited near the supply room door while Norma followed and put the hidden panel back in place.

When Norma straightened, she said, "Don't you want to know how I found out about it?"

Sage reached for the doorknob. "You can tell me on the way back to the ward."

"The person who used to bring you here showed it to me."

Sage let go of the doorknob and gaped at her. "Rosemary used to . . . I mean, I used to come here?"

"Don't try to trick me. You know you did."

"No, I don't. I told you, I can't remember anything from before. Who used to bring me here? And why?"

"You know who."

"Please. You have to tell me. Was it that janitor, Eddie?"

Norma shook her head.

"Then who?"

"If I tell you, you can't tell anyone we came here, remember?" She held up her pinky to remind Sage of their deal. "Wayne made me promise. He said it's our secret."

Alarms went off in Sage's head. "*Wayne* used to bring me here?"

Norma nodded and then said in a proud voice, "After you disappeared, he brought me here and said *I* could be his girlfriend instead."

Nausea churned in Sage's stomach. As if Willowbrook weren't horrible enough. She braced herself to ask another question, despite being fairly sure what Norma's answer would be. "Was Ro . . . was I his girlfriend before I left?"

Norma made a face, confused by the question. "That's why I brought you here. So you'd know you're not his girlfriend anymore. You left without telling me, so I wanted to hurt you back. And now I did."

Sage pressed her lips together, her heart crushed by the knowledge of everything Rosemary had suffered.

"Did I hurt your feelings?" Norma said.

Sage started to tell her it was okay, that she hadn't hurt her feelings, but she didn't want to upset Norma, not now, when she was finally getting somewhere. She took a deep breath and struggled to remind herself that Norma was in Willowbrook for a reason. And it was easy to

197

understand why she'd cling to even the tiniest fragment of affection in such a terrible place, no matter how depraved and inappropriate. She probably had no idea it was wrong. "Does Wayne . . . does he hurt you when he brings you here?"

Bewilderment crumpled Norma's face. "What do you mean? He would never hurt his girl-friend."

Feeling sicker by the minute, Sage thought about explaining what she meant but decided against it. It didn't take a rocket scientist to figure out why Wayne would take a female resident into a hidden room. No wonder Nurse Vic and Leonard thought he knew something about Rosemary's disappearance. But if they knew what he was doing, why hadn't they put a stop to it? And did they know about this room? She needed the answers to those questions—but right now, she had to get all the information she could out of Norma. "Does Wayne know why I left? Did he tell you where I went?"

"No, but he knew I was sad when you tried running away without me."

"Is that what he told you? That I tried to run away?"

"No, *you* told me. You said you were going to escape. But you promised to take me with you. And then you didn't."

Sage felt dizzy. A thousand thoughts and questions and feelings spun around in her head. "Did I tell you how I was going to escape?"

"No. You wouldn't, no matter how many times I asked. You just kept saying I'd find out when the time came. Then you left me here alone."

"How did you find out I was gone?"

"I woke up in the morning and you weren't there anymore."

"What did Marla and Nurse Vic say?"

"They didn't say anything. They never tell us what's going on. And you know people disappear here all the time. Sometimes they come back, sometimes they don't. But everyone was looking for you."

"And Wayne didn't know anything about it?"

"I don't know. He didn't say."

"Are you sure?"

Norma nodded.

"I really want to remember what happened," Sage said. "So will you tell me if you remember anything else?"

Norma smiled and held up a pinky. "I will."

Sage hooked her finger through hers and shook it. Then she put a hand on Norma's arm. "Listen," she said. "I know you like Wayne, but you shouldn't come here with him anymore. And you need to tell someone he's been bringing you here."

Norma's smile dropped from her face. "No," she said, shaking her head furiously. "A promise is a promise. And I keep *my* promises. Not like you."

"But what if he's . . ." She almost said "what if he's Cropsey," but stopped herself. Wayne was a sexual predator—a rapist, even—but it didn't mean he was a serial killer. She didn't think so, anyway. Still, she had to try to protect Norma. "What if he's dangerous?"

Anger twisted Norma's features. "You stop that," she spat. "He's not dangerous. He's nice to me. Look." She went over to a cloth bag hanging next to a straitjacket, reached in, and pulled out a handful of Pixy Stix. "He gives me a prize every time we come here."

Sage closed her eyes for a moment, sick and furious at the same time. How could she make Norma understand without upsetting her? "Listen to me," she said. "You have to tell someone what he's doing. It's not right. He's not supposed to do that."

"I said stop it," Norma said. "You're just mad because he loves me now." She put the handful of Pixy Stix back in the bag, then took one out, ripped it open with her teeth, and dumped the contents into her mouth.

"No, I'm not mad. I promise. I don't even like him. I just don't want him to hurt you anymore. And what if you . . . what if he . . ."

"Puts a baby inside me?"

Sage nodded.

Norma laughed. "You know that can't happen." She put the Pixy Stix in her mouth again, shaking it until it was empty.

"Of course it can."

"No, I had the operation, remember? Retards aren't allowed to have babies."

Sage's stomach turned over again. As if medical experiments and lobotomies weren't bad enough, female residents were being forcibly sterilized? Then a sudden realization hit her. If Rosemary had been sterilized, she'd have a scar. Maybe *that* was how the two of them could be told apart! Adrenaline buzzed through her. Finally, she knew how to prove she wasn't her sister. *If* Rosemary had the operation. And *if* Sage could find a doctor or nurse to check for a scar. "Do all the girls in Willowbrook have the operation? Did I have it?"

Norma shrugged. "I don't know." She crumpled up the empty Pixy Stix straw and threw it back in the bag. "Maybe."

Then Sage remembered that Marla had said residents couldn't see a doctor unless they were bleeding or dying—sometimes not even then. And Tina said the same thing. Not to mention Sage had seen enough injuries and illnesses to know that the residents rarely got medical attention. Slowly but surely, her heart sank again. It had been impossible to get anyone to listen to her about anything; how would she ever get someone to look for a scar? She looked at Norma again—poor, broken Norma who couldn't understand her own dreadful predicament.

"Okay," Sage said. "But even though you had that operation, you can't let Wayne bring you in here anymore. It's not right."

"I told you to stop it," Norma said. "I'm his girlfriend now, not you." Her voice was getting louder and louder. "So just stop it."

Sage held up her hands. "Okay, okay," she said. "Be quiet or you'll get us in trouble."

"Then quit making me mad," Norma hissed.

"I'm not trying to make you mad. But if you don't tell someone what Wayne is doing, I will."

With that, Norma's eyes went wild and she bared her teeth. "You promised you wouldn't tell! You pinky swore!"

"I know," Sage said. "And I'm sorry, but I can't let him get away with it. Someone needs to stop him."

"So you lied again," Norma said, practically breathing fire. "And now you want to break another promise. But no one will listen to you!"

Norma was probably right, but Sage had to try. She started to say Marla might listen, but stopped. She'd seen that trapped-animal look in Norma's eyes before, the day she smashed the wooden chair and cut her wrist, when she looked ready to die to defend herself. To avoid an argument—or worse—Sage dropped the subject and reached for the doorknob. They needed to go back to the ward. Then she remembered the keys.

"I'm sorry," she said. "But why don't we make a deal? I won't tell anyone about you and Wayne if you give me Marla's keys."

"What?" Norma said, her eyes huge. "Why do you want the keys? To leave me again? I told you they don't work on outside doors."

"No, that's not it," Sage said. "I—"

Before she could finish, Norma shoved her backward with both hands, knocking her off her feet. Sage hit the shelves behind her, the wood smashing into her spine and shoulder blades like a row of sledgehammers. The serving trays on the shelves rattled and fell, clattering across the floor. Norma froze for a second, eyes wide with fear, then ran out of the supply room. Sage scrambled to her feet and chased after her.

Out in the hall, Norma slipped through the double doors and disappeared. With a growing sense of horror, Sage realized Norma could lock her in the seclusion hall. And if she got caught, someone might think she escaped from one of the rooms. She raced to the double doors and pulled on one of the handles. Her shoulders dropped in relief: Norma had forgotten to lock the doors behind her. But she could still lock Sage out of the ward. And if Nurse Vic or Marla caught her out there alone, they'd think she was trying to escape again. She scurried to the end of the hall and peered down the main corridor. It was empty. And Norma was nowhere to be seen. She started around the corner, then stopped, turned around, and pressed her back against the wall, breathing hard.

No one but Norma knew she was out there, and she'd probably locked her out of the ward by now. If Sage went in the other direction, maybe she'd find a way out. She looked left and right, trying to decide which way to go. To the left was the nurses' station, the dayroom, and the door to the tunnels. To the right—who knew what she'd find? Maybe an open window, an unlocked door, or another way into the tunnels. She leaned against the wall again, trying to decide if it was worth the risk.

"What are you doing?" someone said in her ear, making her jump.

It was Norma.

"Jesus Christ," Sage said, one hand over her racing heart. "You scared the shit out of me."

Norma stared at her with furious eyes. "I know what you're thinking," she said. "And if you try running away again, I'll get Nurse Vic. If you tell on me, I'll tell on you."

Sage's stomach fell. Suddenly she had to choose between protecting Norma and a chance at escape. But there was no guarantee she'd find a way out. The only guarantee was that Norma *would* tell on her if she tried. "I was looking for you, that's all." She started down the main hall. "Let's get back before someone notices we're gone."

Norma scoffed and moved around her, bumping her shoulder like a bully in school, then hurried toward the corridor leading to their ward. Sage followed, her heart still in her throat. When they reached Ward D, Norma turned at the door to face her.

"You should be careful," she whispered. "Or I'll tell Nurse Vic and Wayne you're not taking your pills."

"But I am," Sage said.

"No, you're not. You're lying again. I saw you breaking them on the floor and spreading them under the couch."

Before Sage could respond, Norma unlocked the door and slipped back inside Ward D. Sage took a deep breath and followed, immediately dropping to her knees. By some miracle, Marla was still sleeping and Norma was able to return her keys without incident.

After Sage crawled back into bed, she stayed awake half the night trying to figure out if Wayne might know where Rosemary was or what happened to her. She tried to remember how he'd acted when he first saw her—she'd been near hysteria, so she couldn't be completely sure if her memories were accurate. She thought he'd seemed surprised, but not necessarily shocked, which probably meant he hadn't kidnapped or killed Rosemary. But he still might know where she had gone. Then she had another thought, and her heart pounded harder: Unless he *knew* she was Rosemary's twin because he knew where Rosemary was, and as long as Sage was there, he wouldn't be caught or get in trouble for whatever he'd done. Her mind reeled with the possibility.

When she finally fell into an exhausted sleep, her dreams were nightmarish and frantic— running through endless halls calling for Rosemary, knowing she'd never find her. Rosemary in the corner of their bedroom at home, crying and laughing and screaming. Rosemary sitting on a rock next to a tree, her hair hanging over her face, and when Sage brushed back Rosemary's hair to talk to her, it was Tina, her skin marled and scarred.

Long before dawn, Sage was startled awake by a high-pitched shriek and hysterical crying.

CHAPTER 9

While Sage waited in line for her pills the next morning, she kept an eye on the dayroom door, hoping Eddie would be the janitor again instead of the man with the orthopedic shoes. When Eddie emerged a few minutes later pushing a mop and bucket, she said a silent prayer of thanks. At least he hadn't gotten in trouble for speaking to her, and now that he was back, maybe they'd get a chance to talk. At the nurses' station, Nurse Vic had returned to dole out the daily meds. More than anything Sage wanted to tell her about Wayne—what he'd done to Rosemary, and what he was doing to Norma. But if something became of it, Norma would tell Nurse Vic and Marla that she wasn't taking her pills. At the same time, the thought of him getting away with everything made her ill. And who knew how many other girls and women he'd assaulted? Maybe Sage could tell Nurse Vic about him without mentioning specific details, like the location of the secret room or Norma's involvement. *If* Sage could get her to listen at all. Earlier she'd thought about saying something to Marla, but Norma had been watching her like a hawk in the ward.

"I know you won't listen because you think I'm

Rosemary," she said to Nurse Vic as she stepped up to the counter. "But you and Leonard are right about Wayne. I think he knows what happened to my sister."

As suspected, Nurse Vic had "ignoring the residents" down to a science. She kept working, her caked-on face powder and thick eyeliner like a mask. "Take your pills and move along," she said without looking up.

"I'm pretty sure he was having sex with her before she disappeared. He took her somewhere so no one would find out. And now he's doing it to another girl, too."

With that, Nurse Vic raised her head, a strange fire burning in her eyes. Sage couldn't tell if it was fear, anger, or something else. "If someone is hurting you," she said, biting off every word, "that's something you need to talk to your doctor about. Not me."

"When am I supposed to do that?" Sage said. "I haven't seen Dr. Baldwin since he locked me up."

Nurse Vic gave her an icy glare. "Take your pills and move along."

Sage knew she ought to be careful, but she couldn't help herself. Her anger was too raw. "What's wrong with you?" she said. "I thought you were a nurse. I thought you were supposed to take care of people."

"Oh, I can take care of you," Nurse Vic said.

"I can give you something stronger to calm you down if I think you need it."

Fuming and feeling helpless, Sage took a plastic cup from the woman in the gray skirt, put the orange pills in her mouth, and, once she was far enough away, spat them into her hand again. It seemed like Eddie was her only hope.

She fixed her eyes on him. Would he acknowledge her today, or just give her the same strange look he'd given her while smoking with Wayne? Maybe he'd ignore her completely so he wouldn't get yelled at again. When he walked by, pushing the mop bucket, he winked at her but kept going. It was a small gesture, but it gave her a tiny bit of hope.

If he came into the dayroom again, she'd find a way to talk to him this time, no matter what. And she'd stay as far away from Norma as possible. Wayne too.

In the dayroom, she tried again to talk to poor Tina, who was back to sitting in the middle of tables with her eyes closed, but got no reply. Tina no longer looked at her; she didn't speak or sing or cry. Sage wondered if they had taken out her tongue too. Nothing would surprise her.

When Wayne circled close by on his rounds, she stared at the floor, certain he would read the truth in her eyes: She knew he was a sexual predator, a rapist who took advantage of his position. She suspected him of doing something to Rosemary, but even if that suspicion turned out to be wrong, Sage was still going to expose him. As soon as she could prove her true identity and everyone realized she'd been telling the truth all along, she would reveal his secrets and make him pay.

Around midmorning, she spotted Norma following him around on the other side of the room, like a puppy dog chasing a toy. When he headed back toward his cubicle, Norma touched his shoulder and he stopped and turned toward her. She whispered something in his ear, and he glared at Sage with furious eyes. Then he grabbed Norma by the arm and snarled angry words in her face. Norma shrank back, crying and trying to pull free. Wayne yanked on her arm one last time, then let go and stomped away. He sat down in the cubicle and lit a cigarette, then took a long drag and glared at Sage, his leg jerking up and down.

What the hell had Norma done?

Just then, Eddie entered the room with the janitor cart. Sage had to fight the urge to run over to him and tell him everything. There was no guarantee he'd believe her, but she could try. Maybe it would help that he was a janitor, just a normal guy with nothing riding on the welfare of the residents. She'd recognized the concern in his eyes when he first approached her in the hallway. He cared about Rosemary. Surely he'd want to know what Wayne had done to her. Maybe he could help find her, if Sage could convince him she was still missing. With nerves gnawing at her insides, she got up and moved toward him, keeping one eye on Wayne. If he saw what she was about to do, he might stop her—or worse.

But when Eddie saw her heading in his direction, he shook his head ever so slightly, warning her to stay away. She stopped, confused, and retreated. Eddie went over to the cubicle, emptied the garbage, and shared another cigarette with Wayne. While they talked, he dug something out of his pocket and handed it to Wayne, who nodded, grinning. Then Wayne glanced over Eddie's shoulder and winked at her, a malicious gleam in his eye.

Fear swirled beneath her rib cage. Maybe she was wrong. Maybe she needed to stay away from Eddie too, especially if he and Wayne were friends. Maybe he already knew about the hidden room. Maybe he knew about Wayne and Rosemary, and Norma too. Maybe he was in on all of it.

When Eddie finished talking to Wayne, he put out his cigarette, tied the garbage bag to his cart, and headed toward the exit. Sage chewed on the inside of her cheek, frantic and trying to decide what to do. Even if Eddie knew about the secret room, she still needed to ask him about Rosemary. She still had to tell him who she was and why she was there. She started toward him again, but he was too far away. He had already unlocked the door and was pushing his cart into the hall. Then he was gone.

Swearing at herself for waiting too long, she returned to the back of the room. Hopefully Eddie would come back tomorrow instead of the man with the orthopedic shoes. But the next time she saw him, she resolved, she wouldn't let anything stop her from talking to him. Even if he warned her away with that shake of his head, even if Wayne was watching, she'd hurry over to him as soon as he entered the day room, no matter what.

Suddenly Wayne appeared in front of her, sweat glistening on his bald head and thick neck. She startled and stepped back.

"You can't listen to a damn thing Norma says," he said. "She's crazy as a loon and she's lying because she's jealous."

"I . . . I don't know what you're talking about," she said.

He moistened his lips. "I guess I'll have to remind you then," he said, grinning as if they were old friends. "In the meantime, your little boyfriend left you a note." He held up a folded piece of paper, pinched between two fingers like a cigarette. "Eddie seems to think he can get away with a lot of shit around here, but take my word for it, he's just a punk."

Sage opened her mouth to reply, but her voice failed her. When he said he would remind her, was he threatening to take her to the secret room? She reached for the note, but he snatched it away and laughed. She dropped her hand and waited, unwilling to be provoked.

He looked disappointed by her reluctance to play along. "What's the matter?" he said. "You lose your fight?"

He lowered the note, ready to tease her again, but a wild-haired girl in ruffled dress grabbed it out of his hand and ran off with it, laughing hysterically. Wayne chased after her, furious. The girl stopped in the center of the room and started to unfold the paper, turning it over and over, round and round, her head cocked to one side as she tried to figure out how to open it. When she saw Wayne coming, she dropped the note and sprinted away, knocking over an older woman and bumping into the other residents. Wayne picked up the piece of paper and tramped back to Sage, the blue vein bulging in his forehead.

"Keep your mouth shut about this too," he snarled, handing her the note. "Or else."

She grabbed it and rushed over to the other side of the room, where she found an empty seat and smoothed the paper out on her dirty, skinned knee. It read:

When everyone leaves to go back to the wards, stay here. We need to talk. Rip this up after you read it.

With her heart thudding in her chest, Sage looked around to see if Norma or anyone else had noticed her reading the note. A sudden screech tore across the room. Wayne had cornered the wild-haired girl who'd taken the note, and he had her pinned against the wall, his fist gripping the collar of her ruffled dress. The girl grimaced and shielded her head with her hands. Wayne shook her and shouted something in her face, then let her go. When he turned to leave, the girl crumpled to the ground, crying and laughing at the same time. Sage tore the note into tiny pieces, shoved half of them under a sagging couch cushion and the other half behind the backrest, then hurried over to the wild-haired girl to see if she was all right. The girl screamed at her and scrambled away.

After the frenzy of breakfast, lunch, dinner, and what felt like a hundred chaotic hours, the daily battle of trying to survive the dayroom finally came to an end. Wayne unlocked the doors, propped them open, and started shouting at the residents to move toward the hall. Sage hung back, nervous sweat dampening her forehead and upper lip. Did Wayne know what the note had said? Was he going to let her stay behind, or would he think she was causing trouble? As usual, he ordered the able-bodied residents to push the carts and the wheelchairs out the door while he herded the slow and uncooperative residents from behind, pushing and shoving them forward. Sage prayed he wouldn't notice her or check for stragglers before he left. Then she had another thought and her blood ran cold.

What if he stayed behind too? What if he and Eddie had come up with a vicious plan to get her alone and rape her? The only thing she knew for certain about Eddie was that he was a janitor who knew Rosemary—that was it. And she'd based all her trust on that. What if he was as bad as Wayne?

No. She couldn't give in to her doubts and fears. There was no reason to believe Eddie and Wayne wanted to trap her there. And this could be her last chance for who knew how long to get someone to listen. She moved toward the back the room, her nerves on fire, and sat down in a chair.

When the last resident left the room, Wayne released one of the double doors and closed it. After releasing the other side, he stood in the open door for a moment, blank-faced, his eyes locked on her. Then he shot her a lecherous grin, like a cat about to eat a mouse, before slamming and locking it.

She jumped out of the chair and raced toward the double doors, a sudden surge of panic filling her chest. She was trapped, and at a stranger's mercy. Despite knowing they were locked, she tried the handles, then pounded on the doors with both hands.

"Let me out!" she shouted.

On the other side of the doors, the muffled sounds of the residents lumbering down the hall moved farther and farther away, the screams, cries, wails, and laughter growing fainter and fainter. She pounded on the doors again.

"Someone, please! Let me out of here!"

No one came.

She turned and leaned against the door, struggling to control her terror. Without the residents, the vast, empty dayroom looked like a war zone. Shit and blood and claw marks marred the walls, overturned chairs and vomit littered the pock-marked floor. The perfect place to commit a murder. No one would even notice more blood.

She felt sick with fear. What if Wayne came back to make sure she kept her mouth shut about the secret room? What if he was Cropsey? What if he had killed Rosemary and was going to get rid of her next? She wrapped her arms around herself and tried to stop shaking. *Don't be ridiculous. Cropsey isn't real.* And even if Wayne and Eddie wanted to shut her up, they wouldn't be able to get her body out of there without being seen.

Except . . . she and Norma had wandered the halls last night without seeing a soul, hadn't they? Plus, the residents seemed to outnumber the staff by seventy to one, and no one counted heads at the end of the day. Wayne and Eddie could easily hide her body in the room and return for it later without anyone noticing.

She tried to reason away her terror: If her presence was helping Wayne get away with hiding Rosemary, surely he wouldn't want to harm her.

Just then, a key clunked inside the lock and one of the doors rattled. She stepped back, searching for something—*anything*—to use as a weapon. There was nothing but the plastic chairs. She grabbed one and lifted it above her head.

Eddie slipped inside. When he saw her wielding the chair, he stopped short, one hand up to protect himself. "What the hell?" he yelped. "What are you doing? It's just me."

"What do you want?"

"What do you mean, what do I want? You've been missing for days. I want to know where you've been."

"I'm not Rosemary," she said. "I'm her twin sister, Sage."

"Okay, if you say so. Just put the chair down so we can talk."

"It's the truth," she said. "I know you don't believe me. No one does. I came here as soon as I found out Rosemary was missing, but Dr. Baldwin locked me up because he thinks I'm her. They all do."

"Okay," he said, lowering his hand. "Just let me lock the door, then you can tell me everything, all right?"

She nodded.

He locked the door, then studied her face, his clear blue eyes filled with concern. When he edged closer, she lifted the chair higher, ready to strike him if he tried anything. But he stopped, and after a few tense moments, he finally said, "Holy shit."

"What?" she said.

"I can see it now. You're really not her."

"You can tell I'm not Rosemary?"

He nodded, shocked. "Yeah, I can."

Her shoulders loosened and she lowered the chair, but only partway. "You're not trying to trick me, are you?"

He shook his head. "I'm not, I promise."

Nearly crumpling with relief, she put the chair down, but still kept her distance. Finally, someone believed her. Someone might listen and help—unless he was lying so she wouldn't bash his head in. Her doubts came flooding back. Maybe she was right about Wayne knowing who she really was; maybe he'd already told Eddie. "Why do you believe me? No one else does."

"Because your voice is different," he said. "It's deeper and a little rougher. And even though you're scared shitless right now, your eyes are softer, more peaceful. Not like Rosemary's. I've never seen anyone with eyes like hers."

"What do you mean? How are her eyes different?"

"Her eyes always look haunted, like her head is full of ghosts."

Goose bumps prickled along Sage's arms. What he said made perfect sense. Rosemary always looked like she was seeing people and things that weren't there. And the odds that Wayne had noticed that about Rosemary's eyes were pretty low, which meant Eddie had figured out who Sage was on his own. "Do you know what happened to her?"

He shook his head. "I don't. I wish I did."

"But you're friends with her." It was a more of a statement than a question.

He shrugged. "Sort of. I guess."

"What does that mean?"

"She always said hi to me when she was in line for her meds. And sometimes she came over to talk to me when I was in here emptying the garbage."

"And that's how you got to know her so well?" she said. Doubt edged her voice.

Sensing her skepticism, he gave her an irritated look. "When people see each other nearly every day, they're bound to form some kind of connection, whether it's good, bad, or indifferent. We never spoke to each other where anyone could see us for more than a minute or two, but Wayne let us meet alone like this a couple times. I felt bad for her, she seemed pretty normal. And I talked to her because I wanted to. I liked her. She was nice."

"Did she tell you she had a sister?"

"Yeah, but I thought she meant Norma. I didn't know she had a real sister."

A twinge of sorrow squeezed Sage's heart. Maybe Rosemary had gradually come to believe that Sage was imaginary. Maybe she was angry with Sage for not visiting. Or maybe she'd forgotten the life she had before being abandoned to live in this horrific place. If that was the case, it was probably for the best. You couldn't miss something you never knew you had.

"Wayne said you're Rosemary's boyfriend."

"Wayne doesn't know what he's talking about. He's always trying to start shit."

"Were you having sex with her?"

He blanched. "What? No!"

"Why didn't you talk to her in front of other people?"

"You heard Marla bark at me when I said hi to you the other day. And everyone in this place loves to spread gossip."

"Was Rosemary friends with Wayne too?"

"I wouldn't say they were *friends,* but she put up with him to stay on his good side. And so he'd let her talk to me."

"What do you mean she 'put up with him'?"

"You know, he flirted and joked around with her a lot, like guys do. He could get vulgar and offensive sometimes, but she brushed it off because she didn't want to make him mad. I'm sure you've seen his temper."

"Is that why Nurse Vic and Leonard think he had something to do with her disappearance?"

"Who knows? Like I said, the only thing that actually works around here is the rumor mill."

"Did you know Wayne was having sex with her?"

Something that looked like pain flickered across his eyes. "Who told you that?"

She started to tell him, then remembered Norma's threat and stopped. "If I tell you, you have to promise not to tell anyone else. Not until I get out of here or we find Rosemary. Because I'll . . ." She paused, not sure how to continue. "I'll get in a lot of trouble if you tell someone too soon, and then we might never find her."

"Okay," he said. "I promise not to tell anyone until you say it's all right." He gave her a weak grin and held up two fingers. "Scout's honor."

She studied his eyes. He seemed honest enough. Maybe even a little naïve. Maybe that was why Rosemary had been drawn to him. And if Rosemary trusted him, hopefully she could too. "It was Norma. She said Wayne used to take Rosemary into a hidden room over in the pit."

He looked doubtful. "You realize Norma is batshit crazy, right?"

"I've seen the room myself."

"How?"

"That doesn't matter right now," she said. "I saw the mattress on the floor, and the dead

221

pigeons and mice lying around." There was no need for him to know about Norma stealing the keys and the two of them leaving the ward in the middle of the night. Not yet, anyway. And what if he told on Norma? She'd tell everyone Sage was destroying her pills. "I know Norma has . . . problems, but she said Wayne takes her there because she's his girlfriend now that Rosemary's gone."

He shook his head, seeming both puzzled and slightly amused. "You must be talking about that empty space off the supply room where Nurse Morris keeps her cats during her shift on the second floor. Everyone talks about how she steals from the cafeteria for those flea-bitten things and lets them shit all over in there. Some of the staff used to meet in there to get high, but they got caught a few times so they stopped doing it as often. Still, if Wayne was taking her or Rosemary in there, someone would have found out and we all would have heard about it."

"Are you sure? Norma wanted me to know about the room because she thinks I'm Rosemary. She wanted to hurt my . . . I mean, her feelings for leaving without telling her. If Rosemary wasn't actually going there, what would be the point?"

"Of course I'm sure. I've seen the damn cats myself. Harry is orange, and Tabby's black and white with seven toes on one foot. And who knows what goes on inside Norma's head. Wayne said she's convinced someone different is coming to kill her every other day. One day it's Jack the Ripper, the next it's the Creature from the Black Lagoon. You can't believe anything she says."

Heat crawled up Sage's face. How could she have been so stupid? She'd seen proof of Norma's mental state from the beginning—running around naked, destroying a chair with her bare hands. It shouldn't have come as a surprise to learn that she'd made up the whole thing. And clearly she was more paranoid than Sage thought or understood, which would explain why she'd mentioned Cropsey too.

Sage groaned inside. Eddie must think she was an idiot. Or a crazy person. The last thing she needed was for the only person who believed her to think she was out of her mind. "So you don't think Wayne is capable of doing something like that?"

"I think *everyone* is capable of doing terrible shit, so I can't say for certain either way. The only things I know for sure are that Norma is nuts and Wayne's a bully and a prick. I only talk to him to stay on his good side because I don't want to deal with his shit."

"He's more than a bully and a prick. He physically abuses the residents. I've seen it with my own eyes."

"I know. But that's because force is the only

way he knows how to maintain control. It's the same with a lot of the attendants here. They never had training. They weren't taught any different. And you know how bad it can get. Some of the residents would kill each other if the attendants let them."

"Why does it sound like you're defending him?"

"I'm not. But you need to know what you're up against. There aren't enough staff to go around, so the attendants end up taking care of way more residents than they're supposed to. That's why Wayne's supervising this dayroom. The attendant here is supposed to be female, but the people in charge have to work with what they've got. And it's not much, believe me."

Sage wanted to tell him that she knew what she was up against, that the dead weight of fear and despair she carried every second of every day in Willowbrook made her bones heavy as lead, but she didn't want to waste time talking about herself. Then she remembered something.

"Norma said Wayne always gives her Pixy Stix when they go in there. She hides them in the supply room."

"Pixy Stix?"

She nodded. "They're in a cloth bag hanging up with the straitjackets. Go over there and see for yourself."

"Shit," he said. She could tell by the look on

his face that he believed her now—about Wayne taking Norma into the hidden room, anyway. There was no way to prove he'd taken Rosemary there, too.

"Now you know why I think Wayne might have had something to do with Rosemary's disappearance," she said. "But I can't do anything about it if I'm locked up in here. Will you help me get out?"

He gaped at her. "How am I supposed to do that?"

"You're a janitor. You must have all kinds of keys."

"I have some keys, but not all of them. And moving someone around *inside* the building is easier than taking someone *out* of it. In case you haven't noticed, the main exits are guarded and locked. And there's a guard at the main gate too."

Shit. Apparently Norma was telling the truth about the keys too. "Did Wayne ever say anything to you about Rosemary disappearing?"

He shook his head. "Not much. He just wondered where she went, like everyone else."

"Did Rosemary ever say anything to you about him?"

"Not really, nothing in particular. But I know she was scared of him."

"How do you know?"

"That was one of the few things she did

mention. And I could tell. She acted different when he wasn't around, more at ease."

"I don't blame her. I'm scared of him too. He said he's still going to make time for me, whatever that means."

He wrinkled his forehead. "Did he act surprised when he first saw you? Wouldn't he have freaked out if he had anything to do with Rosemary's disappearance?"

"He acted surprised, but not really shocked. And I was thinking, what if he *knows* I'm not Rosemary? What if he just isn't saying anything because he wants everyone *else* to keep thinking I'm her?"

"How would he know? And why would he want that?"

She shrugged. "I don't know, but I keep thinking . . . maybe he knows I *can't* be her because he has her locked up somewhere. But as long as everyone else thinks I'm her, they won't realize she's still missing. It would make sense, wouldn't it?"

"Jesus," Eddie said. "I didn't think of that."

"Will you ask him if he knows who I am?"

"I don't think that's a good idea, for a whole lot of reasons."

"Why not? I thought you were friends."

He let out a sarcastic laugh. "Yeah, right. I just told you, I only talk to him so I can stay on his good side. Because if there's one thing I've learned about working here, it's that there's a pecking order. And the cleanup crew, that's me, is at the bottom. No one trusts anyone else. The attendants don't trust the nurses because the nurses answer to administration. And the nurses don't trust the attendants because administration will hire anybody who can stand upright and talk in complete sentences. We've got ex-cons working here, and most of the doctors are a joke. Normal hospitals won't hire them. Did you notice the doctors and nurses don't touch the residents? They have the staff bring them in to be seen, then make the staff hold them and move them around so they don't have to get close to them because they're afraid of getting hurt or catching disease. And don't even get me started on the criminally insane who get dumped here. Sometimes it seems like the only difference between the residents and the staff is that the staff have keys. So I just stay out of the way and try to get along with everyone."

Something cold and hard twisted in her stomach. Ex-criminals? Bad doctors? Criminally insane residents? That wasn't what she wanted to hear. She thought about asking him why the hell he'd continue to work there, but that wasn't important right now. Then she remembered the track marks on Wayne's arms. "Did you know Wayne's a drug addict?"

"Yeah. So's half the rest of the staff. Sometimes

I think using is the only way they can cope with working here. Most people don't last long. We lose at least a dozen every month."

"Why don't the staff report each other? Would they report Wayne if they found out he was doing something to Rosemary?"

He hesitated. "Do you want the truth, or do you want me to make you feel better?"

"The truth."

"No one's going to report Wayne for doing drugs, or anything else for that matter. A lot of them party together. They buy and sell drugs at work. They screw around with each other too. They might fight once in a while, but they don't snitch and they don't rat each other out. Some of them find that out the hard way when their tires get slashed or their cars get set on fire, they get beat up in the parking lot, or worse. To report something, an employee would have to be able to prove it beyond a reasonable doubt, which is almost impossible. And everybody's afraid of guys like Wayne. *And,* besides all that, it's really hard to fire a state employee because the union backs them. I don't know everything because like I said, I try to stay out of trouble, but I hear things. And I know things."

His words ricocheted like pinballs inside her head. She could hardly keep up or believe what she was hearing. If the employees were getting away with doing drugs and having sex with each other at work, what else were they getting away with? Kidnapping? Murder? And who was going to listen to her if no one cared about what they already *knew* was happening in Willowbrook? She started to tremble, the grating edge of anxiety fraying her nerves.

"Then why do you think Wayne let you talk to Rosemary, and now me, in private?"

He shrugged. "Because I don't give him any shit?"

"And because he wouldn't care if you were having sex with a resident?"

"That too. I'm pretty sure that's exactly what he thinks is going on in here."

"He must not be worried that you'll believe me either. What about Dr. Baldwin? Do you think you can convince him I'm not Rosemary?"

A frown line deepened between his brows. "He won't listen to me."

"Why not?"

"Because he blames me for her running away. Or whatever she did. I honestly don't know what she was thinking. Or where she could have gone."

She hesitated, confused. "But Wayne said Dr. Baldwin blamed *him*. That he almost got fired because of it."

"That's because Baldwin has no idea what happened, and he's trying to figure it out."

"So why would he blame you?"

"I don't know."

Sage studied him, then said, "Yes, you do. Please, you have to tell me."

A hardness tightened his jaw that wasn't there before. "He thought we were . . . doing things we weren't supposed to be doing. Just like you thought it, and Wayne thought it."

"Well, if she liked you, I don't care," she said gently. "Honestly, it'd make me feel better to think she'd found a little happiness in this shithole. So please . . . tell me the truth."

"She kissed me in the hallway once, that was it. I pushed her away, but it was too late. Everyone saw it. That's why Dr. Baldwin thinks she left, so we could be together. He thinks I'm hiding her somewhere."

"Are you?"

"Of course not."

"And you're sure you don't have any idea where she might be?"

"I told you, I don't," he said. "I really wish I did. She asked me to come into her ward one night so we could talk, but I told her no, that we'd get in trouble if we got caught and then I'd never see her again. But she insisted. She said she'd do something drastic if I didn't show up. She said someone was sneaking into the ward and hurting her, and she thought it would stop if they saw me there."

"*Hurting* her?" Sage said. She felt sick. "Do you think it was Wayne?"

"I don't know. She never got the chance to tell me, because that was the night she went missing. Now I can't help thinking the worst, and it's killing me." His eyes grew glassy and his voice caught. "She had problems for sure, but she just wanted to be loved."

A lump lodged in Sage's throat. If the one person in this horrible place who cared about Rosemary was thinking the worst, what was *she* supposed to think? "If Dr. Baldwin thinks you were messing around with Rosemary," she said, "why didn't he fire you?"

"Because he's grasping at straws. And because my mother donates a lot of money to this place, and my uncle is Willowbrook's program director and the head of the physical therapy department. He warned me to stay away from Rosemary because she's psychotic and paranoid and she'll be afraid of everything and everyone for the rest of her life, but I didn't listen. But I think the biggest reason Baldwin didn't fire me was because my uncle said he'd go to the press."

"Go to the press? About what?"

"About her going missing. And all the other things that go on in Willowbrook."

Sage's eyes went wide. "Are you saying they haven't told anyone she's gone?"

He nodded.

"Not even the cops?"

"Hell no, *especially* not the cops! That would

be a stain on Willowbrook's reputation. And administration would never allow that." His voice was filled with sarcasm.

"Oh my God. So they never even brought in a search party?"

He shook his head. "The staff was instructed to check every building on campus. And they sent some of the security guards out to search the lawns and woods, but that was it."

"I don't understand. Why wouldn't they ask for help? Why wouldn't they get the cops to come with dogs and horses and officers who know what they're doing?"

"Because that would have brought reporters, which would make it harder to hide all the bad shit that happens here. You've seen the way residents are treated. This isn't a school. It's a warehouse for incurables. Only a handful of kids over in the experiment ward get any sort of education, and those lessons only last a couple hours a day, if that. And the only reason they're getting any lessons at all is because their parents signed papers allowing Dr. Krugman to give them experimental vaccines in exchange for better accommodations. Meanwhile the doctors are putting feces from hepatitis patients in the chocolate milk."

She put a hand over her stomach, certain she'd vomit if she tried to speak.

"But they're not getting better care over there.

They're dying," he continued. "The public has no *idea* how many residents die in this place every year. Some of them make it into the local paper, like the ten-year-old who was scalded to death in the shower because of the crappy plumbing, and the twelve-year-old who strangled himself while trying to get free from a restraining device. But most don't, like the eighteen-year-old who died last week after another resident punched him in the throat. And your sister isn't the first to disappear."

Sage wanted him to stop talking. At the same time, she had to know the truth, even as hopelessness swept through her like a brutal wind. "That's what Norma said. But she . . ." She stopped herself. Norma thought Jack the Ripper and the Creature from the Black Lagoon were real. "Never mind. It doesn't matter what she said."

"Obviously it mattered to you, so tell me."

"Norma said it was Cropsey." As soon as the words left her mouth, she regretted them. Cropsey was nothing but another rumor. Deep down she knew that, but being at Willowbrook made the unthinkable seem real.

Something that looked like sorrow filled Eddie's eyes, or maybe it was concern; it was hard to tell. She wanted him to say something—anything—to let her know he didn't think she was as crazy as Norma. "See, I told you it wasn't important," she said. "It's just a stupid urban legend I heard when I was a kid. I was just surprised when Norma mentioned it."

"I don't think it's stupid," he said. "I grew up hearing about Cropsey too. And honestly, those stories scared the shit out of me. My older brother and his friends used to drag me into the tunnels beneath the old Seaview Sanatorium and leave me there to find my way out. They said they wanted to catch Cropsey. I was the bait."

"Oh my God. That's horrible!"

He shrugged. "Well, my brother was an asshole, but I survived."

Sage pushed the thoughts of Cropsey from her mind and steered the conversation back to her sister. "Did anyone question Wayne and the rest of the staff when Rosemary disappeared?"

"Of course. Dr. Baldwin had lots of us questioned, some more than once, including me. But nothing ever came of it."

"Do you think she could have escaped?" She was grasping at any shred of hope, but she had no choice. She had to keep going, to keep searching for the truth. Otherwise she and her sister would both be lost.

"As far as I know," he said, "the only way residents leave Willowbrook is by dying."

She swallowed. "Are you saying . . . are you saying you think Rosemary is dead?"

"No," he said, regret creasing his forehead.

"I'm sorry. That's not what I meant. I've just never heard of anyone escaping, that's all."

She let out a frustrated, exhausted sigh. Talking about Cropsey and everything that was wrong with Willowbrook wouldn't get her released or find her sister. She had to take action. "If you can't get me out of here, will you do something else for me?"

"If I can."

"Will you call my stepfather and tell him I'm here? Dr. Baldwin said he called him, but I don't know if he's telling the truth. And even if he did, he would have just said that Rosemary was back safe and sound. If you tell my stepfather you work here and they locked me up because they think I'm my sister, maybe he'll give a shit."

"Where does he think you are?"

"At a friend's, probably. He doesn't care as long as I'm out of his hair. His name is Alan Tern and his number is 212-567-2345. Can you remember it?"

He nodded and repeated the number. "Will he believe some guy on the phone he's never met?"

"I don't know," she said. "But I have to try something. I'm warning you though, he can be a real asshole, especially when he's drinking, which, if he's home to answer the phone, he will be."

"What should I say?"

"Tell him I came here on the bus and my purse

was stolen. Tell him I'm not with Heather or Dawn or Noah."

"Okay. Anything else that might convince him?"

Imagining Alan's reaction to Eddie's call, she suddenly remembered how he refused to answer the phone if he thought debt collectors were calling, which was usually the case. "If he doesn't answer, would you be willing to go in person and talk to him face-to-face?"

"If you think it will help."

"It *has* to help," she said. She told him the address. Then she had another idea. "If you can get me a pen and paper, I could write him a note."

Footsteps sounded out in the hall.

"Wayne's coming back," Eddie said.

She moved away from him and stood behind the chair she'd wielded earlier, her mind racing as she tried to think of anything else she should tell him. The footsteps stopped on the other side of the door. A key entered the lock.

"When will we be able to talk again?" she said.

"Soon. In the meantime, try to stay out of trouble. I'll do whatever I can to help, but if you get sent to the pit, it'll be a lot harder."

She nodded.

The deadbolt clunked, one side of the double doors opened, and Wayne stepped into the room.

"All right, lovebirds," he said. "Time to get dressed and call it a night."

Eddie gave her a reassuring look, then turned to leave. Wayne shot her a lewd grin and held the door open for him.

"Thanks," Eddie said to him.

"Anytime," Wayne said, thumping him on the back. "Anytime."

When Eddie disappeared into the hall, Sage started toward the door, anticipation and fear making her tremble. If she could make it through another twenty-four hours until Eddie told Alan she was there, she'd be going to the press about Willowbrook and her missing sister. And Wayne.

Before she could exit, Wayne stepped in front of her, blocking the doorway. "What's your hurry?" he said.

She stopped and took a step back, dropping her eyes to the floor.

"Looks like your little boyfriend missed you while you were gone," he said. "Come to think of it, now that I've lost the urge to wring your neck, I missed you too."

She took another step back, ready to run or fight if he shut the door and came after her. She'd scream and grab a chair to bash him over the head like she'd almost done to Eddie. Maybe Eddie would hear her and come back. "Please leave me alone," she said.

Wayne leaned against the doorframe, leering at her as if waiting to see if she'd try something. After what felt like forever, he moved aside to let her pass. "Lucky for you I've got better things to do with my evening," he said.

She skirted around him and rushed out the door. No one was in the hallway except Eddie, who was mopping the floor several yards away. She started toward him, walking fast.

"Why so skittish?" Wayne called after her, locking the door. "You got ants in your pants?"

She ignored him and kept going.

"You okay?" Eddie said as she neared.

"Can you walk me back to the ward?" she whispered. "I don't want to be alone with him."

He shook his head. "Sorry. Marla would blow a gasket."

Sage kept going. Hopefully someone would be at the nurses' station.

"Jesus, Eddie," Wayne said, laughing as he followed her. "What'd you do to her? She's trottin' like her ass is on fire."

Eddie wrung out the mop and slapped it onto the floor. "Not a thing, my friend," he said. "Not a damn thing."

"Uh-huh," Wayne said. "Sure."

When Sage neared the nurses' station, Nurse Vic leaned over the counter and peered down the hall toward Wayne. "What's going on?" she said.

"Just taking this straggler back to her ward," he said. "She was hiding in my cubicle while I was rounding up the others."

Nurse Vic came around the counter and waited

for them to reach her. "Was she trying to escape again?"

"I wouldn't put it past her," Wayne said. "She's a sneaky one."

Sage made eye contact with Nurse Vic, hoping she'd see the fear on her face. Nurse Vic glanced at her briefly but didn't react. Instead, she took a pack of cigarettes out of her uniform pocket.

"Got a light?" she asked Wayne.

"Sure," Wayne said. He stopped to dig his lighter out of his pocket.

Sage kept going.

"Whoa, slow down there," Wayne called after her. After lighting Nurse Vic's cigarette, he sprinted to catch up.

Sage glanced over her shoulder to see if he was getting close. To her surprise, Nurse Vic walked casually down the hall behind him, taking a long drag from her cigarette and watching them. Wayne slowed when he caught up to Sage, then followed a few feet behind her. When she turned the corner and went down the hall toward her ward, she looked back again. Nurse Vic strolled past the hallway intersection, keeping an eye on them until they reached Ward D. As soon as Wayne unlocked the door and pushed it open, Nurse Vic turned around and disappeared.

Once Sage was inside the ward, Wayne shut the door behind her, locking it before he left. Near the back of the room, Marla was holding a screaming woman down on a mattress and waiting for her to stop struggling, her face pinched with determination. Grateful that Marla was too busy to notice her late return, Sage hurried toward her sister's bed, surprisingly relieved to be back in the noisy, overcrowded ward. At least Wayne couldn't reach her there. Then she remembered what Rosemary had told Eddie about someone sneaking in there at night.

She wasn't safe anywhere.

CHAPTER 10

At the nurses' station the next morning, Sage took another chance with Nurse Vic. "Thank you for looking out for me when Wayne took me back to the ward last night," she said. "I felt safer knowing you were there."

As usual, Nurse Vic ignored her and kept working, filling the plastic cups with orange pills, putting the trays on the counter.

"He really scares me," Sage said.

Nurse Vic stayed silent.

"You know I'm right," Sage said. "You know Wayne is dangerous and I'm telling the truth about what he was doing to my sister. That's why you followed us last night."

Nurse Vic lifted her chin to look out over the crowd of residents. "Marla?" she shouted. When she saw Marla, she motioned her over. "Can you come here, please? I need you to take someone to the pit."

Sage went rigid. "No," she said. "You don't need to send me there. I'll shut up."

"Then shut up," Nurse Vic said.

Sage dropped her eyes. Eddie was right: The staff wouldn't rat on one another, no matter what they knew about what their coworkers were doing. And if the look in Nurse Vic's eyes was any indication, she was afraid of Wayne too. Sage took a plastic cup from the woman in the gray skirt, popped the pills into her mouth, grabbed the wheeled cart she was pushing, and moved on. Anger and frustration boiled like acid in her throat.

After spitting the drugs into her hand, she watched the dayroom door for Eddie, anxious to find out whether he'd gotten in touch with Alan. If he hadn't, she wasn't sure what she'd do— break down and weep? Scream at the top of her lungs? The thought of spending another night in Willowbrook was more than she could take. She tried to remember if Eddie worked every day or every other day, but the days and nights jumbled together, like waking from one frightening nightmare to find yourself lost in another, more terrifying one.

When the janitor in the orthopedic shoes came out of the dayroom door pushing the mop bucket, she nearly wept. What if Eddie had been fired after all? What if he'd moved away or been run over by a car? Or maybe he decided not to get involved. Maybe he requested a transfer to another ward. No. She had to stop being so paranoid. Either he had the day off or he was working in another building, that was all. With any luck, he was on his way to Willowbrook with Alan. The two of them could be in Dr. Baldwin's office at that very moment, explaining the situation and giving him hell.

After parking the cart in the dayroom, she sat in the far corner and tried to make herself invisible. Thankfully, the other residents left her alone for the most part, but every now and then someone tried to talk to her, or picked at her hair and pulled at her clothes. When that happened, she kept quiet and waited for them to go away, afraid she'd say or do something to set them off and get punched or slapped or kicked. Thankfully, Norma stayed away from her too, and so far she hadn't snitched on Sage for destroying her pills. At least she didn't think she had. She thought briefly about asking Wayne if he knew where Eddie was, but decided against it.

During the long, horrible hours of uncertainty, she survived by closing her eyes, putting her hands over her ears, and pretending she was somewhere else. She thought about her father—about going to South Beach with him and Rosemary, the sea-green water foaming on the sand, the sun a dazzling high point in the sky. She could see her dad, tall and tanned in his swimming trunks, chasing them through the waves. And Rosemary, building a sandcastle with a moat and a railing and windows made out of seashells. She thought about piggyback rides, picking out toys at yard sales, and riding her banana-seat bike to Farrell's Ice Cream Parlour. She imagined sitting in the darkened theater at Lane Theater waiting for the movie to start, breathing in the smell of fresh popcorn. She remembered curling up on the couch to watch *The Brady Bunch*, downing root beers at the A&W, dancing and going out for pizza with her friends.

The memories helped until she was forced back to reality to eat ground-up mush or avoid a conflict with another resident. Each time she had to pull herself from inside her head to reenter the cruel abomination of Willowbrook, and the realization that Eddie might not help after all, a desperate sadness swept over her, so profound it made tears swell in her eyes and she felt physically ill. It nearly tore her to pieces.

When Wayne strolled over to her later that afternoon with a shit-eating grin on his face, she barely had the willpower to face him.

"Your boyfriend wants to see you again," he said. "You two are really getting hot and heavy these days, aren't you?"

With that, overwhelming relief loosened her tense muscles and adrenaline revived her spirit, but she said nothing. She kept her eyes on the floor and waited for him to go away.

But instead of leaving, he reached down, his fingers grazing her cheek, and lifted her chin. "How about you share a little more of that sugar with me before he comes back?"

She slapped his hand away. "Get away from

me," she said, then jumped up and got behind the chair.

He moved closer and pushed the chair into her legs, herding her back into a corner. "Oh, come on now," he said. "Eddie's just a boy. I'll remind you what it's like to be with a real man. You liked it last time. You liked it a lot. I can take you to our secret place again, or we can just do it right here. Nobody'll even notice."

Gripping the back of the chair, she pressed herself into the corner, her knuckles turning white. "Leave me alone or I'll scream."

He laughed. "You think anyone is gonna pay attention to screaming in this place? Scream all you want." He tore the chair out from between them, grabbed her shirt, and yanked her toward him, his laughter replaced by something fiercer, blacker.

She pounded on him with her fists, hitting his rock-hard face and chest and shoulders. "Let me go!"

A strange mix of fury and glee twisted his face. "So you want to play rough this time, huh?" he said, catching her arm in his plank-thick hand. He started to wrench it behind her back, but she pulled away and ran, nearly tripping over a girl on the floor. He pushed the residents out of his way and chased after her.

"I love it when you play hard to get," he shouted.

She raced toward the cubicle, zigzagging and fighting her way through the ever-shifting crowd. If she could get to the phone before Wayne caught up to her, maybe she could call for help. Then the dayroom door opened and Eddie entered. She hurried toward him. Wayne slowed his pursuit, then stopped and laughed. He grabbed a girl who was banging her fists against her head and made her sit on the floor.

"He tried to attack me," Sage said when she reached Eddie, breathing hard.

"Who did? Wayne?"

She nodded, still shaking. "He said he'd take me to a secret place, just like Norma said."

Eddie's face went hard. He yanked off his work gloves and marched over to Wayne, who was trying to stop two girls from pulling each other's hair. Eddie pointed at him and said something. Sage was too far away to hear, but it looked like he was giving Wayne a piece of his mind. Wayne seemed amused. He let go of the girls, crossed his massive arms over his chest, and smirked down at Eddie. Sage held her breath and waited for one of them to take a swing. If they got in a fight, it might send the other residents into a frenzy. And if Eddie got hurt or fired, he wouldn't be able to help her. She started toward them, desperate to defuse the situation.

Then, to her surprise, Wayne ruffled Eddie's hair and laughed. He looked up and saw her coming, then winked at her, clapped Eddie on the shoulder, and walked away, still grinning.

Eddie met Sage halfway across the room, anger creasing his forehead. "Let me know if he bothers you again," he said.

"What did you say to him?"

"That I'd go to my uncle and find a way to get him fired if he got anywhere near you again."

Near the door, Wayne started shouting orders at the residents, telling them to grab wheelchairs and carts and get ready to return to the ward. A mass of residents started toward him all at once, like a sudden outgoing tide, rushing by and tumbling into Sage and Eddie. Suddenly, a woman with whisper-thin hair grabbed Eddie's wrist.

"Take me with you," she said.

Eddie shook his head and gently pulled away.

"Please," the woman begged. "I need to go. It's time for me to leave."

"I'm sorry," he said. "Go away."

The woman turned, a sad look on her face, and shuffled toward the door.

"I hate it when they do that," he said.

"Do what?" she said.

"Ask me to sneak them out of here. They ask all of us, really, the other janitors, and the laundry workers too."

So she was right. The residents asked him for help all the time. A rush of fear washed over her. What if he was just being agreeable because he liked Rosemary? He said Rosemary was "nice," but that didn't mean he'd risk his job or get in trouble with his uncle for her, much less for Sage. "When you didn't show up earlier, I thought you'd changed your mind about helping me."

"Sorry, I had to cover someone's shift over in House Eight."

She chewed the inside of her lip, nervous about the next part of their conversation. "Please tell me you talked to Alan."

"I called, but he didn't answer, so I went to your apartment. The TV was blaring inside, so I don't know if he could hear me or not, but I pounded on the door for over half an hour and he never opened it. Maybe he was sleeping."

Tears welled in her eyes. How much longer would she be trapped in this nightmare? "He probably got shitfaced and passed out," she said. "Or he was at the bar with his buddies. I should have told you about the TV. He leaves it on all the time, even when he's not home. He thinks it keeps us from getting robbed." Knowing Alan, he was going out with his friends every night now that she was gone. He'd probably told them she had run away so they'd pat him on the back, tell him how sorry they were, and buy him another beer. The same way he'd let everyone keep buying him drinks after her mother's wake, while she sat in the corner of the restaurant crying and waiting to go home.

"I slipped a note with my phone number on it under the door before I left," Eddie said.

"I thought I was going to write it."

"Did you want me to wait until I could get you a pen and paper?"

She shook her head, realizing how foolish that sounded. She thought it might have helped if Alan recognized her handwriting, but who knew if he would? All that mattered now was that Eddie had left a note telling him she was there. She just prayed he'd believe it.

"He had to have seen it this morning," Eddie said. "When I get out of work tonight, I'll go back and make sure. Hopefully he'll answer the door this time."

She wiped her eyes, trying to control her emotions. For some reason, beyond the obvious desperate need to get out of Willowbrook, she wished Alan had knocked down the institution doors and demanded her release by now. Part of her hoped he loved her—even a tiny bit. Enough to care if she were dead or alive anyway. She should have known better. He had never cared about anyone but himself. Her *real* father would have been there to rescue her in a heartbeat. Then again, he never would have sent Rosemary away in the first place.

"Don't worry," Eddie said. "We're not done yet. I'll talk to my uncle to see if he can help somehow. He's at a conference right now, but he'll be back tomorrow."

"Will he believe you?"

"I'm sure he'll warn me for the hundredth time to stay away from the residents, but I'll try. And I'll let you know as soon as I find out anything. In the meantime, we don't want Nurse Vic to wonder why you're lagging behind again, so you better go."

Sage looked over at Wayne, who was herding everyone out the doors and into the hall, one eye on her and Eddie. By the smirk on his face, he had no intention of heeding Eddie's warning. "Wayne doesn't look very worried about your threat."

Eddie glanced over at him, fury flashing in his eyes. "He thinks I'm joking because we both know what happens when employees rat on each other. If I turn him in, even if he does get fired, I'll need to be careful walking alone to my car."

"In other words," she said, "there's nothing you can do."

"I'm sure my uncle and I can figure something out, but even if I could prove Wayne guilty beyond a shadow of a doubt, I don't want to draw more attention to you right now. And I wouldn't want to get him fired yet anyway. Think about it, he lets us talk to each other. Someone else might not. Plus, he could easily send you to the pit for no reason and then we'd be screwed."

"What are you saying? That I should do whatever he wants?"

"No! That's not what I'm saying at all."

"What then?" she said. Her chin started to tremble. "How am I supposed to keep him away from me?"

He gently took her hand, his fingers wrapping around her palm, and looked at her with worried eyes. "I don't know," he said. "All I can do is try to get you out of here as soon as possible."

It was the first time in what felt like forever that another person had touched her in a kind, comforting way, but it did little to calm her nerves. She pulled her hand away. "I'm sorry. I know. And I'm grateful for your help."

"Just hang in there, okay?" he said. "We'll figure this out. But I better get back. I need to clock out." He started to turn toward the door.

Then she remembered something. "Wait," she said. "Norma said some of the female residents were sterilized. Do you know if Rosemary was? If I can show Dr. Baldwin I don't have a scar, he'll know I'm not her."

He seemed surprised by the suggestion. "I don't know," he said. "But the only way you're going to see a doctor is if you're bleeding profusely or you're on the verge of death."

"I know," she said. "Marla said the same thing." She held out her arm, wrist up. "So cut me. You must have a knife or something in your cleaning cart."

He recoiled. "What? No."

"Then tell me where it is and I'll do it."

He shook his head. "Janitors aren't allowed to carry anything that's sharp. But even if I had something, I wouldn't let you do that."

"Then I'll get Wayne to beat me up. Please! I have to get out of here. I don't care how."

He grasped her by the shoulders and looked her in the eye, his face stern. "The only thing you'll get by doing either of those things is a nice, long stay in the pit. Is that what you want?"

She covered her face with her hands and shook her head, swallowing the sobs that threatened to tear from her throat.

"I'm sorry," he said. "I know you're scared, but you're going to be okay."

She dropped her hands and gaped at him. "How can you say that? I'm locked up in a loony bin, I feel like I'm dying, my sister is still missing, and my stepfather, the only person who can get me out of here, doesn't give two shits where I am. He's probably glad to be rid of me." She couldn't hold back any longer, tears fell down her cheeks. "The only people who might care are my friends. Would you go see them and tell them I'm here?"

"I can try," he said. "Where do they live?"

She wiped her face and tried to pull herself together. "Dawn lives in the housing units over on Belmont Avenue in Mariners Harbor. She's in apartment 5B. And Heather lives about ten blocks from there on Gooseneck Drive, above the Starlight Liquor store. Do you know it?"

He nodded. "I've driven by it."

"You should probably try Dawn's place first because Heather's father is an asshole. If he doesn't know you, he'll just tell you to get lost."

"Okay," he said. "If your stepfather doesn't answer the door this time, I'll go see your friends afterward."

"Do you think Dr. Baldwin will listen if they come?"

"I don't know," he said. "But all we can do is try, right?" He gave her a reassuring smile.

She nodded and tried to return the smile, but her lips quivered and her eyes filled again.

CHAPTER 11

By Sage's fifth day in Willowbrook, Ward D had gone two nights without heat and no one had showered since the day she'd arrived. Four residents had been wrestled into straitjackets and hauled off to who knew where. Two residents had died; one broke her leg. Yesterday, they'd been given only half portions of the ground-up meals, and a strange, itchy rash had started on Sage's feet and ankles. She'd been spit at, screamed at, grabbed, slapped, and punched. She knew every wall and corner and piece of furniture in Ward D and the dayroom like a prisoner knows the inside of his cell. She knew who relieved themselves on the floor, who liked to piss off the attendants, and who refused to take off their soiled clothes. She knew who watched television and who acted like it didn't exist.

After another exhausting morning of waiting in line for pills and forcing herself to eat one more watery bowl of mealy oatmeal, she sat in her usual corner in the dayroom, her eyes locked on the double doors, watching for Eddie, praying he'd talked to Alan or Heather or Dawn. She imagined Dr. Baldwin coming into the dayroom, apologizing, and taking her to meet Alan or her friends in the lobby.

When Eddie finally appeared, it was all she could do not to cry out and run over to him. But they couldn't talk about their plans in front of Wayne—no matter how hard it was, she had to wait a little longer. After emptying the trash and sharing a cigarette with Wayne, Eddie finally made his way over to her.

"I went to your stepfather's after work again," he said. "He didn't answer and I didn't hear the TV this time, but I pushed another note under the door, then talked to the building supervisor. He said Alan went up to the Adirondacks to go ice fishing with his buddy . . . what's his name?"

"Larry?"

"Yeah, that's it."

She opened her mouth to reply but couldn't speak. Despite knowing how little Alan cared for her, the news that he'd left on a fishing trip knocked the wind out of her lungs. Surely he'd seen the first note Eddie had slipped under the door. But he'd left anyway. When she found her voice again, it cracked. "Of course he did," she said. "Now that I'm not around, he's free to do whatever he wants. Did the super say when they were coming back?"

"No, he saw them packing up a truck yesterday morning. I'm sure Alan will call Dr. Baldwin when he gets back, but I'll stop by after work again in case they come home tonight."

"What about Heather or Dawn? Did you talk to them?"

He shook his head. "No one was home at Dawn's. I tried to leave a message for Heather, but her father tore it up and told me to get lost."

"That sounds about right. What about your uncle? Have you talked to him yet?"

He nodded.

"And?"

"It's like I thought. He told me not to get involved. And unfortunately, even if he believed my story about you and Rosemary, which I'm not sure he did, he can't do anything to help anyway."

She felt like she couldn't breathe again. "Why not? I thought he was the head of some department here?"

"He is, but he has to be really careful right now because his coworker, Dr. Wilkins, just got fired."

"What does that have to do with me?"

"It means my uncle can't look into your case yet . . . I mean, your sister's case, because he needs to keep a low profile for a while. The people in charge are already watching him because he and Dr. Wilkins tried to persuade Dr. Hammond, the director of Willowbrook, to demand more help from the state. Wilkins and my uncle were trying to make things better around here and now no one wants anything to do with them, not even the nurses or the attendants. After the parents picketed yesterday, Baldwin found out Dr. Wilkins was meeting with the parents' association to talk about patient rights and the abuse happening here, so he fired Wilkins. And if anyone finds out my uncle was meeting with the parents too, he'll get fired next."

"I thought it was impossible to get someone fired here?"

"It is if you're ratting staff out to administration. But Wilkins and my uncle have been ratting to the parents' association about the administration. And the director of Willowbrook will do anything to protect those in charge. Now Dr. Baldwin's trying to cover up the truth by spreading rumors that Dr. Wilkins molested one of the younger female residents. It's a bald-faced lie, but my uncle doesn't want the same thing to happen to him. If his career gets ruined, he won't be able to help anyone."

A throbbing lump filled her throat. "Well, if your uncle can't help and you can't find Alan or talk to one of my friends, what am I supposed to do? I don't know how much longer I can take this."

"I know," he said. "But don't worry. We'll figure something out, I promise."

Sage couldn't tell if she was awake or dreaming or dead. All she knew for sure was that she was on her side on a floor or a hard mattress and someone was shaking her, a heavy hand gripping her shoulder. She blinked and opened her eyes, the deep murkiness of a desperate, exhausted sleep clouding her mind. A weak shaft of moonlight fell across rows of iron beds filled with twisted, lumpy forms. At first she thought she was looking at an abstract painting, a monochromatic study of gray and black. Then she heard the cries and murmurs, the shrieks and laughter, and she remembered. The twisted forms were people. And she was locked inside Willowbrook State School.

The hand shook her shoulder again. "Wake up," a low voice whispered. A hot breath puffed over her ear, moving her hair and making her shiver.

She turned her head toward the voice, certain it was Norma, and got ready to tell her to go away. But the person was too close. Their facial features were a blur, a disembodied head floating in the dark, yet somehow she knew it was a man. *Wayne.* She bolted upright and yanked the blanket to her chin, terrified. Then she saw the dark hair and broad shoulders.

It was Eddie.

"What are you doing?" she said. "How did you get in here?"

"I have my ways," he said.

She scanned the shadow-filled ward, terrified

that someone would see him and sound the alarm. Then she remembered that Wayne—or someone else—had been sneaking in to hurt Rosemary and no one had done anything to stop him. As usual, Marla was asleep inside the cubicle, her head tilted back against the wall, her mouth open. "What's going on? Did you talk to Alan?

"No, he's still not back yet. But I have a plan. I'm going to get you out of here."

She drew in a sharp breath. "Right now?"

"No, but soon. I wanted to tell you so you'd be prepared."

Adrenaline raced through her body, making her tremble. "How soon?"

"Tomorrow or the next day."

"What's the plan?"

"I overheard my uncle talking to Dr. Wilkins a few hours ago. Apparently Wilkins is meeting with a reporter to tell to him everything about Willowbrook. He's hoping the reporter will bring in a camera crew to show the world what's happening here. If the reporter agrees, Wilkins is bringing him here, to House Six."

"But how would a reporter get inside? They won't even let parents in to see their kids."

"Dr. Wilkins still has his keys. And when Nurse Vic and Wayne see the reporter and TV crew coming in, all hell's going to break loose. That's when I'll sneak you into the tunnels. From there we'll go to my car, over in the employee parking lot next to the medical treatment center."

"The tunnels they brought me through when I first got here?"

He nodded. "They're all connected, like a giant maze beneath the buildings. That's how food and laundry, pretty much everything, gets moved around."

She hated those damn tunnels, but she'd crawl through a cave full of rats and snakes if it meant escape. Maybe the tunnels weren't as constricted as she remembered; maybe the drugs had given her a distorted view of things, like the cakes and bottles of liquid in *Alice's Adventures in Wonderland.*

"Wait," she said. "When the reporters come inside, why don't I just tell them I'm being kept here against my will? I'll tell them about Rosemary and—"

He shook his head.

"What?" she said. "They're looking for a good story, aren't they?"

"They're breaking into an institution for the mentally retarded. Do you really think they'll believe you?"

Shit. He was right. No one was going to believe a resident of Willowbrook who said they were someone else. Going into the tunnels was her only choice. And anything was better than being locked up in this awful place for even a minute longer than necessary.

"What if someone catches us down there?" she said.

"That's a chance we'll have to take," he said.

She thought about her options. She could wait until Alan returned, or until Eddie was able to talk to Heather or Dawn. But who knew if her friends would believe him or know how to help? They might even think she was playing a prank on them for teasing her about Cropsey.

"Okay," she said. "Then what?"

He shrugged. "Then I'll take you home."

CHAPTER 12

Desperate to control her nerves, Sage followed Eddie through the narrow tunnel, ready to turn and run if someone should appear around a corner. Between the fear of getting caught and the ever-present gnaw of claustrophobia, it was all she could do to put one foot in front of the other. It seemed like only yesterday she'd been dragged through the tunnels to the unimaginable hell of House Six, but at the same time, it felt as if an entire lifetime had passed, as if she'd aged a thousand years.

Eddie walked slowly ahead of her, listening for footsteps or voices, putting a hand up whenever he heard a sound. So far, to her relief, the tunnels had been deserted.

The cave-like odor of mold and wet stone filled the cold air, and fat rats scrambled along drainage ditches next to walls striped green and gray with gritty water and mildew. Metal conduits and rusty pipes ran along the ceiling, dripping a brownish fluid that reminded her of sewer water, onto the cement floor. Dusty lightbulbs in metal cages emitted a weak, jittery glow that seemed, at times, like it might blink out at any second and leave them in complete blackness.

If that happened, she thought she might scream. Luckily, Eddie had a flashlight in his back pocket just in case.

Naïvely, she'd hoped she'd only imagined the tunnels being tight and low, that they would actually be tall and wide, like the subway system beneath Manhattan. Unfortunately, her memory was accurate. She felt like a giant crawling through a rabbit hole. Getting out of there couldn't come soon enough.

Only ten or twelve minutes had passed since the reporter and TV crew had burst into the day-room of House Six, followed by a panicked Nurse Vic, who had no idea what to do other than frantically—and uselessly—ordering them to leave. When a cameraman's floodlight pierced the dimly lit space, one of the men said, "My God, they're *children*."

Another man said, "Welcome to Willowbrook."

The reporter and cameramen stood wide-eyed and staring, clearly shocked and appalled by what they were seeing. As the floodlight panned the room, desperate figures were framed in direct light, then lost in a shadowy blur. The bright, moving light gave the residents a jumpy, surreal quality, like the scope of a hunting rifle revealing skittering prey. There was a twisted, spindly leg. There was a grossly swollen head. There was a mass of dark blotches smeared across the wall. There was the grimy white fabric of a straitjacket on a dark figure in the corner. That child crouching on the floor with her back to them was naked, and so were the two next to her.

When the reporter ordered the cameraman to start filming, Wayne tried to intimidate them into leaving. He shoved the reporter by the shoulder, but the man warned Wayne that if he interfered, his face would be shown on every news station as a perpetrator when the story came out. With that, Wayne put up his hands in surrender, stood back, and let everything happen.

During the chaos, Eddie and Sage slipped out through the double doors. They could hear Nurse Vic shouting in the dayroom behind them as they darted along the hallway toward the nurses' station; residents cried and screamed, and the voice of a reporter, stunned and shaking, began describing the chaos around him. After hurrying to the other side of the nurses' station counter, Sage followed Eddie into the supply room. She thought she'd scream while he fumbled with his keys, trying to find the one to the tunnel door. Finally, he unlocked it, and they went through. He slammed the door shut behind them, muffling the growing uproar in the dayroom, and locked it again. A bulky paper bag sat at the top of the staircase that led down to the tunnels; Eddie picked it up and handed it to her.

"What's this?" she said.

"Extra clothes. Hurry up and put them on."

Inside the bag was a pair of corduroy trousers, a long wool coat, and a worn pair of men's boots. After pulling on the pants, which were too loose around her waist and almost worn through at the knees, she slipped her arms into the coat and pushed her bare feet into the boots. The boots were too big, but it felt good to have something on her feet again. When she was ready, they went down the crumbling steps into the tunnels.

Now, it seemed like they'd been in the tunnels for hours, turning left and right and left again. "Are we almost there?" she whispered.

"Not yet," Eddie said over his shoulder. "After we pass the morgue and the autopsy room, we need to go under the emergency surgery and dental halls. Then we'll come up near the parking lot next to the hospital."

She cringed. "The morgue and autopsy room?"

He nodded.

"Jesus." As if she weren't scared enough.

Behind them, an engine roared to life, making her jump. Grinding gears echoed in the narrow shaft like a screeching animal. "What was that?" she said too loudly.

He turned and held a finger to his lips. "It's just a generator. Nothing to worry about."

She swallowed the bitter taste of fear and kept going.

After turning right again, they crept down another dank tunnel, past swinging double doors below a sign that read: MORGUE. She tried not to look through the windows in the top half of the doors, but couldn't help it. Behind the stainless steel autopsy table, bottles labeled EMBALMING FLUID lined the counter next to a three-basin sink. In the far corner, a body storage vault with six doors took up nearly a quarter of the room; its hinges and handles rusty and tarnished, the wood under each door stained with something that looked like tar, as if something inside had rotted and leaked out. The odors of mold, formaldehyde, and something that smelled like warm pennies hung in the air outside the room. She put a hand over her nose and mouth, the sickening-sweet odor reminding her of biology class when they'd dissected frogs and she gagged so much the teacher had to send her to the nurse. Pulling her eyes from the morgue doors, she tried not to think about what happened in that room, or wonder whether any dead bodies lay cold and stiff inside the vault.

At the end of that tunnel they turned left, went halfway down another tunnel, then took another right, threading their way around old wheel-chairs, rolling carts, rusted gurneys, and vinyl-covered seats with belts and wheels. The farther in they went, the bigger the piles of discarded equipment grew. Moldy cardboard boxes and plastic jugs littered the floor, and shards of cement and old paint crunched beneath their feet.

"Why the hell does it stink so bad down here?" she said.

"It's the rats," he said. "More places to hide over here. The only reason anyone ever comes this way is to put things in storage. Most of it's junk, but we're not allowed to get rid of it."

At the end of the hall stood a wide metal door that looked like the entrance to a service elevator. She breathed a sigh of relief. Finally, they were getting out of there. But instead of heading straight to the elevator, Eddie stopped, took the flashlight from his pocket, and turned it on.

"What are you doing?" she said.

He shined his flashlight into another tunnel. "We need to go that way," he said. No lights ran along the ceiling of that narrower, murkier corridor. Beyond the flashlight beam, the walls and floors disappeared into blackness.

"Are you sure?" she said.

"Of course I'm sure," he said. "It's a shortcut to one of the employee parking lots that no one uses anymore."

"What about the elevator?"

"Doesn't work," he said. "That's why this tunnel's full of junk. There's a ladder leading up to a manhole cover at the end of this." He pointed at the narrow, shadow-filled passageway. "Once we go through that, we're home free." He turned to look at her. "Don't worry. It's going to be fine."

She wanted to believe him more than anything. But she wouldn't breathe easy until they were out of the tunnels, in his car, and driving away from Willowbrook. Even then, she wouldn't feel safe until she found out what happened to Rosemary and who was responsible for her disappearance. Her first stop would be the police station, but what if the cops didn't believe her? What if they called Willowbrook and Dr. Baldwin convinced them she was an escaped resident? What if he sent someone to drag her back and lock her up again?

"Let's just hurry up and get out of here, okay?" she said.

Eddie nodded, then turned and headed into the black tunnel. She followed, keeping her head down in case the ceiling was lower than it seemed. This passageway looked older than the others, with stone archways and crumbling, narrow walls that made walking side by side impossible. Clots of black mold streaked the floor, and a foul, musty stench filled the air. It smelled like something had died down there. She stayed close behind Eddie; the only light was from the flashlight beam in front of his silhouette, bouncing up and down and back and forth on the stone walls and wet floor. It was impossible to shake the feeling that someone was behind her, as if at any second, a pair of strong arms with clawed hands would come out of the darkness and pull her into a hidden pit. Then she would learn, once and for all, what had happened to Rosemary. Instinctively, she reached for Eddie—for his shirt or belt buckle or hand, *anything* to hang on to so she wouldn't trip and fall or get snatched from behind. Sensing her touch, he stopped and took her hand, then kept going, his arm trailing behind him as he held on. Cobwebs brushed across her face and she wiped them away. No wonder no one used this tunnel anymore. It was creepy as hell and it smelled like dead animals. The farther in they went, the worse the odor grew.

"How much further?" she said.

"We're almost there," he said. "Come on."

"I can hardly see anything."

"Just hold on. I'll lead the way."

Suddenly he stopped and let go of her hand. "Oh my God," he said. "Jesus." His voice came out rattled. He turned around, still holding the flashlight up, blinding her.

She held up her arm to shield her eyes and he lowered the beam, standing to one side as if trying to block her view. His eyes were wide, his face white. "What's wrong?" she said.

"It's, um . . ."

"What?"

"We need to turn around," he said.

"Why? Is there something in the way? Let me see!"

"That's not a good idea. Come on, let's go back. I know another way out."

"Why, what is it?"

"Just do as I say, okay?"

The deep crease across his brow and the strange way he was looking at her made her heart beat faster. She had to know what he saw. She grabbed the flashlight, shoved past him, and aimed the beam into the dark void of the tunnel.

Wedged between the wall and a stone outcropping, the pale, naked body of a young woman sat on a ledge. She was facing out toward the passageway, blue eyes wide open, as if she were sitting there waiting for them. Despite the fact that it had been chopped off to mere inches, the strawberry-blond hair was as familiar to Sage as her own. She knew the slim legs and long fingers, the dimpled knees and slender toes. It was as if she were looking at her own body. But the girl's mouth had been painted circus red, caked lipstick stretching up toward her ears in an exaggerated, clown-like smile. Black slits ran along her wrists, and streaks of blood ran like dark rivers along her thighs and calves. Another jagged, black line ran along her willowy neck, and blood dripped down her chest, striping her breasts and the soft mound of her abdomen.

Sage dropped the flashlight and her face went hot, sweat instantly coating her skin. Her limbs went slack and for a second, she thought she might fall to the ground right next to her sister. The gorge rose in her throat; she bent over and vomited until there was nothing left but dry heaves. Then she backed up, leaned against the tunnel wall, and put a hand to her neck, willing her hammering pulse to slow.

"Oh my God," she cried. "Oh my God." She fell to her knees and started to scream.

Eddie knelt beside her. "Don't," he said. "Please."

She buried her face in her hands and wailed. She was too late. Rosemary was gone—for real this time. Murdered. But who would do such a thing? And why?

People still search the woods for the remains of lost children.

Heather's and Dawn's words shrieked in her mind. She gaped up at Eddie, grief and fear tightening her throat. "Do you think it was Cropsey?" she croaked.

"No." He shook his head violently back and forth, his features contorted by shock.

Then a sudden realization gripped her. "What if it was Wayne?" she said with a trembling voice.

"I don't know who it was. But let's not stick around to find out." He reached under her arm to help her up. "Come on, get up. We have to keep going."

She pulled out of his grasp and scrambled away from him on her hands and knees. Tiny pebbles and sharp rocks dug into her palms. She got up and turned to face him, panting and out of breath. "What are you talking about?" she cried. "We *can't* keep going. It's *Rosemary!* It's my sister!"

"I know," he said. "And I'm sorry, but we need to go."

"We can't go! We have to tell someone!"

"We will," he said. "I promise. But we need to get you out of here first."

She shook her head, his face a blur through her tears. "No. We need to tell someone she's down here. We need to tell someone she's been murdered!"

"Who the hell are we going to tell?" he said, close to yelling. "Someone who works at Willowbrook? What do you think Baldwin will do when he finds out? Do you think he'll call the cops and let everyone know one of the residents was killed? A resident who hasn't even been reported missing yet?"

"I don't know," she cried. "I don't know." She couldn't think straight. And she couldn't stop shaking.

"Well, I know. He'll make this all go away and keep you here. He'll send Rosemary to be cremated and it'll be like it never happened."

She felt faint. He was right. No one had reported Rosemary missing. And if Dr. Baldwin was capable of making up lies about a doctor molesting a resident to cover up what was happening in Willowbrook—who knew what else he would do? Norma and Eddie both said residents died there all the time and no one looked into how or why. And Rosemary wasn't the first to disappear—what was one more?

But Rosemary had been *murdered*. She'd been taken down into these awful tunnels and someone had slit her wrists and throat. Whether it was Cropsey or Wayne or someone else, people had to know. They had to be warned. Then she had an idea. "Do you think the news crew is still here?"

"I don't know. Maybe."

She got to her feet and headed back the way they had come, her legs trembling, her hands clutching the damp tunnel walls to keep from falling. "We need to tell them before they leave."

"Wait," he said. "What if they're gone and someone sees us?"

"We have to try!"

"Okay. But it'll be faster if we go this way." He pointed back the way they'd been headed. "If we hurry, we can run across campus and maybe catch them on their way out."

He was right. They'd taken so many twists and turns, it felt like they'd walked a hundred miles. Going aboveground and taking a straight shot back to House Six had to be faster.

But that would mean walking past her dead sister.

There was no other choice. She returned to where Eddie stood. "You go first."

Staying close to the opposite wall, he moved past Rosemary, then turned and held out his hand to Sage. "Come on," he said. "We've got to hurry."

She took a deep breath and, keeping her eyes on him, slipped past Rosemary's body. Then she turned and took one last look at her.

"I won't leave you here," she said. "I promise. And I'm going to find out who did this to you if it's the last thing I do."

Then she followed Eddie a few more yards, climbed up a utility ladder through a manhole cover, and crawled out of the tunnels.

CHAPTER 13

A bitter wind whipped across the snow-covered campus, stinging Sage's eyes and pushing tears across her cheeks as she ran. After spending so much time inside the dark walls of Willowbrook, she squinted against the sun, a high pinpoint of light in the sky that blinked and flickered behind scudding clouds. Her feet slid back and forth inside the too-big boots, grating against her heels and the balls of her feet like sandpaper. She ignored the pain and kept going, past four-story buildings and shuddering trees, across snowy roads and drifted yards. When her feet broke through a crusty snowdrift, she nearly fell but caught herself before tumbling forward, her hands scraped raw by ice. Eddie stopped and reached back to help her.

"Keep going," she shouted. "Get to the reporters before they leave!"

He hesitated for a moment, unsure, then turned and kept running. She stood and tried to keep up, but it was no use. Between too little sleep, too little food, and the shock and grief of discovering Rosemary's body, her strength was nearly spent. Her chest ached from the frigid air, and a stitch caught in her side. When she saw House Six in the distance, she slowed.

Eddie stood in the road next to a Chrysler New Yorker parked in front of the building, looking toward the campus entrance with one hand on the top of his head, as if he were lost. No news van sat in front of the building or trundled along the road toward the exit. No men with cameras and microphones surrounded Eddie or House Six.

The reporters were gone.

"Damn it," she said, stopping to catch her breath. The cold air felt like a knife in her lungs. What were they supposed to do now? If Eddie told Dr. Baldwin about Rosemary and he didn't believe him or tried to cover it up, getting out of Willowbrook and finding out who killed her sister would be impossible. Eddie looked back at her, throwing his arms up in frustration. She wiped her wet cheeks with frigid hands and started toward him. They would have to take their chances with Dr. Baldwin. They had to go to his office and tell him what they found. There was no other choice.

Then Sage stopped in her tracks. Wayne and Marla were coming out of the main doors of House Six, followed by Dr. Baldwin, who look red-faced and disheveled. She crouched in the snow. If Dr. Baldwin thought she was running away, he'd have Wayne and Marla drag her back to Ward D and pump her full of drugs before she could convince him what happened. Yes, she and Eddie were going to tell him about Rosemary, but first they had to get their story straight.

"Just pretend you're going to work and enter the building, Eddie," she said under her breath. "Act like nothing happened. Then you can come back out and get me and we'll go to Dr. Baldwin's office together."

She pressed her nails into her palms, waiting to see what Eddie would do. As she had hoped, he turned down the sidewalk toward a door at the end of one wing. But Dr. Baldwin had already spotted him. He raised his hand and called out. When Eddie stopped, Dr. Baldwin started toward him.

Sage held her breath. Did they know she was missing from House Six? Had they counted the residents after the news crew left?

She was too far away to hear what was being said, but Dr. Baldwin started shouting at Eddie, his hands in fists, his face twisted in anger. Then he thrust out his arm and pointed at House Six as if ordering him inside. Eddie took a step back, but Dr. Baldwin seized his wrist and wouldn't let go. When Wayne and Marla hurried over and grabbed him by the arms, Sage drew in a sharp breath. Why were they treating him that way? Did they think he was the one who let the reporters inside?

She wanted to yell at them to leave him alone,

to tell them Eddie hadn't done anything wrong, but she clamped a hand over her mouth. Dr. Baldwin wouldn't listen to her, and if he thought Eddie was helping her run away, they'd both be in big trouble.

Glancing toward the distant gate of Willowbrook's main entrance, she wondered if she should make a run for it. The problem was, even if she could get there without being seen, she'd never get past the guard in the middle of the day. Maybe she should wait until dark. She eyed the nearby buildings and trees. If she could hide behind something, she could stay put until nightfall, then sneak out. Even if the gates were closed by then, she'd find a way out through the woods somehow. And once she was free, she'd go to the police, bring them back here, and show them Rosemary's body. After that, Dr. Baldwin would have to release her. He'd have no choice.

When she looked back at House Six, she startled. Wayne and Marla were plowing toward her, clambering over snowbanks and trudging through drifts. Terrified, she froze. Then she jumped up and ran toward a stand of trees, slipping and sliding in the oversize boots. The cold air stabbed her chest as she ran and tripped and almost tumbled. By the time she was halfway to the trees, she was certain she'd gained ground. She risked a look back and let out a shriek. Wayne was only a few feet away, his breath billowing out in the cold, his muscular arms reaching for her. She tried to run faster, but her feet caught in the snow and she fell face-first into a drift.

Wayne stood over her, beast-like and breathing hard, then grabbed her arm and yanked her up. "You and your little boyfriend took it too far this time," he said. "No one makes me look bad and gets away with it."

"Let go of me!" Sage shrieked. "We found Rosemary!"

"Sure you did," Wayne said. He dug his fingers into her biceps and hauled her back toward House Six. She pounded on his face and shoulder and chest, but couldn't get away.

When Marla reached them, winded and panting and limping worse than ever, she took Sage's other arm. "What'd you get your damn self into this time?" she said.

"We found my sister!" Sage said. "She's dead!"

Marla rolled her eyes. "Oh, Lord have mercy. Not the sister story again."

Sage started to say more, but she could hardly catch her breath. It didn't matter if Wayne and Marla believed her or not, anyway. The person she needed to convince was Dr. Baldwin, and that would take every ounce of strength she had left. Exhausted both physically and emotionally, she stumbled and tripped, staggering like a drunk, nearly falling every few steps. Exasperated, Wayne picked her up and carried her across the yard. She squeezed her eyes shut and tried not to think about his hands cutting Rosemary's throat, his arms carrying her bloody body. When they reached the icy sidewalk in front of House Six, he put her down and shoved her forward. Eddie hurried over to catch her before she fell.

"There's no need to be rough," he snarled at Wayne.

"What are you going to do about it, punk?" Wayne sneered. He pushed Eddie away and dragged Sage over to Dr. Baldwin, who still looked shaken by the news crew's surprise visit. His hair stuck up on one side and his shirt collar was cockeyed. He glared at Sage, anger hardening his face.

"What the hell are you doing out here?" he said.

Sage looked at Eddie. Had Dr. Baldwin asked him why he was out there? Did he know they were out there together? Eddie's face revealed nothing. She had no idea if he would have lied or told the truth. "I . . . I found Rosemary," she said. "Someone killed her."

Dr. Baldwin jerked back his chin and gaped at her like she had three heads. "Good Lord," he said. "Now I've heard everything." He glanced toward the snow-covered lawn. "Where is she, over there behind the trees? Buried in a snowbank somewhere?" Sarcasm colored his voice.

"I know you don't believe me," Sage said.

"But it's true. She's in the tunnels. And she was murdered."

Dr. Baldwin smacked his palm against his forehead, grinning like he was on the edge of losing his mind. "Of course she is," he said. "Why didn't I think of that? How foolish of me." Then his face went dark and he addressed Wayne. "Take her inside and put her in the pit. She needs to learn once and for all to stop running away. I don't care how long it takes. Right now I need to find out how those damn reporters got inside and deal with that. Then I'll get to the bottom of her latest stunt."

Wayne seized Sage again. Marla grabbed her other arm.

"No!" Eddie said. "She's telling the truth. Her sister's body is in the old maintenance tunnel leading out to the employee parking lot near the hospital." He looked at Dr. Baldwin. "We can show you."

"How do you know?" Dr. Baldwin said. "Were you in the tunnels with her?"

Eddie nodded.

Dr. Baldwin looked like the top of his head was going to blow off. "What were you doing down there? Helping her run away again?"

"After we show you the body," Eddie said, "I'll explain."

"Jesus Christ," Dr. Baldwin said. "I don't need this shit right now. A bunch of damn reporters just broke into House Six and you were fucking around in the tunnels instead of doing your job? What the hell were you thinking?"

"If you give me a chance, I'll—"

"Just shut up," Dr. Baldwin yelled, his face scarlet. "I don't want to hear it!"

"What do you want us to do, Doc?" Wayne said.

Dr. Baldwin turned on him. "For Christ's sake," he snarled. "You saw what just happened in there. It was chaos! I've got bigger fish to fry than someone trying to escape again! Do as you're told and put her in the pit." Then he glared at Eddie. "You. Come to my office. You've got some explaining to do."

"No!" Sage said. "Please! Don't send me to the pit! We're telling the truth. My sister is dead. We can show you where she is!" She started to say Wayne had killed Rosemary, but stopped. If he was taking her to the pit, letting him know she suspected him was a bad idea.

Dr. Baldwin ignored her and started toward the New Yorker, raking his hands through his hair and straightening his collar. Wayne and Marla pulled Sage toward House Six. She dug in her heels, but Wayne tightened his grip and walked faster, nearly dragging her and Marla up the stairs. She looked over her shoulder at Eddie. He was standing on the sidewalk next to the car, watching her being taken away, his face lined with anxiety. There was nothing he could do.

He turned and got into Dr. Baldwin's car. Sage started to struggle again, desperate to get away, but it was a waste of energy and she needed to preserve what little strength she had left to get through the next few hours. After Eddie showed Dr. Baldwin Rosemary's body, everyone would know the truth and they'd let her go. She had to believe that. The alternative was unthinkable.

Inside House Six, Wayne and Marla led her across a tiled lobby into a wide hallway where Wayne unlocked a riveted steel door leading to the left wing. After the door slammed shut behind them, the metal bang echoing along the empty corridor, Wayne locked it again, then took them through two more locked doors into the main hall leading to Ward D. When they reached the nurses' station, Nurse Vic got out of her chair and stared at them from behind the counter, her eyes wide.

"What the hell is going on?" she said. "Did she slip out with the reporters?"

"We're not sure," Wayne said. "But Eddie was with her."

Nurse Vic sucked air in between her teeth. "That little shit. What was he thinking?"

"That's the problem," Wayne said. "He wasn't thinking. Baldwin took him to his office. I'm pretty sure his ass is in a sling."

"All our asses might be in a sling," Marla said, worry edging her voice.

"Is Eddie the one who let the reporters in?" Nurse Vic said.

"I don't know," Wayne said. "But I wouldn't put it past him."

Nurse Vic shook her head in disbelief, then addressed Marla. "You better get back to Ward D and do damage control. Those cameramen scared the shit out of all of us, and the residents are going nuts."

She gestured toward Sage. "Take her with you and restrain her. We've had enough excitement for one day."

"Dr. Baldwin wants her in the pit," Wayne said.

Sage shook her head. "You don't have to put me there. I won't try running again, I promise. After Eddie shows him Rosemary's body, Dr. Baldwin will have to let me go. You'll see." An image of Rosemary flashed in her mind again: her slim, naked corpse; her eyes staring; her legs and chest and abdomen covered in dark blood. "Please," she said around the growing lump in her throat. "I'm begging you."

Nurse Vic looked confused. "What's she yammering about now?"

"She and Eddie claim they found a body in the tunnels," Wayne said. "If you ask me, they both need to be locked up for a few months."

"Are you shittin' me?" Nurse Vic said.

"Nope," Wayne said. "I heard them say it."

Marla nodded in agreement.

"Well, that's a new one," Nurse Vic said, incredulous. "I'll get the meds and meet you in the pit. Get back to your ward, Marla. Don't make me say it again."

"Yes, ma'am," Marla said, and started down the hall, limping toward Ward D.

"Please," Sage said to Nurse Vic. "You don't have to do this. I'll behave, I promise."

No one listened to her.

Wayne dragged her along the hallway, then took a right toward the pit. After unlocking the double doors and taking her through, he stopped at the third seclusion room on the right and dug his keys from his pocket again, his free hand like a vise on her arm. Behind the other riveted steel doors, voices cried and shouted and prayed. Someone hit one of the centered door panels so hard it sounded like a gong, making Sage jump. Down the hall behind them, the double doors opened and shut, and footsteps hurried toward her and Wayne. She turned to look, praying it was Dr. Baldwin coming to set her free—but she knew there hadn't been enough time for Eddie to have shown him Rosemary's body. And as she feared, it was Nurse Vic, carrying a syringe on a metal tray.

Sage woke with a start, her head throbbing and her forehead covered in sweat. She was lying on her side with her hands clamped together under her chin as if she'd fallen asleep praying. Something that felt like a leather strap tied her wrists together. No cot or mattress or blanket lay beneath her, but she was still wearing the shoes and coat Eddie had given her. Then an image of Rosemary's body flashed in her mind, and a hot rush of grief lit up her chest. Her sister was dead.

With no idea how long she'd been in the pit or how much longer she would be kept there, she turned her head, blinking to clear the haze from her eyes, and tried to tell the time of day. But no light reached her. The room was pitch-black, the air heavy and rank. She squeezed her eyes shut and opened them again. It made no difference. The darkness was complete and relentless. The surrounding walls felt thick and close, like the cushioned insides of an oversize coffin. Straightening her arms, she rolled over, leaned on her bound hands, and pushed herself onto her knees. Dizziness descended on her, and she closed her eyes and counted to ten, praying it would stop. When she regained her equilibrium, she blindly reached out to touch a wall. It was padded and rough, as if covered with canvas.

"Help!" she shouted. "Someone, please! Let me out of here!"

No one answered. No one unlocked the door or came into the room. She yelled again. Still nothing. How long had it been since she and Eddie had found Rosemary's body? Two hours?

Four? A day? A week? Panic gripped her, then she reminded herself that her imagination was probably making it feel longer than it actually was. She pushed herself onto her feet and edged forward, arms out, feeling for the door. When her hands landed on the padded door, she pounded on it, to no avail.

"Hello?" she yelled. "Is anyone out there?"

No one answered.

She pounded on the door again, focusing on the sliding panel in the center. Nothing. Standing in the dark—she felt like she was swaying but couldn't be sure—she tried to think logically. They wouldn't keep her in the pit forever. Surely Eddie had shown Dr. Baldwin her sister's body by now. And when Dr. Baldwin realized she'd been telling the truth all along, he'd come over to the pit and release her—apologizing profusely, of course. Unless Eddie was right. Unless it would be easier for Dr. Baldwin to leave her locked up in House Six and get rid of Rosemary's body than it would be to explain how a resident had been murdered. Dr. Baldwin and the people in charge would do anything, Eddie had said, to protect their jobs and reputations. He also said residents died in Willowbrook all the time, and no one cared. So what would one more death be among so many?

No. She couldn't think that way. Eddie wouldn't let that happen. If Dr. Baldwin tried to cover up Rosemary's murder, Eddie would call the cops, who would demand her release and find the killer. Then, finally, this nightmare would be over. She wouldn't let Dr. Baldwin get away with it either. No matter how long he kept her in the pit, she would wait this out and survive. Then, somehow—with or without Eddie's help—she'd escape and find her sister's murderer.

She sat down on the cold floor again. Leaning against a padded wall, she pictured the door opening, Eddie and Dr. Baldwin entering and helping her out of there, and Wayne and Marla and Nurse Vic all watching in awe and disbelief.

Finally, after what felt like forever, the sliding panel in the center of the door rattled and a thin sliver of light found its way through. The high-pitched shriek of metal sliding against metal made her cringe as the panel slid all the way up, and she blinked against the glare coming in from the hall. Then Nurse Vic's makeup-caked face filled the opening, her dark brows and red lips like a cartoon character close up.

"You awake?" she said.

"Yes," Sage said. "How long have I been in here?"

"Since yesterday morning."

"What time is it now?"

"Six p.m."

Sage stiffened, shocked and distraught that she'd been in there that long. Why hadn't they released her yet? What was taking so long? There had to be a good explanation. Maybe they were waiting for the drugs to wear off so she could leave on her own two feet. "Are you here to let me out?"

"No," Nurse Vic said. "Doctor's orders. You have to stay until Dr. Baldwin can talk to you. Then he'll decide what to do."

"When will that be?"

"I'm not sure."

"But I need to talk to him right now. It's urgent."

"Sorry, no can do. He already left for the day."

A savage twist of fear ripped through Sage's stomach. "What do you mean he already left? How could he?"

"The same way he does every day at five o'clock. He gets in his car and drives home."

"But what about my sister? What about her body?"

The line between Nurse Vic's penciled brows got deeper. "Don't start up with that nonsense again."

"It's not nonsense! It's the truth!" She could hardly contain her panic. Why hadn't Nurse Vic heard about Rosemary's murder? Why wasn't Willowbrook crawling with cops? "What about Eddie?" she said. "Can I talk to him?"

"No. And you won't be seeing him around House Six for a while either."

"Why not?"

"He's not coming back here after he messed around with you. It's not right."

"We weren't . . ." She pressed her bound hands against her forehead, anxiety and frustration making it hard to think straight. "Eddie and I are just friends."

"Uh-huh."

Sage tried to focus. What Nurse Vic thought about her relationship with Eddie was the last thing that mattered right now. "Did Dr. Baldwin call the cops yet?"

"Don't be ridiculous. The cops can't do anything about those reporters. They were only here for a few minutes and they didn't do any damage or take anything. I know it was upsetting when they broke in, but you didn't have to run. They weren't here to hurt anyone. They were just trying to get a story." Worry flashed across her features. "But I think they got more than they bargained for," she said, more to herself than to Sage.

Sage felt like screaming. "I'm not talking about the reporters!" she cried. "I'm talking about Rosemary. Did Dr. Baldwin call the cops about her?"

"Oh my God. Stop it already. I just came to see if you were awake yet. But if you're going to go on like that, maybe you need another shot."

"No, you don't understand," Sage cried. "I

didn't run away from the reporters. Eddie and I . . . we . . . when the news crew came in, we went into the tunnels because he was going to help me escape. But we found Rosemary and . . . we found her body, I mean. She's dead. Someone killed her."

"Oh, I understand perfectly. You were imagining things. But everyone was shook up about those reporters, including me. A lot of the residents didn't know what was happening. Some of them thought they were being taken away. One girl had to be sent to the hospital because she thought the camera's light was Jesus coming to take her to heaven. She ran toward it, tripped, and broke her arm, just like that." She snapped her fingers in front of her face.

"You're not listening," Sage said. "I was trying to *leave.* If you don't believe me, call Dr. Baldwin. Eddie was going to show him my sister's body. He was going to tell him everything!"

"Uh-huh. Sure. You can tell Dr. Baldwin all about it tomorrow. In the meantime, I'll have Wayne bring you something to eat." She started to close the panel.

"No!" Sage said, shaking her head violently. "Not Wayne. Please, anyone but him. He was going to rape me in the dayroom, but Eddie stopped him. I told you he was having sex with Rosemary. He's having sex with Norma now too.

He takes her to a secret place behind the supply room down the hall. I wouldn't be surprised if he was the one who killed Rosemary."

"Like I said before," Nurse Vic said, her voice firm. "You need to talk to Dr. Baldwin about that, not me. But if it makes you feel better, I'll bring your food myself." Before Sage could respond, Nurse Vic pushed down the panel and disappeared, leaving her alone, drowning in an ocean of black.

CHAPTER 14

Other than stacked rows of black filing cabinets, the thirteen-inch television on a metal stand, the bulky desk with the captain's chair, and the two folding chairs, Dr. Baldwin's office was sparse and clinical. No decorations hung on the whitewashed walls, no family photos or landscape paintings, no inspirational posters or framed degrees. The aged industrial clock read 5:15, but Sage had no idea if it was morning or night. Within the confined, gruesome world of Willowbrook, none of that mattered. Every minute and every hour, every day and every week jumbled together into one constant horror. Darkness pushed against the glass of a single window.

Sitting in a folding chair in front of Dr. Baldwin's desk, she twisted a tear-soaked tissue between her fingers, tearing it into tiny white shreds. Her nose was stuffed up from crying, her eyes sticky and swollen. According to Dr. Baldwin, she'd been locked in the pit for fifty-six hours. It felt like fifty-six days.

During those long, desperate eons alone in the pitch-black, she'd had one meal and little sleep. And she'd convinced herself that Cropsey had killed Rosemary. He knew Sage had found her sister's body and he was going to kill her next, to keep her quiet—Eddie too, wherever he was. An eternity later, when the panel in the door flew open a second time, she nearly screamed, certain it was Cropsey. He'd come to haul her into the secret room and slit her throat. Either that or it was Wayne, who'd rape her before Cropsey killed her. When Nurse Vic's powder-caked face filled the opening again, Sage burst into tears of relief.

Now, Dr. Baldwin leaned back in his captain's chair and regarded her with a stern look. "What were you doing in the tunnels?" he said.

"I told you, I was trying to get out of here."

"What about the coat and shoes you're wearing. Where did you get them?"

"Eddie gave them to me."

"You didn't steal them from one of the other residents?"

"Of course not. I'd never do that."

"Were you hiding in the tunnels the last time you went missing?"

She shook her head so hard her eyes hurt. "No, I wasn't hiding anywhere because that wasn't me. I didn't even know the tunnels existed until I was dragged through them after you sent me to House Six. Eddie took me down there because he knows I'm not Rosemary, which is why he was helping me. I know he told you everything."

"Eddie and I have talked about what happened, and he's been dealt with in an appropriate manner. I warned him not to get involved with you again because it would only mean trouble, but he wouldn't listen. A lot of people think I don't know what goes on around here, but I'm well aware that the two of you have been friends for a while now, long before you went missing this last time."

"He was friends with Rosemary. Not me. I just met him a few . . ." She hesitated. Had it been a few days since her first horrible morning at Willowbrook? A few weeks? A month? She wasn't sure. "I met him after I came here looking for my sister and you locked me up in House Six. He knew Rosemary better than anyone else here did, including you. That's why he can tell us apart. That's how he knows I'm not her."

"I'm sorry to burst your bubble, Miss Winters, but Eddie is not a doctor or a psychologist. Therefore, he's not qualified to make that distinction."

She leaned forward in her seat, fighting the urge to yell at him. "Did you call the police about my sister yet? Did you tell them her killer is still on the loose?"

"There was no reason to call the police."

"What do you mean there's no reason to call the police? Someone murdered Rosemary!" She couldn't believe what she was hearing. Eddie was right. Dr. Baldwin only cared about protecting Willowbrook and his job.

"Yes, that's what you keep telling me."

"Because it's true!" she cried. "Eddie and I found her body. I know he showed you."

"For argument's sake, let's say you're telling the truth. How did 'your sister' get into the tunnels?" He made quotation marks with his fingers around the words "your sister." She wanted to punch him in the face.

"I don't know," she said, throwing up her hands. "The killer must have taken her down there."

"Let's back up a bit, shall we?"

Her face felt on fire. "Back up? What good is that going to do? You need to find out who killed my sister and stop asking stupid questions."

"Asking questions is part of my job, Miss Winters. And right now I'm trying to figure out where all this is coming from."

"Where all what is coming from?"

"All this anger and hostility," he said. "I thought we'd worked through that years ago. I'm glad to see that you've improved somewhat, you're no longer flapping your arms around and screaming, but this story about your sister being dead has me wondering if it's some kind of breakthrough. Perhaps you're shedding that part of your personality."

She jumped up and slammed her hands on his

desk. She'd never hit anyone in her life, but right now she wanted to—and it would feel good. "I'm not shedding anything. My sister is dead. I saw her with my own eyes. Eddie saw her too!"

"Please take a seat, Miss Winters. Otherwise, I'll have you restrained."

She glared at him, fighting the urge to scramble over the desk and wrap her hands around his neck. "Why won't you listen to me? What are you doing? Trying to cover this up like you cover up every other horrible thing that happens in this shithole?"

With that, he punched a button on the intercom on his desk, his face lined with anger. When his secretary answered, he said, "Send Leonard into my office and tell him to bring a straitjacket."

"Yes, Doctor," the secretary said. "For Miss Winters?"

"Yes, Evie." Then he released the button, leaned back, and stared at Sage with furious eyes, daring her to try something. "What happens next is your decision. We can either continue this discussion calmly, or I can have you put back in the pit until you decide to cooperate."

She took her hands from the desk and stepped back, her heart pounding so hard she was breathless. Dizzy. Maybe she should turn and run out of the office, shove the secretary out of the way and race screaming out the front door. Except that possibility was nothing more than wishful thinking, her mind playing tricks on her. Every door was locked and bolted, every room a prison. She eased backward and sat on the edge of the chair, ready to flee or fight if need be. Behind her, the door opened. Leonard entered with a straitjacket in one fist, walked over to Dr. Baldwin's desk, and stood near the wall like a soldier awaiting a command. He eyed her suspiciously.

"Are you ready to finish our discussion now, Miss Winters?" Dr. Baldwin said.

She took a deep, shuddering breath and nodded.

"Good," he said. "Now I need you to listen carefully to what I'm about to say. I wanted to break this to you gently, but you've given me no choice. There was no body in the tunnels."

The air left her lungs. "What do you mean there was no body? Of course there is. Eddie showed you!"

"The head of security and I went into the tunnels with Eddie and we did a thorough search. We found nothing. So you see, it wasn't real. It was just a hallucination, brought about by your illness and the stress of the reporters breaking into your building."

"No!" she cried. "That's not true. I saw her! Her hair was chopped off and her throat was slit and she was dead. I'm not making it up. And I don't have an illness. I'm not crazy. She was there and someone killed her!"

"I'm sorry, Miss Winters, but I'm afraid you're wrong. You *wanted* to see a body because it reinforced your delusions."

"I'm not having delusions!" A white-hot pressure boiled through her like a murderous rage. It was all she could do to stay in the chair. "What did you do?" she cried. "Did you get rid of her body so no one would find out you never reported her missing?"

"I can assure you I did no such thing," he said.

This was lunacy. A nightmare to end all nightmares. He didn't believe anything she said. Not one word. What could she say to make him listen? With desperate eyes, she scanned the floor, the desk, the dark window, as if the answer might be hidden there. She felt light-headed. Panicked. Confused. Desperate. For all she knew the killer could be outside the window right now, watching this exchange, waiting to see if she would be set free so he could slit her throat too. Maybe she needed to try a different approach. "I know this sounds crazy, but have you ever heard of Cropsey?"

An amused smile flashed briefly across his face, then disappeared. "Of course I've heard of Cropsey. But he's not real. And I have to say, hearing you mention that ridiculous rumor makes me wonder if you've fallen into a new kind of neurosis, which, to be honest, is rather worrisome."

She shook her head. "I'm not falling into anything," she said. "I'm perfectly sane. I know who I am and I know what I saw. Eddie saw Rosemary too. He told you the truth. I know he did. And you're right, Cropsey isn't real, but some of the residents here seem to think he is, and *someone* killed my sister. It might even be someone who works here, like Wayne. Did you know he was having sex with my sister and now he's having sex with Norma? Did you know he's a drug addict and he tried to rape me? Do you even care? Of course not, because you don't listen to anyone, which makes me think Eddie is right. You just want to hide all the abuse and neglect that goes on here, no matter who suffers."

"I'm sorry you feel that way, but I can assure you that I have no reason to hide anything. And speaking of Eddie, you don't have to worry about him bothering you anymore. He'll no longer be anywhere near you."

"He wasn't bothering me. He was *helping* me. That's why we were down in the tunnels. He knows I don't belong in this place."

"As I said, that's not for Eddie to decide. I just want you know you won't be seeing him again."

The room started to spin around her. Who would help her now that Eddie had been fired? She reached blindly for the back of the chair, moving farther into the seat and holding on to the cold metal for dear life to keep from sliding into a whimpering heap on the floor. How was she going to prove him wrong? How could she ever convince him she was telling the truth? She looked at Leonard to see his reaction to everything he'd heard. He stood with his eyes on the floor, refusing to look at her.

"Ask Leonard," she said to Dr. Baldwin. "He knows. He and Nurse Vic were talking about how Wayne might know where Rosemary was hiding. Maybe he knows who killed my sister. Maybe he and Wayne are two of the ex-criminals you hired without doing background checks."

Leonard glanced at her, then shifted on his feet, clearly uneasy.

"Don't be ridiculous," Dr. Baldwin said. "We don't hire ex-criminals."

"Yes, you do. Eddie told me. He also said Dr. Wilkins was fired because he told some of the parents about their children being mistreated. Then you spread a lie about him molesting a resident to cover up the truth. So don't tell me you're not trying to hide anything."

Dr. Baldwin's temples pulsed in and out. "Eddie has no idea what he's talking about. He's always stirring the pot around here."

"Did Eddie tell you anything about Rosemary?" she said, grasping for straws. "Did he tell you how we're different?"

He shook his head. "There was no need to discuss anything like that."

"Did Rosemary have a scar from being sterilized?"

"I'm a psychiatrist, Miss Winters, not a general practitioner. So I don't know."

"Who was the doctor who did those operations?"

"I can assure you I don't know that either. We have many doctors here; none of whom are assigned to any specific resident."

She stood on trembling legs, yanked up her shirt, and pulled down the waistline of the corduroy trousers. "I don't have any scars."

"Please cover yourself, Miss Winters."

"Just look," she cried. "You know what a scar looks like, don't you?"

His face flushed with anger. "If you wish to continue this discussion, you need to cover yourself and sit down."

She lowered her shirt and sat. "If Eddie didn't explain how he knows the difference between me and my sister, then what did he tell you? Anything?"

"He said he was with you in the tunnels, and he took us to the spot where you claim to have seen a body."

"He saw her body too. I heard him tell you that, before Wayne and Marla dragged me back inside House Six."

Dr. Baldwin glared at her for a tense moment, as if trying to decide how much to say. "If Eddie was actually trying to help you escape, why would I believe anything he says? Either way, the fact remains that there was no body."

She shook her head again. "You're lying," she said. "You're lying because you don't want anyone to find out Rosemary was murdered and you never reported her missing." Then she had another thought and her blood ran cold. Why hadn't she thought of it before? "Or maybe *you* killed her!"

"Now you're being completely irrational, Miss Winters. And this conversation has told me two things. We have more work to do. And you can no longer be trusted." Venom edged his voice, making his meaning clear—he'd send her back to the pit if she didn't calm down.

She dropped her flooding eyes to the floor. There had to be something she could do or say, something that would make him listen. Then she looked up at him again. "I know how the news crew got inside House Six."

"Of course you do," he said.

"It's true, I swear. Eddie told me the night before it happened."

He looked doubtful. "There's no way Eddie could have known anything about that."

"You're wrong. He overheard some of the doctors talking about it. That's how we knew when the news crew was coming and that we'd be able to get into the tunnels without anyone noticing."

His chin lifted slightly, acting unfazed, but she could see the surprise in his eyes. "What did Eddie overhear?"

"I'll tell you, but only after you do something for me."

"What's that?"

"Call my stepfather."

"I called your stepfather when you first came back to let him know you'd been found. If I feel the need to call him again, I will."

"But calling him would prove I'm telling the truth. It's just one simple thing and you won't do it. When you called him, did you ask him if Rosemary had a twin?"

He shook his head. "It didn't come up. When I told him you'd been found safe and sound, he was relieved. That was it."

"He didn't say his other stepdaughter had run away?"

"No."

"So call him again. Right now, while I'm sitting here. Ask him if Rosemary had a twin."

"I'm afraid that would do more harm than good, Miss Winters. I don't want you to get your hopes up."

"I think you're afraid of what he'll say."

"I can assure you I am not."

"Then call him. But only if you want to know how the reporters got in."

He clenched his jaw, his nostrils flaring. After

a long moment, he pushed the button on the intercom again. When his secretary answered, he said, "Get Alan Tern on the line for me, will you, Evie?

"Yes, Doctor," Evie said.

"Call me back when you have him." After releasing the intercom, he folded his hands on the desk. "There. I've done what you asked. Now tell me, how did the news crew get in?"

"Not until you talk to him," she said.

"That wasn't the deal. Evie is going to get him on the line, so I'm holding up my end of the bargain. And unless you share what you know before she reaches him, I'll have her tell him she called him by mistake."

She chewed her lip. If Eddie's uncle got fired, he and Eddie would never be able to help her. Then again, she only had to tell Dr. Baldwin *part* of what she knew, not everything.

"But before you answer," Dr. Baldwin said, "do you remember where I sent you when you assaulted that attendant a few years ago?"

"No," she said. "Because that wasn't me. It was my sister."

He scowled, losing patience again. "I sent you to our state security hospital, where you remained for a year. Clearly it didn't teach you anything, but if you lie about how the reporters got in, I'll have them send someone to pick you up in the morning."

She swallowed. If the state security hospital was considered *punishment,* how much worse must it be than Willowbrook? "It was Dr. Wilkins," she said. "He's friends with that reporter. They met at a diner and Dr. Wilkins gave him a key to House Six."

Dr. Baldwin pressed his lips into a hard, thin line. Before he could respond, the phone on the desk rang, making Sage jump. Dr. Baldwin stared at it, fuming, then picked up the receiver.

"Yes?" He listened for a moment, then frowned. "I see," he said. "Yes, all right. We can try again later. Thank you, Evie." He hung up and looked at Sage. "Your stepfather isn't answering."

"Maybe he's still at work."

"On a Saturday evening?"

Heat crawled up her cheeks. She had no idea what time of day it was, let alone what day of the week. She was about to tell him Alan was probably at a bar when someone knocked on the office door.

"Yes?" Dr. Baldwin said.

The door opened and Evie rushed in, her lime-colored dress and platinum hair glowing in the drab office. "I'm sorry to interrupt, but you need to see this," she said. She hurried over to the television and turned it on.

"What is it?" Dr. Baldwin said.

Evie shushed him, turned up the volume, and backed away from the television so he could see.

"Is that goddamn reporter coming on?" Dr. Baldwin said. "The one who took the news crew into House Six?"

Evie nodded, chewing her manicured thumbnail and staring at the screen.

Dr. Baldwin's face went pale, like a man about to lose his last dollar in a bet. He got up, went around the desk, and stood beside Evie, who put a hand on his back, concern lining her brow. Standing next to each other, they looked more like a couple than a secretary and her boss.

On the television screen, a reporter behind a desk said, "And now we have a special report from Eyewitness News correspondent Geraldo Rivera."

Then Willowbrook's six-story headquarters appeared on the screen behind the headline: WILLOWBROOK: THE LAST GREAT DISGRACE, the ominous-looking building growing larger and larger as the camera got closer. A second later, a reporter with dark hair and a mustache came on and said into the microphone in his hand: "It's been more than six years since Robert Kennedy walked out of one of the wards here at Willowbrook and told newsmen of the horror he'd seen inside. He pleaded then for an overhaul of the system that allowed retarded children to live in a 'snake pit.' But that was way back in 1965 and somehow we'd all forgotten. I first heard of this big place with the pretty-sounding name because of a call I received from a member of the Willowbrook staff. The doctor told me he'd just been fired because he had been urging parents with children in one of the buildings to organize so they could more effectively demand improved conditions for their children. He invited me to see the conditions he was talking about, so, unannounced and unexpected by the school administration, we toured building number six."

On the screen, he and another man made their way through a thicket of trees, then stepped over a concrete barrier, their coats flying as they jumped down. After crossing a road and a lawn, they walked toward a U-shaped brick building: House Six.

The reporter went on. "The doctor had warned me that it would be bad, it was horrible. There was one attendant for perhaps fifty severely and profoundly retarded children. And the children, lying on the floor naked and smeared with their own feces . . . they were making a pitiful sound, a kind of mournful wail that is impossible for me to forget."

Suddenly the shadowy interior of House Six appeared and a horrendous wailing vibrated out of the television speaker, like a million tortured shrieks echoing from outer space or inside a colossal underground cave. The camera lights revealed pale figures, like hunted creatures in the crosshairs of a night rifle—half-dressed girls slumped in chairs and on the floor, a naked young woman jumping up and down, another crouched against the wall, her fingers tapping her face. A skeletal girl sat on the floor with her arms tied in what looked like a bed sheet while a nurse tried to calm her down. Then a line of sinks against one wall, children lying and squatting below them with their pants around their ankles, their buttocks and legs covered in filth.

"This is what it looked like," the reporter said. "This is what it sounded like, but how can I tell you about the way it smelled? It smelled of filth, it smelled of disease, and it smelled of death."

Sage leaned back and closed her eyes, wishing she could sink into the chair and disappear. The bizarre combination of being inside Willowbrook and seeing it on the television screen at the same time made her feel faint. And that horrific sound, like a giant, dying animal going on and on and on, vibrating through the speaker as if the television were about to explode was more than she could stand. Even if she survived and got out of there, she knew she would hear that haunting, anguished wail for the rest of her life, twisting and spinning throughout her thoughts and nightmares. Fighting the urge to plug her ears—she wanted to hear what else the reporter said—she sat still as a stone, her heart banging hard in her chest.

"We've just seen something that's probably the

most horrible thing I've ever seen in my life," the reporter said. "Is that typical of ward life?"

A man off-screen said, "Yes, there are five thousand three hundred patients at Willowbrook, which is the largest institution for the mentally retarded in the world. The ones that we saw were the most severely and profoundly retarded. There are thousands there like that, not going to school, sitting on the ward all day, not being talked to by anyone. Only one or two or three people to take care of seventy people on a ward. They're sharing the same toilet, contracting the same diseases. One hundred percent of patients at Willowbrook contract hepatitis within six months of being in the institution. Most patients, at some time in their lives, have parasites. The incidence of pneumonia is greater than any other group of people that I think exists in this country. Trauma is severe because these patients are left together on a ward unattended, fighting for a small scrap of paper on the floor to play with, fighting for the attention of the attendants who are overworked trying to clean them, feed them, clothe them, and if possible pay a little attention to them and work with them to develop their intelligence. But what in fact happens is that they go downhill."

Sage didn't know if she could listen to any more. The horrible knowledge that Rosemary had spent so many years struggling to survive such an unspeakable existence was bad enough, but now *she* was locked inside Willowbrook too, with little hope of escape. She counted backward in her head, trying to ignore the voices coming out of the television, but every once in a while she still heard snippets of what was being said: "Willowbrook has lost eight hundred employees in two years. . . . The attendants are trying their best, but the staff is just too small. . . . I've visited penal institutions all over the country. I visited hospitals all over the country. I've visited the worst brigs in the military. I've never seen anything like it."

When the report was over, Sage brushed the moisture from her cheeks, unable to move. Shock and terror anchored her in place, and the dreadful knowledge that she might not escape unless Rosemary's body was found made her feel like throwing up.

Unleashing a stream of profanities, Dr. Baldwin clicked off the television, trudged back to his desk, and put his head in his hands.

"Is there anything I can do for you, Doctor?" Evie said.

He gazed up at her and shook his head. Then he addressed Leonard, who still stood like a soldier in the same spot. "Take Miss Winters back to House Six," he said. "I can't deal with her right now."

CHAPTER 15

Between the lack of water and crying for what felt like a thousand days, Sage had no tears left to shed. Either she was severely dehydrated or had used them all up. She lay under the grimy blanket on her sister's bed in Ward D, shell-shocked and desperate, unable to think or feel. Numb.

The thought of spending the rest of her life in Willowbrook was too much to bear. She'd rather die. She'd rather let Cropsey—or Wayne, or whoever had killed Rosemary—slit her throat. It was only a matter of time before he came after her anyway, so why not get it over with? Maybe she should just stop eating.

Except . . .

Except she couldn't give up yet. She just couldn't. Eddie was still out there somewhere. And he knew the truth. He could still tell Alan what happened. He could still tell the police. He could still save her and help figure out who killed Rosemary. She just had to hang on a while longer.

Suddenly she sensed a presence near the bed and yanked the blanket off her head. A shadowy form moved nearby, edging closer and closer. She scrambled off the other side of the mattress, certain Wayne had come to shut her up for good.

"Relax," a voice whispered. "It's just me."

She squinted into the darkness, desperate to see. A pale shaft of moonlight filtering in through the Plexiglas fell on one side of Eddie's face, revealing his familiar features. She sat back down, breathless with relief. It was all she could do not to hug him. "You scared the shit out of me," she said. "I thought Dr. Baldwin fired you."

"He wanted to, but he moved me to another building instead."

"Jesus, that was close. He kept lying to me, telling me there was no body."

He put his hand on shoulder. "I hate to tell you this," he said, his voice grave. "But he was telling the truth."

"What do you mean? We both saw Rosemary's body! Did you take him in the right tunnel? Did you show him the exact spot?"

"Of course I did," he said. "I don't know how it happened, but by the time we got down there she was gone. Which means whoever killed her moved her body."

Panic ripped through Sage like a knife. She reached for his shirt, pulling on it and shaking her head as if she could change what he was saying. "No. No. That can't be! How is that possible? You took Baldwin into the tunnels at the same time Wayne and Marla brought me back here. There's no way the killer had enough time to move her."

He took her hands from his shirt and held them. "Unfortunately, that's not what happened. I tried to take him down there right away, but he was in a rage because of the reporters and insisted on making phone calls first. I kept telling him we had to call the cops, that I'd show someone else while he was making the calls, but he wouldn't hear of it. He said he had to do damage control as soon as possible and made me wait outside his office. I could hear him yelling on the phone, trying to find out how the reporters got in and trying to stop them from airing what they filmed."

"How long did you have to wait?"

He shrugged. "Twenty minutes, maybe more. When he came out of his office, he looked like he was about to have a heart attack."

"And that's when you took him down in the tunnels?"

He shook his head. "No, his secretary made him sit down and drink some water first because his face was all red and covered in sweat. By the time we got down there, Rosemary was gone. I couldn't believe it. Baldwin thought I was lying, of course, and there was no talking to him after that."

"Oh my God," she said, suddenly dizzy.

"I'm sorry," he said, his features going dark. "But there's something else."

She took her hands from his and braced herself. "What?"

"The reason he didn't fire me is because I lied to him."

"About what?"

"I said I was in the tunnels getting rid of old equipment and I caught you trying to escape. That you got away from me and I was going to House Six to get Wayne. It was the only way I could convince him not to fire me. But I had to take a position in the main building, otherwise I'd be gone."

The hairs on the back of her neck stood up. "Thank God you came up with the lie, otherwise I'd be screwed and trying to figure this out on my own. Have you gone to the cops yet?"

"To tell them what? That I was trying to help someone escape from a mental institution and we found a body that's no longer there?"

"Yes. And that I don't belong here." It sounded crazy, but she didn't care.

"They'd never believe me. And even if they called Dr. Baldwin, he'd just lie his way out of it. Then he'd fire me for sure."

"So don't tell them who you are. You can report a crime anonymously, can't you?"

"I don't know. I've never had to report one."

"If they ask for your name, just make something up. Use one of the phones here and tell them you're Dr. Baldwin."

"That might work, but I'd need to use a phone in one of the offices or a nurses' station without someone seeing me, which won't be as easy as it sounds."

"What about Alan? Did you try to talk to him again? Dr. Baldwin had his secretary call him, but he didn't answer."

He nodded. "I went to your apartment again. He's still not home, but I'll keep trying."

"Did you try to see Heather or Dawn?"

"Yeah, they weren't around either. Dawn's mom thought they went bowling, but she wasn't sure where."

She groaned. Telling their parents they were going bowling meant they were doing something else, like drinking in the park or driving around getting high. They hadn't been bowling in years. "Where the hell is Alan?" she said. "He can't still be ice fishing, can he?"

"I have no idea. But he has to come back sooner or later, right?"

"I guess. Unless he left town while he had the chance."

"Don't think like that. He probably just took a few days off to go on that fishing trip. I can't believe you managed to get Baldwin to call him."

She cringed inside. If she admitted that she'd told Dr. Baldwin about Dr. Wilkins giving the reporter a key, Eddie might stop helping her. Even if she could convince him that she hadn't mentioned his uncle, he might still be angry enough to desert her. For now, she couldn't take that risk. If the truth ever came to light, hopefully he'd remember she'd been fighting for her life.

"I couldn't believe he agreed to it either," she said. "Maybe he's scared because that story about Willowbrook came out on the news. His secretary turned it on while I was in his office and he was pretty upset. Did you see it?"

He nodded. "Hopefully it'll help change things around here, but I'm not holding my breath."

"What about your uncle? Have you told him what happened to Rosemary?"

"If I say one word to him about being down in the tunnels with you, he'll force me to quit working here. And how am I supposed to make him believe your sister's dead when her body has disappeared?"

"I don't know," she said, her voice filled with desperation. She couldn't stop thinking about the way Rosemary had been sitting in the cramped tunnel, like she was waiting to be found. And Sage had failed her. Again. She looked at Eddie. "Do you think I'm right? Do you think Wayne did it? Maybe she threatened to tell someone what he was doing to her."

"I don't think that would be reason enough for Wayne to kill her. He knows no one would believe her, that's why he gets away with the things he does."

"What if he had another reason?"

He furrowed his brow. "Like what?"

She thought for a moment, then gasped, surprised it hadn't occurred to her before. "Maybe she didn't have that operation. Maybe he got her pregnant."

"Well, if he killed her, he moved her body too. How long was he in House Six with you after he and Marla took you back inside?"

"He stopped at the nurses' station to talk to Nurse Vic for a minute, then he took me to the pit and restrained me while she gave me a shot. One of them bound my wrists together, but after that I don't know what happened." A sick feeling swirled in her stomach. She hadn't thought about the fact that she couldn't remember anything after she was drugged. When she'd woken up, she was still wearing the trousers, and as far as she could tell, she hadn't been violated. But who knew what Wayne might have done while she was unconscious? "I don't think Nurse Vic would have left him alone in there with me. I hope not anyway."

"If he did it, he would have needed enough time to make it all the way over to Rosemary and move her before Baldwin and I went down there. And the only way he could have done that without Nurse Vic wondering where he was would be if he left the residents alone in the dayroom."

Sage nodded. "Which sounds exactly like something he would do."

CHAPTER 16

The next day, Sage sat alone in Dr. Baldwin's office, anxiety clawing at her nerves. Earlier that morning, Leonard had retrieved her from the ward and taken her into the tunnels, refusing to answer her questions about where they were going and why. At first she thought he was taking her to the morgue to identify her sister—that, somehow, Rosemary's body had miraculously been found. But then he turned in the other direction, took her up into the main building, and led her along a maze of hallways and elevators until they reached Dr. Baldwin's office. After Evie let them inside, Leonard told Sage to sit, then left her there while Evie locked the door behind him.

When they were gone, Sage jumped up from the chair, went around the desk, and picked up the phone. Hands shaking, she tried to think. When Dr. Baldwin asked Evie to get Alan on the line last night, he said it was Saturday. That meant today was Sunday. Trying to call Alan again would be pointless, but Heather or Dawn should be home. Please God let one of them be home. She put the receiver to her ear, her heart pounding so hard it felt like it was about to burst through her chest. Except, for some reason, she couldn't remember Heather's number. And she'd dialed it a thousand times. *Shit.* She took a deep breath, squeezed her eyes shut, and pushed the chaos from her mind. Finally the number came to her and she dialed it with trembling fingers, the whirl and click of the rotary like bones grinding in her ears. With the receiver tight in her fist, she kept her eyes locked on the door in case someone came in. But no ringing sounded on the other end of the line. No one picked up or said hello. She hung up briefly and got ready to try again, then realized for the first time that there was no dial tone. Frantic, she pressed the hang up button repeatedly. Still nothing. Scanning the extension buttons beneath the dialer, she prayed one of them would connect the phone to an outside line. She pushed the one next to the red HOLD button. After what felt like forever, the phone rang on the other end. Once, twice, three times. Finally someone picked up.

"Dr. Hammond's office," A female voice said.

Sage froze, unsure. Then, in the steadiest voice she could manage, she said, "I'm sorry. I'm trying to dial out. Can you connect me?"

"This is the head of administration's office," the woman said, "not the switchboard."

"How do I get the switchboard?" Sage said. *Please don't ask who you're speaking to.*

"You need to dial zero."

"Thank you," Sage said, and hung up.

Suddenly Evie's voice came over the intercom, making her jump. "Get off the phone, Miss Winters. I can see you're trying to use it."

Ignoring her, Sage picked up the receiver again and dialed zero.

Another female voice answered. "Operator, how may I direct your call?"

"I . . . I need to dial out," Sage said.

Then the line clicked and Evie's voice came on. "Operator, this is Dr. Baldwin's secretary. There will be no outside calls from his line for the time being. I'll let you know when he returns to his office and you can open it up again."

"Yes, ma'am," the operator said. "I understand." Then she hung up.

"Hello?" Sage said. "Hello, operator?" She pushed the hang up button again and again, but the line was dead. She slammed down the receiver. "Damn it!" she yelled, tears of frustration burning her eyes. She pressed the button on the intercom. "Please, Evie. I just need to make one phone call, that's all. Just one. Please."

"I'm sorry," Evie said. "But you know I can't allow that."

"Will you at least tell me why Dr. Baldwin sent for me? Please?"

Evie said nothing.

Desperate, Sage released the intercom, picked up the phone again, and dialed Heather's number, knowing it was a waste of time but hoping for a miracle. Nothing happened. No ringtone on the other end of the line. No dial tone. No clicks or other sounds. She hung up the receiver, then stood and went over to the window, where a shaft of sunlight filtered in below a yellowed shade. If she could open the window or break the glass, she could climb down or jump out and go to the police. Then she pulled up the shade and realized the office was at least five stories up if not more. The blanket of snow and shoveled brick sidewalk below looked a hundred miles away. If she fell, she'd fracture her skull or break a leg, which would make running impossible.

She tried opening the window anyway to let in some fresh air, but it wouldn't budge. Cursing under her breath, she turned and paced the floor, a hundred scenarios running wild in her mind. Was she in Dr. Baldwin's office because they'd found Rosemary's body? Was Alan coming to get her? Were they sending her to the state security hospital as punishment for trying to escape?

She surveyed the doctor's desk. No files sat on the blotter. No papers or other clues that might help her figure out why she was there. She hurried behind the desk again, sat in the chair, and tried the middle drawer. It was locked. She tried the other drawers. Also locked. She stood and looked at the stacks of black filing cabinets. The answer to why she was in the office wouldn't be in there, but maybe some helpful information about Rosemary would—*if* the filing cabinets were unlocked. Peering at the tattered labels, she found the drawer labeled "W" and pulled. To her surprise, it slid open.

What looked like a thousand crumpled files filled the long drawer, packed together so tightly it seemed impossible to take one out, let alone put it back again. Quickly scanning the faded names on the tabs, she looked for the one labeled "Winters." With every sound on the other side of the office door, every scrape of a chair and thump of a drawer in the waiting room, she shut the drawer, scrambled around to the front of the desk, certain Dr. Baldwin would catch her.

Finally, she found two files with the name "Winters" and tugged on the first one, trying to get it out. The tab started to rip. She stopped and pulled out the next one, which was sticking up just enough to get a good grip. She opened the file. Affixed to the first page was a black and white photo of a young boy, a toddler with crossed eyes and a cleft lip. On the wall behind his head were five digits on a white sign. Below the photo was a date: November 3rd, 1955; the name "Gregory Winters"; and words in bold type: "SEVERELY RETARDED." Gregory looked like he was laughing in the photo, his first teeth showing in a gummy grin, his nose crumpled in delight. Sage swallowed, wondering if Gregory was still alive. She closed the file and took out the other one labeled "Winters." When she opened the cover, she nearly dropped it.

Rosemary looked back at her with frightened eyes, her lips pressed together as if she were trying hard not to cry. Written beneath her name in bold type was: "MANIC-DEPRESSIVE SCHIZOPHRENIC WITH SPLIT PERSONALITY DISORDER." Even with the terrified expression, Rosemary looked exactly like Sage remembered her, with translucent skin and light wisps of hair framing her dainty features. It was like looking at a photo of herself. Blinking back tears, she turned the page and started reading.

December 10, 1965: Resident seems in good physical health. Did not settle into the ward easily. Responded well to Thorazine. No longer hostile after three days of treatment, although hallucinations and delusions continue to occur. Continued daily treatment recommended.

May 12, 1966: Resident is fairly cooperative and eats and sleeps well. No complaints from nursing staff. Continued daily treatment recommended.

Sage drew in a sharp breath. No one had reevaluated Rosemary for *six months* after she had been admitted? Unbelievable. Out in the waiting room, Evie's phone rang, making Sage jump. She skimmed over the next few pages, reading as fast as possible.

June 2, 1967: Resident is definitely paranoid in her thinking and continues to have delusions. Has developed a fixation on another patient, claiming she is her sibling. Continued daily treatment recommended.

July 10, 1968: Resident continues to be paranoid and delusional. Also seems to have developed split personality disorder, with three separate personalities detected so far: Trixie, Belinda, and Sage. Staff advised not to contradict. Continued daily treatment recommended, along with dose of Prolixin as needed.

September 1, 1969: Along with continued paranoia, schizophrenia, and split personality disorder, resident has developed violent tendencies. After causing a disturbance in the dayroom, during which she assaulted an attendant and several other residents were injured, she was confined to seclusion for four days in an attempt to adjust paranoia. Continued daily treatment recommended, along with dose of Prolixin as needed.

September 6, 1969: Seclusion failed

to curb violent tendencies. Temporarily transferred to state security hospital.

October 12, 1970: Resident attempted escape. Confined to seclusion for eight days. Continued daily treatment recommended, added dose of Prolixin as needed.

January 6, 1971: Resident went missing. After two days found in House Fourteen, dazed and highly paranoid. Continued daily treatment recommended, additional dose of Prolixin until readjusted.

Despite having been told that the residents rarely saw doctors, seeing it in black and white made Sage even more furious. How could the doctors let an entire year pass between evaluations? It was outrageous and cruel. Willowbrook would never help anyone with that method. She flipped through the last pages, looking for anything that might tell her more. Other entries in a dozen different scripts included medication logs; physical characteristics like height and weight; and medical situations that needed attention: compound fracture, dysentery, eye injury, hepatitis test, suicidal ideation.

A thick lump formed in Sage's throat. Rosemary had wanted to kill herself? That didn't sound like her. Rosemary had always loved life. Then she remembered the complete and utter misery she'd felt when she thought she was damned to spend the rest of her life in Willowbrook. In some ways, she could understand why her sister would want to end her suffering.

She closed Rosemary's file and shoved it, along with poor little Gregory's, back in the cabinet, not caring if they got crumpled or torn. After shutting the cabinet, she went around the desk and sat down to wait for Dr. Baldwin. Unfortunately, finding Rosemary's file had only deepened her grief over the loss of her sister and added to her despair over her short, tragic life. And now, sometime in the next few minutes, she was about to find out if she was being released or sent to the state security hospital, which meant her life would be as disastrous as Rosemary's.

No, that wasn't true. Unlike her sister, she'd had the chance to go to school and make friends, to go dances and ballgames and museums, to learn about the world and the people in it. She'd gone to the movies and to all-night parties; she'd laughed and gossiped with her best girlfriends. She'd walked under the stars at midnight while drinking wine and felt that bottomless hope of a world full of possibilities. She'd fallen in love and made love to a handsome boy. It was more life than most of the Willowbrook residents had ever experienced. And she'd taken it all for granted.

She squeezed her eyes shut to stanch her tears and wiped her cheeks, determined to stop thinking that this was the end. If someone was coming to take her to the state security hospital, they would have just taken her from the ward. Leonard must have brought her here because Dr. Baldwin wanted to talk to her again. And more than anything, she needed to know why.

Ten more minutes went by. Fifteen. Thirty. She couldn't take it anymore. She got up and pounded on the door.

"Hello?" she shouted. "Evie? Where is Dr. Baldwin?"

No answer. Just the muted clicking of type-writer keys.

She rattled the handle and pounded on the door again. "I know you're out there. When is he coming back?"

Still nothing.

She went to back to the desk and pressed the intercom button. "Please talk to me, Evie."

When Evie answered, she said, "He'll be back soon. You need to be patient."

"Do you know what's happening? Is someone coming to pick me up?"

"I'm sorry," Evie said. "But you know I can't help you."

"Can you at least tell me if got hold of my stepfather yet?"

"You'll have to ask Dr. Baldwin about that."

Sage let go of the button and sat down hard in Dr. Baldwin's chair.

Just then, a door shut and footsteps sounded in the waiting room. A male voice asked if there'd been any calls. Sage jumped up and went back to the folding chair. The door unlocked and opened, and Dr. Baldwin entered.

"What's going on?" Sage said. "Why did you send for me?"

Dr. Baldwin went around his desk, pulled out his chair, and sat down, flipping his jacket away from his waist, then looked at her, his face unreadable.

Her heart boomed in her chest. "Did you find Rosemary?" she said.

"You know we didn't," he said.

"Did you talk to my stepfather?"

He shook his head. "I've had Evie call several times. Still no answer."

"Then why am I here?"

"You'll find out soon enough."

Someone knocked on the office door.

"Yes?" Dr. Baldwin said.

The door opened partway and Evie stuck her head inside. "They're here."

Sage felt something click inside her head, as if her brain were shoring up, preparing for shock. Who was there? Someone from the state security hospital? She stood and moved toward the wall, her hands reaching blindly behind her, as if searching for a hidden exit. "You can't send me away. I didn't do anything wrong."

Dr. Baldwin ignored her. "Let them in, Evie," he said.

Sage slumped against the wall, certain she was about to break into a thousand pieces and fall to the floor like shattered glass. "No," she said. "I was telling the truth about Dr. Wilkins. I promise I won't cause any more trouble."

When Evie opened the door all the way, two men entered the room, one in a police uniform, the other in a wool overcoat and black goulashes. Sage went rigid. Did they send cops to help take residents to the state security hospital? Was she about to be handcuffed and hauled away?

Then she had another thought, and a tiny spark of hope ignited inside her. Maybe Eddie had made the anonymous call to report Rosemary's murder.

Evie stood in the doorway nervously chewing her thumbnail, her other hand on the knob.

"You can go now, Evie," Dr. Baldwin said.

Evie nodded and reluctantly closed the door, worry written on her face. The man in the wool coat gave Sage the once-over as he moved toward Dr. Baldwin's desk, holding out his hand. He looked to be in his midthirties, with unruly hair and stubble on his cheeks. The uniformed cop stood straight-backed and steady near the door.

"I'm Detective Sam Nolan with the NYPD, 121st Precinct," the man in the wool jacket said. "This is my partner, Sergeant Clark."

Sage's breath caught in her throat. He wasn't from the other institution.

Dr. Baldwin stood, shook the detective's hand, and gave the sergeant a brief nod. "Dr. Donald Baldwin, Willowbrook's psychiatric director."

"I'm here on what could be a sensitive matter," Detective Nolan said. He glanced at Sage. "May I talk freely?"

"Yes, please do," Dr. Baldwin said. "I have nothing to hide."

"As I told your secretary earlier," the detective said. "We received an anonymous call from one of your employees early this morning. He said he found a body in the basement, a young woman named Rosemary Winters. Do you know anything about that?"

Sage nearly cried out in relief. Eddie had done it. He'd called the police. *Thank God.* Now she just had to make sure Dr. Baldwin didn't lie his way out of it. She stood up straight and stared at the detective, willing him to read the truth in her eyes.

Dr. Baldwin let out a halfhearted chuckle. "I was told that as well," he said. "But I can assure you there are no dead bodies in our basement. Or our attic for that matter." He forced an uneasy smile. "Our head of security and I did a thorough search and found nothing amiss or suspicious."

"It was my sister," Sage said. "I saw her body down in the tunnels, but someone moved her."

Nolan turned toward her. "And you are?"

"Sage Winters. It was my twin sister, Rosemary." She eyed Dr. Baldwin. "But he doesn't believe me."

"Detective," Dr. Baldwin said, smiling. "Let's remember that Miss Winters is a Willowbrook resident for a reason. She truly has no concept of reality."

"He's lying!" Sage cried. "I came here looking for my sister because she went missing and he locked me up because he thinks I'm her!"

"That's simply not the case," Dr. Baldwin said. "Miss Winters is a paranoid schizophrenic. She thinks everyone is 'out to get her,' including me."

With a look of concerned concentration, Detective Nolan took a pad of paper from his pocket, jotted something down, then turned his attention to Dr. Baldwin. "You said you were told there was a body down there as well," he said. "May I ask who told you that?"

"Certainly. It was Miss Winters." Baldwin gestured toward Sage. "That's why I wanted her here in my office when you arrived. She needs to learn once and for all that her antics have real-life consequences. You see, we caught her trying to escape, not for the first time, I might add, so she has come up with an elaborate story about finding her twin sister's body in the tunnels to distract us."

"That's not true," Sage said, her voice rattled by anger. "She was there! I saw her!"

Nolan looked at the doctor for a moment. "So you're telling me there's no body?"

"That's exactly right. There's no body. Miss Winters has been going by numerous names for years now. She claimed one of the other residents was her sister, but I believe they've had a spat. And now, suddenly, she says she has a twin sister. A *dead* twin sister. But you have to understand, thinking that way is a result of her many conditions. She also has what's called split personality disorder, among other problems."

Sage furiously shook her head. "He doesn't know what he's talking about. My sister was ill, but I swear to you, I'm not. I'm perfectly sane. You can't believe anything he tells you because he's trying to cover up what happens here. This place isn't a school. It's like a concentration camp! A prison! Didn't you see it on the news? The staff abuses the residents and—"

"Miss Winters," Dr. Baldwin interrupted, his voice granite. "Do I need to send you into the waiting room?"

She hesitated. She had to be careful. "Please," she said, turning to him, her eyes filling. "I'm begging you. Just tell them the truth."

"You know perfectly well that I *am* telling the truth," he said. "But I'm also losing patience with you. So I suggest you keep quiet until a staff member arrives to take you back to your ward." He looked at the detective. "Please continue, Detective Nolan."

"So you're saying Miss Winters made up a story about the body in the tunnels, correct?"

"She either made it up or actually believes she saw it. It's hard to tell with someone who suffers from her illness."

"But the person who called the station said he was an employee. And he was male. How do you explain that?"

Dr. Baldwin shrugged. "Unless you can give me a name, I can't."

"The call was made anonymously."

Sage opened her mouth to tell them it was Eddie, then stopped. She didn't want him to get fired for calling the cops.

"It's quite possible that one of our employees caught wind of Miss Winters's story," Dr. Baldwin said. "Because as you can imagine, a place like this is ripe with gossip. And sadly, there are employees who like to start trouble for those of us in charge." He looked at Sage. "Who else did you tell about this wild idea of yours?"

She ignored him and kept her eyes on the detective. "You need to check the tunnels again. Or the morgue. No one would even notice another dead body in this place because people die here all the time and they cover it up. My sister was down there, but someone moved her. I swear I'm telling the truth."

Another knock sounded on the door. Sage ignored it. "Please, you have to listen to me."

"What is it?" Dr. Baldwin shouted, scowling at the door.

A man's muffled voice came from the other side. "Picking up."

"Enter." Baldwin looked at Nolan. "Excuse me, Detective, but someone is here to take Miss Winters back to her ward. I just wanted her here long enough to see the trouble she's caused. She needs to know that giving a false report is not only wrong, it's against the law."

The door opened, the uniformed cop moved to the side, and Leonard came into the office. When he saw the cop, he hesitated for a moment, then dropped his gaze and lumbered toward Sage. She gripped the back of the chair and held on, her knuckles turning white. If Dr. Baldwin wanted her to leave, he'd have to wrench her loose from it.

"Please," she begged Nolan. "Don't let them do this. I'm not crazy." Leonard grabbed her by the arm and began trying to pry her fingers from the chair. She struggled to hold on, her eyes locked on the detective. "They're keeping me here against my will because I look like my twin sister. But I found out she's dead and I think I know who killed her. I saw her body in the tunnels. I swear on my life."

Leonard yanked the chair from her grasp and pulled on her arm, jerking her toward him. She let her knees buckle to make herself heavier.

"Please do as you're told, Miss Winters," Dr. Baldwin said. "Or I'll have a nurse sedate you."

Before Sage could stand again, Leonard heaved her upright. He wrestled her arm behind her back and steered her toward the door, his knuckles digging into her spine. She yelped in pain and, using everyone ounce of strength she had left, tried to get away.

Nolan gaped at Dr. Baldwin, his forehead lined with concern. "Is it necessary to manhandle her like that?"

"Sometimes, yes," Baldwin said. "If a resident is being difficult, we have no choice."

Nolan held up his hand. "Hold on a minute," he said. "I'm not sure what's going on here, but I want to hear what this girl has to say."

Sergeant Clark took a step sideways to block the exit. Leonard stopped shoving Sage toward it and looked back at Baldwin, awaiting his next order.

Bent over and in pain, Sage turned her head toward the detective and tried to catch her breath. "My sister's throat and wrists were slit," she said. "Her hair was chopped off, and her lips were painted red. I think one of the attendants killed her. His name is Wayne. Please, you have to help me. Dr. Baldwin doesn't want anyone to know she was murdered because he never reported her missing."

"My apologies, Detective," Baldwin said. "I'm very sorry you have to witness this. As I said, Miss Winters is a manic-depressive schizophrenic with violent tendencies, and today has not been one of her better days. She believes everyone from Jack the Ripper to Cropsey is trying to harm her. I probably should have waited until she was gone before we spoke any more about the reason for your visit, but I didn't expect this reaction. And if she doesn't return to her ward soon, she'll miss breakfast."

"He's lying!" she said. "Call my stepfather and ask him about me. His name is Alan Tern and his number is 212-567-2345."

Dr. Baldwin shook his head, looking slightly amused. "I've spoken to her stepfather numerous times and I can assure you he has never mentioned having twin stepdaughters. Call him if you'd like, but Miss Winters has wandered off before and we've always returned her to Ward D safe and sound."

"So she *was* missing?"

Dr. Baldwin hestitated, as if caught off guard. "For . . . for a day or so, yes."

"But you never reported it?"

"There was no need," Dr. Baldwin said, his voice smooth and confident again. "We knew she was somewhere on campus and thankfully, this time she came back of her own accord."

"That's not true," Sage said. "I came here on the bus after I found out Rosemary was gone."

Nolan looked back and forth between Baldwin and Sage, trying to decide what to do. She tried to imagine how she must look to him, a filthy-faced girl in men's boots and an oversize jacket with snarled hair and terrified eyes. Believing Dr. Baldwin would be easy. When the detective told Sergeant Clark to open the door, she nearly passed out.

"No! Please!" she screamed. "You can't believe anything he tells you! He's just worried about his job! Call the bus station! They have my name and number because my purse was stolen on the way here!"

But no one listened. Sergeant Clark did as he was told, stepping away from the door, and Leonard forced Sage out of the office into the waiting area. She dragged her feet and tried to get away, but he wrenched her arm higher behind her back. Evie shut the door behind them, muffling the men's voices, as Leonard lugged her out of the reception area, through a maze of halls, down into the tunnels and back to House Six.

CHAPTER 17

For three days Sage waited—for Eddie to sneak into the ward again with news, for Dr. Baldwin to tell her that the cops had found Rosemary's body, for Alan to show up and get her out of there.

Struggling to hang on and barely eating, she slogged through the wretched dark nights and the long, treacherous days in silence; every endless passing hour chipping away at her hope. Thankfully Wayne did little more than watch her, as if waiting for her to run or hide again. And she tried to be grateful that at least she'd been given another shower and had long pants and a coat to keep her warm, and boots to protect her feet from the human waste and Pine-Sol on the floors. But how much longer would she last?

On the fourth day, Marla entered the dayroom late in the morning, spoke to Wayne briefly, then made her way toward Sage.

"You need to come with me."

"What for?" Sage said.

"Dr. Baldwin wants to see you. Damn if I know why. I'm just doin' what I'm told."

For a second, Sage couldn't move. This was it. She was about to find out if she was going to be set free or locked up forever. With her heart in her throat, she followed Marla out of the room and down to the tunnels, then up through the maze of halls and elevators in the main building. As usual, Marla took fast, steady strides despite her limp, but it still felt like a snail's pace. Sage wanted to run. She wanted to get to Dr. Baldwin's office as fast as possible.

When they finally reached the waiting area outside his office, Evie's desk sat unattended. Marla knocked on his door instead of making Sage wait to be called in. When Dr. Baldwin's muffled voice ordered them to enter, Sage held her breath. Surely he was going to apologize and tell her they had found Rosemary's body. Surely Alan was there to take her home. But when Marla opened the door to let her inside, Sage didn't know what to think.

Detective Nolan sat opposite Dr. Baldwin's desk, and Sergeant Clark stood in front of the window, blocking the light. Seated behind his desk, Dr. Baldwin was writing something down. When he finished, he looked up, his face pale, his forehead lined with something that looked like dread.

"I'll have Leonard return her to Ward D when we're finished here," he said to Marla.

"Yes, Doctor," Marla said, then left, closing the door behind her.

Sage stood in the center of the room, nearly hyperventilating. If he was going to send her back to the ward when they were finished, she wasn't being released. "Did you find my sister?" she managed.

Detective Nolan stood and offered her the chair.

She shook her head. "I'm fine. Please, just tell me what's going on."

"Have a seat, Miss Winters," Dr. Baldwin said, his voice firm. Then he sat up straight and took a sip from the cup of coffee on his desk, like he was getting ready to make a speech or an announcement.

The last thing she wanted to do was sit, but there was no point in arguing. The sooner she did as she was told, the sooner they'd tell her why she was there. She perched on the edge of the chair. Nolan leaned against the wall and lit a cigarette. He took a long drag, then blew out the smoke and studied her with pity-filled eyes, running his thumbnail along his lower lip.

"I've summoned you here at Detective Nolan's request," Dr. Baldwin said. "I'm not sure why he wanted to speak to you, but I won't be accused of impeding a police investigation." He picked up a pen and held it in his fist, his thumb repeatedly pushing the top up and down. *Click. Click. Click.*

"An investigation?" she said.

"Yes," the detective said, straightening. "Two days ago, Dr. Baldwin's secretary, Evie Carter, was reported missing by her husband. He found her car parked behind the main building with the door open and the keys in the ignition. Her purse was on the ground, and there were signs of a struggle."

Sage nodded to show she was listening, but a storm raged inside her. What about her sister? Why weren't they looking for her? Had the detective called Alan yet, or did he believe everything Dr. Baldwin said? At the same time, she was curious: Who would hurt Evie, and why? Could it have been the same person who killed Rosemary?

"After no trace of Mrs. Carter was found in any of the buildings or surrounding lawns," Nolan continued, "a search party was sent out to look for her."

Sage took a deep breath and held it, fighting the urge to point out that no search party had been sent out for Rosemary.

"To make a long story short, we found her body in the woods near a clearing at the far end of the Willowbrook campus."

Sage exhaled long and hard, then looked at Dr. Baldwin and tried to choose her next words carefully. "That's horrible," she said. "And I'm truly sorry. I'm sure you'll miss her." She turned back to Nolan. "How was she killed? Maybe it was the same person who killed Rosemary."

"How do you know she was killed?" Dr. Baldwin said, his thumb still clicking the pen.

"Maybe she became ill and wandered off." *Click. Click. Click.*

Sage frowned and glanced at Nolan. "Oh. I just assumed—"

"You assumed correctly," he said. "That's why I wanted to talk to you. Evie Carter's injuries and some other findings are similar to the ones you described the last time I was here."

Baldwin threw down the pen and stood. "This is preposterous," he said. "Are you going to tell me you're asking a mentally disturbed individual to help with your investigation? Whatever she thought she saw was her overworked imagination, nothing more."

"I understand your concern," Nolan said. "But I'm not asking her to help, exactly. I just need to understand how she knew about the similar injuries." He regarded Sage again. "I'd like you to describe them to me again, if you can." While the detective had studied her with pity before, now something in his eyes had changed. Her skin turned clammy. He didn't want her help—he thought she killed Evie.

"I . . . I'll help however I can," she managed.

"Tell me about the body you saw in the tunnel. Include everything you can remember."

Dr. Baldwin sat down hard in his chair, shaking his head in disgust.

She swallowed. "It was my sister, Rosemary. Her hair had been chopped off, like it was done with a knife or dull scissors. And her lips were painted red. Not normal, but more like a clown face, with the lipstick going up her cheeks, like this." She touched the corners of her mouth and traced lines toward her ears.

"And her injuries?"

"Her wrists and throat had been slit, and blood was running down her legs and chest."

Nolan glanced knowingly at Sergeant Clark, then looked back at Sage. "Do you have any idea who might have killed your sister?" he said.

Baldwin slammed a hand on his desk. "That's enough, Detective," he said. "I can't allow this type of questioning. It's just feeding into her delusions."

Nolan ignored him. "Miss Winters? Who do you think killed Rosemary?"

She glanced nervously at Dr. Baldwin. If Eddie was right and he'd somehow covered up Rosemary's murder by getting rid of her body, he would make her pay. And if Nolan thought Sage had killed Evie, she could go to prison. "I . . . I don't know for sure. I wish I did, so I could tell you. But like I said before, if I had to guess, I'd say it was that attendant Wayne. I don't know his last name."

Nolan turned to Baldwin. "What's Wayne's last name?"

Dr. Baldwin grumbled in disgust. "This is ridiculous."

"Maybe. But I need his last name."

"I'm not sure," Baldwin said. "I'd have to look it up."

Nolan's eyebrows went up. "You don't know who takes care of your patients?"

"We have over two thousand employees working on campus, Detective. I can't be expected to remember everyone's names. And we prefer the term *resident,* not *patient.*"

Nolan shot him an exasperated look. "I'm going to need you to look that up," he said. "And I'd also like to know how Miss Winters found her way into the tunnels in the first place. Is it possible for a patient . . . excuse me, I mean, a *resident,* to find their way down there without being noticed?"

"Of course not," Baldwin blustered. "We keep all doors locked. Only employees have access to the basement and tunnels." He took another sip of coffee. When he set the cup back down, his hand trembled.

"I had help," Sage said.

"From who?" Nolan said.

She glanced at Baldwin. "I'd rather not say. Not yet anyway."

"Do you know who she's talking about?" Nolan asked Baldwin.

Dr. Baldwin squeezed his forehead between his thumb and fingers, closing his eyes as if he were getting a headache, then pulled himself together and regarded Nolan again. "Look, you have to understand something. A news crew broke into Miss Winters's building that day and all hell broke loose. She tried to escape but got caught, and now she claims to have found a body. A body *we* didn't find anywhere. As far as her getting into the tunnels, someone could have easily left the door unlocked with everything that was happening. And as her doctor, I'm telling you that whatever she said to me, and whatever she says to you now, you need to understand that it's all part of her delusions. Her story."

"I understand your position," Nolan said. "But regardless of that, the similarities between the conditions of the body she described as her sister's and Evie Carter's body are too much of a coincidence to ignore. And due to the fact that Mrs. Carter's body was found on Willowbrook property, you might as well get used to the idea that there will be a full investigation. So from here on out, I'll be talking to your employees and your residents, if need be. I'll have some questions for you too, Dr. Baldwin, so be prepared. And I'll be sending someone to check out the tunnels. In the meantime, I'm hoping Miss Winters will agree to look at Mrs. Carter's body." He turned to her. "Do you think that's something you can do? Only to point out any similarities, of course."

"Good God," Baldwin said. "You're being unreasonable, Detective. Miss Winters is *unwell*.

And I would never allow you to take her off the premises. It's too big a risk and she's too unstable. Not to mention we've already caught her trying to escape several times. You're welcome to bring the body into our morgue for her to examine if you wish, but that's it."

"I'm afraid that's not an option," Nolan said. "Evie Carter won't be going to Willowbrook's morgue. The coroner will be taking her body to the city morgue. But that's irrelevant right now, because we're still investigating and photographing the crime scene, which includes the body. And *that* means I won't need to take Miss Winters off the premises."

Baldwin balked. "Are you saying you want to show her the crime scene?"

"That's exactly what I'm saying, yes," Detective Nolan said. "If she's willing, of course. I don't want to force her to do anything she's not comfortable with."

"As her doctor, I cannot allow it," Dr. Baldwin said. "It could send her into another psychotic episode."

Nolan let out an irritated sigh. "Did I mention I called the bus station and they did indeed have Miss Winters's name and Alan Tern's phone number on record? I believe it concerned a stolen purse."

Sage gasped. He'd actually listened to her the last time he was there.

Dr. Baldwin rolled his eyes. "That doesn't mean anything. She could have easily hopped on the bus while it was on campus and taken a joyride."

"Do the residents ride the bus for free?"

"Actually, we do have a few residents who go home with relatives on occasion for short visits, and we always pay the bus fares for them. Maybe the driver allowed her on by mistake and she told him one of her imaginary stories."

Sage groaned inside. As usual, he had an answer for everything. She looked at Detective Nolan. "Did you call the number they gave you?"

"I did," Detective Nolan said. "Several times, but there was never any answer."

Sage nodded, not surprised. She'd realized by now that Alan was not going to be the one to save her. She had to save herself. And if looking at another dead body would help find Rosemary's killer, she could handle it. She could handle anything. "I'll go," she said. "I want to help however I can."

"Again," Dr. Baldwin said, "as her doctor, I don't think that would be wise."

"Are you advising Miss Winters to hinder our investigation, Doctor?" Nolan said. "I have to warn you it wouldn't look good, especially not after the statements made by Evie Carter's husband."

"What statements?" Dr. Baldwin said, his face going dark.

"I'd rather not get into the details of that right now," Detective Nolan said. "Just be aware of the fact that he believes his wife was romantically involved with someone at Willowbrook."

"Who?" Dr. Baldwin said. "I'll have them fired right away."

"And that's precisely why I'm not going to tell you. I don't want the person in question to know we're on to them."

Frustration hardened Dr. Baldwin's features. "All right, I'll allow you to take Miss Winters to the crime scene, but only under heavy security. She's tried to run away too many times, and I won't risk it happening again."

"Of course," Nolan said. "That's not a problem."

"What about Eddie?" Sage said. "Shouldn't he come too? He was with me when we—"

"No," Baldwin interrupted. "This situation is preposterous enough without getting him involved. I won't hear of it."

"Eddie who?" Detective Nolan said. "And what does he have to do with this?"

"Eddie King," Dr. Baldwin said. "He claims he caught Miss Winters attempting to escape, but it's not the entire truth. In any event, he's been properly dealt with, I can assure you."

"In what way?"

"He mops floors and empties the trash in a different building now. And his actions have been noted in his file."

"Is he the person who helped you?" Detective Nolan asked Sage.

She nodded. "Yes, but I didn't want to say anything until now because I didn't want to get him in more trouble."

Detective Nolan took out a notepad and wrote down Eddie's name. "Did Eddie King also state there was a body in the tunnels?"

"Yes," she said. "He told Dr. Baldwin about it too."

"Eddie was involved with Miss Winters despite numerous warnings to stay away from her," Dr. Baldwin said, his voice filled with scorn. "So he was clearly trying to protect her."

"Why didn't you mention him before now?"

Baldwin shrugged. "It wasn't necessary. He's been reprimanded for his involvement. And there is no body."

"You do realize I could come after you for not disclosing important information during an investigation, don't you?" Detective Nolan said, irritated.

"I can assure you, Eddie has nothing to do with any of this."

"I'll be the judge of that. I'll need to speak to Mr. King as soon as possible. And this Wayne person, when you find out who he is."

"I'll arrange it."

"No, I don't want to give them a heads-up. You can take me to them after we're done at the crime scene."

"All right," Baldwin said. "But just so we're clear, you're being sent on a wild-goose chase, Detective. Whatever she, or they, say they saw in the tunnels was either a hallucination or a downright lie."

"I hope you're right, Doctor. Because if not, you could have a mass murderer on your hands."

CHAPTER 18

Wrapping the wool coat Eddie had given her around herself and wearing the too-big boots tied extra tight, Sage trailed Detective Nolan and Dr. Baldwin through the mist-filled forest, along slushy paths winding around frozen tree roots and icy rocks, up slippery embankments and back down again. Layers of sleet from an earlier storm gathered in the shadows of trees, but the snow on the branches and ground was starting to melt and drip, filling the air with the scent of soil and wet pine. Sage took deep, cleansing breaths as she hiked, letting the salty hint of the distant ocean and the fresh winter air evict the heavy stench of Willowbrook from her lungs. Muttering about the cold, Marla followed close behind, carrying a fistful of leather straps to restrain Sage if she caused any trouble.

Every now and then Sage slipped in the slurry of snow and mud but managed to grab a tree or find her footing before she fell. Dr. Baldwin, on the other hand, wearing a wool peacoat and tweed newsboy cap, slipped every few steps, the soles of his brown Oxfords like grease on the slush. Every time he slipped, Sage wanted him to fall on his face, but it never happened. Detective

Nolan had to keep stopping and waiting for them to catch up, and his patience was clearly wearing thin.

After climbing a rocky mound and taking several more twists and turns through the woods, they came to a marshy clearing surrounded by tall pines, leafless oaks, and thick shrubs. Yellow police tape roped off part of the area, wrapping around tree limbs and brush. When a cop at the edge of the clearing saw them coming, he held up a hand.

"Turn around, folks," he said. "You don't want to see this."

Detective Nolan took out his wallet and showed him his badge. "Stand down, Officer. That's why we're here."

"Sorry, Detective," the cop said, and stepped back to let them pass.

Nolan and Baldwin hurried into the clearing, but Sage slowed, her heart pounding. She had no desire to see another dead body, but she had no choice. She needed to see if Evie's throat was slit. Needed to see if her hair had been chopped off, if her lips had been stretched into a clown smile.

Nolan and Baldwin went under the police tape and trudged over to the crime scene, where another cop and two men who looked like part of a search team stood talking. When they reached the crime scene, Dr. Baldwin immediately turned away like he was about to be sick. Nolan looked back at Sage and gestured for her to follow. Marla nudged her impatiently from behind.

"Move it along so we can get this done and I can get out of this damn cold," she said, her teeth chattering.

Swallowing her fear, Sage went under the police tape and edged closer to Detective Nolan.

Evie lay in a shallow grave between a fallen tree and an outcropping of jagged rock, her shoulders jammed forward as if she had been crammed into the tight space by sheer force, her arms straight in front of her, her sliced, bloody wrists touching. Blood pooled dark and gelatinous between her broken collarbones at the base of her neck, which had been slit from ear to ear. A few jagged inches of platinum hair remained on her head, and random blotches of icy dirt muddied her face and eyes. Clumps of wet leaves covered her legs up to her waist, and a long section of bark from a hollowed-out tree rested over her feet and ankles like a recently removed coffin lid.

Sage backed away, unable to pull her eyes from Evie's twisted lips and the circus-red lipstick smeared like clown makeup toward her ears. Finally, she went back to the police tape, slipped under it, and stood near Marla, the icy air suddenly finding its way through her wool coat.

"Was it Miss Evie?" Marla said.

Sage nodded.

"Damn," Marla said. She crossed herself and muttered a quick prayer, shaking her head.

Detective Nolan and Dr. Baldwin returned to where she and Marla stood.

"Well," Detective Nolan said, watching Sage closely, "is Mrs. Carter's body in the same condition as the body you saw?"

She nodded. "Yes, the hair, the lipstick, everything. Exactly the same."

Dr. Baldwin scoffed. "What did you expect her to say?" He yanked a handkerchief from his pocket and wiped his mouth. "She'll agree to anything if it backs up her story."

"Do you have any other explanation for her knowledge about the condition of Mrs. Carter's body before today?"

"There's only one explanation I can think of."

"What's that?"

"You know perfectly well what it is," Dr. Baldwin snapped. "I told you before that Miss Winters has violent tendencies."

Nolan's brows shot up. "What are you saying? That you think *she* killed Evie Carter?"

"It's the only explanation that makes sense," Dr. Baldwin said. "And for the safety of the other residents, I am going to have her sent to the state security hospital until there can be a full investigation."

Sage went rigid, fear and anger shooting through her blood like lightning, bright and white-hot. She glared at Dr. Baldwin. "Are you really going to stoop that low? I didn't touch Evie and you know it. You're just making up lies to cover your own ass!"

"I guess we'll find out who's lying, won't we?"

"Miss Winters isn't going anywhere right now, Doctor," Nolan said. "Not until we get to the bottom of this."

Breathing hard, Sage tried to calm down. Screaming at Dr. Baldwin wouldn't get her anywhere. "Do you believe me now, Detective? About my sister?"

"I'm not going to say one way or another, but your story has certainly gained more credibility."

Nolan turned to Dr. Baldwin. "Do the residents at Willowbrook have access to the newspaper?"

Looking confused by the question, Dr. Baldwin shook his head. "Most can't read. And even if they could, making the newspaper available would only cause more problems. Why do you ask?"

"What about television?" Nolan said. "Are they able to watch the news?"

"No. The attendants shut the televisions off when the news reports come on and distract the residents in other ways."

"That's bullshit," Sage said. "The attendants never shut off the TV. They do whatever they want. He has no idea what goes on in the dayrooms."

"And *you* have no idea what you're talking about," Dr. Baldwin said. "It is my *job* to know exactly what goes on in every building. That's why the nurses and attendants report to me every day. Isn't that right, Marla?"

"Yes, sir," Marla said.

Nolan held up a hand. "All right, all right. I'm only asking because I wondered if Miss Winters had somehow read about the other victims we've found and that's how she . . ." He dropped his eyes to the ground and trailed off, finishing the thought inside his head, if at all. Then he looked up at them again. "It's the same MO."

"Other victims?" Suddenly light-headed, Sage looked around for a log or tree stump to sit on, but there were none nearby.

"Yes," Detective Nolan said. "We've found three other women in the same condition over the last couple of weeks on the island. As a matter of fact, not far from here." He addressed Dr. Baldwin. "So unless Miss Winters has been leaving the premises on a regular basis, I don't see how your theory that she has something to do with this has a leg to stand on."

"Who knows what's she's been doing?" Dr. Baldwin said. "I've never had a resident give us this much trouble."

"With all due respect, Doctor, that seems like a bit of a contradiction. A minute ago, you were adamant that you know everything that goes on inside Willowbrook, but now you're saying you don't know what Miss Winters has been doing. So which is it?"

"That's not what I—" Dr. Baldwin started, then took a deep breath. "I mean that she's been exceptionally underhanded and deceitful."

Sage nearly went limp with relief. Finally, someone was challenging Dr. Baldwin's authority instead of believing everything he said. Finally, she seemed to have someone who could help on her side.

On the other side of the clearing, twigs snapped in the woods, drawing everyone's attention in that direction. A few seconds later, a handful of cops came out of the trees, along with a man in a black jacket with the word CORONER across the back. A cop with a German shepherd on a leash began checking the area outside of the police tape, forcing Sage, Marla, Dr. Baldwin, and Detective Nolan to step out of the way. Then three men in business suits and long coats came to the edge of clearing, their shiny shoes slipping and sliding on the mud and snow. Anger, confusion, and something that looked like fear lined their faces. As if on cue, gray clouds started to gather in the sky, darkening the already dim day.

"Who are they?" Nolan asked.

"Administration." Dr. Baldwin sounded defeated. "And the king of Willowbrook, Dr. Hammond."

The men in business suits began to enter the clearing, but a man in jeans and hiking boots pushed his way past them, went under the police tape, and ran toward Evie's makeshift grave. A cop stepped in front of him to block his way.

"And that," Dr. Baldwin said, his voice sounding even more miserable, "is Evie's husband, Dr. Douglas Carter, Willowbrook's program director."

"Shit," said Detective Nolan. "Stay here." He ducked under the police tape and went over to Dr. Carter, who was struggling to get past the cop blocking his way. Realizing that he was Eddie's uncle, Sage looked for some resemblance. They had the same dark hair, but from this distance it was hard to tell if he and Eddie shared any other features, especially because Dr. Carter's face was contorted with agony. After putting a firm hand on Dr. Carter's shoulder and speaking to him briefly, Nolan nodded once at the cop, who stepped aside. When the doctor saw his dead wife, he clutched his hair and made a sound deep in his throat, a low, flat moan of despair that nearly made Sage cry. Then he fell to his knees, his arms loose at his sides, and gaped down at her body, stunned and heartbroken and sobbing.

Nolan returned to Sage, Dr. Baldwin, and Marla just as the men in business suits and muddy shoes reached them. The first man glowered at Dr. Baldwin, then addressed Detective Nolan.

"Would someone like to tell me what's going on here?" he said, his voice firm with authority.

"And you are?"

"Dr. Hammond, head of administration."

"Well, Dr. Hammond," Nolan said, "we found a recently deceased female on Willowbrook property and we believe she was murdered. She was one of your employees."

"It's my secretary," Baldwin said. "Evie Carter."

Hammond's face went dark. "Wasn't her husband involved in that trouble with Wilkins and the parents' association?" he said.

Dr. Baldwin nodded. "Yes, and I have reason to believe Dr. Wilkins is responsible for the reporters breaking into House Six."

"Good Lord," Hammond said. "Do you have proof?"

"No." Dr. Baldwin glanced at Sage. "But I'm sure Dr. Carter can enlighten us."

"Excuse me, gentlemen," Nolan said, sounding irritated. "But right now you have more pressing matters that need your attention. I suggest you concentrate on the fact that one of your employees has been found murdered in the woods surrounding your institution."

"Yes, yes, of course, Detective," Dr. Hammond said. Then he pointed at Sage as if noticing her for the first time. "Why is this resident out here, by the way? What does she have to do with this?

And why am I paying an attendant to be out here with her?"

"I found my sister's body in the tunnels," Sage said. "She was a resident here who went missing. But I bet Dr. Baldwin didn't tell you about that."

Hammond glared at Baldwin. "What on earth is she talking about?"

Before Baldwin could reply, Dr. Carter came rushing toward him, yelling, "What did you do to her?" He tore under the police tape and reached for him, his face twisted in fury and grief.

Dr. Baldwin blanched and took a step back, nearly falling in the snow, but Marla caught him before he went down. Nolan grabbed Dr. Carter and held him back, gripping the lapel of his sport coat. Carter fought to get free of him, his arms flailing, his hands in claws. "I'm going to kill you!" he raged. "I know you were fucking her! I *know* you were! I'm going to kill you for what you did!"

Baldwin shook his head and glanced nervously at his colleagues. "I have no idea what he's talking about. I didn't have anything to do with this."

While Dr. Baldwin continued to make excuses, two cops rushed over, grabbed Carter, and dragged him away. At the other side of the clearing, they shoved him down and made him sit in the snow. "Don't make me cuff you," one of them said.

When Carter put his head in his hands and started to sob, the cops let go. Despite knowing nothing about the man, Sage wanted to go over there and comfort him, to let him know he was not alone in his grief and promise him she'd do her best to find Evie's killer because he had murdered her sister too. But it would have to wait.

Nolan addressed Hammond, pulling his attention away from the spectacle. "I know you have a lot of questions about Miss Winters and Evie Carter," he said. "And I'll explain everything once we're finished here and I have more answers. I have some questions for you too. So for now, I just need to know where to find you."

Dr. Hammond looked down his nose at the detective. Clearly he was not accustomed to being put off. "My office is in the administration building," he said. "Top floor. If I'm not there you can find me at my residence, the two-story Victorian at the far end of the Willowbrook campus."

"Got it," Nolan said. "And as part of the investigation, I'll need a statement from you."

"I'm not sure how I can help. But I'm willing to cooperate."

"I'll need one from each of you too," Nolan said, turning to Baldwin and Sage. Then he looked up at the sky, scowling at the gathering clouds. "Now if you'll excuse me, Dr. Hammond,

I need to wrap this up before the weather changes again."

"I'll leave you to it then," Dr. Hammond said. "But I expect a full report. On everything." He shot Baldwin a livid glance.

"I'll share what I can as soon as I can." Detective Nolan ducked back under the police tape and returned to the crime scene, leaving Dr. Hammond standing in the snow, annoyed and confused.

Hammond turned to Baldwin, his face pinched. "I'll expect you to stop at my office too. And for your sake, I hope you didn't have anything to do with bringing more unwanted attention to my institution." Then he turned and left the clearing, picking his way out through the wet slush. The other men followed.

After they were gone, Sage, Dr. Baldwin, and Marla silently watched the coroner photograph the body, while two other cops combed the surrounding woods. When paramedics arrived carrying a stretcher, one went over to Dr. Carter—who was still sitting in the snow, white-faced and silent—and wrapped a blanket around his shoulders. After glancing over at Carter, Nolan caught sight of Sage and the others, shook his head, and returned to where they stood.

"I'm sorry," he said. "I was in such a hurry to get away from Dr. Hammond I forgot to say you don't need to stay out here any longer. I'll report back as soon as we're finished." Then he looked at Sage. "Are you okay?"

"Me?" she said, surprised to hear someone sound genuinely concerned about her.

"Yes," Detective Nolan said. "You."

She tried to think. *Was* she okay? If only she knew. Detective Nolan seemed like he was starting to believe her story about Rosemary after she'd described Evie's injuries, but what did he really think? That she was telling the truth? That she was lying about killing Evie? How could she prove anything without her poor sister's body? And along with everything else, if the killer realized she and Eddie were onto him, they could be next. There were no words to explain the storm of emotions inside her head, so she just nodded.

"Are you sure?" he said. "You're white as a sheet. You might be going into shock."

Suddenly one of the cops yelled, "Over here!"

Sage jumped, startled, and everyone looked in that direction. At the far end of the clearing, near a tangled mass of grapevines and sumac just outside the police tape, the German shepherd was digging through the snow and dirt. Two cops ran over to see what was going on, then hurried back to get shovels out of their equipment bags. Nolan rushed over to where the German shepherd was digging, then turned and yelled over his shoulder, "We got another one!"

Sage went rigid. Another what? Another body?

When the coroner headed over to Detective Nolan, she knew. She started around the outside of the police tape, her legs suddenly elastic. She'd taken only a few steps when Marla grabbed her by the arm.

"Where do you think you're going?" Marla said.

"Let me go," Sage said. "I need to see who it is."

Marla looked back at Dr. Baldwin, a question on her face.

"It's all right," he said, sounding weary. "She won't get anywhere with all these cops around."

Sage pulled away and hurried toward the far end of the clearing, slipping in the slush and tripping over brambles and dead logs. When she neared the grapevines and sumac where the cops were still digging, she slowed. What if it was a little kid? What if the cops had stumbled upon a graveyard of Cropsey's—or Wayne's—victims? What if the dog was wrong, and it was nothing but a dead deer? Shaking, she gathered the coat tighter around her waist and edged close to Detective Nolan. When he turned and saw her, he gently guided her backward, but not before she saw a pale arm in the icy dirt.

"Just hold on," he said. "I'll let you know when, or if, you can look."

After what seemed like an eternity, the cops

finished digging and backed away to make room for Nolan and the coroner. She thought she'd scream waiting for the detective to say something. Finally, he turned toward her, his face unreadable, and motioned her forward. She put a hand over her stomach, certain her insides were falling out, then walked up to the mound of mud and sticks and peered over the edge.

When she saw who was lying like a discarded rag doll inside the shallow grave, she fell to her knees.

CHAPTER 19

Waiting beside Sergeant Clark outside the morgue, Sage shivered and looked through the top half of the doors at the stainless steel autopsy table and the counter filled with bottles of embalming fluid. Even out in the tunnel, the sickening-sweet odor of formaldehyde and warm pennies made her nauseated. Still, she wanted to go in there more than anything, to get this nightmare over with once and for all so she could get the hell out of there.

Inside the morgue, Dr. Baldwin and Detective Nolan stood in front of the storage vault with their backs to the entrance. A third man in a white coat opened a vault door and slid out a sheet-covered body on a steel slab. When Nolan turned and motioned her inside, Sergeant Clark pushed the door open and held it, waiting for her to go through. Suddenly she couldn't move. Everyone waited in silence. They probably thought she was rude or crazy, but she couldn't help it. Seeing Rosemary's mutilated corpse had been bad enough the first and second times.

"I'm sorry about this," Nolan said. "But we need an official identification."

"I cleaned her up as much as I could," said the man in the white coat.

"Just think of it as something you're doing for her," Detective Nolan said. "One last service. You just need to look at her long enough to know it's her. It'll be over in a second."

Dr. Baldwin stared at Sage with miserable eyes but said nothing.

Finally, she took a deep breath, put a hand over her nose and mouth, and entered the cold room.

"Are you ready?" Nolan said.

She nodded, still holding her breath.

The man in the white coat lifted the sheet and stepped aside. Sage's knees went weak and she instinctively grabbed the detective's arm to keep from falling.

He put his hand over hers. "Are you okay?"

She nodded again, not at all sure she was okay.

Despite further signs of decay, there was no mistaking the jagged strawberry-blond hair, just inches long, and the slender, pale face of her twin sister. Rosemary's once impossibly long eyelashes were gone, and without the caked-on clown lipstick, her lips looked like they'd been chewed on by a rat. Under the fluorescent lights of the morgue, the dark remnants of blood on her neck and the black rot on her paper-thin skin leapt out like ink on snow. It was almost more than Sage could take. She turned away, the gorge rising in her throat.

"It's her," she managed. "It's my sister, Rosemary." A band of hot sorrow tightened around her chest again and she buried her face in her hands. Detective Nolan put a hand on her back and led her out of the morgue.

Nolan glanced over his shoulder to address Dr. Baldwin, who was following them. "Looks like you've got some phone calls to make," he said, his voice flat.

Dr. Baldwin sat down hard at his desk, his forehead creased with tension, his upper lip shiny with sweat. He looked like he'd aged ten years. Detective Nolan sat on the other side opposite Sage, taking notes and asking questions, while Sergeant Clark stood next to the door, one hand on his holster as if worried someone might try something. After identifying Rosemary in the morgue, Sage had shown them the tunnel where she and Eddie found her body sitting on the stone ledge, but after a quick sweep of the area with powerful flashlights, they found nothing—no dropped knives or lost hairs, no cigarette butts or distinguishable footprints. Afterward, on the way to Baldwin's office, Nolan assured Sage he'd send in a forensics team to make sure they hadn't missed anything.

Now, Nolan regarded Dr. Baldwin with more than a hint of irritation and contempt. "Tell me again why you didn't report Rosemary missing?" he said.

"Because it wasn't the first time she'd run off

and gotten lost on campus. The last time it took us two days to figure out she was in the wrong ward. Unfortunately, due to budget cuts we're at half staff, which means we don't have enough manpower to keep track of every resident as closely as we'd like. This has happened before, multiple times, and we've been able to handle it on our own."

Nolan raised his eyebrows. "You've found dead girls in the tunnels before?"

Dr. Baldwin shook his head, more miserable than ever. "Of course not," he said. "That's not what I meant at all. I meant we've had patients wander off before. But we've always found them and returned them safely to their wards. We didn't know where Miss Winters was for three days this time, so who knows what she was up to. And it had been a while between my last evaluation of Rosemary and the day when I first saw Miss . . . her sister, Sage, so I automatically assumed she'd returned, as did several of my other colleagues. Like I said, we're understaffed. The governor and medical director are always pressuring us to make room for more residents, then they make more budget cuts because they think sending bullets and guns to Vietnam is more important than—"

"Let's stay on track, shall we?"

"Yes, yes. Of course." Trying to hide his anxiety, Baldwin took a sip from the cup he'd been drinking from earlier, then grimaced when he discovered it was cold. He put the cup down, picked up a pen, and opened the center drawer to put it away. Sergeant Clark put his hand on the gun in his holster.

"Please don't reach into your desk, sir," he said.

Dr. Baldwin nodded shakily, set the pen down, and placed both hands on the blotter.

"I'll need the name of your colleagues who thought Sage was Rosemary," Nolan said.

"Initially it was Dr. Whitehall, Nurse Moore, and several attendants. But Nurse Vic, Marla, and Wayne saw Rosemary every day and they all thought the same thing. More importantly, neither Rosemary's mother nor her stepfather ever mentioned the existence of a sister. I was under the impression she was an only child. So clearly you can't fault any of us for not knowing the Winters girls were identical twins."

"Uh-huh," Nolan said, writing down the names. "I'll need to speak to all of them." He turned his attention to Sage. "When you found out your sister was missing, you immediately came here looking for her, is that right?"

She nodded. "I came on the bus the next morning, after I overheard my stepfather talking about it."

"And how long ago was that?"

Sage tried to think. It felt like she'd been trapped in this nightmare for a hundred years.

"I'm not sure what day it is now, but I arrived on December 27th."

"So fourteen days." Nolan wrote it down, then looked at Baldwin again. "And why did you move the body instead of calling the police?"

Dr. Baldwin went white. "I did no such thing."

"Then who did?"

"I can assure you I have no idea."

"And you have no idea who would want to harm Rosemary Winters or Evie Carter?"

"Of course not."

Nolan looked at Sage again. "What about you? Do you have any idea who would want to harm your sister?"

"Like I said before, the only person I can think of is Wayne. I'm pretty sure he was having sex with her against her will. I also found out he's been having sex with one of the other residents from Ward D. Her name is Norma. And who knows how many others. He has plenty of opportunities to do whatever he wants. He's alone with the residents all the time."

"Do you have proof that he's having sex with a resident?"

"No, but I can show you a hidden room in the seclusion area. Norma took me there and told me what he was doing to her."

Nolan eyed Dr. Baldwin. "Did you know about this?"

"Miss Winters mentioned it, but I thought she was either lying or making it up."

"I need you to take me to see Wayne as soon as we're done here."

"Whatever you say," Dr. Baldwin said.

"Same with that Eddie King we talked about earlier," Detective Nolan continued. He pulled a pack of Camels out of his coat pocket, lit one, and addressed Sage. "How well did you know this Eddie King?"

"I met him the day after I got here. I think that's when it was anyway. And we talked a few times. That's it."

"But you knew him well enough to go down into the basement with him?"

"He was going to help me escape."

Detective Nolan took a drag of his cigarette, eyeing her through the smoke. "Why would he do that?"

"Because he knew I was Rosemary's twin and I didn't belong here."

"He *caught* her trying to escape," Dr. Baldwin interrupted. "He wasn't helping her."

Nolan shot him an irritated glance, then returned his attention to Sage. "Was he having a relationship with your sister?"

"As far as I can tell," she said, "I think they were just friends."

"How exactly does someone who mops the floors become friends with a resident?"

She frowned at him. "What do you mean? Have you looked around here? Have you been inside House Six?"

He shook his head.

"Well, maybe you should do that before asking me a question like that," she said. "Then you'll understand why my sister looked for whatever bit of kindness she could find in this hellhole."

"I'm sorry," the detective said. "But if I'm going to find your sister's killer, I need to ask questions like that."

She dropped her eyes, heat crawling up her neck. He was on her side and she was beyond grateful, but unless someone spent a day locked up in Willowbrook, they'd never understand that the residents were not only fighting for their sanity behind these walls, they were fighting for their lives. Luckily, he seemed unfazed by her outburst.

He turned to Baldwin again. "Why didn't you listen to her and this Eddie King when they said they found a body in the tunnels? That sounds like something you should have paid closer attention to."

"As I said before, a news crew had broken into House Six that day. They were filming the residents, and the reporter was saying terrible things about the conditions. The next thing I know, she and Eddie were coming across the yard toward House Six, telling me they found a body.

I'd be lying if I said I was thinking rationally right then."

"What about when you talked to Sage the second time and she insisted?"

"I didn't believe her, of course, because I thought she was . . . well, I thought she *was* Rosemary. As a side note, she keeps saying Eddie helped her into the tunnels, but he said he caught her down there. All I know for sure is that I do my best to run a tight ship around here and the last thing I needed was a scandal. I would have called the police if there had been an actual body in the tunnels. But there wasn't. So what was I supposed to think?"

"But why didn't you check it out right away instead of waiting?"

"I already told you, I was trying to deal with the reporters showing up. I was making phone calls to the administrators of Willowbrook and the heads of the news stations, trying to find out if and when they were airing the story. By the time I got down there, the body had already been moved."

Someone knocked hard on the door. "Oh, for Christ's sake," Dr. Baldwin said. "What is it?"

Sergeant Clark stepped aside and Nurse Vic entered. When she saw Nolan and Clark, her eyes widened, but she quickly put on her professional face and announced why she was there.

"Excuse me, Dr. Baldwin, I'm sorry to bother

you, but Wayne Myers from House Six seems to have disappeared."

Dr. Baldwin's face fell. "What do you mean, disappeared?"

"He's emptied his locker and left, sir. He's gone."

Sage's heartbeat quickened. She'd been right all along.

"Is that the attendant you were talking about?" Nolan asked her.

She nodded.

"Shit," said Baldwin and Nolan at the same time.

"How long ago did he leave?" Nolan said.

"We're not sure," Nurse Vic said. "When I entered the dayroom in House Six to speak to him about something, he wasn't there. The residents had been left without supervision for who knows how long and they were in a frenzy. Three of them had to be sent to the infirmary."

"Wonderful," Dr. Baldwin said, his voice filled with gloom. "Did you get another attendant over there to cover for him?"

"Yes, sir. We took care of that right away."

"And the residents are under control?"

"For now, yes. But I'm afraid we had to send them back to their wards and sedate quite a number of them."

"All right. Thank you, Nurse Vic. I'll be over as soon as I'm finished here."

"Yes, Doctor," she said, and left the office.

After the nurse left, Sage turned to Nolan. "I told you it was him."

Flustered and red-faced, Baldwin started gathering the papers on his desk. "As you can see, Detective, I'm a very busy man. I need to check on things over at House Six right away. Can we finish this later?"

"I can see that you're busy," Detective Nolan said. "But one of your employees was murdered and her husband, who also happens to be an employee, seems to think you had something to do with it. Now a third employee has disappeared on the same day we found two bodies on Willowbrook property, which means I need to take a look at that employee's records so I can send someone to check out his residence. In the meantime, you need to call Miss Winters's stepfather and let him know what's happened here. Then you can sign her release papers. Now that her sister's body has been found, there's no need to hold her here any longer." He looked Sage. "Do you feel strong enough to go home?"

A burning lump formed in Sage's throat. At long last, she was getting out of Willowbrook. It felt like being rescued after a thousand days lost at sea. But she'd seen too many movies where things went wrong at the last minute. She wouldn't believe the nightmare was over until she was on the other side of the gate. And it wouldn't have mattered if she felt weak as a kitten or sick as a dog, she never would have said so. She refused to stay one second longer than necessary.

"Yes," she managed. "I feel fine."

"Are you positive? You've been through quite an ordeal. I'm sure Dr. Baldwin could ask one of his colleagues to examine you before you leave."

She shook her head. "No, I'm perfectly healthy. I just need to get out of here."

"Do you want your stepfather to pick you up, or would you rather have one of my officers take you home?"

"Please have someone take me home. I want to leave as soon as possible."

"All right. Dr. Baldwin will call your stepfather to let him know you're coming, and—"

Sage interrupted. "I don't know if he's home, and he won't care anyway. I'm used to taking care of myself."

Dr. Baldwin fixed weary eyes on her. "I want you to know I'm sorry about everything that happened here. I meant no harm to you or anyone else. I thought I was doing the right thing. And as soon as I get Rosemary's death certificate from the coroner, I'll send it to your stepfather and add a copy to her file."

Maybe it was her imagination, but the remorse in his voice sounded phony. Considering he was a man who allowed so many to suffer under his watch, his deceit didn't surprise her, but she could also tell he was scared. Scared of what would happen when word got out about the murders. Scared of what she might do to him for keeping her there against her will. Maybe she could sue him for everything he was worth. She wanted to ask if that was all he had to say to her, but she didn't have the energy. She just wanted to go home. Knowing he was afraid would have to be enough—for now.

Changing the subject, Baldwin turned to Nolan and said, "You wanted to see Wayne's employee record?"

"Yes, I need his address."

Baldwin looked at Sergeant Clark to make sure he wouldn't grab his gun again, then stood and went to the black filing cabinets behind him and pulled open one of the drawers.

While the doctor's back was turned, Nolan dropped his cigarette butt into the cold cup of coffee on Baldwin's desk.

After a quick search, Dr. Baldwin pulled out a folder, sat back down, and opened it. As he thumbed through the papers inside, he wrinkled his brow, his face getting redder by the second.

"Is there a problem, Doctor?" Detective Nolan said.

"I'm afraid so," Baldwin said. "Wayne Myers's employee record is missing."

CHAPTER 20

By the time Sage was officially released, the pale sun had dropped lower in the sky, and the gray clouds from earlier had been replaced by the deep, cold blue of the coming winter dusk. Dr. Baldwin had called Alan earlier to tell him about Rosemary, but got no answer, which was no surprise. He was probably at work—unless he'd skipped town and left her without a place to live. Maybe he was shacked up with some floozy or still fishing with Larry, which seemed unlikely but would have been fine by her. She'd give anything to have a few days alone in the apartment before she had to deal with him.

Standing next to Detective Nolan inside the main foyer of the administration building, watching for the cop car that would finally take her home, she felt like a hundred years had passed since she had come through the same doors looking for Rosemary. When the black and white car finally pulled up to the curb, she choked back tears. She was actually leaving Willowbrook. She started to open the door, then hesitated and looked up at Detective Nolan.

"Thank you for listening to me," she said, her voice catching.

"No problem, kiddo. I'd take you home myself, but I still need to talk to Dr. Hammond and Eddie King."

"I know," she said. "But I'll be fine. Tell Eddie thanks for me, will you?"

He nodded. "Sure thing. Just stick around the island, okay? We'll need to talk to you again in the next couple of days." He dug in his jacket pocket and handed her a card with his name and phone number. "And give me a call if you need anything or remember anything that might help, okay?"

She nodded, pushed open the door, and walked out of Willowbrook. She stopped briefly on the top step and took a deep breath, never more grateful to be outside in the fresh air. Somehow, it seemed as though she could smell *everything*—the cold wetness of the snow and the earthy aroma of bare tree limbs, even the pavement on the roads. A cool breeze caressed her face, bringing with it the noises of traffic in the distance, engines running, tires humming, horns honking. More tears sprang to her eyes as she went down the stone steps, hurried along the sidewalk, and climbed into the back of the cop car without looking back. The cop in the front briefly put his hand to his nose as if smelling something bad, then looked at her in the rearview mirror.

"I'm Officer Minor," he said. "You doing all right?"

She nodded, wondering why he'd put his hand to his nose. Then she realized she probably smelled bad. Dr. Baldwin had called someone in laundry to bring her a clean outfit—a flowered dress and a pair of brown leather shoes that looked like they belonged to someone's grand-mother—and she had thrown out her filthy underwear and bra, but she was still wearing the coat from Eddie, which was stained with dirt and blood and shit, and her hair was matted and filthy.

"Detective Nolan said you're going to Green-way Apartments over in Mariners Harbor," the cop said. "Is that right?"

"Yes."

"Okay. You got it." He put the car in gear and drove away from the administration building.

She sat back in the seat and gazed out the win-dow, praying the officer wouldn't try to make conversation. She had nothing to say and no energy to say it. She just wanted to go home. Outside the car window, the row of bare willow trees along the frozen stream bent toward the earth as if hanging their heads in shame for being part of the beautiful campus that hid Willow-brook's terrible secrets. Then came the brick houses with swing sets and monkey bars outside, and Sage looked away, unable to stop thinking about the young children living tortured lives behind those dark walls.

When Officer Minor drove the vehicle into the wooded area between the campus and the main gate, she thought back to the day she'd arrived. It seemed like another lifetime ago, when she had been another person. Gone were the days of caring about hairstyles and the latest fashions, or worrying about who was dating who and keeping up with the most popular music. How could she ever look at life the same way again?

If only she'd stayed on the bus that day. If only she'd swallowed her pride, gone back home, and asked Heather and Dawn for help. Except, except . . . She had wanted to save her sister more than anything in the world. She'd wanted to find out where she was and make everything up to her, to apologize for not knowing she'd been sent away, for not coming to see her, and for not helping her get better. She'd been naïve and hopeful and bold. How could she fault herself for that?

Or maybe she'd just been stupid.

As they passed through the rest of the woods, she remembered how she'd thought of her father that day too, how he would have loved all the trees and wildlife, how he never would have sent Rosemary away. What would he think if he knew one of his daughters was dead? What would he think if he knew all the agony Rosemary had suffered? Surely he would be furious and heartbroken. If only she knew where to find him.

Then she remembered Alan. How was she going to face him after what he'd done? How was she going to live in the same apartment?

She took a deep breath and tried to clear her thoughts. Right now she needed a shower, a change of clothes, and sleep. She was on her way home and that was enough. She would figure everything else out later. Like how she would deal with Alan, if he was still around. How she would tell her friends what happened. How she would find the strength to go on living a normal life.

When they passed the guardhouse at Willowbrook's main gate, the guard gave them a friendly wave, like a carnival worker outside a haunted ride, smiling to hide the horrors inside. Then a sudden realization hit her. At least she was getting out. At least she had a chance to live a normal life. The days and weeks ahead might be difficult, but they would be nothing compared to what Rosemary and the thousands of poor souls locked inside Willowbrook suffered day after day after day. They never stood a chance. She wiped her flooding eyes. How could life be so unfair? How could God let anyone, let alone innocent children, live lives full of nothing but suffering? It was incomprehensible.

When they'd driven far enough away from Willowbrook to return to civilization, to houses and businesses and traffic lights, to people on the shoveled sidewalks and cars on the plowed streets, to miniature lights twinkling on manicured trees and landscaped bushes, tears filled her eyes a second time. She'd thought she'd never see those things again.

Before going to Willowbrook, she'd hated it when she and her friends sometimes had no money for a cab and they had to walk to wherever they were going. But thinking about it now, she remembered how they'd laugh and talk about boys and parties, the briny ocean breeze rippling through their hair. She would never walk down a sidewalk again without giving thanks that she was free to do it. Then again, how could she— or anyone else—go on with their lives, working and getting married and playing and shopping, with the horror of Willowbrook only a few miles away? She watched the pedestrians pass by the car window: the man with the white dog on a pink leash; the young couple holding hands and laughing, their breath pluming out in the cold air; the gray-haired lady carrying a mesh bag full of oranges. Didn't they know people were being abused in that place? Didn't they know people were dying there every day? Didn't they care?

Just then, a bald man hurried past the gray-haired woman, bumping into her shoulder and nearly knocking her over. The woman stopped and found her footing, but the man kept going without even stopping to see if she was okay.

Sage drew in a sharp breath and slumped down in the seat, her heart suddenly ricocheting in her chest. The bald man looked like Wayne. What if he knew she'd been released from Willowbrook? What if he was out to get her? Coming for her, to cut her throat and shut her up? She craned her neck and peered at the man as they drove past, then sat back again and let out a sigh of relief. It wasn't him. Her imagination had run away with her.

When Officer Minor turned a corner and stopped at a red light, a van pulled up beside them and she was sure it was Wayne in the driver's seat, staring back at her with menacing, hostile eyes. She closed her eyes until the car started moving again, then looked up and down the sidewalk and road, eyeing the other pedestrians and drivers, scanning them one by one. He could be tailing her, a sharp knife in his pocket, waiting to make his move. It only made sense that he would want her dead. She had told everyone about the secret room and Norma, and that she thought he had killed Rosemary—and Evie too. It only made sense that he would want her to pay.

By the time Officer Minor stopped in front of her apartment building, she was a bundle of nerves. Wayne was everywhere. He was the man in the baseball cap and leather jacket, the man walking into the liquor store, the man knocking on the neighbor's door. Paranoia had taken hold of her, but she couldn't help it. She opened the car door, slid off the seat, and stood on trembling legs. Officer Minor got out too.

"Detective Nolan wants me to walk you up," he said.

She nodded, relieved she didn't have to ask, then looked up and down the street. Alan's truck was nowhere to be seen, unless he'd found a spot in the crowded parking lot behind the apartment buildings, which seemed unlikely. She glanced at the kitchen window in their apartment. The curtains were drawn and the window was dark, which meant he was gone. Because despite his habit of leaving the TV on all night, he was a stickler about shutting off lights. She breathed a sigh of relief.

If she was really lucky, he had stopped for drinks after work and wouldn't come home until late. Right now it was early enough that she didn't think he'd be passed out yet; if he was, the deadbolt and chain would be secured and she wouldn't be able to get in. Then she remembered that her apartment key was in her stolen purse.

"Shit," she said.

"Is there a problem?" Officer Minor said.

"I don't have a key and my stepfather is still at work. I'll have to ask the super if he can unlock the door."

As if on cue, a window curtain moved to one side in the superintendent's apartment, then fell back into place. At least she wouldn't have to knock on his door. Once he saw the police car, he'd meet them in the lobby, like he had done that time the cops brought her home after Dawn broke her ankle peeing in the sink at a dive bar downtown. Sage had lied to him then, saying there had been a fight at the bowling alley and the cops brought her home just to make sure she was all right. Luckily, he'd believed her and never mentioned the incident to Alan.

As predicted, the super was waiting in the lobby, wearing sweatpants, a sleeveless T-shirt, and ratty slippers. When he saw Sage's filthy coat and matted hair, his mouth fell open.

"What the hell happened to you?" he said.

"Alan can tell you later," she said. "Can you let me into my apartment? I lost my key."

"You in some kind of trouble? Alan said you been visiting his sister up in Long Island for a while. Said you two weren't gettin' along too well."

Of course he did. And if anyone had called or stopped by asking for her, he'd probably told them the same thing. But Heather and Dawn should have known he was lying. They should have known she'd gone to Willowbrook to look for Rosemary—unless they hadn't called at all. Unless they'd just gone on with their lives.

"You can't believe everything Alan tells you," she said. "He doesn't even have a sister." And then, filled with a sudden sense of reckless-ness, she added, "I was kidnapped."

The super gaped at Officer Minor, eyes bulging. "That true?"

"I'm only escorting her home," he said. "I don't know the details of the incident."

"Can you just let me into the apartment?" she said.

"Alan working today?" the super said. "I ain't seen him in a few days."

"Must be," she said. "Unless he's not back from his fishing trip yet." *Or he's shacking up with some floozy.*

"Is that where he went?"

She frowned. "I thought . . . You told a friend of mine he went ice fishing with Larry."

He shrugged again. "I ain't talked to nobody about nothing. One thing about me is I mind my own business."

"Uh-huh," she said, sarcasm in her voice. It was hard to tell if he had forgotten about talking to Eddie, or if he was playing dumb in front of Officer Minor. Considering his past and the shady-looking friends he often had over, she sus-pected the latter.

"Are you sure you didn't tell someone he went on a fishing trip?" she said. "A young guy with dark hair? I'm sure he said you were the one who told him."

"Oh, wait," the super said. "Yeah, I remember

him now. Good-lookin' kid. But that was a while ago. He and Larry came back, but I didn't see no fish." He laughed. "Maybe they went fishing for something besides perch and pike."

"Can you just unlock my door please?" she said.

"Oh, sure. Hang on." He disappeared inside his apartment.

She glanced at Officer Minor. "Sorry about this."

"It's no problem."

Finally, the super came out and gave her a key. "I need it back," he said. "So find yours by tomorrow morning."

She thought about telling him it had been stolen, but it was too much to explain. And it didn't matter right now anyway. "I'll try," she said, turning toward the stairs that led up to the fourth floor.

"Was it Cropsey who grabbed you?" he said, his voice filled with enthusiasm. "How'd you get away?"

She stopped and looked back at him, a remark about minding his own business on the tip of her tongue. Instead, she said, "No, it wasn't Cropsey. They found my sister and let me go."

"Who's they? And what sister?"

She let out a heavy sigh. She didn't have the energy for this. Then she remembered he'd never met Rosemary. He got the job in the building after she'd died. *No. After she was locked up.* "You wouldn't believe me if I told you," she said, and started up the stairs.

"You kids and your crazy stories," he called after her. "Someday they'll get you in trouble, you'll see. Isn't that right, Officer?"

Officer Minor said nothing and followed Sage up the steps. When they reached her apartment, he stood silently behind her while she unlocked the door. Praying again that Alan wasn't passed out inside, that the deadbolt and chain would be undone, she turned the key. With more than a little relief, she pushed the door open.

"You okay from here?" Officer Minor said.

"I think so," she said. "Thank you."

He smiled and gave her a two-fingered salute, then turned and went nimbly down the stairs and out the door. Once she was certain he was gone, she took off the filthy coat and left it on the hallway floor, refusing to wear it inside, then entered the apartment and switched on the foyer light. After closing the door behind her, she locked it and slid the deadbolt and chain into place, then took off the leather shoes, wiped her feet on the worn doormat, and made her way toward the living room, turning on lights as she went.

The thick, familiar odor of stale beer and cigarette smoke filled the air, mixed with something that smelled like old cheese. Alan had always

391

been a slob, but the apartment looked and smelled worse than ever. Beer cans and pizza boxes and take-out containers filled the coffee table. Crumpled pants and shirts lay strewn over the couch and recliner. After pulling the living room curtains closed, she moved farther into the apartment. At the door to the kitchen, a foul smell wafted into the hall. Something must have spoiled while Alan was gone ice fishing and, like everything else, he had just let it go.

Still, even with the mess and the smell, the apartment felt like paradise compared to Willow-brook. She made her way to the bathroom, anxious to take a long, hot shower and wash her hair. Then she reached Alan's bedroom door and froze. He was lying on his side in the double bed, crumpled into a crescent-shaped mound like a washed-up seal on a beach. *Shit.* He *was* home. But why was he in bed? Normally he passed out in the living room and slept on the couch until morning. Maybe he was sick.

Squinting, she peered into the dim room, praying he was asleep. Then her shoulders dropped in relief. What she had thought was Alan was just the dirty sheet and worn comforter, twisted into a gray pile.

Shaking off her nerves, she went into the closet-size bathroom at the end of the hall, turned on the water in the mold-speckled shower, and relieved herself in the toilet. After stripping out of the dress from Willowbrook and dropping it into the wastebasket, she stepped into the shower and let the stream run over her shoulders and back. The water was hot, the kind of hot that made goose bumps rise on her arms, but it felt like silk on her grimy skin. She tipped her head back and nearly gagged when her nostrils filled with the sour stench of Willowbrook seeping out of her hair like a cloying, heavy perfume. She grabbed a half-empty bottle of Prell shampoo, relieved Alan hadn't used it all up, and squeezed a heaping pile of it into her palm.

Using both hands, she lathered her head, scratching at her scalp to get at the dirt, pressing and rubbing and massaging until gobs of suds slid down her body. Then she rinsed her hair and washed it again, taking deliberate, deep breaths to fill her nose with the floral perfume of the shampoo. While the lather worked on her head, she scrubbed every inch of her body and face with Dial soap and a washcloth until her skin was nearly raw.

She could tell she'd lost weight. Her legs and arms felt hard where they used to be soft; her stomach was shallow and almost sunken. Purple and yellow bruises covered her elbows and knees; scratches and scrapes and scabbed-over cuts marked her skin. She couldn't remember getting the injuries, but that was no surprise. While imprisoned, her mind had been in overdrive, frantic to survive and escape, while her body had no choice but to endure the everyday grind of rough hands grabbing and pulling and yanking on her arms and torso and head, while her feet and legs took the brunt of stumbling and falling over herself and others as they were herded from the wards to the halls to the dayroom and back again, like animals being led to slaughter.

Closing her eyes, she tipped her head back again, and ran her hands through her hair to get out all the soap, Suddenly an image of Rosemary flashed in her mind: her strawberry-blond hair chopped into ragged chunks, her red-painted lips, the black stripes of blood running down her breasts and belly. She gasped, accidentally inhaling water and shampoo, and was overcome by dizziness. Her knees gave out and she grabbed the shower curtain, slapping a hand on the tile wall to keep herself upright. When she thought she could let go, she straightened, but vertigo hit her again and she bent over and retched into the shower, choking and spitting what little amount of liquefied food was in her stomach into the drain.

Finally, the spinning sensation stopped, but grief and gravity threatened to pull her to the shower floor. With one hand on the wall to keep from falling, she finished rinsing herself off and got out, abandoning her plan to shave her legs. After drying off, she wrapped herself in a towel and used a wide-toothed comb to rake the snarls out of her hair. The comb caught and pulled, caught and pulled, but she kept working at it, exhausted but determined to get it over with.

With every gob of hair that ripped free from her head and fell to the bathroom floor, her anger grew. She was furious with Alan and her mother. And Dr. Baldwin. And Wayne. And everyone who worked at Willowbrook. She was even mad at Noah and Heather and Dawn. Every one of them had changed the course of her and Rosemary's lives with their decisions. And there was nothing at all she could do about it.

Maybe she should leave—get off this island, as far away from Willowbrook as possible. There was nothing here for her now. And she didn't want to spend the rest of her life looking over her shoulder for Wayne. Or Cropsey. Or whoever had killed Rosemary and Evie. Her father was still somewhere in New York State. Maybe she could call information and ask for his phone number, starting with the neighborhoods in New York City. If that didn't work, she could pawn the gold necklace and diamond earrings Alan had given her mother when they were dating—if they were real, and if Alan hadn't already sold them—and hire a private investigator to find him. Once she told her father what happened, he wouldn't turn her away, she was sure of it. Yes, Detective Nolan had warned her not to leave, but she had his phone number. She could check in with him to see if they'd found any clues, or if he wanted to ask her more questions. Not that it mattered. Rosemary was dead. That was all she knew and all she could deal with right now.

In her bedroom, she switched on the ceiling light and looked around, her tangerine and lime-green bedspread so bright it almost hurt her eyes. Everything was exactly as she had left it, from the Rolling Stones and the Doors posters on her walls to the lava lamp on her dresser. Except it all belonged to a different girl: a girl who thought having a shitty stepfather was the worst thing in the world; a girl who had hope for the future; a girl who, despite her experiences, thought most humans were good. That girl was gone now. Who knew what kind of girl was going to replace her?

After pulling down the shade on her window and closing the curtains, she switched on her bedside lamp and turned off the ceiling light. At her dresser, she sprayed Wind Song perfume on her legs and stomach and arms and hair, certain that the stench of Willowbrook had seeped into her every crease and pore. Then she put on a pair of sweatpants and a sweatshirt. She knew it would probably be a good idea to eat something, but she was too tired to even think about food. And judging by all the take-out containers in the living room, Alan hadn't bought groceries anyway.

After pulling back her bedcovers and lying down, she reached for the bedside lamp to turn it off. But she couldn't do it. She wouldn't be able to push the nightmarish images away in the darkness. She left the light on, closed her eyes, and put her head on the pillow, her body sinking into the mattress as if her bones weighed a thousand pounds.

More than anything, she longed to escape into sleep, to turn off her mind and disappear into oblivion. Figuring out what to do next could wait until morning.

But her mind had other ideas.

Her heart floundered at the most innocent noises: the click of the numbers changing on her bedside clock, a neighbor's door closing out in the hall, the rattle of her window. She sat up, rearranged her pillows, and lay back down. Maybe she should call Heather or Dawn and tell them what had happened. Maybe she should ask if she could stay with one of them for a few days, just until she figured out her next move. Wayne would never look for her there. Then she imagined the looks on their faces when they learned the truth and her anger rose again. They'd done nothing to help her back when she needed it; why would they help her now? Even if Alan had lied to them about her visiting his nonexistent sister, they should have known better. Calling them would be pointless.

And they were probably out partying anyway.

After tossing and turning for what felt like hours, exhaustion finally pushed her into a restless, troubled sleep filled with nightmares and disturbing images. Sometime later she sat up in bed midscream, her blankets clutched to her chest, certain Wayne was lurking in a shadowy corner of the room, ready to slide a knife across her throat. When she realized she was alone, she fell back on the pillows, breathing hard, and looked over at her bedside clock. It was one o'clock in the morning.

And she was starving. Her stomach growled and twisted in on itself, a gnawing pain eating through her insides. She got up and tiptoed along the hall to Alan's bedroom door. His bed was still empty, thank God, which meant he'd likely be gone all night. She went down to the kitchen, where the musty aroma of rotten garbage drifted out of the overstuffed trash can. Now that she'd washed the stench of Willowbrook from her hair and body, the sickening odor she'd noticed earlier seemed stronger than ever. Pushing back the kitchen curtains, she opened the window to let in some fresh air.

Coffee-coated mugs, soup-crusted bowls, and sauce-covered plates filled both sides of the double sink. The milk-sour refrigerator held three six-packs of Budweiser, a half gallon of curdled milk, a moldy hunk of Velveeta, and a jar of pickled eggs. She rummaged through the cupboards and found an open box of stale cereal and half a sleeve of saltines. She opened the crackers and ate one. They were stale too. She needed something substantial, like eggs and bacon and toast.

Back in her room, she counted the money in her extra makeup bag, ones and fives and quarters that she'd pilfered from Alan or found in the washing machine. Nineteen dollars. Enough to buy food and have a little left over. She pulled her hair into a loose ponytail, put on a pair of thick socks, her winter boots, and her warmest jacket, then left her bedroom and went to the apartment door. She opened the door and looked left and right down the hall. No one was there. After slipping out, she relocked the door, put the key in her jacket pocket, and moved quickly down the stairs.

Just before leaving the apartment building, she hesitated. The nearest 24-hour store was four blocks away, and it was dingy and poorly lit. Her feet felt rooted to the floor. Wayne could bump into her on the sidewalk or in the store, stab her in the neck—or whatever spot she would bleed out fastest from—and then disappear like he was never there. No one would know she'd been knifed until she fell.

She swore under her breath. She had to stop thinking like that. Wayne had no idea where she lived. Even if he did want to kill her, he'd have to find her first. That would take time. And by then she'd be gone.

She pulled her jacket hood over her head, opened the door, went down the steps, and turned left on the sidewalk. No moon hung in the black sky, no pinpricks of white starlight. Other than the snow-dusted cars parked along one side of the road, the streets were empty and quiet. She shoved her hands into her coat pockets and walked with her head down.

Behind her, the headlights of a parked car came on, pulled away from the curb on the other side of the street, and began traveling in her direction, the muffled thump of music pounding inside the vehicle. She walked faster. The car reached her and slowed, the music growing louder as if someone were rolling down one of the windows. Then the music turned down and went off. *Just what I need, some creep harassing me.* Or maybe it was Wayne. She pulled her hands from her pockets and started to jog. Her heart felt like it was going to beat out of her chest.

"Hey," a male voice called out. "Where you going?"

She glanced at the car—a red Mustang with black hubcaps and red rims; definitely not from her neighborhood. A guy leaned out the driver's side window, his hand on the outside of the door.

"Hey," he said again. "Don't run. It's just me."

She slowed and looked again. Then she stopped. It was Eddie.

"What are you doing here?" she said, trying to catch her breath. She pushed back her hood.

He stopped the car. "I thought you might need a friend," he said, flashing a quick grin.

"Why didn't you come up instead of waiting out here?" she said. "You scared the shit out of me."

"Sorry. I didn't know if your old man was home."

"So what were you going to do? Sit out here forever?"

He shrugged. "I knew you'd have to come out sooner or later. But it's the middle of the night. Where are you going?"

"To the store. I'm starving and there's nothing to eat in the apartment."

"Hop in, I'll give you a ride."

She gathered the collar of her jacket under her chin and tried to decide what to do. As much as she would have appreciated a ride in a warm, safe car, she didn't want anything more to do with anyone or anything associated with Willowbrook. It was the only way she could put the traumatic ordeal behind her—that, and getting justice for her sister, which would be hard enough. Still, she had to admit that seeing Eddie made her feel a little less lonely and a whole lot safer. "That's okay. It's only a few blocks."

"You got money?"

"Some."

"Come on. I'll drive you. Just tell me where to go and what you need."

Her eyes grew moist. What she *needed* was her sister. And her father. She *needed* to go back to the way things used to be when they were young. But that was impossible.

His face fell, as if he'd read her mind. "Dr. Baldwin told me about Rosemary. I'm sorry you had to go through that again."

She shrugged. No one could do anything about the fact that she'd had to see her sister's mutilated corpse three times. She would have to work through that on her own. "I'm sorry about your aunt Evie, too. How is your uncle doing? He was having a really hard him when I saw him at the crime scene."

He furrowed his brow. "Oh," he said. "Thanks. He's doing okay, considering."

"Did you talk to Detective Nolan yet?"

He nodded. "Yeah, but there was nothing I could tell him that you hadn't already told him."

"Did they tell you Wayne Myers ran off?"

"I heard."

"Do you think he did it?"

"Why else would he have left? I'll tell you one thing, if I ever get my hands on him, I swear I'll strangle him. Rosemary didn't deserve what he did to her. Neither did Evie. No one does."

A gust of cold wind blew along the sidewalk, rattling the tree branches and pushing the snow along the street. She lifted her hood again and turned her face away from the cold.

"Come on," he said. "Let me give you a ride. It's freezing out here."

She glanced down the block, along the dark sidewalk and empty pavement, at the patchy pools of weak light cast by the few streetlights that worked. The street was dead quiet, everyone safely ensconced in their homes. Wayne could be waiting and watching from anywhere, hiding behind a bush or parked vehicle. And the sooner she got to the store, the sooner she could get back to the locked apartment.

Sensing her surrender, Eddie put the car in park. She studied him, trying to make a decision. Right now he felt like her only friend. He'd been willing to help her escape, and he was the only person who knew what she'd been through. Not to mention he'd experienced the shock of finding Rosemary's body too. Things like that didn't happen to people every day. Neither of them would ever forget it. And if she was being honest, she still felt like the walking dead, exhaustion weighing down every muscle and bone like they were made of granite. When she started toward the car, he got out and opened the passenger door. She went around the front and got in. It felt good to sit. Her legs were unsteady, as if she'd just walked a thousand miles. She took a deep breath and let it out slowly, trying to calm down while Eddie got back in.

To her surprise, the interior of the Mustang looked brand new, with black leather seats, gold crosses and oversize dice hanging from the rearview mirror, and a shiny eight-track player mounted under the radio. When Eddie slid back in and closed the driver's side door, the scent of his cologne came with him, filling the car. She wondered if he wore extra because he, too, was haunted by the stench of Willowbrook. For the hundredth time, she asked herself how he could stand to work there.

"This is a nice car," she said, trying to act normal, feeling anything but. "Is it yours?"

He nodded.

"Did you steal it?"

"Ha ha. Very funny."

"Well, I know where you work, remember? You can't make that much money mopping floors." As soon as the words left her mouth, she regretted them. He was trying to help her, again, and she had repaid him by saying something rude.

Thankfully, he ignored the comment. "I've been saving for a car since I was old enough to know what one was," he said. "I finally bought this a few months ago." He put the car in gear, let up on the clutch, and started driving, one hand on the wheel.

"I'm sorry," she said. "I shouldn't have said that."

He let out a slight laugh. "It's fine. I'd be suspicious if I were you too. But let's not talk about me. You're the one trying to figure out how to run away."

She furrowed her brow. "I'm not running away," she said.

"Not yet," he said. "But you're planning on it."

She chewed her lip and stared out the windshield. How did he know? She could feel him glancing at her, waiting for her to say more.

"Sorry," he said. "Maybe I'm just assuming that because after everything you've told me and everything that's happened, I wouldn't blame you for wanting to get away from your stepfather. I just want you to know I'm willing to help however I can."

"The only thing I care about right now is finding out who killed Rosemary."

"I care about that too," he said.

They stopped at a red light and he peered along the shadowy street. "Where's the store you want to go to?"

"It's at the end of the next block. Johnny's Superette."

The light turned green and he released the brake and continued down the street. When they reached the superette, he slowed. A bearded man sat on the sidewalk, leaning against the ice chest next to the grimy front door and drinking from a paper bag.

"Well, that looks a little sketchy," Eddie said. "Why don't we go somewhere for breakfast instead?"

"No, this is fine. I'm just grabbing eggs and bread."

"You sure? My treat."

She started to refuse again, then hesitated. She hadn't eaten anything but a stale cracker since her last horrible meal at Willowbrook and she was starting to feel nauseated. Going to a diner would be faster than lugging food home and cooking it. Besides, a free meal was a free meal. And saving money however she could until she had a concrete plan about what to do next seemed like a good idea.

"Come on," he said. "You look like you could use someone to talk to. And a stack of pancakes with bacon." He smiled at her again, his eyes full of understanding.

"I guess that would be okay," she said. "I don't have the energy to cook anyway."

"Great," he said. "I think there's an all-night diner not far from here."

"The Top Hat?"

"Is that the name of it?"

She nodded.

He grinned, then revved the engine and drove faster. "Do you like Pink Floyd?" he said, reaching for the eight-track player.

She nodded again and tried to return the smile. She couldn't have cared less what he played.

"I saw them live in April," he said. "They were amazing."

He pushed in the eight-track and turned up the volume, then drummed on the steering wheel with one hand as they sped along the streets. Considering how reserved he'd always been at work, it was strange seeing this side of him. He'd seemed older at Willowbrook, but now she couldn't help wondering if they were closer in age. She thought about asking him, but it didn't matter. She'd probably never see him again after this, unless they had to testify at Wayne's trial.

She leaned back in the seat and looked out at the sidewalks, at the dark houses and buildings passing by. Here and there, soft lights glowed behind windows, illuminating the homes from within. She imagined families getting up in a few hours to sit at breakfast tables and have coffee and talk, to read newspapers or do last-minute homework, like she and Rosemary used to do while their parents got ready for the day. But that had been another lifetime ago, when she'd had a normal family. Now she had no one.

With that thought, a sudden swooning sensation swept over her. She grabbed the edge of the seat to steady herself, certain she was about to faint. Sweat broke out on her forehead, and her chest constricted. She couldn't breathe. The air inside the car was too thick, the music too loud. She rolled down the window and pushed her face into the rushing cold, trying not to hyperventilate.

Eddie turned down the music and slowed the car. "You okay?" he said. "What's wrong?"

She clutched at her throat. "Can you pull over for a minute?" she said. "I need . . . I just need to get out for a second."

He pulled the car over to the curb and stopped. She opened the door, jumped out, and bent over on the sidewalk, her hands on her knees. For a moment she thought she was going to be sick, but the feeling passed as quickly as it had come. Eddie got out and came around the front of the car.

"What is it?" he said. "Do you need a doctor?"

She shook her head. "No! No doctors. I'll be fine. I just couldn't catch my breath for a minute."

"After everything you've been through, it's no wonder," he said. "Are you sure you're okay?"

She straightened and wiped her fingers across her mouth, nodding. Then, suddenly roasting, she ripped off her jacket, threw it over her arm, and started down the sidewalk.

"Where are you going?" he said, following her.

She walked a few yards, then stopped, took several deep breaths, and turned back toward the car. "Nowhere. I just needed some fresh air."

He followed her back to the car and opened the

passenger's side door, concern lining his face. She climbed in and slumped down in the seat, her energy spent. Whatever that was all about, she never wanted to feel that way again. Maybe she just needed to eat something. Or maybe being locked up in Willowbrook and finding her sister murdered had messed her up for the rest of her life. She swallowed hard, wishing for water—no, wishing for schnapps, or whiskey.

When they turned into the diner parking lot, she sat up and peered over the dashboard, trying to see in the front windows. She and her friends used to come to the Top Hat after a night out. But they normally showed up around 3:00 a.m.; it was still relatively early for the drunk crowd. To her relief, no groups of late-night partiers crowded the booths. No wasted kids gathered outside the door. Only neon signs flashed inside the wide windows.

Eddie pulled the Mustang into a parking spot near the door, popped out the eight-track, and turned off the engine. "This okay?" he said.

"Yeah," she said.

"You sure? You seem on edge. I mean, I'm sure you're on edge but . . ."

"No. I mean, yes, it's fine. I'm fine. It's just, I used to come here with my friends."

"We can go somewhere else if you want."

"No, it's all right, really. I need to eat." She opened the car door, got out, and put on her coat.

He did the same, following her across the gravel lot and hurrying in front of her to open the door. The strong aromas of coffee and fried food wafted over them as they stepped inside, and a waitress wiping down the soda fountain looked up. It was Iris, one of the two waitresses who normally worked the night shift. Blinking against the bright fluorescent lights, Sage looked for the best place to sit. An old man sat at the counter eating a slice of pie à la mode, but other than that the place was deserted. She moved toward a spot at the far end of the diner and slid into a booth, her knees shaking beneath the Formica table—from anxiety or a chill, she wasn't sure. Hopefully she'd feel better after she ate. Eddie slid in across from her and pulled the menu out from behind the metal napkin holder. She did the same.

Sitting on her hands, she scanned the list of burgers and milkshakes and eggs, trying not to jump out of her skin at every little noise. The ding of the cash register, the piped-in music, the neon lights clicking on and off, the glasses and silverware clinking. Maybe this was a bad idea.

Iris appeared with a pot of coffee and turned over their cups. "Hey," she said. "You both want coffee?"

"Sure," Eddie said. "Thanks."

"Just orange . . . I mean, milk for me," Sage said. The last thing she needed was caffeine. And she'd never touch orange juice again.

Iris filled Eddie's cup, then smiled at Sage. "This your cousin?" she said.

Sage frowned. "Sorry?"

"I thought maybe this handsome young man was your cousin," Iris said. "I assumed he and your aunt came back with you from Long Island to stay for a while. You know, for support and all."

Sage's cheeks grew hot. Had Alan told everyone that lie? "Who told you that? And why would I need support?"

Iris dropped her gaze, her face flushing. "No one told me," she said. "I overheard your friends when they were in here talking about why they hadn't heard from you. They said your stepfather sent you away because you had a break . . . I mean, you needed time to get over learning the truth about your sister."

"That's not true," Sage said. "I—"

"There's no need to explain, darlin'," Iris interrupted. "It's just a shame your mother didn't tell you and Alan about sending your sister to that awful place."

Sage seethed with anger. "Alan is a liar," she said. "He knew where my sister was all along."

"I'm sorry," Iris said. "I didn't mean to upset you. But the part about your sister being sent to Willowbrook is true, right? 'Cause your friends said—"

"Can we just order, please?" Eddie said, irritation edging his voice.

"Sure," Iris said. "Sorry." She set the coffeepot on the table and pulled her order pad out of her apron. "What can I get you?"

He ordered pancakes and bacon, and Sage said she'd have the same. After Iris picked up the coffeepot and left the table, Sage unzipped her coat and took her arms out of the sleeves, suddenly sweating again.

"See?" she said. "I told you Alan doesn't give a shit about me. He was so glad I was gone he lied to everyone to make it look like I had a breakdown. And he's telling everyone he didn't know Rosemary was in Willowbrook? How low can that bastard go?" Her eyes flooded. "I hate him so much."

"I'm sorry you had to hear that," Eddie said. "But try not to think about it right now. Everyone will know what a loser he is when the truth comes out. The newspapers will be all over what happened to your sister, and you can tell your side of story about everything, including him. Was he home when you got there?"

She wiped at her eyes, refusing to let Iris see her cry. "No, thank God. And I hope I'm gone before he comes back."

"I don't blame you. He seemed like a real asshole."

She frowned, confused. "I thought you never talked to him?"

He picked up the sugar and put three spoonfuls

in his coffee. "I didn't," he said. "But anyone who would ignore all those letters and phone calls has to be an asshole."

"Oh," she said. "Right."

"You said you hope you'll be gone before he comes back." He put down his spoon and took a sip of coffee. "I knew you were going to leave. So where you going?"

Damn it. She'd said too much. "I'm not sure yet. I'll probably just stay with a friend for a while, until I can get in touch with my real father."

"Well, if you need a ride somewhere," he said, "don't hesitate to ask." He reached into his jacket pocket and took out what looked like a page from a newspaper. "Remember I told you how my uncle's friend got fired for telling parents about the conditions at Willowbrook?"

She nodded.

He unfolded the paper and slid it across the table to her. "Well, take a look at this."

It was an article from the *New York Times*. She picked it up and began to read.

Commissioner Won't Reinstate
Two Dismissed at Willowbrook

Acknowledging that reconciliation efforts had failed, Dr. Alan D. Miller, State Commissioner of Mental Hygiene, announced yesterday that a doctor and a social worker dismissed from the Willowbrook State School for mental defectives will not be reinstated.

The two, Dr. Michael Wilkins and Mrs. Elizabeth Lee, were dismissed Jan. 4 by Willowbrook's director, Dr. Jack Hammond, who said he found them "impossible to work with."

Dr. Hammond has said he dismissed the two from the state school on Staten Island because of repeated violations of departmental regulations. They contend they were dismissed because they showed newsmen and citizens' groups the deplorable conditions in which Willowbrook's mentally retarded patients live.

Other Willowbrook employees, feeling that the Wilkins–Lee charges blamed them for poor patient care, approved Dr. Hammond's dismissal of the pair. Dr. Miller's change of mind about the reinstatement drew a strong protest from Anthony Pinto, president of the Benevolent Society for the Retarded Children of Willowbrook, a parents' organization. Mr. Pinto charged that Dr. Miller had "relinquished his administrative authority and bowed to the union."

Dr. Hammond is scheduled today to

414

testify for the second time before the Richmond County Society for the Prevention
of Cruelty to Children. This organization,
incorporated only last month, has been
conducting public hearings all week on
conditions at Willowbrook.

Dr. Hammond promised Monday that
he would return today with detailed information about patients who have died at
Willowbrook.

She looked up at Eddie, her eyes wide. "Is he
going to talk about Rosemary?"

"I doubt it," he said. "I just wanted you to know
that Baldwin isn't the only one who's covering
things up. The lying comes all the way from the
top down."

"But Dr. Hammond is going to give them
information about patients who died at
Willowbrook." She pointed the article. "It says
so right here."

"Do you honestly think Hammond's going to
start telling the truth all of a sudden? Do you
think he'll admit to a resident being murdered
any sooner than he has to?"

She shook her head. He was right. If the people
in charge could find a way to cover up two
killings, they'd do it in a heartbeat. Residents
died from abuse and medical experiments at
Willowbrook all the time, which was pretty much

the same thing as murder, so Rosemary's death would have little effect on their conscience.

Just then, headlights flashed across Eddie's face and they both looked out the window. A car drove into the lot and parked next to his Mustang.

"Shit," Sage said, hoping it wasn't anyone she knew. Then an image flashed in her mind: Wayne storming into the dinner and charging toward them with a knife. She slid down in her seat and pulled her coat around her shoulders, trembling.

As she watched, the car doors opened and a young couple got out and headed toward the diner door. She straightened and breathed a sigh of relief. It wasn't Wayne, and she didn't recognize the couple. The bell over the entrance chimed as they entered, their arms draped around each other. They looked high, or drunk, or both. Laughing and kissing, they fell into a corner booth.

"Are you sure you don't want to go someplace else?" Eddie said. "We can still leave, you know."

"No," she said. "I'll be fine." She glanced over at the food pickup window, hoping their order wouldn't take too long. Iris went over to wait on the young couple, pad and pencil in hand. She looked annoyed.

"You're not fine," Eddie said. "You look like you're about to scream."

"I just need to eat something," she said. "And we have more important things to talk about than how I'm feeling. What did your uncle say when you told him about finding Rosemary?"

He pulled a straw out of the dispenser next to the napkin holder and twisted it between his fingers. "He was shocked, but not surprised, that Baldwin tried to cover it up. He was pretty upset with me for helping you, but he said we were lucky we found Rosemary when we did, because no one uses that tunnel anymore and who knows how long she would have been down there. It could have been years." He bent the straw in half and chucked it at the napkin holder.

A chill crawled up Sage's spine thinking about Rosemary trapped in the bowels of that nightmarish institution, cold and alone for weeks and months and years, slowly decaying. Not that being buried in the woods was much better, but at least it wasn't in the tunnels beneath Willowbrook. At least it was outside with trees and animals and all the things Rosemary loved. Plus, if they hadn't found her, Sage would have been kept locked up, possibly for the rest of her life. Thank God she'd tried to escape. Thank God Eddie had helped by taking her into the tunnels. Because as much as she hated the fact that her sister had been killed, she was beyond ecstatic to be free.

As soon as the thought crossed her mind, guilt slammed into her heart. How could she feel relief when the price of her freedom was Rosemary's life? What kind of person thinks that way? And about her own sister, no less?

Suddenly the aromas of fried food and coffee made her sick to her stomach. She looked over at the pickup window again. Thankfully the waitress was headed their way, two plates balanced in one hand, a glass of milk in the other. When Iris put their food on the table, Sage was going to ask if they could get it to go, but Eddie had already started eating. He wiped his mouth and looked at her.

"You okay?"

She nodded and picked up her fork.

He covered his pancakes with syrup, then held the bottle over her plate. She nodded and he poured some on hers. "So do you think he'll come looking for you?" he said. "After he finds out about Rosemary, I mean."

The blood drained from her face. *Oh my God. He thinks Wayne wants to kill me, too.*

"What is it?" he said, alarmed. "What's wrong?"

"You think Wayne is going to come looking for me?"

His eyes went wide. "No! Not Wayne. I was talking about Alan! You said you might stay with a friend for a while."

"Oh." Her shoulders loosened. "I . . . I doubt it. Why would he?"

"I don't know, to apologize?"

"Yeah, right." She stared at her plate, at the greasy bacon and sticky syrup, and the swooning sensation stirred in her head again. *What if Wayne Myers is Cropsey? What if he killed all those missing kids too?*

"What about your sister's funeral?" Eddie said.

If he got away with all those murders, surely he'll get away with killing Rosemary and Evie. And me.

"Sage?" Eddie said. "Did you hear me?"

She blinked and looked at him. "I'm sorry. What did you say?"

"I asked if you would go to your sister's funeral."

She put down her fork and took a sip of milk, trying to think straight. "Alan won't pay for a funeral. He'll just let them cremate her, or whatever Willowbrook normally does with deceased residents."

"I'm pretty sure they send anyone who isn't claimed by family to the city crematorium."

"Well, that's what he'll let happen, then. And honestly, I haven't had time to think about that." It was the truth. But she should pay her respects and say goodbye to Rosemary. For real, this time. "I guess I should be there to say a prayer or something." Her eyes grew wet again.

"I'm sorry," he said. "I shouldn't have brought it up."

"It's okay," she said. "Maybe you can go with

me when the time comes? It'd be nice to have someone else there who cared about her."

"Okay," he said. "Sure. If you want." He picked up his fork and started eating again. "And, you know, you can stay with me for a while if you want, instead of hoping one of your friends will take you in." Instantly realizing how his offer probably sounded, embarrassment colored his face. "Just until you figure out what you're going to do, I mean."

Taken aback by the offer, Sage wasn't sure how to say no without seeming ungrateful. She could never live with someone who worked at Willowbrook anyway, even if it was just for a little while. "I appreciate that," she said. "But I hardly know you, and we were together when we found my sister, so it might not look good."

"No problem," he said. "But what do you mean it wouldn't look good? Wayne is the number one suspect. Not you. Not me."

"I know," she said. "But Dr. Baldwin tried to make Detective Nolan think I killed her and Evie because I knew their injuries were the same."

"What the hell? Did he think you were sneaking out and killing people or some bullshit? Doesn't he realize that if you could have gotten out of that place you would have left a long time ago?"

"I don't know, I'm just telling you what he did and what I think. Did you get the feeling

Detective Nolan suspected you during his questioning?"

He looked at her like she'd grown an eye in the middle of her forehead. "No, not at all. But then again, Wayne had already run off at that point."

"That's true. I hadn't thought about that. Did you know Detective Nolan wanted to send a cop over to his place? But his file was missing."

"Wayne's file?"

She nodded.

"That's odd."

"Do you know where he lives?"

"No," he said. "But now I know why Detective Nolan asked me the same question. I thought it was just because we worked together and he wanted to know if we were friends. I didn't know his file was missing."

"Can I ask you something?" she said.

"Sure, anything."

"How the hell can you stand working at Willowbrook?"

He shrugged. "I don't like it. But I'm working there because I got into trouble last year. My uncle got me the job, said he'd keep me in line while I earned my GED."

"What kind of trouble?"

His scrubbed a hand on his leg, looking uncomfortable.

"Never mind," she said. "You don't have to tell me."

"I got in a fight," he said. "A bad one. Put some jerk in the hospital for a few days. Got expelled, you know the drill." He fixed his eyes on her as if desperate to be understood. "I'd never been in a fight in my life before, but the guy was a real asshole and deserved what he got. He wouldn't leave this girl alone. She was a little heavier, you know, and he was tormenting the shit out of her. I finally pushed him away from her, but he wouldn't back off, so I punched him. He pulled a knife, we wrestled, and he fell on the blade. Went into his chest and just missed his aorta. And, of course, his friends told the cops *I* was the one who pulled the knife."

She almost said something trivial and appropriate, like *I'm sorry,* or *how awful.* But the way he was looking at her, both troubled and distracted at once, made her stop. She knew what it was like to have no one believe her. "What about the girl you were sticking up for? Did she tell the truth?"

He shook his head. "You know how it is. The kids who get picked on keep quiet, otherwise they get picked on even more."

Yes, she knew how it was. It didn't matter how many times she had been teased in grade school for being taller than everyone, including the boys; she'd never told anyone. There was no point. If she had told a teacher or principal, the teasing would have just gotten worse. It reminded her of

422

the employees at Willowbrook, how they were afraid to snitch on one another. "That sucks," she said. "I take it your mother didn't believe you either?"

He let out a humorless chuckle. "She was more worried about the family name. She's a big deal at the Richmond County Yacht Club, and she likes to think of herself as a great philanthropist who'll always be remembered for her good deeds. She'd never forgive me if I caused a scandal. Said she'd disinherit me if I messed up again. Eventually it came out that the knife wasn't mine, but the school didn't want me back, and my mother wanted to put me in the military, so my uncle put me in an apartment and got me the job. My mother gave me two years to turn my life around before she cuts me off completely."

"She sounds . . . pleasant."

"Yeah, she and Alan would get along great." He grinned. "Maybe we should introduce them."

"Somehow I can't picture Alan hanging out at a yacht club," she said. A smile spread across her face for the first time since she had been imprisoned at Willowbrook and she almost laughed. It felt strange. Maybe she and Eddie had more in common than she thought.

She picked up her fork and cut into the pancakes. When she took the first mouthful, she had to stop chewing and push the food to the side of her cheek, certain she couldn't swallow over the sudden lump in her throat. The combined flavors of maple syrup and moist pancake seemed amplified a thousand times, making her taste buds explode. It surprised her, and she had to catch her breath before she choked on the joy of something so simple and delicious. She put her fingers over her closed lips and sat back in the booth.

"What's wrong?" Eddie said.

She shook her head. "Nothing," she said. "I'm just happy to eat real food again, that's all."

CHAPTER 21

By the time they finished eating and Eddie paid the bill at the Top Hat, it was 2:30 a.m. Ten minutes later, Eddie pulled the Mustang into an open parking spot half a block from her apartment building, put the car in park, and shut off the engine.

"Sorry I couldn't get closer," he said.

"It's all right," she said. "Thanks again for breakfast."

"Anytime."

She wanted to say more—wanted to thank him for helping her, for keeping her safe and sane. If he hadn't been working at Willowbrook, if he hadn't been kind to Rosemary and gotten to know her a little bit, Sage might have spent the rest of her life locked up. But at the same time, she didn't want him to get the wrong idea. She opened the car door and started to get out, then hesitated and looked up and down the empty sidewalk and deserted road, scanned the thick clumps of bushes and the black trunks of trees. It was nearing 3 a.m., the darkest hours of the night, full of strange shadows and sinister secrets. But no deranged killer with a bald head and tattooed arms was waiting for her outside.

None that she could see, anyway.

She turned in the seat to look back at Eddie. "Would you mind walking me up?"

"Of course not," he said, then opened his door and got out.

After he came around the front of the car, she climbed out and started along the sidewalk, the pancakes like a rock in her stomach despite the fact that they were the most delicious food she'd eaten in a long time. After the bland food and small portions at Willowbrook, she should have ordered something less heavy, like a turkey sandwich or a bowl of chicken noodle soup. Of course, being anxious didn't help.

Walking fast, she kept her hand wrapped around the apartment key in her coat pocket. Eddie walked silently beside her, every now and then looking toward the trees or over his shoulder, which only made her more nervous.

When they finally reached the lobby of her apartment building, she relaxed, but only a little. At least they were inside. In the fourth-floor hallway, she put the key in her apartment door, then turned to face him.

"Thanks again," she said.

"My offer still stands," he said. "You can stay at my place tonight if it'll make you feel safer. I'll bring you back in the morning."

She shook her head. "No, it's fine. I'm okay. You've already helped me enough." She was about to say good night when a door slammed above them and heavy footsteps stomped rapidly down the staircase. In an instant, she had spun around, unlocked the door, and rushed inside, her heart in her throat. Eddie followed her in just as quickly, shutting the door behind him. With trembling hands, she locked the door, slid the deadbolt in place and fastened the chain, then took a step back and stared at the door, waiting for Wayne to break it down.

Out in the hall a man shouted something about leaving and never coming back, then clomped down the next set of stairs. He sounded angry and drunk. Sage glanced at Eddie, relieved and embarrassed.

"Sorry," she said. "But that scared the shit out of me."

"It's okay," he said. "It rattled me too. Are you sure you want to be here alone? I can stay if you want. On the couch, of course. I promise I'll leave first thing in the morning. You won't even know I was here."

She studied his face. Sincerity filled his eyes, along with genuine concern. Maybe he was right. Maybe she'd feel safer if he stayed. If he slept on the couch, maybe she could get some sleep instead of jumping at every little sound. "Okay," she said. "But excuse the mess and the smell."

"I don't care about that," he said. "I just want to help if I can."

In the living room, she cleared away the wrinkled magazines and newspapers from the couch, straightened the cushions, and picked the empty beer cans off the coffee table. "I'll get you a pillow and blanket," she said. "You can turn on the radio if you want, and there's Budweiser in the fridge if you want a beer."

"No thanks," he said. "I've got to work in the morning."

"Oh," she said. "I didn't realize . . ."

"I clock in at six, so I'll only be here a few hours. Unless you want me to call in so I can stick around longer."

She shook her head. "No, I'll feel better in the morning. I just need a little more sleep." She put a hand on her abdomen. "And I need to digest all that food."

He laughed. "Me too. I can check back after work to see how you're doing, if that's cool with you."

She shrugged. "You can try, but I'm not sure I'll be here."

"Okay. Do you want me to leave my number in case you need anything?"

"Sure." She motioned toward an end table, where a notepad and pen sat next to the telephone.

He went over, picked up the notepad, and wrote down his number. "If you do end up leaving, just give me a call to let me know you're all right, okay?"

She nodded, then started out of the room. "I'll be right back." She went down to the kitchen to throw away the empty beer cans, nearly gagging when she opened the garbage lid, then fetched an extra pillow and blanket. Back in the living room, she said, "If you need anything, my room is at the end of the hall on the right, past the kitchen and bathroom."

He sat on the couch and started taking off his shoes. "Okay. Go get some sleep. I'll be right here if you need me."

"Thanks," she said. "Good night."

In her bedroom, she closed the door and crawled under the covers, admitting to herself that she was glad she'd allowed Eddie to stay. Even a few hours of sound sleep would be worth him possibly thinking they could be more than acquaintances. Besides, even if she left to stay with one of her friends or somehow found her father, this was far from over. She'd be seeing Eddie again if and when Detective Nolan found Wayne, to testify in court and whatever else they had to do to make him pay.

The sound of a closing door startled Sage awake. She sat up in bed, her jaw aching from grinding her teeth, and looked at the clock on her bedside table. 5:00 a.m. Outside, darkness pressed against the glass between her curtains. The noise she'd heard was probably Eddie leaving for work. She scrubbed her hands over her face and tried to shake off the remnants of nightmares. Even with Eddie in the living room, sleep hadn't come easy. And what little rest she had found was assaulted by images of Rosemary's decayed corpse and Wayne chasing her through the tunnels with a bloody knife. She pulled back the tangerine and lime-green bedcover and got out of bed. If those grisly dreams awaited her every time she closed her eyes, she'd rather stay awake.

After dressing in sweatpants and a bulky sweater, she padded down to the living room. She was right: Eddie was gone. The notepad with his number on it sat on top of the folded blanket, along with a twenty-dollar bill and another note that said:

> I hope you're feeling better. I'll be back as soon as I get off work. If you don't want to wait, please call and let me know where you are so I know you're okay. Sorry I couldn't leave more cash, it was all I had on me.

She picked up the twenty-dollar bill, guilt coiling beneath her ribs. Eddie had done so much for her. And she still needed his help to get justice for Rosemary. But he wanted something she couldn't give—a true friendship; maybe more. She'd be forever grateful to him, but she had to leave Willowbrook—and everyone associated with it—behind her as soon as she could. There was no other choice. Not that she blamed him for Rosemary being killed or everything that had happened, and was continuing to happen, in Willowbrook, but he would always remind her of that place, no matter what. And somehow, even if she hurt his feelings, she had to move on, to heal and put this part of her life behind her. Willowbrook would not claim her as another victim.

After putting the money in her makeup bag, she went to Alan's room to look for the spare apartment key so she'd have it when the super showed up. Then she'd pack and leave. She'd go either to Heather's place or Dawn's—she hadn't decided which—tell them the truth about where she'd been and beg to stay with them for a day or two. If they turned her away, she wasn't sure what she would do, but she had to be gone before Alan came home. She also needed the extra key to get back in while he was at work so she could pick up more of her things.

When she entered the bedroom, she switched on the ceiling light and wrinkled her nose. For some reason, the rank odor that seemed to permeate the rest of the apartment was noticeably stronger inside the room. Had Alan shit the bed in one of his drunken stupors, or puked in a corner and not cleaned it up? Had a rat died inside the walls?

Just thinking about it made her queasy. She held a hand over her nose and mouth, stepped around a pile of dirty laundry spilling out of a plastic hamper, and went over to the dresser.

Her mother's white jewelry box sat on the dresser, along with a bottle of Tylenol, a smudged glass full of hazy water, a dust-caked vase filled with even dustier fake roses, a *Playboy* magazine, a pile of unopened bills, and a Zippo lighter. After blowing the dust off of the jewelry box, she opened it and rummaged beneath the hinged upper shelf for the spare key, the slight hint of Chanel No. 5, mixed with a faint metallic aroma, wafting up from the pink fabric interior. The scent reminded her of playing dress-up with Rosemary, how Alan had slapped them for breaking one of their mother's necklaces and spilling her perfume inside the jewelry box. Even now, with her mother dead and gone and Alan out of the house, looking inside it still felt wrong.

The spare key was beneath a turquoise pendant on a silver chain, the last Christmas gift her father had given her mother before he left. She took out the necklace and put it on, lifting the collar of her sweater and dropping the pendant underneath. Not because it was her mother's— she'd never worn it, not once—but because Sage and Rosemary had helped their father pick it out. As she'd expected, the diamond earrings and gold chains were gone. Alan had probably sold them years ago.

Stepping on magazines and more dirty clothes, she went around the double bed to check inside the bedside table where Alan kept his drinking money. Searching for cash was probably a waste of time—he'd probably spent it all on the ice-fishing trip—but it couldn't hurt to check. The dingy bed comforter was partially draped over the bedside table, one corner lying in an ashtray full of cigarette butts. She pulled it aside and stepped forward to open the drawer—then went stiff.

Her foot had landed in something impossibly sticky yet somehow dry. Praying it wasn't shit or vomit oozing between her toes, she looked down.

A pool of dark blood mottled the beige carpet. More blotches and streaks splattered up the white wall and the yellow bed skirt, the bottom of which looked saturated, as if it'd been dipped in a vat of red paint. She gasped and leapt back, then scraped her foot along a clean section of the rug and the dirty clothes, desperate to get rid of the blood darkening her toes and the creases of her skin. What the hell was going on? Why was there blood on the floor? She hurried around the bed toward the door, her muscles tight, her body ready to run. Another dark puddle of blood stained the rug near the footboard, along with a crumpled blue shirt and a worn pair of pants. It looked like the blood was coming from under the bed.

Someone, or something, was under there. And they had been bleeding. Profusely.

Had Wayne been out in the hall waiting for Eddie to leave? Had he killed Eddie and shoved him under the bed? Was he still in the apartment? She stared at the blood, temporarily paralyzed by panic, then dropped to her knees and reached for the bed skirt to look underneath. But when her fingers touched the fabric, she yanked back her hand.

She couldn't do it. She had to get the hell out of there. She had to call the cops, get the superintendent. But what would she say? That she wanted to know why there was blood on the floor? It could have been there for any number of reasons. And maybe it was less than it seemed. She'd learned in health class that a tablespoon of menstrual blood could look like a cup; they didn't want the girls to think they were dying during their periods. Maybe Alan had cut his finger on a beer tab or gotten injured during a drunken brawl. Before she called the cops, she had to know why or if she needed them. Steeling herself, she lifted the bed skirt.

At first she couldn't tell what she was seeing. Then she noticed a pale hand frozen into a bloody claw. Her eyes followed the hand up a pale arm to a bloody neck, from there to a white face with wide, horror-filled eyes. And a painted-on clown smile.

It was Alan.

She let out a shriek and scrambled backward, hitting her head on the dresser, then got to her feet and bolted out of the bedroom. She ran down the hall to the kitchen, grabbed the phone, and dialed the operator, her hands shaking so hard she could hardly turn the dial. Waiting for the operator to pick up, she felt faint. Dizzy. After what felt like forever, someone answered.

"You need to send the police!" she said, gulping for air. "I found my . . . my stepfather under the bed. He's dead! Someone killed him!"

"All right," the operator said. "Calm down and tell me your name and address. I'll send someone over right away."

"My name is Sage Winters," she said. "I'm at the Greenwood Apartments on Dryer Road. Apartment 4C. Mariners Harbor."

"Okay, I've got it," the operator said. "Are you alone?"

She spun around and scanned the cramped kitchen. "I . . . I think so."

"Are you safe?"

"I'm not sure." She moved toward the knife drawer, but the phone cord was too short.

"Can you go to a neighbor's to wait for the police? Will someone let you in?"

She shook her head. "No. I mean, yes. I can try."

435

"All right. You need to go somewhere safe until the police come, okay? A unit is in the area and can be there in just a few minutes."

"Okay. Tell them to hurry!"

She hung up the receiver, hurried over to the knife drawer, and pulled out a butcher knife, her fist clenched around the handle. Holding her breath, she edged toward the doorway.

"Is someone out there?" she shouted.

No one answered.

"I have a knife and I'm not afraid to use it!"

Still nothing.

She peered around the doorframe. No crazed killer waited in the hallway. No man with a razor-sharp ax. She crept slowly into the hall and made her way to the living room, the knife ready. At the living room door, she stopped and looked around the edge, terrified Wayne would be waiting there. No one sat on the couch. No one stood by the television or the window. The room was empty. She started toward the front door, then stopped halfway there. What if Wayne was hiding in the coat closet? What if he jumped out when she got near?

Trying not to make a sound, she tiptoed toward the exit, her eyes fixed on the closet handle, her heart beating so hard she thought she'd pass out. Just a few more steps and she would be at the door. Just a few more steps and she would be out of the apartment. Unless Wayne heard the deadbolt opening. Unless he jumped out of the closet and slit her throat. A floorboard creaked beneath her foot and she froze. When nothing happened, she let out her breath and kept going. Just three more feet and she would—

Out in the hall, footsteps stomped up the staircase. Someone pounded on the door.

"Police! Open up!"

She rushed forward, her hand shaking as she struggled to open the deadbolt, the chain guard, and the lock. Finally, she turned the knob and an officer burst inside, his gun drawn and pointed right at her.

"Drop the weapon!" he shouted.

She dropped the knife and put her hands in the air. "It's not me!" she said. "I'm the one who called you!"

"Is there anyone else in the apartment?" he said.

"I don't know."

The cop moved forward, his gun still at the ready. "Dispatch said there's a body?"

She nodded and pointed down the hall. "In the bedroom on the right. Under the bed."

CHAPTER 22

Sitting in a hard plastic chair next to a cop's desk with a scratchy wool blanket around her shoulders, Sage wrapped her hands around a paper cup filled with stale coffee. Not that she drank any or she was cold, but the cup was warm and kept her hands from shaking. The 121st Precinct station was actually hot and humid, with a sweaty, sour smell that hung in the air like the inside of a men's locker room. Still, she couldn't stop shivering. And it seemed like she'd been there for hours—first waiting to talk to someone, then answering a million questions while the image of Alan's horror-filled face flashed over and over in her mind. The cop at the desk gazed at her with doubt-filled eyes, his pen poised over the report he was filling out.

"So you're saying you were just released from Willowbrook State School and your twin sister was murdered there?" he said.

She nodded. "Yes, she was killed the same way Evie Carter was killed. Evie was a secretary at Willowbrook and they just found her body. You must have heard about her."

He wrote something in the report.

"Did you call Detective Nolan yet?" she said.

438

"He can tell you what's going on. He knows I'm telling the truth."

"Yes, they did," a man's voice said behind her.

She turned in the chair, and sagged in relief. Detective Nolan was heading toward them.

"Thank God you're here," she said.

The cop at the desk got up to let Nolan take his chair.

"I just came from your apartment," the detective said.

"And?"

"It looks like whoever killed Rosemary and Evie might have killed your stepfather too."

"Might have?" she said. "It *had* to be the same person! His neck and . . . and the lipstick and—"

"I know, I know. It looks like the same MO, but we can't be one hundred percent sure."

"Have you found Wayne yet?"

He shook his head. "We found his address and went to his residence, but he's disappeared. Neighbors haven't seen him in a few days."

"Oh my God," she said. "He must have broken into my place and killed Alan while I was sleeping."

Detective Nolan shook his head again. "There was no sign of forced entry. And Alan's been dead for a while now. A few days at least."

Her eyes widened. How was that possible? Then she remembered the rank, sour odor when she first arrived, how she'd searched for the source but couldn't find it. Now she knew. The smell had been coming from Alan's corpse. Her stomach clenched. "Why would Wayne want to kill him? I mean, he was an asshole, but—"

"Tell me what happened," he said. "Give me every detail."

She told him everything she could remember: how she had been getting the spare key out of her mother's jewelry box so she could give the other one back to the super, how she decided to look for money, how she stepped in blood and saw more on the bed skirt, how she found Alan under the bed.

"I woke up early because I thought I heard Eddie leaving for work," she said. "Then I found Alan and I wondered if what I'd heard was the person who killed him. I was terrified because I didn't know if he was still in the apartment. But if Alan has been dead for a while, it must have been Eddie leaving after all."

Detective Nolan raised his eyebrows. "Did you say Eddie?"

She nodded. "Yeah, he came by after Officer Minor dropped me off. I'm not sure what time he got there, but he was waiting outside when I left to go to the store. He wanted to buy me breakfast, so we went to the Top Hat to get something to eat, then he slept on the couch because I was scared to be alone and—"

"Are you talking about Eddie King from Willowbrook?"

"Yes," she said. "I know I probably shouldn't be hanging around with him, but he was the only one who would listen to me. If it weren't for him . . ."

Detective Nolan pinched the bridge of his nose and squeezed his eyes shut as if stricken by a sudden headache.

"What?" she said. "You don't believe me?"

"It's not that," he said. "It's just—"

"What is it then?" she said, on the verge of tears again. "Did something happen to Eddie? Is he dead? Did Wayne kill him too?"

He took the notebook out of his coat pocket and grabbed a pen from the desk, his frown lines growing deeper. "No, he's not dead. What time did you say he was at your apartment?"

"It was a little after one in the morning when I went outside and he pulled up beside me. I was walking to the store to pick up a few groceries, but he offered to take me to breakfast."

He wrote down the information. "You said he pulled up beside you?" he said.

She nodded.

"In what?"

"A red Mustang. I was surprised because it looked brand new. I didn't think he could afford it working at Willowbrook as a janitor. But he said his family is rich. His uncle works there, too, so that's how he got the job."

Nolan kept taking notes, his face unreadable. "And he took you to the Top Hat?"

She nodded.

"Did you see anyone you know at the diner? Talk to anyone?"

"Just the waitress, Iris. She said Alan told everyone I was visiting his sister out on Long Island. That's why no one was looking for me when I was at Willowbrook. But Alan doesn't . . . didn't have a sister."

"When did Iris talk to Alan?"

"She didn't. She overheard my friends talking about it. She thought Eddie was my cousin."

"Any idea when your friends might have talked to Alan?"

"I don't know. Maybe a few days after I went to Willowbrook? Iris didn't say when they were there, and I didn't ask."

"Do you know Iris's last name?"

"No."

"I need your friends' names and addresses."

She gave him Heather's and Dawn's information. "I'm not sure who else was with them, but they're the ones who would have asked Alan about me."

"So there was no one else in the diner when you were there?"

"There was an old guy eating pie, and the cook, but he never came out of the kitchen. Oh, and a young couple I didn't recognize."

"What time did you leave?" he said.

She shrugged. "I don't know. We weren't there that long—maybe forty-five minutes?"

He scribbled something else down, then ripped the piece of paper out of the notebook, stood, and looked at a group of cops on the other side of the room. "Hey, McNally!" he shouted. "I need you to check something out for me."

A thin, baby-faced cop hurried over and eagerly took the paper from him.

"Go to the Top Hat diner and ask for a waitress named Iris. Ask her if she remembers seeing Miss Winters there last night with a young, dark-haired guy named Eddie. I need to know what time they were there, what time they left, and what they were driving. Find out what she said to Miss Winters about her stepfather, Alan Tern, too."

"Yes, sir," the baby-faced cop said, then turned on his heels and left.

Nolan looked at Sage. "I need to ask your friends when they talked to Alan. And you and I need to talk to Dr. Baldwin."

She shook her head. No. Not Dr. Baldwin. She never wanted to see or talk to that man again. "Why? Eddie helping me again is none of his business. And why are you sending someone to ask Iris about us being at the diner? Don't you believe me?"

Before he could reply, a cop yelled from an

open office on the other side of the room. "Nolan! Call for you on line three."

"Hold on," he told her. "Don't go anywhere."

She rolled her eyes. Where would she go? Back home where Alan's dead body was under the bed? Back to where Wayne could find and kill her? Except for stopping at the apartment to get a few things, living there was out of the question for a hundred different reasons, least of which that she had no way of paying the rent on her own.

He punched a button on the phone and picked up the receiver. "Detective Nolan," he said, impatience edging his voice. He frowned as he listened then gave Sage a worried glance. "Are you sure?" He dropped his gaze to the floor, still listening.

She kept her eyes on his face. Obviously the call had something to do with her. And it wasn't good.

"Where?" he said. "Uh-huh. Uh-huh. Okay. Yes, Dr. Baldwin, we'll be right over." He hung up the phone and stared at her, his expression a strange mix of shock and confusion.

"What is it?" she said.

"We need to get over to Willowbrook right away," he said.

"Why? What's going on?"

"I'll know more when we get there."

"No, I'm not going back there."

"Well, you're a minor. And I hate to be blunt,

but your parents are dead. We can't just let you out on the streets. Do you have family nearby who can come pick you up?"

She shook her head.

"Do you have any idea where your biological father is?"

She shook her head again. "No, but I can stay with one of my friends."

"Sorry, I can't let that happen. You need to remain under my custody or I'll have to call Social Services before I leave so they can find you a temporary place to stay until we sort this out. More than likely they'll put you in the children's home, so you might as well come with me."

Slouched in the back seat of the unmarked Ford LTD behind Sergeant Clark, who was driving, and Detective Nolan, who rode in silence, Sage stared out through the snow-pelted windshield. The wipers slapped back and forth so fast they nearly made her dizzy. Despite the fact that it was midmorning, it looked like dusk outside, the winter sky filled with murky clouds so low they seemed to touch the ground. Wind and sleet clawed at the car, pushing it all over the road as if trying to get inside. A perfect day to return to the nightmare of Willowbrook. The only thing missing was thunder and lightning.

No. She wasn't going to think like that. She'd

made up her mind back at the police station to be brave. She wasn't returning as a patient. She was free and sane and everyone knew it now. At least she thought they did.

Detective Nolan had said the phone call had something to do with Rosemary's case, but he wanted to wait until he could check the evidence before he confirmed it. Deep down she worried it was a trick; that he and Dr. Baldwin had come up with a plan to lock her up again. What was one more soul lost in Willowbrook? Especially if Dr. Baldwin still thought she had something to do with the murders. Especially if he thought she was insane. Locking her up would be easier than going through a trial to prove she was guilty.

But that was ridiculous. Detective Nolan knew she was innocent. And she'd made the choice to return with him instead of being picked up by Social Services. She needed to stop being paranoid. Still, she couldn't help wondering it if was too late to ask Sergeant Clark to turn around.

As they sped along the snowy, one-lane road, getting closer and closer to Willowbrook's front gate, the more she wished she'd stayed at the station. Maybe she could have snuck out before anyone arrived to pick her up. Maybe she could have called Heather and convinced the other cops she was her sister so they'd let her go. She cracked her window open to get some fresh air, certain she was suffocating. Sleet flew in through the narrow opening, hitting her eyes and forehead like tiny wet bullets. She rolled the window back up.

"You okay back there?" Nolan asked over his shoulder.

"I'm fine," she lied.

And she would be fine, as soon as they left Willowbrook again. As soon as they found Wayne and put him behind bars. Outside the windshield, the pillared gates to Willowbrook stood open, gaping, and hungry for their next victim, like the mouth of a hushed, breathing beast. Sergeant Clark slowed the car, stopped next to the guardhouse, and rolled down his window. The guard stepped out partway to wave them on, squinting against the snow.

Detective Nolan leaned across the seat to talk to him through the open window. "What's the quickest way to the hospital?"

"After the administration building keep going straight," the guard said. "It's at the far end of the campus on the same road."

"Thanks." Nolan gave the man a quick wave.

Sergeant Clark rolled up the window and drove on. "They need to tighten security in this place," he said.

"I agree," Nolan said. "But like everything else funded by the state, it probably all comes down to money."

Sage sat forward, growing more and more

nervous. "Why are we going to the hospital?"

"That's where Dr. Baldwin said to meet him," Nolan said.

She sagged back in the seat, her anxiety building as they drove along another lonely length of road into a wooded area filled with snow-covered trees and low brush. When they came out on the other side and the first brick building came into view, she pressed her nails into her palms. Never in a million years would she have thought she'd be back on the Willowbrook campus, and certainly not so soon. Yet here she was.

Here and there in the low-slung houses, jittery, weak lights shone in the windows. Shadows moved behind the grimy glass—ashen silhouettes lurching back and forth, or side to side, up and down, slowly and methodically, fast and frenzied. The misery and pain of the people trapped behind those dark walls, weeping and misused and afraid, abused and desperate and dying, was palpable—a living, breathing thing. It put a boulder in her chest and a sour pit in her stomach.

Then the administration building appeared like a ship through the wind and snow, the massive structure dark, the windows black, the outside lights shining like a ghostly warning. It looked deserted.

When Detective Nolan spoke, she jumped. "From what I understand, this campus is over three hundred acres," he said to Sergeant Clark. "So the hospital is probably quite a ways down this road."

After the administration building, they passed more resident "houses" on both sides of the road—a thousand more dim windows and moving shadows, a thousand more miles of brick walls hiding squalor, abuse, neglect, misery, and death. She'd never been this deep inside the campus; seeing one resident house after another, along with side roads lined with even more houses, she was again reminded of a concentration camp, with row after row of identical barracks. Hearing the numbers was one thing, but seeing the houses firsthand was something else entirely. She had no idea there were so many.

When they reached the hospital—another imposing building with the same number of floors and wings as the administration building— Nolan told Sargent Clark to park in the back. "Baldwin wants us to come in through a delivery door," he said.

"What the hell?" Clark said. "What's with all the secrecy?"

"Beats me. Maybe with that news report he's had enough publicity for the year."

After driving around one wing of the hospital into an empty parking lot scoured clean by the wind, Clark stopped the Ford next to a white van. The only other vehicle in the lot was Dr.

Baldwin's New Yorker. Clark shut off the engine and looked at Nolan.

"Need me to come inside?" he said.

"No, I'll get it from here. We shouldn't be long."

"I'll be here if you need me," Clark said, then cracked the window and lit a cigarette.

Sage wished more than anything that she could stay in the car. What if they were at the hospital so Dr. Baldwin could give her a lobotomy? What if he had phoned the police station because he knew she'd be there? What if he told Detective Nolan to lie about the reason for his call? She wiped at her eyes, determined not to cry, and told herself to be reasonable. She was at the police station because someone had murdered Alan. Dr. Baldwin and Detective Nolan had nothing to do with that. At least she didn't think Dr. Baldwin did. Maybe she should refuse to go inside. She could wait for Detective Nolan to tell her about the evidence, if it was that important.

Detective Nolan got out of the car, opened the back door, and waited for her to get out, holding on to his hat so the wind wouldn't blow it away.

She looked up at him. "Can't you just let me know what you find out?" she said.

He shook his head. "I need to you to tell Baldwin about Eddie."

She sighed miserably, then climbed out of the back seat, pulled up her hood, and trailed the detective across the parking lot on shaking legs. Sleet pelted her face, and she put her head down to follow his quickly disappearing tracks. Thankfully, when they reached the back of the hospital, the massive building blocked most of the wind.

Nolan tried the nearest delivery door. It was locked. He pounded on it with the side of his fist.

"It's Detective Nolan," he shouted. "You in there, Dr. Baldwin?" He pounded again.

After what felt like forever, the handle rattled and the door opened. When Dr. Baldwin saw Sage, he frowned. "What's she doing here?" He had a breathless, anxious look about him.

"She was at the station when you called. I'm afraid I've got some bad news. Her stepfather has been murdered. Same injuries as Rosemary and Evie."

"Jesus Christ."

"There's more," Nolan said. "She says Eddie King was at her apartment last night."

Dr. Baldwin furrowed his brow. "But that's impossible. He's—"

"I haven't told her yet. I thought it'd be better coming from you."

"Told me what?" Sage said, her chest tightening.

"Come inside and we'll talk," Dr. Baldwin said.

She shook her head. "I don't want to talk. I want you to tell me what the hell is going on."

"Don't be ridiculous," Dr. Baldwin said. "It's freezing out there." He stepped back and held the door open.

Nolan jerked his chin toward the door. "It's all right. You're with me." He entered and waited beside Dr. Baldwin.

"Just tell me about Eddie," she said. "Then I'll come inside."

"After I show Detective Nolan why I called him," Dr. Baldwin said, "I'll explain everything."

She rolled her eyes, annoyed and frightened at the same time. They knew they had the upper hand. And if she was being honest with herself, she knew she had to go inside—she owed it to Rosemary to do whatever she could to get to the bottom of this mess. Not to mention, the sooner they caught Wayne, the sooner she could try to move on with her life. Clenching her jaw, she went through the delivery door into Willowbrook's hospital.

A dim yellow glow filled the narrow corridor, reminding her of the dank tunnels below. The air felt as cold as the parking lot. Dr. Baldwin locked the door behind them, tested it, then put the keys in his pocket. He looked at her, his forehead lined with concern. To her surprise and dismay, he seemed almost worried, though whether it was about her or something else, she couldn't tell.

"When did you say Eddie was at your place?" he said.

Something about the tone of his voice set off alarms inside her head. It seemed casual, as if he were talking to a friend at a dinner party. "Last night," she said. "A little after one o'clock. But I already told Detective Nolan that." She crossed her arms and looked from him to Nolan and back again. "Will one of you please tell me what we're doing here? Did you find Wayne yet?"

"If you want answers, follow me." Dr. Baldwin started down the corridor, Nolan following.

Sage stood rooted to the floor, her heart jumping around in her chest. Something wasn't right. She could feel it in her bones.

Detective Nolan stopped and looked back at her. "You coming?"

She shook her head. "Not until you can guarantee I'll be leaving again."

He took off his hat and came back to where she stood. "He's not going to lock you up again. We're just trying to solve this case, that's why we're here."

She studied his face, trying to decide whether or not to believe him. It seemed like he was on her side. And he was a cop—surely he wanted to find the killer, whether it was Wayne or someone else. Plus, what would he gain by letting her be locked up? Reluctantly, she started down the corridor toward Dr. Baldwin, who was waiting next to what looked like a service lift. When she and the detective reached him, he pushed the up arrow and the door shuddered open to reveal a large elevator with peeling walls and a black floor. Dr. Baldwin got in and kept the door from closing with one hand.

She swore under her breath and followed him inside the elevator, where the smell of hot rubber and a rank mixture of sour milk and stale blood filled the air. After Detective Nolan got on, the doors jerked closed and the elevator lurched once before starting up the shaft. A few seconds later, it stopped and the doors opened to a deserted hallway. Dr. Baldwin held the door while they got out, then moved around them and kept going. Detective Nolan and Sage followed, walking past closed doors with doctors' nameplates or signs that read: LAB, ELECTRIC SHOCK THERAPY, and LOBOTOMY. She pulled her eyes away from the signs and looked straight ahead, trying not to think about what went on inside those rooms. Finally, Dr. Baldwin stopped outside a set of steel doors below a sign that read: MORGUE. She swallowed. How many morgues did Willowbrook need?

"Is Rosemary in there?" she said. "Did you find something on her body that will help catch her killer?"

"No," Dr. Baldwin said, then opened one of the doors and went inside.

"Wait out here," Detective Nolan said, following him.

Sage moved a few yards away and leaned against the wall, relieved at least that she didn't have to look at another dead body. Then she became aware of the rank stench of formaldehyde seeping under the doors, remembered where she was, and moved away from the wall. Being inside Willowbrook's hospital was bad enough; she didn't want to touch anything in there, didn't want any part of her exposed to the poison that had surely permeated its bricks and mortar. Not her coat or her skin or her hair. She shoved her hands in her coat pockets and started to pace. Obviously Dr. Baldwin was showing Detective Nolan a body. But whose was it? And what was taking so long? What if they were lying about Eddie? What if he was in there, dead?

At long last, Detective Nolan came back through the doors and, without a word, marched down the hall toward the elevator, Dr. Baldwin on his heels. She hurried to catch up.

"Is it Eddie?" she said.

Nolan pushed his hat back on his head. "No, it's not Eddie."

"Who is it then?"

"It's Wayne Myers."

CHAPTER 23

Back in the service elevator, Sage took deep, even breaths, struggling to fight the dizziness and confusion that swirled inside her head. Wayne was dead. Which meant they were back at square one. "Where was he?" she asked Dr. Baldwin, whose colorless face was impossibly pale.

"The morgue attendant found him in the vault this morning," Dr. Baldwin said.

"How did he die?" She looked back and forth between him and Nolan. "Did someone kill him?"

"We can't be one hundred percent sure," Nolan said. "But it certainly looks that way. From what we can tell so far, his throat was cut. But he's a mess, so there could be other injuries we can't determine yet." He addressed Dr. Baldwin. "How many of your employees have keys to the morgue?"

Baldwin knit his brows together, thinking. "It's hard to know for sure," he said. "The attendants who transport bodies, several of the doctors, and the hospital janitors."

"And as far as you know," Nolan said, "Wayne Myers was not a patient in this hospital?"

"Of course not," Dr. Baldwin said, shaking his head. "He was an employee."

"Is it possible he was injured at work and taken over there?"

"I suppose it's possible," Dr. Baldwin said. "Anything is possible. But Nurse Vic would have known about that."

"Are you informed every time a resident or employee is sent to the hospital?"

"Well, no, but—"

"Why not?"

"Because I'm a psychiatrist, not a general practitioner, and I'm only one of many doctors who work here. I'm also in charge of numerous buildings and residents. I can't keep track of everyone."

"But you're informed when a resident dies?"

"No, the general practitioners in charge of each building are supposed to be informed, not me." He jabbed the button for the first floor and the elevator door lurched shut.

"Supposed to be?" Nolan sighed loudly and looked up as if trying not to lose his temper. Then he gave Baldwin a stern look. "My God, man. How do you keep track of anything here? I thought mistaking someone for a missing patient was bad enough."

A thin sheen of sweat broke out on Dr. Baldwin's forehead. "You do realize, Detective, that between residents and workers, we have nearly eight thousand souls here at Willowbrook. There's no way I or anyone else, for that matter, can possibly stay on top of everything. I'm not sure where you're going with this, but I don't like it. And Wayne Myers emptied his locker before he left, remember?"

"Or someone emptied it for him."

The elevator jerked to a stop and the doors opened. Sage hurried out and waited for Dr. Baldwin in the dim corridor. "I'm not sure why I had to come in here to find out Wayne was dead," she said when he got out. "But now that I know, what do you need to tell me about Eddie?"

Detective Nolan locked eyes with Dr. Baldwin, and a silent understanding passed between them. Whether it was concern or sympathy was hard to tell. The exchange happened so fast someone else might not have noticed, but she did. Her mind screamed, *Run!* But there was nowhere to go. And she needed to know what they were hiding about Eddie.

"I think it would be best if I showed you," Dr. Baldwin said.

Outside, the sleet had stopped and the wind had died down. When Sergeant Clark saw Nolan and Sage heading toward him across the parking lot, he started the vehicle. After they got in, Dr. Baldwin walked over and tapped on the window. Detective Nolan rolled it down.

"Follow me over to House Thirteen," Dr. Baldwin said. "We'll park behind the left wing and

I'll let you in through the employee entrance."

Sage stiffened. "House Thirteen?" she said. "Why do we have to go there?"

"You'll understand when we get there," Dr. Baldwin said.

Before she could say more, he turned and walked to his car. "I'm not going inside that building," Sage said to Detective Nolan. "You can't make me."

"Suit yourself," he said. "But the only way we're going to find out who killed your sister and stepfather is by you helping me find answers about what's really been going on in this place. Because to tell you the truth, at this point I'm as confused as you are."

She bit the inside of her lip hard enough to draw blood. She wanted to find Rosemary's killer too, but she didn't want to lose her sanity or her life in the process. Coming back to Willowbrook and going inside a resident building was too much.

When Sergeant Clark pulled onto the main road again, she wanted him to keep driving, right out the front gate and back to the city. But wanting something wasn't going to get her anywhere. And there was no getting out of this mess now anyway. She could either help Nolan find the killer or look over her shoulder for the rest of her life until he was caught.

"But I don't understand," she said. "What does House Thirteen have to do with Eddie?"

Nolan lit a cigarette, then turned and held the half-empty pack out to her, his arm across the back of the seat. Unfiltered Camels. Not her brand, and she hadn't smoked a cigarette in over two weeks, but she didn't care. She picked one from the pack with trembling fingers, let him light it, and took a long drag.

"I'm not sure," he said. "But Dr. Baldwin thinks it's important to *show* you what we're talking about, not tell you." He took a drag of his cigarette, held it for what seemed like forever, then forced the smoke out between his lips. "And I agree."

"But after that we're getting the hell out of here," she said. "Right?"

"Yup. As soon as we get this next bit cleared up." He squinted through the windshield, reading the stenciled numbers on the buildings.

Whatever that means, she thought. She took another drag of the cigarette, but it tasted awful and made her dizzy. She held on to it for another minute, then quickly rolled down the window and threw it out.

When they reached the right building, Clark parked behind the left wing next to Baldwin's car.

"Wait here," Nolan said. "This shouldn't take long."

He got out and opened her door, but Sage sat motionless in the back seat trying to find her courage. The images from House Six would haunt her for the rest of her life; she didn't need more to add to the torture. What if House Thirteen was worse? What if going inside made her have another anxiety attack like the one she had in Eddie's car? Thinking Dr. Baldwin might want to lock her up again didn't help.

Detective Nolan leaned down and looked at her through the open door. "You coming?"

She nodded and got out, then followed him to the back of House Thirteen. Keeping her eyes on the ground, she forced herself to put one foot in front of the other until they reached the employee entrance. Once inside, Dr. Baldwin led them down a hallway past metal doors, some open and some closed, others slightly ajar. In one room, industrial-size barrels of Pine-Sol and janitors' carts filled with mops and brooms lurked against the far wall like warped circus wagons. In another, lockers lined the walls, along with a time clock and a timecard rack, practically empty.

At the end of the hall, they turned right into another corridor, this one wider and with fewer doors. It looked exactly like the main hallway in House Six. For a second, she felt light-headed, overcome by the powerful sensation that she was about to fall to the floor. Half convinced that she'd just been jarred awake from a long dream to find herself still locked inside Willowbrook, she reminded herself to breathe and stayed close to

Detective Nolan. At least there were no moaning residents in wheelchairs and carts lining the hall.

When they passed the turnoff leading to the seclusion ward, she half expected Wayne to be standing there with a shit-eating grin on his face, ready to throw her into a straitjacket and drag her into the tunnels to slit her throat.

But Wayne was dead. So who would be waiting there instead?

At the far end of the hall, they came to a set of riveted double doors below a sign that read: ADULT WARD D. BURNED OUT CHRONIC.

"I thought Willowbrook was for children?" Detective Nolan said.

"It is, mostly," Dr. Baldwin said, unlocking the doors. "But children grow up."

He pushed open one side of the double doors and held it, and the familiar stench of feces and Pine-Sol immediately wafted over them, along with the nightmarish sounds of muttering and wailing and screaming. Nausea stirred in Sage's stomach. It was all she could do not to turn around and run.

After she and Nolan went through, Baldwin locked the door again and led them down a wide corridor, past more doors with square windows covered with metal bars. A woman screamed behind one door. A man pushed his face up to a window and barked at them. Another man let out of string of profanities.

Sage walked in the center of the corridor with her hands over her ears, the floor and walls reeling in front of her. Detective Nolan looked left and right, sometimes hesitating, sometimes walking fast. While he tried to maintain a professional detachment, the horror in his eyes betrayed him.

After they passed a nurses' station and took a left, Dr. Baldwin stopped at a door with a sign that read: CONSULTATION ROOM.

"You can wait in here," he said, unlocking the door and letting them through.

Inside, a pockmarked table surrounded by four wooden chairs sat in the center of what looked like a small waiting room, with three more chairs against one wall, beneath a painting of a pond surrounded by wildflowers. Detective Nolan took a seat at the table, turning the chair sideways to face the door. At first Sage couldn't decide whether to pace or sit. Then she got dizzy, so she sat in one of the chairs lining the wall, her hands tightly clasped in her lap, her knuckles turning white. A thousand thoughts and questions ran through her head, jumbling together so fast she couldn't think straight. She took a deep breath and let it out slowly, trying to stop trembling.

Within minutes, Dr. Baldwin returned, followed by an attendant gripping the arm of a young man. The young man shuffled into the room with his eyes down, his face devoid of emotion. When

Sage saw who it was, she felt something shift inside her head, as if Dr. Baldwin had reached into her brain with his ice pick and altered reality. She couldn't breathe.

"Eddie?" she managed. "What are you doing here?"

When Eddie looked up, he stopped in his tracks, his eyes wide.

She gaped at Dr. Baldwin. "What's going on? Why did you lock him up? He's not crazy. He was only trying to help me!"

"Sit down over there, Eddie," Dr. Baldwin said, pointing at the chair opposite the detective.

Eddie dropped his eyes but stayed put. The attendant yanked him forward and forced him into the chair, then stood behind him.

"It's all right," Dr. Baldwin said, nodding at the attendant. "I can handle this. Wait outside in the hall and shut the door behind you." After the attendant left, Baldwin stood in the middle of the room, halfway between Eddie and Detective Nolan.

Sage could only stare at Eddie, the roar of her blood growing louder and louder in her ears. She felt light-headed. Confused and sick. "Will someone please tell me what is going on?"

"Just a moment, Miss Winters," Dr. Baldwin said. "I think Detective Nolan might have a few questions first." Then he addressed Eddie. "I expect you to cooperate."

Eddie shrugged. "I did yesterday, didn't I?"

"Yes, but things have changed since then," Dr. Baldwin said. "We just came from—"

Nolan held up a hand to stop Dr. Baldwin from saying anything more, then regarded Eddie. "He's right, things have changed," he said. "And I appreciated your cooperation yesterday evening, but due to recent developments, I have some more questions. Sage says you paid her a visit last night. What do you have to say about that?"

"What do you want me to say about it?"

"Just answer the question," Dr. Baldwin said. "Did you go to Sage's apartment or not?"

He shrugged. "I don't know."

"Eddie, please," Sage said. "Tell them the truth. They can't fire you for something you did on your free time!"

Nolan held up a hand to silence her, keeping his eyes on Eddie. "She said you went to her apartment after she was released and stayed overnight on the couch."

Eddie shrugged again. "Okay."

"What the *hell* is going on?" Sage glared at Dr. Baldwin. "Did you drug him? Is that why he's acting so strange?"

Dr. Baldwin shook his head.

"Yeah, right. What did you give him?"

The doctor ignored her.

She began pleading with Eddie. "Why aren't

you telling them what happened? You showed up in front of my house when I left to go to the grocery store a little after one in the morning. We went to the Top Hat to get something to eat, then you slept on my couch because I was scared, remember? And then this morning . . . this morning I found Alan dead under his bed!"

Finally, Eddie acknowledged her. "I'm sorry to hear that," he said. "I really am." His voice was emotionless and cold, nothing like the Eddie she thought she knew. And he wouldn't meet her eyes.

Panic and anger rose like bile in her throat. She wanted to grab him by the neck and shake him until he told the truth. What was he trying to pull? Did he want Dr. Baldwin to think she was crazy?

Eddie looked at Detective Nolan. "Was it Wayne? Did you catch him yet?"

"Yes, we found him," Nolan said.

"Wow, that was quick. Did he confess?"

"No, he didn't confess. He's dead. They found him in the morgue this morning."

Eddie's mouth fell open. Then a smirk played around his lips and he eyed Dr. Baldwin. "Did *you* put him there?"

"Enough of the bullshit, Eddie," Dr. Baldwin said. "I warned you to cooperate."

"How am I not cooperating?" Eddie raised his hands in the air. "It's a legitimate question."

Dr. Baldwin shook his head, like a teacher dealing with a disobedient student.

"Sage said you were driving a red Mustang," Detective Nolan said.

"Cool," Eddie said. "Except I don't know how to drive."

A miserable clutch of fear twisted in her stomach. "What are you doing, Eddie?" she said. "Why are you lying?"

Dr. Baldwin looked at Detective Nolan. "Do you want to tell her, or do you want me to do it?"

"Tell me *what?*" She felt like throwing up.

Baldwin cleared his throat. "I'm sorry, Miss Winters, but what you're saying is impossible. Eddie doesn't work at Willowbrook. Well, he does, but he's not a paid employee. He's been a resident here since he was nine years old, when he was found at Grand Central Station with a sign around his neck that said, *Take Me to Willowbrook.* And like a number of the long-time residents, he empties the trash cans and mops the floors because we're understaffed and it keeps him out of trouble. At least it did, until you came along. He doesn't have a driver's license, let alone access to a vehicle, so he couldn't possibly have been at your apartment last night."

The floor seemed to drop out from beneath her. She couldn't feel her legs. This was a setup after all. They didn't believe her. They thought she was crazy. But what she said was true. Eddie had been there. He'd taken her to the Top Hat. He'd folded the blanket on the couch before he left.

Unless.

Unless . . .

She started to shake. Unless she'd imagined the whole thing. Unless being locked up in Willowbrook had unearthed the hidden parts of her brain that were twin to Rosemary's. Unless *her* head was full of ghosts too. She gaped at Eddie, tears blurring her vision.

"Why are you doing this?" she said. "Why aren't you helping me?"

"I'm not doing anything."

A booming noise filled her head. It was too loud. Too overwhelming. All of this was too much—too unbelievable, too ridiculous. She looked at Dr. Baldwin. "If he doesn't work here, how did he take me down into the tunnels? How did he get a key?"

"Detective Nolan and I discussed that with Eddie yesterday," Dr. Baldwin said. "He says someone left the door to the tunnels open when the reporters broke into House Six, and you must have taken advantage of the situation to try to escape. I can assure you he never had a key."

"That's not true," she said. "We planned the whole thing together. Remember when I told you he overheard the doctors talking about Dr. Wilkins giving the reporter the key to House Six?

Eddie and I knew we could get into the tunnels when they arrived because he had a key. He said he lied to you about it because you would have fired him for helping me, but you made him work in another building instead."

"Well, he's not an employee so he couldn't have been fired," Dr. Baldwin said. "But I did prevent him from working in House Six again, that part is true. But that is neither here nor there. Residents are not allowed to have keys."

"But he came into the ward in the middle of the night. He *must* have one!" she said. "And I saw keys in his hands! He also called the cops because he knew you'd try to cover up Rosemary's murder. And I don't care what he says or what you say, he came to my house last night!" She turned to Eddie. "Tell them!"

"Sorry," Eddie said. "I don't know what you're talking about."

"You're lying!" she said, close to screaming. "You picked me up in a red Ford Mustang and drove me to the Top Hat for breakfast! You even paid the bill!" She pointed at Detective Nolan. "He sent someone to the diner to talk to the waitress, so you might as well tell the truth!"

"Maybe Detective Nolan sent someone to check out your story because he knows it's impossible," Dr. Baldwin said. "He's known since last evening that Eddie is a resident."

Nolan gave Dr. Baldwin an irritated look, then

said, "I'll confirm one way or the other when I hear back from Officer McNally."

"Then call the station," she said. "See if he's back yet."

"I will. As soon as we're done here."

"Excuse me for stating the obvious," Dr. Baldwin said, "but how on earth can anyone prove it was Eddie at the diner? It could have easily been some other boy."

"Iris knows my friends," Sage said. "She thought Eddie was my cousin." She turned to Nolan. "Will Officer McNally ask her about that? Will he ask her if I was with one of my usual friends?"

"Maybe," he said. "But unless Iris knows Eddie or has seen him before, technically Dr. Baldwin is correct. There's really no way to prove it was him."

Tears welled in her eyes. "It was him, I swear on my life."

"I'm sorry, Miss Winters," Dr. Baldwin said, using the same tone he'd used when he thought she was Rosemary. "But there's no way Eddie came to your apartment last night. And you see how this looks, don't you?"

"Of course I see how it looks," she said. "But Eddie's lying!" She turned to Detective Nolan. "You believe me, don't you?"

"I want to," he said. "I really do. But at this point your story is a little hard to swallow. If

Eddie could leave Willowbrook to go to your house, why would he come back here?"

"I don't know!" she cried. "Maybe you should ask him that! But I didn't imagine it! I'm not sick like my sister!"

"No one said you were sick," Nolan said.

She leapt up, ran toward the door, and tried the handle. It was locked. She spun around and stared at the men, all of them watching her with pity. "Let me out of here! I want to go home!"

Dr. Baldwin started toward her.

"No," she cried. "Eddie, please! Tell them you were there. Tell them we went to the Top Hat." She looked at Baldwin and Nolan with wide, tear-filled eyes. "We had pancakes and . . . and he played Pink Floyd on the eight-track!"

Eddie made a face. "Pink Floyd? Is that a band?"

"You know it is!" she shouted. "You said you saw them in concert!"

"Just calm down, Miss Winters," Dr. Baldwin said. "Everything is going to be all right."

She shook her head violently back and forth. "No! No, you're not locking me up again."

"No one said anything about locking you up," Baldwin said. "We just want to help you get through this latest shock."

She pleaded with Nolan. "But you went to the apartment. You saw the pillow and blanket on the couch where he slept."

"I saw a blanket and pillow on the couch, yes. But that doesn't mean anything. *You* could have slept there, for all I know."

"No, I slept in my bed. What about the note? He left me a note and twenty dollars!"

"We found a note on the floor, but it wasn't signed by anyone," Nolan said. "And there was no date on it."

She gaped at Eddie. "Please, don't let them do this. Please!"

"We're not going to do anything to you," Dr. Baldwin said. "But I think it would be best if you stayed here for a couple of days, overnight at the very least. We've got a few short-term rooms in the main building for temporary admissions. I won't put you in House Six again unless it becomes necessary, so don't worry about that. It's not likely that you'll fall into full-blown psychosis like your sister, but we want to be on top of the situation to prevent that from happening."

She shook her head again, gaping at Detective Nolan, horror filling her throat like oil. "You said you wouldn't let him lock me up again!"

He pressed his lips together and nodded, looking sheepish. "Let me run out and have Sergeant Clark give the station a call on the radio to see if McNally's returned from the Top Hat yet," he said. He stood and started toward the door. "It'll only take a few minutes."

"If you insist," Dr. Baldwin said. "But it's a waste of time."

Sage stood rooted to the floor, blocking the exit. "Take me with you!"

He shook his head. "It'll be faster if I go alone. I'll be right back."

"I'm begging you," she said. "Don't leave me here."

"The sooner you let me by, the sooner I'll find out if McNally talked to Iris or not," he said. "That's what you want, isn't it?" His voice had turned patronizing, as if he were talking to a child.

She nodded, her chin trembling, and reluctantly moved aside. He tried the handle, but it was locked. Dr. Baldwin unlocked the door and let him out, then stuck his head into the hall and spoke to the assistant waiting there.

"You can take Eddie back to his ward now."

The attendant entered and Dr. Baldwin shut the door behind him, guarding it so Sage wouldn't try to escape. Eddie stood, his face blank, and let the attendant take his arm and lead him toward the door. She moved to a chair and sat down, watching him, praying he would change his mind and tell the truth. But he kept his eyes straight ahead, as if no one else were in the room, as if his words and actions had no repercussions. And then, without a second glance at her, he was gone.

Dr. Baldwin shut the door, locked it, and took

a seat across from her. She stared at the floor, refusing to look at him.

"You know I only want to help," Dr. Baldwin said. "But I can't help if you won't let me."

She ignored him.

"It wouldn't surprise me at all if you had a hallucination about Eddie last night," he said. "Or maybe it was a dream that you think was real. After all, he was a big part of your time here and—"

"Don't talk to me," she said. "I have nothing to say to you."

"But talking things out is the only way to get through everything you've experienced. It's the only way to find out what's really been happening here."

"Nothing is happening, except for you taking Eddie's word over mine. And if I ever need to talk to someone, it sure as hell won't be you."

He made a wordless noise of disgust. "We'll see about that," he said.

Finally, after what felt like the longest few minutes of her life, someone knocked on the door. Dr. Baldwin got up and unlocked it. Detective Nolan entered and looked down at Sage, wind-blown and out of breath.

"I'm sorry," he said. "But Iris is off today. The owner of the Top Hat said she's gone out of town for a few days."

Sage felt like someone had hit her in the chest

with a sledgehammer. No one but Iris could back up her story.

Nolan addressed Dr. Baldwin. "I'll make a call to Social Services so they can work on finding her a temporary place to stay. That was the plan to begin with because she has no other family we can reach right now."

"With all due respect, Detective," Dr. Baldwin said, "I know a mental breakdown when I see one. The right thing to do here is to let Miss Winters get the help she needs. That way you can kill two birds with one stone, giving her a place to stay until you check out her story. You're welcome to return tomorrow to see if the situation has changed, but if I were a betting man, I'd bet good money that you're going to learn there is no way Eddie King was at that diner with her, or anywhere else near her, for that matter."

"I'm not having a mental breakdown," Sage said, trembling with rage and fear. "I'm upset because Eddie is lying and you don't believe me. Why is that so hard for you to understand?"

The detective looked at her with apologetic eyes. "Maybe Dr. Baldwin is right. Maybe it'd be for the best if you stayed here, just for one night, at least. That will give Social Services a little extra time to find you a temporary foster home, instead of sticking you in the children's home for who knows how long."

"No!" she said. "I won't do it!" She got up, ran

to the door again, and shook the handle. "Let me out of here!" She pounded on the door. "Please! Someone let me out!"

Strong hands pulled her away from the door, then turned her around. It was Detective Nolan. He wrapped his arms around her, holding her so tight she could hardly breathe, his face in her hair. She struggled to get free, but it was no use.

"Calm down," he said in her ear. "You're acting like a lunatic and making this worse than it has to be. I want to believe you and I want to help, but I can't if you don't cooperate."

She stopped struggling and leaned against him, sobbing and trying to stay upright.

"I'll let go," he said. "But you have to pull yourself together and listen to me, okay?"

She nodded and he released her, but kept his hands on her arms, as if afraid she'd fall. She pushed her hair from her eyes and swallowed her sobs, her shoulders hitching.

"You can't go back to the apartment right now anyway," Nolan said. "It's a crime scene. And like I said, we can't just let you out in the streets. I know it's not what you want to hear, but for right now, I think you should stay here. I'll find out where Iris went and call her myself. And as soon as your story about the diner checks out, I'll come back and take you out of here, no matter what Dr. Baldwin says, all right?"

"No!" she sobbed. "You've seen how horrible

this place is. Don't let them keep me here again!"

Detective Nolan shook his head. "I'm sorry, kiddo, but it's the best solution right now."

She moaned and closed her eyes. Then her knees gave out, she fell to the floor, and everything went black.

CHAPTER 24

At first, Sage was vaguely aware of the stiff material beneath her cheek and the strong, acidic smell of Pine-Sol and bleach. Then she realized she was shivering, despite the fact that she was under a blanket and fully dressed, except for her winter boots. She turned her head and opened her eyes. A strip of fluorescent lighting hung above her, a bright line of white against a gray-tiled ceiling.

Then she remembered returning to Willow-brook. Panic slammed into her chest, knocking the air from her lungs. She gasped and sat up. Had Dr. Baldwin locked her up again? Was she in House Six? She looked around. No other residents lay in white beds beside her. No other furniture filled the room; only the iron bed beneath her. She wasn't in a ward, but what building was this? And how long had she been out? The barred window beside her revealed a dark sky. At least she wasn't strapped down this time. She got up and tried the steel door. It was locked. She pounded on it.

"Hello?" she shouted. "Is anyone out there?"

No sounds came from the other side.

"Please!" she shouted as loudly as possible.

"Can someone let me out of here?" She pounded on the door again, this time with both hands. "Hello?"

No one answered. No one came and unlocked the door.

She went over to the window and looked out. The full moon hung round and pale behind drifting gray clouds. Several floors below, Willowbrook's snow-covered campus stretched out like an endless blanket, the white expanse broken up by an occasional streetlamp, dark clusters of bare trees, and the sinister hulk of two resident buildings. The city lights of Staten Island sparkled in the distance, cold and remote, white as ice, and as far out of reach as the stars in the sky.

She pressed her forehead against the window, slammed the side of her fist against the thick glass, and closed her flooding eyes. Why had she come back here? Why had she trusted Detective Nolan? One thing was for sure: When she saw Dr. Baldwin again, she'd lie and say she was wrong about Eddie. He had never come to her apartment, had never slept on the couch. Anything to get out of there. She'd say she took a sleeping pill and made a mistake. She'd say she was confused and scared and grieving. She'd say it was all just a dream.

If she saw Dr. Baldwin again.

Behind her, a key turned in the lock. She spun

around. *Thank God.* Someone had heard her call for help. Someone was going to let her out. Maybe Detective Nolan had already talked to Iris and realized she was telling the truth. She started toward the door, then slowed. What if it was a nurse coming in with a syringe? What if it was Marla coming to take her back to House Six? The door opened partway and she froze, holding her breath. Then a familiar man quickly slipped inside and closed the door behind him. She took a step back.

It was Eddie.

"What are you doing here?" she said.

"I came to see you," he said, sounding like the old Eddie again.

Her heart thumped faster. She didn't trust him or anything he said. Not only had he been lying to everyone, including her, he'd made her look crazy and let Dr. Baldwin lock her up again. It was all she could do not to slap him across the face. At the same time, she needed to be careful. Who knew if he had a serious mental problem or was just playing games? And what else was he lying about? "How did you get in?"

He held out his hand to reveal a ring of keys. "The same way I get in and out of everywhere."

She pressed her lips together, holding back her fury and the words she wanted to say. "Where did you get them?"

"A janitor needs keys."

"But you're not a real janitor," she said. "You're a—"

"A what? A resident? A retard? A piece of human garbage someone threw away?"

She shook her head. Despite sounding like the old Eddie, something in his eyes had changed. Either that, or she'd been so blinded by desperation when she was in House Six that she'd seen concern in his eyes instead of coldness, kindness instead of deceit. "That's not what I was going to say," she said. "But why have you been lying to me?"

"Would you have trusted me if I'd told you the truth?"

"I don't know. You were nice to me and you were trying to help. That was all that mattered to me. And you were nice to my sister too. At least I think you were."

"I was," he said. "But now you know who I really am. Now you know I'm a long-term resident of Willowbrook State School. Except I've got these." He held up the keys and shook them. "And that makes all the difference."

"Is that how you got out and came to my house?"

He grinned. "Maybe."

"And the Mustang?"

"I stole it."

"What about the money you used to pay for breakfast?"

"Found it in the glove box of the Mustang."

"But if you've had those keys this whole time, why didn't you just let me out of here?"

"I could have, but I wanted to make it look like you escaped on your own."

"Why?"

He looked at her like she was crazy. "*Why?* Do you know what they'd do to me if they found out I set you free? They'd pump me full of Thorazine and Prolixin and lock me up in the state security hospital. Then I'd be done for."

"So you were protecting yourself."

"Damn right I was. I don't have a choice."

"And now you're protecting yourself again, by letting them think I'm sick like Rosemary," she said, suddenly incapable of hiding her anger. "By letting them think I imagined the whole thing . . . you coming to the apartment and taking me to the Top Hat. You sleeping on the couch. You let them lock me up again instead of telling them what really happened."

"I'm sorry," he said, tilting his head like he was sad. "But you didn't really expect me to give up my freedom for you, did you?"

"What are you talking about? You're not free. You've been in Willowbrook since you were nine years old."

"That's true, I have," he said. He held up the keys again. "But freedom looks different to everyone."

She furrowed her brow. It was her turn to

look at him like he was crazy. "There's nothing about being locked up here or anywhere else that means you're free, keys or no keys. What I don't understand is, why don't you leave? Why would you stay here when you can get out so easily?" As soon as the words left her mouth, she regretted them. Maybe, impossibly, he hadn't thought about leaving and now that she'd suggested it, he would. Not that he deserved to stay locked up in Willowbrook—no one did—but what if he wanted to leave with her? What if he thought he could be part of her life?

He shook his head, suddenly serious. "I can't leave."

She breathed a silent sigh of relief. But his answer made no sense. Who, in any capacity of their right mind, would want to stay? Maybe he really did have a psychological problem. "Why not?" she said.

"Because I can't abandon them."

"Abandon who?"

"Everyone. The staff. The residents. They all need me."

She started to say he was being ridiculous, that everyone would get along fine without him, but stopped herself. Not only did she want to avoid encouraging him, but suddenly she was frightened by the way he stood so terrible and still. He was dead serious. Delusional. And who knew what else.

"What do you mean they need you?"

He groaned, long and loud, as if it took too much effort to explain. "Because I *help* them. I help the staff by working. And I help the residents when they've had enough of this place."

"What do you mean you help the residents? How?"

"I help them escape."

Her eyes widened. "Through the tunnels?"

"No, not like that. Taking *you* through the tunnels so you could escape was different. You'd be all right out there in the real world. But the other poor sons-a-bitches in this place? They'd never survive out there, and they know it. That's why they come to me when they're ready to be set free."

She shook her head, confused. What was he talking about? Did he get them more drugs? Move them to the experimental wards where there were drapes on the windows and silverware in a dining hall? "I don't understand."

He rolled his eyes. "How long were you locked up here, a couple of weeks? Imagine living in this place for years. Decades. Your entire *life*. Imagine coming here as a child. Then the day comes when you're no longer cute. You're big and smelly and even more broken from years of abuse and daily drugs. It's different for someone like me, I'm perfectly sane and I don't have any mental or physical handicaps. I understand what the staff wants. I know how to stay out of trouble. But the others? They have some real problems for sure, but it's this heartless institution that makes them act the way they do. They want love and compassion and kindness just like everyone does. Sure, they get angry and confused and upset, but it's the way they're treated that makes them crazy. Hell, animals get treated better than the residents do in this place. I give them a way out of this nightmare."

Her skin prickled as a hint of realization took shape in her mind. He couldn't be saying what she thought he was saying—could he? "How do you . . . 'give them a way out'?"

He gave her a stern look, like a teacher scolding a lazy student. "I told you before that no one has any idea how many residents die in this shithole every year. Do *you* know how many? Hundreds. Four hundred died last year. *Four hundred.*" A pained expression pinched his face. "Do you think anyone cares why, or how, or what happened to them? Their death certificates say they stopped eating or died from pneumonia or measles or some other bullshit virus that was given to them on purpose, like they were no better than lab rats. Their death certificates never say 'kicked in the head by an attendant' or 'starved to death.' Never 'beaten to death' or 'given too many drugs.' Because that might make the city and state suspicious. That might make someone dig into what's happening here."

She swallowed, feeling sick. Despite her reluctance to hear more, she needed to know exactly what he meant. She needed him to spell it out in black and white, to put the last piece of the puzzle in place so she could be sure. "I understand what you're saying, but how do you help the residents escape?"

"The fact that no one cares how they die makes it easy to do what I do. That's why the residents need me. I want Willowbrook shut down, but I don't see that happening. And no one leaves here unless they die. That's why the residents think of me as their angel of mercy."

She couldn't believe what she was hearing. "Angel of . . . ?"

"Angel of mercy. Cropsey. Whatever you want to call me."

She drew in a sharp breath. "What . . . what are you saying?"

"You know perfectly well what I'm saying. But you need to remember that *Willowbrook* is the culprit here, not me. Willowbrook makes life a living hell."

She went rigid, her body turned to ice. He was out of his mind. And now she knew his secret. She glanced at the door, praying he hadn't locked it. She had to get out of there. "And Rosemary? Did you . . . did you—"

"Your sister had an unbearable existence," he

said. "When she wanted to escape it, I hid her for days, trying desperately to talk her out of it because I truly cared about her, but she begged me to end her pain."

Sage clenched her teeth, holding back a scream. It was easy to understand why Rosemary had wanted to end her dreadful life in Willowbrook, but surely she hadn't wanted her throat slashed. Surely she hadn't wanted to bleed out, to be left to rot in a pitch-black tunnel before being buried in the cold, muddy ground. Grief tore at her heart again. Her poor sister had endured so much.

"By slitting her throat?" she managed.

He shook his head, his face waxen, brittle. "No. When I gave her the freedom she longed for, I decided to kill two birds with one stone."

"What . . . what do you mean?" She glanced around the room, looking for something she could use as a weapon. There was nothing.

"I wanted to make it look like Wayne killed her." His eyes grew glassy. "You know what he was doing to her. I wanted him to pay. But I promise, she didn't feel a thing. She swallowed a handful of pills before I cut her throat."

A burning lump blocked Sage's windpipe. She felt like she was suffocating. "If you were trying to make it look like Wayne killed Rosemary," she said, "why did you move her body?"

He shrugged. "Because I panicked. And because I decided I wanted you to stay."

Oh God. That's why he had lied. That's why he let Dr. Baldwin lock her up again. She had to get out of that room. Had to get away from him. Had to tell someone what he'd done. But she wanted to understand how he did it, and she needed to know how to find more proof.

"How did you have time to move her before taking Dr. Baldwin into the tunnels?" she said. "You said you were waiting outside his office while he was making phone calls."

"I was. But there's so much you don't know about this place, like that fact that Dr. Baldwin's secretary, little Miss Evie Carter, was a lying slut. While Baldwin made the phone calls, I told her she had to let me leave for a few minutes, otherwise I'd tell her husband about her extra-curricular activities with Baldwin and Wayne. Of course I promised to come right back."

An image flashed in her mind—Evie's husband out in the woods, threatening to kill Dr. Baldwin. "Dr. Baldwin said Evie's husband was helping Dr. Wilkins. So he's your uncle, right? The one who told you about the reporters having a key to House Six? Or was that a lie too?"

"Dr. Carter is good to me, like an uncle is good to his nephew, or a father to his son. He's a decent man who wants to do right by the residents. He deserves a loving, faithful wife."

"So you . . . you killed Evie too?"

"Maybe."

Horror and bewilderment twisted in her mind. "But why? She just worked here. She wasn't a resident. She didn't do anything to you."

"Like I said, she was a slut. And it helped make Wayne look guilty."

She stared at him, unable to shake the feeling that she'd disconnected from reality. Even though he was standing right in front of her. Even though he was saying the words. "Then why did you kill Wayne if you were trying to frame him?"

"Because he deserved it and I needed to stop him. After you told me about Norma, I couldn't let him get away with it anymore. He was a fucking pig."

"But it worked. Everyone thought he was the killer until you put him in the morgue. Why would you—?"

He shrugged one shoulder. "To fuck with Baldwin. The more bodies found on Willowbrook property, the more attention on him and everyone who works here."

"And Alan?"

He frowned, confusion lining his face. "I thought you hated him?"

"That doesn't mean I wanted him dead!"

"Well, he was an asshole. When he was finally home to answer the door, he was so drunk he could barely stand. He told me to get lost and slammed the door in my face."

"So you never left him a note about me being here?"

"Oh, I did, but after I gave him what he deserved, I found them in the apartment and got rid of them."

Putting a hand over her mouth to hold back her revulsion, she pictured him slitting Alan's throat, painting a clown smile on his face, and shoving his body under the bed. No matter what he said about "helping" people, he was clearly a cold-blooded killer. Then she had another thought and shivered.

"What about . . ." But she hesitated. No. She couldn't ask him that.

"What?"

"Nothing," she said, then crossed her arms and began to pace, hoping she could get closer to the door without him noticing.

"Tell me what you were going to say," he said. "I want to know."

"I don't remember," she said.

"Yes, you do. Tell me."

She stopped and considered him, unsure how to word the question. On one hand, she didn't want to hear his answer; on the other hand, she had to know. "Have you snuck out of Willow-brook before? I mean, before you came to my house?"

"Of course. Why?"

"What for?"

"I had my reasons. Why do you want to know? What difference does it make?"

"You said I could call you Cropsey. Did you . . . other than Alan, did you kill anyone else? Outside of Willowbrook, I mean?"

He dropped his gaze to the floor, then looked at her with pain-filled eyes. "Do you know how many people have shitty lives out here? How many kids have parents who beat and abuse them, or don't make enough money to feed them? How many have parents who are alcoholics or drug addicts?"

"Oh my God." Terror rose to a fever pitch in her mind. And she'd given him her friends' addresses! "Please tell me you . . . you didn't hurt Heather and Dawn, did you?"

He shook his head. "I thought about it, but they weren't worth my time."

Relief swirled through her, along with the growing cyclone of panic and fear.

"Remember after the first time I saw you in the hall, you didn't see me the next day?" he said. "I freaked out because I thought you were Rosemary's ghost. I didn't tell Dr. Baldwin why I was so upset, but he had to sedate me for a while."

She said nothing. If he was looking for sympathy, he was asking the wrong person. Then she thought of something else.

"So you *wanted* me to see Rosemary's body in the tunnels. But why?"

"Because . . ."

She waited.

"Because I thought you deserved to know she was dead instead of wondering what had happened to her. I can tell you're a good person. And not knowing what happened to someone you love is worse than knowing."

"If I'm a good person, then why are you doing this to me?" Her voice broke. "I don't deserve to be locked up again."

"I'm sorry. But I don't know what else to do. I can't tell them the truth." He moved toward her, reaching for her with one hand, his eyes sad.

She forced herself to stand stock-still, as if ready to accept a comforting gesture, then skirted around him at the last second, raced to the door, and tried the handle. It was locked. She spun around to face him, her back pressed against the cold steel.

He let out a humorless laugh. "Did you really think I'd be stupid enough to leave it unlocked?"

"Please, just let me go. I'll never survive in this place. I have to get out of here." Then she forced a smile, hoping to convince him they could still be friends. It felt like a twitch. "I'm . . . I'm not going far. You've still got keys. You can sneak out and come visit me whenever you want."

He moved closer, staring at her with a pained expression. "You're lying," he said. "You're afraid of me, I can see it in your eyes. And you're smart to be afraid, because I can't let you or any-one else come between me and what I was put here to do. If you tell them, they'll make sure I can never help anyone else. And I can't let that happen."

"I won't tell," she said. "I promise."

"Of course you will. You think I'm a monster. And you want to make me pay for killing your sister. You're a good person, remember? You want to see justice served. But you need to under-stand that this is bigger than you and me."

She shook her head furiously back and forth. "No. I just want to go home. That's all, I prom-ise."

He took a step back and reached into his pocket. "I almost forgot. I brought you something." He held out his closed fists as if playing a guessing game. "Pick one."

"I don't want to," she said.

"Come on. Didn't your parents teach you it's rude to turn down a gift?" He tried to hide his irritation, but anger edged his voice.

"The only gift I want is to be free." As soon as the words left her mouth, she regretted them. As he had said, freedom could mean different things.

"I'll set you free, I promise, but first you have to pick one."

She shook her head again.

He opened his fists. A red cylinder lay in one palm. It looked like a fat tube of lipstick. She raised her eyes to meet his, and the vicious gleam she saw there drained the blood from her veins. Then, horribly, he began to laugh.

She turned and pounded on the door. "Help!" she screamed. "Someone, please! Help me!"

He grabbed her arm and yanked her toward him. She fell to her knees, kicking and screaming and trying to get away. He yanked her up, dragged her over to the bed, and pushed her onto the mattress. "You're making this harder than it has to be," he snarled. He put a sweaty hand over her mouth, held up the lipstick tube, and popped off the cap with his thumb. A hawkbill blade shimmered in the light.

She tried to scream, but he pressed his hand harder over her mouth and climbed on top of her, straddling her like a horse. She bucked beneath him, but it was no use. He was too heavy, too strong. She tried to snatch the weapon from his fist, her arms flailing, her hands grabbing but finding only air. He moved the blade back and forth, slicing her skin and lifting the knife out of her reach. Then he held it up high.

"Not the color you expected?" he said.

In that second, while he taunted her, she opened her mouth wide and bit down as hard as she could, catching two of his fingers and not letting go. He yelped and she bit down harder, kicking and shaking her head like a mad dog until his flesh broke between her teeth. He bent forward in agony. She tried to grab the blade and he swiped at her arms, cutting her again.

She reached up and shoved her thumb into his eye. He tried to pull her thumb away with his free hand, but accidently cut his own temple, just missing his eye socket and gouging out a thick flap of bloody skin. He cussed and reached for his face, dropping the blade. It clattered to the floor. She pressed her thumb harder into his eye and dug her fingers into his wound. He finally tore her hand away and clutched his bloody head, his face contorting in pain. She unclenched her teeth from his fingers, then slammed both hands into his chest as hard as she could. He grunted in surprise and half fell, half stumbled off the bed, landing on his side.

She scrambled upright and frantically searched the floor for the blade but didn't see it anywhere. Then she saw it, only a few feet behind him. He turned over and got to his feet, one hand over his bleeding temple, one eye squeezed shut. He was looking for the blade too, his uninjured eye gaping and bloodshot. Sage lunged forward, grabbed the knife, and plunged it into his side, grunting with the effort. He looked down and tried to pull it out with a blood-covered hand, staggering back and forth like a drunk. She yanked it out of his side and retreated with it in her fist, ready to stab him again if he got close.

Eddie lurched forward, his hands clawed and

ready to grab her. She pulled back the blade and jammed it into his neck as hard as she could. He went rigid, blood instantly gushing out from below his ear. She stepped back, gasping for air and trying to stay upright.

He stared at her with a feral-looking mixture of desperation and rage until, finally, the fight left his eyes. He fell to his knees, one hand grasping his neck. Blood poured between his fingers, running down his arm and chest in red rivers. Then, in what seemed like slow motion, he fell face-first on the floor.

Sage backed up and leaned against the wall, a scream welling up in her throat. The warm, coppery tang of blood filled her mouth, and she spat several times to get rid of the taste. She wiped her mouth with the back of her hand, leaving a watery streak of saliva and blood on her skin. Streaks of blood striped her arms and clothes, dripping dark and heavy on the floor.

Feeling faint, she examined her injuries. Ragged slashes crisscrossed her forearms and wrists, along with several deep lacerations on her hands. She hadn't felt a thing when it had happened, but now the wounds felt on fire. Pressing her forearms into her sides to slow the bleeding, she looked at Eddie.

He lay on his stomach in the middle of a growing puddle of blood, his face turned to one side, his legs and arms at odd angles. She stared at his back, straining her eyes to see if he was still breathing. His gore-splattered shirt lay flat and still. At least it seemed like it did. It was hard to tell when her heart was pounding so hard and so fast that the room throbbed with every beat.

She edged forward, trying not to step in his blood, and nudged his shoulder with one foot. He lay still as a stone. She searched the floor for the keys, looking under the bed and along his body, between his legs and in his hands, but didn't see them anywhere. *Damn it.* The only place she hadn't looked was in his pants pockets. Kneeling down, she reached into one pocket but couldn't reach in far enough. She lifted his shoulder, put a hand under one of his thighs, and heaved him over, flopping him onto his back.

When his body hit the floor again, he exhaled, long and loud. She shrieked and scrambled backward. He was still alive! Then she realized the deep sigh was his last breath being expelled from his lungs. She closed her eyes for a second and tried to calm down, then sat up and moved toward him again, keeping her eyes off his face. Holding her breath, she reached into his right-hand pocket. *Thank God.* The keys were there, cold and hard on her fingers. She yanked them out, straightened, and started toward the door, praying it wouldn't take long to find the right one.

Then she looked back at Eddie—she couldn't

stop herself. His eyes were open as if staring at her, his lips bloody and sagging, like the upside-down smile of a clown. With trembling fingers, she tried the keys one by one in the door, until at last she found the right one.

CHAPTER 25

Sitting up in the hospital bed, an IV in one hand, Sage stared at the tray of ground-up food in front of her. The nurse had begged her to eat, but the thought of eating one more bite of Willowbrook slop made her stomach turn. Just being in Willowbrook's hospital was enough to make her sick. It might have helped if she could have washed the blood and the odor of Pine-Sol from her skin and hair, but the nurse said a shower had to wait. Seventy-six stitches crisscrossed her forearms and hands, and the bandages went up to her elbows. It would be twenty-four hours before she could get them wet.

And she could even live with *that,* if they'd only let her out of there. She'd called for the nurse to ask when she'd be released so many times that they'd started ignoring her. She didn't care. Maybe they'd throw her out. She pushed the tray of ground-up food away. If they would give her back her clothes, she could leave, but her pants and shirt were in the laundry. The laundry worker who had picked them up warned her that it might be hard to remove the bloodstains. She didn't care about that either. She'd wear a grocery bag if she had to, as long as it meant she could leave.

Of course she had no idea where she'd go, but it didn't matter. She'd think about that on the other side of Willowbrook's gate.

Someone knocked on the door, a quick, insistent rap. She looked up as the door opened.

It was Detective Nolan.

She dropped her eyes to her lap. He was supposed to help her. Instead, he'd gotten her committed again.

"How are you feeling?" he said.

She looked up at him. "How am I *feeling?* Dr. Baldwin locked me up again, and Eddie almost killed me. How do you think I'm feeling?"

"I know, and I'm sorry," he said. "I should have listened to you."

"You think?" She started to cross her arms, but the stitches pulled and stung.

"What can I do to make it up to you?"

"Get me out of here. They want to keep me overnight."

He nodded. "I know. I just talked to the doctor who stitched you up. And I know you want to leave, but you've been through hell and they need to make sure you're okay before they let you go."

"I'm fine," she said.

He pulled a chair away from the wall, shucked off his coat and hung it over the back, then sat down. "You might think you're fine, but you need fluids and rest."

"Then take me to a normal hospital," she said. "Anyplace but here."

"They're not going to lock you up again, I promise. We all know you're telling the truth about Eddie coming to your house now. Along with everything that happened last night, we've also found out that a red 1972 Mustang had been stolen just outside of Bulls Head the night you said he showed up at your apartment. The car was abandoned out on Richmond Avenue. The owner was found dead in his garage with his throat slit."

She closed her eyes, trying to work out the juxtaposition in her mind. Eddie had been sick, that much was clear, but he'd honestly thought he was helping people. Except somewhere along the way, "helping people" had turned him into something else: a killer who ended lives with ease and without remorse. How many people had he murdered? Ten? A hundred? A thousand? Would they ever know? She looked at Detective Nolan again. "Is he dead? Did I kill him?"

He shook his head. "He's in a coma. The doctors think he'll survive, but they're not sure when, or if, he'll wake up."

"And if he does?"

"If he's fit to stand trial, he'll be held responsible for murdering your sister. And the others."

"He'll go to jail?"

"If he's found guilty, yes. Or he might get the death penalty."

"What do you mean, *if?* He told me he did it. He confessed to everything. He killed Evie and Wayne and Alan."

"Alan too?"

She nodded, her eyes filling.

"Did he say why?"

"Because he knew I hated him." She felt sour with shame.

"Jesus."

"There's more," she said. "He killed other Willowbrook residents too. And . . ." She hesitated, not sure how to explain herself without sounding ridiculous. "When he came to my apartment, it wasn't the first time he'd snuck out of Willowbrook. I don't know how many times he left before, but I'm pretty sure he's responsible for a lot of the missing kid flyers on Staten Island. He said I could call him the angel of mercy or Cropsey."

"Good God," Nolan said, shaking his head. "I hope he wakes up so we can crucify the bastard. And find his other victims, of course."

"What about Dr. Baldwin? Is anything going to happen to him and the other people in charge at Willowbrook?"

"Well, thanks to that reporter breaking into House Six, there's been a public outcry. There are rumors that the parents of some residents are filing a class action lawsuit against Willowbrook in the U.S. District Court."

"Good," she said. "I hope they all go to jail."

He sat forward in the chair. "I'm going to need an official statement from you about Eddie, and anything else you can tell me. But right now we need to figure out what's going to happen when you get out of here."

She didn't like the look on his face. "What do you mean 'what's going to happen'?"

"Dr. Baldwin called someone to come in and talk to you."

She shook her head. "I'm not talking to any more doctors."

"She's not a doctor," he said, getting up to open the door. "But she's here to help."

Sage gritted her teeth in frustration. What now? She'd had enough of people trying to "help." Detective Nolan opened the door and gestured someone in from the hall. A pale woman in a tweed coat entered the room, a clipboard held against her chest. She extended her hand and approached the hospital bed, a sympathetic smile on her face.

"Hello, Sage," she said. "I'm Diana Jay. It's nice to meet you." When she noticed Sage's bandaged arms, her smile faltered, but only by a fraction. She dropped her hand. "I don't know if Detective Nolan told you or not, but I'm with the Children's Aid organization of New York City. I'm here to talk to you about where you're going once you're released from the hospital."

"I'll figure something out," Sage said.

As impossible as it seemed, Diana's smile grew bigger and more sympathetic. "I'm afraid that's not the way things work in New York State," she said. "You're a minor, so we can't just let you fend for yourself."

"I'll be fine," Sage said. "I can stay with a friend."

Diana cleared her throat and glanced at Detective Nolan. When he failed to be helpful, she moved closer to Sage. "Listen, I know you've been through a lot and you just want everything to go back to normal. But, unfortunately, that's not possible when you become an orphan at sixteen."

"I'm not an orphan," she said. "It was my stepfather who was killed, not my real father."

"I see," Diana said. She gave Detective Nolan a hard look, then sat on the edge of the chair to write something down, balancing her clipboard on one knee. "Do you know your biological father's full name?"

"Charles Winters," Sage said.

"Middle name?"

"Lee."

"Do you have his phone number?"

Sage shook her head.

"Any idea where he lives?"

She tried to think of an easy, phony answer—he was on a ship off the California coast saving dolphins, or in Uganda on a missionary trip. Nothing came to mind. "No, I haven't seen or heard from him in years."

Diana sighed and rested her hand on the top of the clipboard. "Well, unless we can find him by tomorrow, it looks like we're back at square one."

"Which is what, exactly?" Detective Nolan said.

"Well, unfortunately, there are no local foster home openings at the moment," Diana said. "So she'll have to go to the children's home for now. As soon as we have a foster care opening, we'll move her, but I'm not going to sugarcoat it. Teenagers can be hard to place."

A rush of anxiety lit up Sage's chest. They wanted to lock her up again. "No," she said. "I'm not going to a children's home. I won't."

Diana stood, her sympathetic smile still frozen on her face, if slightly weaker. "I understand your apprehension," she said. "But trust me, our children's home is nothing like Willowbrook."

"I don't care," Sage said. "I'm not going there. And you can't make me." She yanked the IV out of her hand and started getting out of bed. "I need to get to a phone so I can call my friends. One of them will let me stay at their place until I find my father."

Detective Nolan stepped forward and put a gentle hand on her shoulder to stop her from getting up. "It's okay," he said. "We'll figure this out, I promise. Just calm down. We can talk about it more tomorrow."

"I'm sorry," Diana said. "But there's not really anything to 'figure out.' Unless we can find her father by tomorrow, by law she's a ward of the state, which means *we* decide where she goes."

Nolan turned on her. "I said we'll figure it out," he said, his voice hard. "Now, if you don't mind, she needs to rest. You can go now."

Diana's smiled wilted beneath his glare. She gripped her clipboard tighter, her knuckles turning white, then gave Sage one last glance and left the room.

CHAPTER 26

Sitting on the edge of the hospital bed the next afternoon, Sage stared at her boots, numb.

The doctor had agreed to sign her release hours ago. She'd taken a hot shower using gobs of soap and shampoo. A nurse had redressed her arms and given her back her clothes—dark stained and wrinkled, but she didn't care.

Yet no one had come to sign her out. No one had come to take her away. If the doctor hadn't insisted on her needing a ride and the nurses' station hadn't been right outside her room, she would have walked out a long time ago. All she could do now was wait. Wait for someone to show up. Wait for whatever unexpected turn her life would take next.

Detective Nolan said they'd figure out together where she was going, but she hadn't heard from him since yesterday when he took her statement. She cursed him under her breath. He *never* kept his promises, not about stopping Dr. Baldwin from locking her up or figuring out where she would go. Now that she'd done his work for him and found out Eddie was the killer, he'd probably moved on to his next case.

Then footsteps sounded in the hall, and the door

handle turned. Sage looked up, bracing herself. If fake-sympathy-smile Diana entered and tried to put her in a children's home, she didn't know what she'd do. Maybe she'd scream and fight and try to run away—but that would have to wait until they were off Willowbrook's campus. No one was going to lock her up again.

In what seemed like slow motion, the door opened wider. She held her breath. A nurse came in, smiled, then stood to one side and held the door open. When Sage saw who was behind her, she gasped.

Dawn came in first, followed by Heather and Detective Nolan. When the girls saw Sage they slowed, no doubt shocked by her gaunt appearance and bandaged arms.

"It's okay," Sage said. "I won't break."

Heather and Dawn smiled, teary-eyed, then rushed over and threw their arms around her.

"Oh my God," Heather said. "Are you okay?"

"We're so sorry," Dawn said. "If we'd known you were here, we would have come sooner."

Ignoring the pull of her stitches, Sage hugged them back, suddenly aware of how starved she was for physical affection, for warm embraces, and people who cared. Her friends smelled of White Rain shampoo and winter air, of lip gloss and mint gum. Heather pulled away and held Sage's hand in hers. Dawn stepped back too, wiping her eyes.

"We're so sorry about Rosemary," Heather said. "And about Alan too."

"Yeah," Dawn said, nodding. "It's awful what happened."

Sage swallowed hard against the thickness in her throat. "Thanks," she managed.

"Can you ever forgive us for not getting you out of here?" Heather said. "We thought you were pissed at us. When we finally called, Alan said you were visiting some aunt we'd never heard of. We tried a few times to see if you were back, but no one answered."

"Noah would have come today too," Dawn said, "but he just started a new job at the bowling alley."

Sage scoffed. "I'm sure Yvette would have been pissed if he'd come."

Heather frowned. "Yvette? Is that what Noah was talking about when he said to tell you he got your note? He said he'll explain everything and it's not what you think."

Sage's heart lifted a tiny bit, but she pushed the thought of him away. She wasn't sure she could ever trust him anyway. "That's not important right now."

"Okay," Heather said. "You're right. We'll talk about it later."

"I went to your apartment twice," Dawn said eagerly. "I wanted to apologize. We thought you were avoiding us because of what we said about . . . you know, about Cropsey."

Sage tried to smile, her chin trembling. "It's okay," she said. "I'll admit I was upset, but I shouldn't have let it bother me as much as it did. I shouldn't have left the bar that night. And I should have told you I was coming here. It's my own fault no one knew where I went."

"We would have come with you," Heather said. "You know that, right? Noah would have too."

Sage nodded, tears flooding her eyes. If only she hadn't let her pride get in the way, none of this would have happened. "I know," she said, nearly choking on her words. "It was stupid and I was being stubborn. It's all my fault."

"I disagree," Detective Nolan said. "I think it was brave of you to come here to look for your sister. And one decision on your part doesn't account for everything that happened. There were so many things already in place that were *not* your fault. So you shouldn't blame yourself at all. Not to mention, you stopped Eddie."

Sage smiled weakly, grateful to him for trying to make her feel better. He was right, of course. If she hadn't shown up looking for Rosemary, Eddie would still be killing residents at Willowbrook. At the same time, she knew that if she had to spend the rest of her life living in that hell on earth, she would want to die too. She hated to admit it, but it was easy to understand why the residents considered him an "angel of mercy." And if she was being honest, part of her thought

Eddie was doing those poor, tormented souls a favor. But she would never say that out loud. She would keep that opinion to herself. Because unless someone had experienced that brutal life firsthand, they'd never understand. And yes, the way Rosemary had died was horrible, but she'd begged Eddie to end her misery. And Sage's heart would forever be broken over the loss of her twin. But at the same time she was grateful to Eddie for ending her suffering.

Except he had taken it too far. He had become a vicious killer. And she could never forgive anyone for that.

"You're a hero," Dawn said, smiling.

Sage let out a quiet, cynical laugh. She didn't feel like a hero. She felt like a scared, exhausted little girl who had no idea where she was going or what she was doing next. She looked at Detective Nolan.

"So what happens now?" she said. "Is Diana coming to take me away?"

He shook his head. "I told her there was no need to come back."

"Good," Sage said. "Because I never would have gone with her without putting up one hell of a fight."

Detective Nolan laughed.

Sage turned to Dawn and Heather. "Do you think it would be okay if I stayed with one of you for a while?"

Heather nodded. "My mom said you could stay with us if you need to."

"Mine too," Dawn said. Then her face fell. "But not for too long because we don't have a lot of room."

"That's okay," Sage said. "We'll figure it out."

"I'm sorry, girls," Detective Nolan said, "but that won't be necessary."

"What do you mean?" Sage said.

Just then, someone knocked on the door.

Nolan smiled. "Well, that's perfect timing," he said. "What I mean is, I found someone who said you could stay with him for as long as you need." He went to the door and opened it.

Sage fixed her eyes on the doorway. Who in the world could he be talking about?

Then a dark-haired man in a wool coat and shiny shoes came into the room, awkwardly holding a plastic-wrapped bouquet of carnations in his hands. He was tall and broad shouldered, with a touch of stubble on his cheeks, fine wrinkles around his eyes, and streaks of gray peppering his temples. He looked older, but there was no mistaking who he was, even in the fancy clothes.

Sage's mouth fell open. *Daddy?*

Looking nervous and worried, he stopped just inside the door and gazed at her with sad eyes. "Hello, my beautiful girl," he said. "Someone told me you had nowhere to go. You can stay with me, but only if you want to."

Sage put a hand over her mouth to stifle a sob. His presence, his words were so unreal she could hardly believe them. Her heart pounded wildly as her father edged closer, his smile uncertain, his blue eyes wet with tears. Heather and Dawn moved back to give him room, their eyes fixed on his face as if he were a mythical creature. Detective Nolan stood watching with a satisfied grin.

Sage wanted to jump off the bed and run into her father's arms, but too many questions and doubts ran through her head to allow her to follow her heart. As happy as she was to see him, a ripple of anger stirred below the surface of her joy.

"What are you doing here?" she said, tears burning her eyes. "How did you find me?"

"Detective Nolan called me and told me what happened," he said. "I'm so sorry about Rosemary. I promise I had no idea your mother had her put away. She always told me you girls were happy and doing well."

"But why didn't you check on us to make sure? Where have you been?"

"Oh, sweetheart." He took a staggering step forward, then stopped, his face lined with pain. "I wanted to see you. I tried for years to get visitation rights, but your mother fought me every step of the way. I won't get into the ugly details, but she lied to the judge about me. She said you were better off without me and it would be too disruptive for me to keep coming around. The judge said if I really cared about you, I'd stay away and let Alan be your father."

She couldn't hold back any longer. Tears spilled down her cheeks. "We didn't love Alan. And he didn't love us."

The frown line deepened between his eyes. "I'm sorry. About everything. I didn't know."

"What about when Mom died? Why didn't you come to the funeral? Why didn't you try to see us after she was gone?"

"I was working overseas at the time, and by the time I came back I didn't think you wanted anything to do with me. I sent letters for years but never got a reply."

Sage pressed her trembling lips together. So that was why Alan had always prevented her from going through the mail. He said it was none of her business and if anything arrived with her name on it, he'd give it to her. She should have known he was lying. All that time he'd been getting rid of her father's letters.

"So why are you here now?" she said.

"Because I love you. And Detective Nolan said you need a place to stay."

Swallowing the lump in her throat, she regarded Detective Nolan. "When . . . how did you find him?"

"I didn't make detective for nothing, kiddo,"

Nolan said, winking at her. "Just doing my job."

Sage looked at her father again, struggling to control her emotions. "But you have a whole new life," she said in a quiet voice. "You don't need me screwing it up."

"Oh, my girl," he said. "You wouldn't be screwing it up. You'd be fixing it. I swear I thought about you and Rosemary every day." He wiped his eyes. "I can't begin to tell you how much I missed you. And I'm so sorry the world has been so unbelievably cruel to you both."

She put her hands over her face and swallowed a sob. She felt like she was about to explode, the strength of her joy and sadness making her dizzy. She wept silently for a moment, then wiped her face and gazed at him, struggling to keep her voice steady. "What about your . . . your . . . you must have a new family now."

He set the flowers on the bed and sat down on the edge of the mattress. "I have a wife," he said. "Her name is Cathy and she's beautiful and kind, but we never had children. We have two dogs and a nice house on Long Island with a great view of the ocean and an extra bedroom. And your friends can visit whenever they'd like."

Sage glanced at Heather and Dawn and Detective Nolan, who were all staring at her with watery eyes. Dawn looked like she was about to weep uncontrollably. Sage looked at her father again. "Are . . . are you sure?"

He nodded. "Cathy wanted me to tell you just one thing."

"What's that?" Sage said.

He gently took her bandaged hands in his. "That kind hearts are strong hearts, and if you'd like to come, we'll welcome you into our lives with open arms."

Sage couldn't hold back any longer. She let out a sob and threw her arms around her father's neck. "Oh, Daddy," she cried.

He hugged her back, holding her tight and burying his face in her hair. When he started to weep, all the emotions she'd held inside for so long released in a flood of tears—the longing ache for his presence in her life, the grief over losing her mother and sister, the yearning for a parent who cared, the terror and heartache she'd experienced over the past weeks. Even the guilt that *her* father had shown up to save her in the end, unlike the thousands of poor children in Willowbrook who would never be so lucky. Her heart felt like it was about to burst from the magnitude of it all.

CHAPTER 27

April 13, 1972

It was a beautiful spring day, and the cemetery was vibrant with color; the grass a deep green, the yellow daffodils and red tulips swaying in the slight breeze. The distant ocean was sapphire and ice blue, waves curling against the shore like slippery lace. Rosemary would have loved it. She would have pointed out the different colors and shapes, and would have lifted her eyes toward the sun, smiling and drinking it all in.

Sage stood over her sister's grave, one arm hooked over her father's elbow, the other cupped by her stepmother Cathy's gentle hand. They'd had to wait to bury Rosemary until the ground thawed and the media circus surrounding everything that had happened in Willowbrook eased up. But now, finally, the funeral was over and they had time to begin stitching their lives together. Sage would have more time to get to know her father again and learn about her new stepmother, and they would have time to know her.

She wiped the moisture from her eyes. "I hope Rosemary is looking down on us and knows how much I loved her," she said.

"Of course she does," her father said. "And she knows how much I loved her too."

Cathy murmured in agreement, then went quiet again.

Sage only nodded, grateful Cathy wasn't going to try to comfort her. Her grief was as deep as it had been the first time she'd lost Rosemary—maybe even more so, now that Sage knew how much her sister had suffered in the last six years of her life. Even with her father by her side, the heaviness in her heart felt like a lonely ache, a silent wound that no one would ever understand. Unless they saw Willowbrook with their own eyes, they'd never know how awful the last years of Rosemary's life had been. "I tried to save you," she whispered under her breath. "But I was too late."

The only thing that gave her comfort was knowing that Rosemary was no longer suffering and she would never be gone, not as long as Sage and her father remembered her. And Sage had made a decision. From now on she would never think of her sister living through hell inside Willowbrook again. Instead, she would hear her laughter in the ocean waves and the breeze through the trees. She'd be reminded of her smile when the sun sparkled on the snow, and she'd hear her voice in the singing birds.

"We can come back and plant flowers if you'd like," Cathy said quietly.

"Rosemary would love that," Sage said. "Thank you."

Her father bent down and put his hand on the fresh dirt. "We love you, baby girl," he said, then stood and wiped his eyes.

Loss settled deep in Sage's chest, at the same time as her love for her father swelled. He had always called his daughters miracles, the loves of his life, and she knew it was true, even when she hadn't known where he was or why he never called. What mattered was that he was here now, and his heart was broken too. Maybe they could mend their broken hearts together.

CHAPTER 28

March 1987
Saturday

Sipping her morning coffee, Sage stood at the window of her family's Brooklyn apartment, watching the people in short-sleeved shirts walking and riding bicycles on the sidewalk below. By some miracle, spring-like weather had come early to the city, bringing with it a cloudless blue sky, and she'd pushed the window open wide to let in the fresh air. Opening the windows was nothing new, of course—she did it for a few minutes every day, no matter the weather—but today she was grateful that the air was finally warm enough to leave them open longer, despite the fact that winter was surely not over.

In the fifteen years since she'd escaped Willowbrook, her need for fresh air had only intensified, along with her desire to clean. Her husband, Elliot, sometimes joked that she had obsessive-compulsive disorder, but her obsessions had little to do with real OCD. Willowbrook had gotten inside her in a terrible way, and it didn't take much to transport her back to those horrible days—the smell of sour milk, a gas station bathroom, a slight whiff of garbage. So she cleaned. A lot. She burned scented candles and opened windows and never went a day without perfume. Considering everything she'd experienced, she was lucky to have come through it all with only those quirks.

The nice weather also meant they could sit outside at her father's house later this evening, when she and her family went there to celebrate her stepmother Cathy's birthday. Which reminded her, she needed to pick up a present on the way there. Between taking her sons and daughter to sports practices and piano lessons, her job at the foster care office, and finding group homes for the remaining residents of Willowbrook, she hadn't had a chance to go shopping all week. And there was no way she'd show up without a present, not when she owed Cathy so much—for everything from helping her get through the rest of high school to her belief that Sage could make it into and excel at college. Her father had helped too, of course—he had been the rock and safety net she needed—but it was Cathy who had bolstered her confidence and reminded her that the three of them were in it together. The first few years had been the hardest, between the nightmares, getting used to a new school, grieving her sister a second time, and testifying in court about Eddie and the horrors of Willowbrook. But her father and Cathy had been with her through all of it, and thanks to them, she learned what it felt like to have a real family.

She took her coffee over to the couch and sat down. For now, shopping would have to wait. Her husband, bless his soul, had taken the kids roller-skating in the park so she could have the morning to herself. She opened the *New York Times* and spread it out over the coffee table, scanning the headlines for the two articles she hoped to find. When she found the first one buried in section B on page 3, she read it before cutting it out to put in her scrapbook.

State and Families
Reach Final Accord
Over Willowbrook

March 3rd, 1987

A Federal judge in Brooklyn has approved a final settlement involving reforms in conditions at a state center for the mentally retarded that were first sought in 1972 and ordered in 1975.

The agreement, signed by District Judge John Bartels, confirms that by the end of the year the state will close the 60-year-old center, which gained national notoriety as the Willowbrook State School and is now known as the Staten Island Developmental Center.

State officials said yesterday that they have been making progress in moving patients out of Willowbrook, where wards once jammed far beyond capacity now hold only 130 patients.

The new agreement calls for those patients to be moved to group homes with fewer than 16 beds. The state also promised to place about 1,200 other patients who once lived at Willowbrook in smaller institutions by 1992. The 1,200 are now living in other large state-operated developmental centers.

The state will not pay any monetary damages to the families of former Willowbrook patients. The state will also establish a special office to look after the rights of former Willowbrook patients who do not have family or guardians to represent them.

In the 1970s, more than 6,000 patients were crowded into Willowbrook's antiquated wards, which were infested with vermin. When parents sued the state over the conditions, Judge Bartels ruled that Willowbrook was overcrowded and inhumane. In 1975, the state and the families agreed to a consent decree under which Willowbrook's population was to be trimmed to 250 patients.

It was frustrating and hard to believe it had taken fifteen years to get to this point, but it was a start. She was glad that at least she'd been able to help make a difference by finding new homes for some of the residents. It was full-time job just figuring out who was who, due to the abysmal recordkeeping that included missing photos, incorrect names, and the same social security numbers being used for multiple people, but getting someone out of that place was one of the best feelings in the world. She cut out the article and set it on top of the scrapbook where she kept the other articles about Willowbrook that had been published over the years. Then she went back to the newspaper and turned the pages slowly, her heart quickening as she scanned the headlines. When she finally found the other article she was looking for, she picked up the paper, braced herself, and read it slowly.

Edward King, One of the Most Prolific Serial Killers in U.S. History, Dies at 34

The man some called the Angel of Death, some called Cropsey, with nearly sixty confirmed victims, died Wednesday in New York, officials said. He was 34.

Eddie King, who had heart trouble and was in a wheelchair as a result of an injury inflicted by a young victim who survived his last attack, died at a New York hospital. He was serving a life sentence for multiple counts of murder. New York Corrections Department spokeswoman Davis Crowe said there were signs of self-strangulation, but the official cause of death will be determined by a coroner.

A resident of Willowbrook State School for nearly ten years, King denied for years that he had ever killed anyone. In 1975, however, King opened up to Detective Sam Nolan during questioning regarding an unrelated murder. During roughly 700 hours of interviews, King provided details of scores of slayings. By the time of his death, King had confessed to killing ninety-three people. Most of the slayings took place in Willowbrook or the surrounding areas on Staten Island.

Almost all of King's victims were residents of Willowbrook or poor children living on the edges of society. They were individuals, King said, who wanted or needed to escape the horror of their lives. Willowbrook doctors initially classified many of the deaths that occurred on their campus as being due to pneumonia, hepatitis, or unknown causes. King smothered or drugged most of his victims, usually, he claimed, at their request. He slit the wrists and throats of others, including two young women, in an effort to frame an attendant who worked at Willowbrook, Wayne Myers, who became one of King's final known victims.

Nolan has described King as both a genius and a sociopath, saying the killer could never adequately explain to him what his motivation was, other than to say he was "helping people."

Nolan worked tirelessly to create and maintain a bond with the killer during their hundreds of hours of interviews, bringing him his favorite snacks, such as pizza, Dr Pepper, and French fries, and discussing their mutual interest in sports. He also gave King assurances that he would not be executed. Nolan addressed King by his childhood nickname, Eddie, while King called Nolan by his first name, Sam, and once told the Times he'd "found a friend in a New York City cop."

King revealed few details about his own life other than that he was raised in Queens by his father until he was nine years old, at which time he was abandoned at Grand Central Station.

Authorities finally apprehended King after he was injured during an attack on a fellow resident of Willowbrook, Sage Winters. Ms. Winters had been unlawfully institutionalized after King killed her twin sister and a Willowbrook psychiatrist, Dr. Donald Baldwin, refused to believe or confirm Winters's true identity. At the request of Willowbrook's Board of Directors, Baldwin resigned soon thereafter and died a year later of cancer.

King claimed the residents of Willowbrook considered him an "angel of mercy" because he was their only way of escaping a gruesome existence. He said they begged him to end their lives. "I don't think there was another person who would do what I did," he told 60 Minutes. "I was the only one brave enough to set those tortured souls free. And that's not a curse, that is an honor."

Sage put down the paper and leaned back on the couch, her vision blurred by tears. Detective Nolan had called her a few days ago to let her know Eddie had hanged himself, but seeing it in black and white made it real. The "angel of mercy" had decided to end his own suffering—although jail would have felt like paradise to the residents of Willowbrook.

Even though it felt like Eddie had taken the easy way out, she was relieved. The nightmares of him breaking into her apartment to slit her throat had dwindled over the years, but they still jolted her awake sometimes, leaving her sweating and tangled in her sheets. Maybe now they would finally stop.

In the meantime, she would continue to count her many blessings, like Rosemary would have wanted her to, and she would continue to show herself mercy by putting the horrors of her past behind her. She wiped her eyes and stood. Then, instead of clipping out the article about Eddie to put in her scrapbook, she ripped it out, crumpled it up in her hands, and threw it in the wastebasket, where it belonged.

She had a birthday party to get ready for, a happy celebration to enjoy with her beautiful family. She'd made up her mind a long time ago that painful memories were not going to steal the wonderful parts of life away from her, or stain them in any way. And that was a promise she intended to keep, not only for her own sake but also in remembrance of Rosemary—who wouldn't have wanted it any other way.

CHAPTER 29

Sage Joy Winters, Rescuer of Abused Willowbrook Residents, Dies at 89

Sage Winters, a former social worker who found homes for hundreds of mentally disabled people after their mistreatment at the Willowbrook State School on Staten Island became a national scandal in the 1970s, died on Saturday in East Meadow, Long Island. She was 89.

Ms. Winters was a New York State social worker from 1986 to 1993, and she earlier worked with foster families, overseeing services for disadvantaged children. But perhaps her most visible impact was made in rescuing abused Willowbrook residents by finding them safe places to live in group homes.

The deplorable conditions at Willowbrook, a state-run institution, seized the nation's attention in 1972 when Geraldo Rivera, then a reporter for WABC-TV in New York, put a spotlight on them, showing children lying naked on the floor, their bodies contorted, their feces spread on the walls. His reports were broadcast nationally. More than 5,400 people lived on the Willowbrook campus, making it the largest state-run institution for mentally disabled people in the United States.

Willowbrook residents and their parents, aided by civil libertarians and mental health advocates, sued New York State to prevent further deterioration and to establish that residents had a Constitutional right to treatment. The state settled with the plaintiffs and signed a court decree in April 1975 promising to improve conditions at Willowbrook and to transfer residents to new homes.

Logistical and legal difficulties delayed the emptying of Willowbrook until 1987. But working with Roman Catholic and black community organizations, Ms. Winters found more than 100 homes for more than 1,000 Willowbrook residents despite meeting intense opposition in neighborhoods. In some instances, she was pelted with eggs, and her jaw was broken in one confrontation.

Six years after the last residents left Willowbrook, its buildings became a campus of the College of Staten Island.

For Ms. Winters, the assignment was also a personal mission. Her twin sister, Rosemary, spent six years in Willowbrook before being killed by Edward King.

Sage Joy Winters Chambers was born on April 4, 1955, on Staten Island. She graduated from Wagner College as a psychology major. In 1975, she married Elliot Chambers, long-time aide to the mayor of New York, who survives her. She is also survived by her sons, Phillip Chambers and Nathan Chambers; a daughter, Clare Chambers Ireland; four grandsons, Luke, Michael, Wyatt, and Jack, and a granddaughter, Rosemary Sage.

DISCUSSION QUESTIONS

1. An institution for people with disabilities, the Willowbrook State School opened in 1947 on Staten Island, New York, and remained in operation until 1987. Despite having a maximum capacity of 4,000 people, by 1965 it housed over 6,000 intellectually and physically disabled children and adults, becoming the largest state-run mental institution of its kind in the United States. Due to staff and money shortages, there was only one nurse per ward, one or two attendants per 35 to 125 residents, and more than 200 residents living in houses built for fewer than 100. An estimated 12,000 residents died at Willowbrook from 1950 to 1980, approximately 400 a year, due to neglect, violence, lack of nutrition, and medical mismanagement or experimentation. What was your awareness of Willowbrook State School before reading *The Lost Girls of Willowbrook*? Why do you think most people today are unfamiliar with the history of Willowbrook?

2. When Sage discovers that her twin sister, Rosemary, has gone missing from Willowbrook, she takes a bus to the institution to

help with the search. She goes alone because her stepfather is cold and indifferent, and she feels like her friends are unreliable. Do you think Sage's lack of knowledge about the "school" influenced her decision to go there by herself? What would you have done in that situation? Would you have headed to Willowbrook alone?

3. How would you react if, after grieving a loved one for years, you found out they were alive but had been committed to a mental asylum?

4. Willowbrook State School gained infamy after an unannounced visit in 1965 from Senator Robert Kennedy. Despite his vivid descriptions of it as "a snake pit" and his horror over the conditions of the children "living in filth and dirt," the school continued to operate for another twenty-two years. In 1972, Geraldo Rivera filmed the Peabody Award–winning expose *Willowbrook: The Last Great Disgrace*, which aired on national television. This documentary brought widespread mainstream awareness to the institution's abuses, overcrowding, deplorable conditions, and physical and sexual abuse of residents. Shockingly, it wouldn't be shut down for another fifteen years. Were you surprised that Willowbrook was allowed to continue operating for so

long? Why do you think it took decades to shut down the institution?

5. Sage remembers hearing rumors about scientific experiments being carried out on children at Willowbrook. This rumor turned out to be true. Some of the top virologists in the U.S. used the school as an experimental hideout for developing vaccines for hepatitis, measles, mumps, shigellosis, and other diseases and it was funded by the Defense Department. Other experiments involved hormone treatments for dwarfism and electrostimulation, among many others. In 1976, one Willowbrook administrator was quoted as saying he once counted seventy-three separate research projects going on at one time. Did this surprise you? Have you ever heard of any other medical experiments being carried out in the U.S. on the disenfranchised, impoverished, orphaned, or ill?

6. Despite the name Willowbrook State "School," fewer than twenty percent of the children living there attended school at any one time and the quality of education was marginal at best. For the most part, the residents on the experiment ward were the only ones given instruction because their parents had consented to their participation in medical research in exchange for a

"better" quality of life, or as a way around a long waiting list for admittance. The majority of the residents were not taught behavioral modification exercises, social skills, hygiene, or basic grooming. With that knowledge, why do you think the state was allowed to call Willowbrook a school? What do you think were the biggest factors that contributed to the lack of education there?

7. When Sage arrives at Willowbrook, the doctors and nurses think she is her missing sister. She tries everything to convince them that she is Rosemary's identical twin but nothing works. Is there anything else she could have tried?

8. Willowbrook State School is mentioned in the 2009 documentary *Cropsey* as reportedly having housed convicted child kidnapper Andre Rand, who had previously worked there as an attendant. One of Rand's supposed victims, Jennifer Schweiger, was found buried in a shallow grave behind the grounds of the abandoned institution. Have you ever heard of the legend of Cropsey? Do you know of any urban legends centered in or around the area where you live?

9. Several Willowbrook staff stated in interviews that some well-to-do families got their children into Willowbrook because they couldn't deal with the children's behaviors,

even going so far as having IQ scores altered to make them eligible for admittance. And virtually everyone who was examined got in. Have you heard of any hospitals, schools, or centers for troubled kids that exist today? Have any of them been accused of neglect or abuse?

10. Sage's stepfather says one of the reasons he and her late mother lied about Rosemary being committed to Willowbrook was because her mother wouldn't have been able to show her face in public without people whispering behind her back. At the time, ignorance of mental disabilities meant there was still extreme stigma and fear surrounding it. Since then, there have been some changes in the attitudes and treatment of those with disabilities, although we still have a way to go. Why do you think that is? When did the change begin? What else needs to be done?

11. Eddie learns that one of the doctors who was fired for trying to improve things at Willowbrook gave a key to a reporter named Geraldo Rivera, who brought a film crew into House Six to expose the inhumane conditions. How do you think Eddie learned that information?

12. At one point, Sage learns there are kids without disabilities in Willowbrook who were

abandoned by parents and foster homes. It's true that Willowbrook became a place for unwanted or troubled children who then became wards of the state. Some were left in public places with signs that said "Take Me to Willowbrook." Why do you think the people in charge let that happen? Why would they commit nondisabled children?

13. How do you think Sage changed over the course of the novel? Which events do you think were most transformative?

14. While researching this novel, the author discovered that it wasn't unusual for Willowbrook residents to kill themselves—some stopped eating, hung themselves, or simply disappeared. How do you think that information influenced the plot?

15. The idyllic campus of Willowbrook, with its expansive lawns, sweeping stands of trees, and brick buildings, belied the horror that was happening behind its walls. Do you think the citizens of Staten Island knew what was really going on there? Do you think they could have done anything to stop it?

AUTHOR'S NOTE

Willowbrook is a tragic story—one I could only begin to touch on in this novel—but it's a story that must not be forgotten. As an author who endeavors to cast light on social injustices of the past within my novels, I've written previously about state-run institutions, particularly in my book *What She Left Behind*. Even still, much of what I knew before I began researching the dark history of Willowbrook was based on urban legends and rumors, some of which turned out to be true and made it into this novel in ways that surprised even me.

The more I learned about the institution itself, the more I realized that "life" inside was far more complex than I imagined. And the more my sympathy for those who lived and worked there grew. Far from being a school, it was over-crowded, underfunded, and understaffed to such a degree that, at times, residents were forced to take on the role of caretaker for other residents. And while it was primarily a warehouse for people with disabilities, it also became a dumping ground for simply unwanted or troublesome non-disabled children who were abandoned by their parents or sent there by foster homes. The conditions were abysmal for both residents and staff. Out of public sight and completely closed off, it became an underground city with its own hierarchy and society, where employees could buy and sell everything, from drugs to jewelry to meat. It also became a hideout for researchers to carry out controversial medical experiments funded primarily by the Defense Department.

Along with rundown facilities, there was disease, violence, theft, drug and alcohol use, and other forms of crime. There was harm done by physicians who failed to do their medical duty. There was violence done by staff to residents, including rape, beatings, psychological torture, overuse of powerful drugs, and murder. There was violence by staff to other staff members, for a variety of reasons, including personal vendetta, paybacks for snitching, drug-dealing disputes, and mental illness. There was also violence by residents to other residents, which included beating, torture, rape, and murder.

Many who came to Willowbrook lived a short, brutal existence. They died because of neglect, violence, lack of nutrition, and medical mismanagement or experimentation. Some simply disappeared or even committed suicide. Most parents who sent their children to Willowbrook were encouraged by certain doctors to relinquish their disabled children "for the sake of the family" with no idea that they were condemning them to a life of agony, neglect, and abuse by those charged with their care. And any parent who fought with the school to protect their children were labeled "trouble makers" by the administration, then subjected to threats and manipulation to ensure they didn't rock the boat.

Certainly I'm not implying that all doctors, nurses and staff were uncaring or incompetent; as in most institutions, some people did very good things and some people did terrible things. There were reports of employees using their own money to buy necessary items for the residents, including clothes, soap, deodorant, etc. The obituary at the end of this novel book was inspired by a real woman, Barbara Blum, who dedicated her life to finding homes for hundreds of people with disabilities after their mistreatment at Willowbrook.

There were also wonderful doctors who truly cared for the residents, like William Bronston, MD, who worked at Willowbrook and went on to lead the exposure and class action lawsuit against the institution. He later co-authored *A History and Sociology of Willowbrook State School* and in 2021, as I was finishing *The Lost Girls of Willowbrook*, he published *Public Hostage, Public Ransom: Ending Institutional America*, an in-depth account of his work against Willowbrook and institutionalization as a whole.

Sadly, Dr. Bronston and anyone else who tried to improve conditions at Willowbrook fought an impossible mission. Bronston wrote that other doctors organized against him and he was moved to another building as punishment for requesting painkillers, soap, sheets, surgery thread (instead of upholstery thread) for suturing, and non-rotten food for the residents under his care.

After Geraldo Rivera uncovered the deplorable conditions in his award-winning expose, a class-action lawsuit was filed against the State of New York by the parents of 5,000 residents of Willowbrook in federal court on March 17, 1972. In 1975, the *Willowbrook Consent Decree* was signed, committing New York State to improve community placement for the now designated "Willowbrook Class." Under the terms of the agreement, Willowbrook would house no more than 250 patients by 1981, all from Staten Island. The cornerstone of the consent decree was that the state "would be required to spend two million dollars to create two-hundred places for Willowbrook transferees in hostels, halfway houses, group houses, and sheltered workshops." In 1983, the state of New York announced plans to close Willowbrook, which in 1974 had been renamed the Staten Island Developmental Center. By the end of March 1986, the number of residents housed there had dwindled to 250, and the last residents left the grounds on September 17, 1987. During the writing of this book, I talked to several people who work, or have worked, with members of the Willowbrook Class. Sadly it's clear that the former residents' neglect and mistreatment had a profound and lasting effect on their lives. For many, the abuse still continues in smaller group homes and institutions, as reported in a February 2020 investigation by *The New York Times*.

As always, in the writing of this novel I've taken some liberties with historical facts for the purpose of plot. Some medical treatments were performed either earlier or later in the book than was actually the case. Lobotomies were performed at Willowbrook from 1948-1954. I'm not sure if any residents were sterilized, but it happened frequently in similar institutions. Geraldo Rivera's expose actually aired the same day it was filmed because Riviera was worried someone would protest the raid and block the story. There was no cemetery at Willowbrook but some children, mostly babies, were illegally buried there.

I have no knowledge of male attendants working on the female wards in Willowbrook, but considering the huge staff shortages and the fact that women worked as attendants on men's wards, it certainly seems possible. While I drew inspiration from the legend of Cropsey and the true story of convicted child kidnapper and suspected serial killer Andre Rand—who had previously worked at Willowbrook as an attendant—the Willowbrook employees in this novel are purely imaginary. Lastly, it is important to note that the use of words such as "idiot," "moron," "retarded," "feeble-minded," "crippled," and "colored" were used as historically accurate terms to represent the era in which the story takes place.

During the writing of *The Lost Girls of Willowbrook*, I relied on the following books: *American Snake Pit* by Dan Tomasulo; *The Willowbrook Wars* by David J. Rothman and Sheila M. Rothman; *A History and Sociology of Willowbrook State School* by David Goode, Darryl Hill, Jean Reiss, and William Bronston. I also watched Geraldo Rivera's expose, "Willowbrook: The Last Great Disgrace," and "Cropsey," a documentary by Joshua Zeman and Barbara Brancaccio.

Even though Willowbrook was eventually shut down, the fight for disability rights is still ongoing. What happened there should serve as a reminder to us all that we need to be more protective of the most vulnerable among us, and that every human being has the right to learn and grow and, more importantly, to be treated with kindness, respect, and compassion.

If you're interested in learning more about Dr. Bronston's work to abolish institutionalization, you can do so at: PublicHostagePublicRansom.org. And if you'd like to learn more about making the future better for people with disabilities, please check out these resources:

People Inc.
www.people-inc.org

Disability Rights Education & Defense Fund
www.dredf.org

National Disability Rights Network
www.ndrn.org

International Disability Alliance
www.internationaldisabilityalliance.org

Center Point Large Print
600 Brooks Road / PO Box 1
Thorndike, ME 04986-0001 USA

(207) 568-3717

US & Canada:
1 800 929-9108
www.centerpointlargeprint.com